*These gorgeous guys are tough risk
takers, ready to take a chance on love*

Rugged
REBELS

**Three all new novels from fresh
Mills & Boon voices!**

Also available:

Boardroom
HOT-SHOTS

Rugged
REBELS

Stephanie BOND
Jeanie LONDON
Kara LENNOX

MILLS
BOON

Harlequin Mills & Boon Limited, Eton House,
18-24 Paradise Road, Richmond, Surrey TW9 1SR

RUGGED REBELS © Harlequin Books S.A. 2011

Watch and Learn © Stephanie Bond, Inc. 2008
Under His Skin © Jeanie LeGendre 2005
Her Perfect Hero © Karen Leabo 2007

ISBN: 978 0 263 88944 4

010-0111

Harlequin Mills & Boon policy is to use papers that are
natural, renewable and recyclable products and made from
wood grown in sustainable forests. The logging and
manufacturing processes conform to the legal environmental
regulations of the country of origin.

Printed and bound in Spain
by Litografia Rosés S.A., Barcelona

WATCH AND LEARN

Stephanie BOND

Stephanie Bond was seven years deep into a computer career and pursuing a master's degree at night when an instructor remarked she had a flair for writing and encouraged her to submit to academic journals. Once the seed was planted, however, Stephanie immediately turned to creating romance fiction in her spare time.

She now writes for Mills & Boon® Blaze®, having gained notoriety for her spicy romantic comedies. Stephanie lives with her husband in Atlanta, Georgia, her laptop permanently attached to her body. Readers can write to her at PO Box 54266, Atlanta, GA 30308, USA or through her website.

This book is dedicated to all the people at my
publisher behind the scenes, who work so hard
to bring so many great books to readers all
over the world.

1

GEMMA WHITE LOVED to make love in the morning. When the sheets were warm from lazy limbs, when muscles were rested and revived, when the day was yet a possibility. Morning lovemaking was an act reserved for the lucky few—new lovers who ignored the impulse to sneak out in the middle of the night, live-in lovers who still enjoyed waking up together, and married lovers wise enough to take advantage of a time when both partners' bodies were primed for passion.

Gemma smiled and rolled over, sliding a loving hand toward Jason's side of the bed. But when her fingers encountered cold emptiness, her eyes flew open and reality descended with a crash.

Jason was gone.

The desire that had pooled in her belly ebbed as sadness, temporarily banished by the cleansing arm of sleep, swamped her chest. The humiliation and shock of his departure hadn't lessoned over the past few weeks and, if anything, had become more embedded in her heart, like sets of bicycle tracks through fresh mud that had dried into an ugly, permanent cast.

Would mornings ever feel right again?

The wail of the phone pierced the air. She closed her eyes, cursing the person on the other end for intruding on her moment of misery. After four teeth-rattling rings, the phone fell silent…then started up again. Resigned, she swung her legs over the edge of the bed and reached for the handset.

"Hello?" she murmured into the mouthpiece.

"Are you up?" her best friend Sue demanded.

"Yes."

"Literally out of bed and walking around?"

Gemma pushed to her feet. "Absolutely."

"What's on the agenda today?"

"Um…" Gemma turned on a light and glanced around the cluttered bedroom. Dirty clothes occupied every surface. The floor was littered with at least two boxes of tissues crumpled into balls. "I thought I might…clean."

"Good. You want everything to look great in case you have company."

"Are you coming to Tampa?" Gemma asked, panicked. She wasn't ready to deal with the full frontal assault of Sue's personality. Her friend would roll into town from Tallahassee like a tank, armed with endless pep talks. But Gemma was too raw, too exposed, to deal with her failed marriage so matter-of-factly, over cups of frothy coffee and shoe shopping. She needed time to reorient herself.

"I can't get away from work right now," Sue said. "I meant in case Jason stops by."

Gemma tightened her grip on the phone. "Have you seen him? Is he coming here?"

"No, I haven't seen him. But in case he does drop by, you and the house need to look your best."

As if the divorce hadn't fazed Gemma. It was, after all, antifeminist to behave as if her husband's desertion had devastated her. Where was her pride?

"Have you told your parents yet?"

"No."

"What are you waiting for?"

"The divorce isn't final…yet."

"Gemma, you're stalling."

"It will break their hearts—Jason is like a son to them."

"Considering Jason's position in the governor's office, it's bound to hit the local papers soon. Is that how you want them to find out?"

"No." But neither did she want her mother pecking her to death with worry. "I'll tell them…soon."

"Did you find a job?"

Another dilemma. Unemployment was not so unusual for the wife of the state attorney general, but not so realistic for a divorcée with no alimony. "Not yet," Gemma admitted.

A noise outside drew her to the picture window overlooking the side yard. She nudged aside the filmy white curtain and looked down into the overgrown lawn of the empty house next door. A tall man with shiny dark hair was using a mallet to dislodge a faded For Sale sign that had been posted on the lawn for all of the two years that she and Jason had lived here.

"Have you even *looked* for a job?" Sue prodded.

"I will…today."

"Okay." Sue's disbelieving response vibrated over the line. "Gemma, you have to pull yourself together."

"I know, and I will. I just need some time to absorb my new reality." She pushed hair out of her eyes. From his tool belt, she gathered the stranger was a workman, hired, no doubt, by the new owner to fix up the place. She felt a spurt of relief for the sagging Spanish house whose exotic lines she'd always admired. But when the man lifted his dark gaze to her second-floor window, she dropped the curtain and stepped back, her face stinging.

The man had probably thought *her* house was empty. How many rubber-banded newspapers were piled on the front porch? Had weeds overtaken the brilliant birds-of-paradise and ginger flowers in the planting beds? Tending to the exotic plants that thrived in the lush Florida humidity had always been her favorite pastime. But since the final court appearance last week, she'd found it unnecessary to move beyond the front door.

"I'm sure any of the nonprofit agencies that you've helped to raise money for would be happy to hire you in some capacity."

"Probably. But I don't want to take advantage of my relationship with Jason."

"There's nothing wrong with using his name to get the job. You'll prove yourself once you get there."

Gemma understood the practicality of her friend's advice, but something inside her revolted at the idea of using Jason's connections. "I don't want to be in a position where I'd have to feel grateful to Jason, or be around people who might expect me to ask him for favors."

"I have some business contacts in Tampa. I could make some calls," Sue offered cheerfully.

Right—Sue's business associates would be *clamoring* to hire a thirty-two-year-old with an unused degree in art history. She'd save herself and her lobbyist friend the embarrassment of asking. "Thanks anyway. I'll find something on my own."

"Okay," Sue said warily. "Have a good day. I'll call you later."

Gemma returned the receiver with a sigh. She had no

right to be irritated with her friend. Sue was only trying to help in a situation that had rocked both of them to the core. Sue felt betrayed by Jason, too. She had introduced Gemma and Jason when the girls were seniors at Covington Women's College in Jacksonville and Jason was in law school at the University of Florida in nearby Gainesville. Sue had preened as her two friends had dated, fallen in love, graduated, married and evolved into an influential political couple.

I introduced them, she'd gushed to onlookers as camera bulbs flashed at their lavish wedding and over the years at every political appointment and election leading up to Jason being sworn in as state attorney general. When Gemma had called her, blubbering about a divorce, Sue hadn't believed her at first. Like Gemma, she couldn't conceive of Jason turning his back on their ten-year marriage with no warning and no remorse, as if it were simply one of the hundreds of decisions he had to make daily.

If there were fifty ways to leave your lover, he had surely chosen one of the most cruel. He'd asked Gemma to pack a suitcase for him for a last-minute trip and bring it by his office. Then after ensuring she had packed his favorite ties and shoes, he'd turned to her and said, "This isn't working for me anymore. I want a divorce."

Gemma remembered laughing at the comment. Jason had always exhibited a quirky sense of humor. But he'd leveled his pale blue eyes on her with an expression that she'd since realized was pity. "I'm moving to Tallahassee alone, Gemma. It's over."

It's over. As if he was referring to a television show or a song that had run its course.

A banging sound next door jarred her from her circular

thoughts. Gemma wiped at the perspiration on her neck, realizing suddenly that she was sticky all over, that the air in the room was stifling. A check of the thermostat revealed that yet something else had gone wrong when she wasn't looking. She'd have to call a repair service.

She went from room to room on the top floor to open windows, releasing heat that had risen in the house. The bedroom that Jason had turned into his office looked as if it had been violated, stripped of furniture and decorated with cobwebs in strange places. From the walls sprang naked cables that had once provided power to fuel his busy life.

It was exactly the way she felt. Unplugged and unwanted.

When she returned to her bedroom to slide open the side window, she chanced a glance at the house next door, startled when the peeling shutters on the round window twenty feet across from hers were thrown open and the dark-haired man she'd seen earlier appeared. She distantly registered the fact that she was wearing only a thin tank top and no bra, but she was rooted to the hardwood floor when his gaze landed on her. He inclined his head in a polite nod.

Gemma managed a shaky smile, but he was already gone, like the breeze.

Feeling sideswiped, her smile dissolved into an embarrassed little frown. A glance up at the sky had her shielding her eyes in mild surprise. In contradiction to the gloom hovering over her inside, it was a beautiful early spring day outside. The sun was everywhere.

She'd thought she'd be living in Tallahassee by now, settling into a new home close to Jason's new office, socializing in the governor's circle and generally being the helpmate that she'd learned to be…looking good, speaking well.

Being ignored.

The thought slid into her mind unbidden, and instantly she resisted it. She had been an integral part of Jason's life, had helped him achieve his dreams—*their* dreams. She had been relevant. Perhaps Jason had fallen out of love with her, but he hadn't ignored her.

Otherwise, how could she have been happy?

Frowning, Gemma turned away from the window and padded downstairs in search of something cool to drink. The kitchen was dark and hummed with electric white noise as the refrigerator labored to stay cool. The pungent smell of overripe fruit hung in the air. From a wire basket, Gemma picked a pear to munch on, then rummaged in the fridge, past Jason's Red Bulls, for a bottle of tea.

While she drank and waited for the caffeine to kick in, Gemma mentally sifted through the things that had unraveled, things she needed to tend to. Sue was right about one thing—she had to find a job. She was more fortunate than most divorcées in the sense that in lieu of alimony Jason had paid off the house and her car, and left her with a small savings account. But she didn't want to squander what money she had, and the house and car wouldn't run on their own.

Besides, a job would help her to…rebuild. Reclaim. Renew. Her future could be waiting for her in the Help Wanted ads.

She pulled on shorts and a T-shirt, and swept her hair back into a ponytail. Then she unlocked the front door and walked barefoot out onto the covered porch. The light gray painted wood planks were gritty beneath the soles of her feet, the two chairs sitting next to a small table full of leaves and yard debris. Scooping up the rolled newspapers, she turned and tossed them inside. Then she surveyed the weedy, neglected yard that would have to wait until she addressed other items on her mounting to-do list.

How quickly things could go from neat and orderly to utterly out of control.

She walked to the mailbox and, at the curb, turned to take in the house next door. The faded yellow, two-story stucco structure with the red tiled roof and wrought-iron details was one of the last houses in the older, eclectic neighborhood to be rescued. She thought she remembered hearing that the house had been tied up in court, something to do with probate. If properly restored, it would be glorious, she decided, much more interesting than the sturdy but standard home that she and Jason had settled into.

The dark-haired handyman was nowhere to be seen, but his presence was evident. The For Sale sign was gone and two ladders leaned against the front of the house. A pressure washer and other equipment sat near the front door. She smiled, relieved that the house would finally receive the attention it deserved.

Her mailbox, labeled "Jason and Gemma White, 131 Petal Lagoon"—another artifact of the marriage to correct— was stuffed full of high-tech catalogues and news magazines that Jason liked to read. It was taking a while for his forwarding address to trickle down. She loaded her arm with the mail and flipped through it idly as she made her way back to the porch steps. Her hand stopped on a large brown envelope with the county's return address. Walking inside, she closed the door behind her and dropped the rest of the mail on the kitchen table. With a sense of foreboding, she slid nervous fingers under the flap and pulled out a sheath of papers.

Final Judgment and Decree. Gemma swallowed hard

and scanned the four short paragraphs that officially terminated her marriage.

"...it is decreed by the Court that the marriage contract heretofore entered into between the parties to this case, from and after this date, be and is set aside and dissolved as fully and effectually as if no such contract had ever been made or entered into..."

As if the marriage had never existed.

Her eyes watered, blurring the words. This was it then. Proof that the last ten years of her life hadn't mattered. She'd assumed that she and Jason were years away from the menace of a midlife crisis, yet in less time than it had taken to plan her wedding, her marriage had disintegrated.

What now? she wondered, leaning into the granite counter, uncaring that the hard edge bit into her pelvic bone. TV therapists and girlfriend shows referred to breakups as a clean slate, a new chapter, a chance for a woman to find her authentic self.

But what if her authentic self was being Jason White's wife?

It was a notion that she didn't dare say aloud for fear that Oprah herself would appear on her doorstep. She knew that being absorbed into a man's life was considered passé, but she couldn't remember the person she'd been before Jason. She didn't have a point of reference, a place of origin. She recalled only a vague sense of floating aimlessly before she'd moored herself to him.

He had been her first and only lover. He was all that she knew.

The sound of the doorbell pealed through the air, jangling her nerves. She frowned, wondering who could be visiting. Then, remembering what Sue had said about having company, her pulse picked up at the thought that it could be Jason. Had Sue been trying to forewarn her? Perhaps he'd received his copy of the final papers, too, and he'd reconsidered...

Gemma wiped at the wetness on her cheeks as she hurried through the foyer and was smiling when she opened the door.

But at the sight of the man standing on the threshold, her smile faltered.

2

THE SHOULDERS OF THE dark-haired handyman spanned the doorway. His hawkish features and long, work-muscled arms were coated with a layer of gray dust. A tiny gold loop hugged his earlobe, and a black tattoo extended below his right T-shirt sleeve. She put him in his late thirties, and was both taller and bulkier than he'd appeared from a distance. Chiding herself for not checking the peephole before opening the door, Gemma took a half step back. The man's appearance made her suddenly realize how vulnerable she was here alone.

She had to start thinking like a single woman again.

"May I help you?" she asked, trying to sound firm.

"Sorry for the intrusion, Ms. Jacobs," he said, his voice low and as smooth as her worn wood floors. Still, her throat contracted in alarm.

"How do you know my name?" Her maiden name…her old name…her *new* name as mandated by a formal order in the divorce papers.

"It's on your mail," he said, extending a white envelope. "I found this blowing around in my yard."

She took the long envelope, feeling contrite. "Oh…I must have dropped it. Thank you."

"You're welcome."

He nodded curtly and made a movement to go, but after her abrupt greeting, she felt compelled to reach out to him. "Did you say *your* yard?"

"I'll be living in the house for about a month, until it's ready for resale."

So he was planning to turn a quick profit, then be on his way. "It's a beautiful place," she offered.

He nodded. "I've had my eye on her for a while, but it took some time to close the deal."

Speaking of eyes, he had nice ones. The color of raw umber thinned with the tiniest amount of golden linseed oil. She hadn't thought of her paints in years. "I've always admired the bones of the house. I'm glad someone thinks it's worth renovating."

"Chev Martinez." This time he extended his bronzed hand.

After a few seconds' hesitation, she put her hand in his. "Gemma Jacobs." Her old name—her *new* name—rolled off her tongue with astonishing ease. Conversely, the physical contact set off distress signals in her brain. His hand was large and callused, but his grip was gentle…the hand of a man who was accustomed to coaxing a response from whatever he touched. Awareness shot up her arm, and she realized with a jolt that he was looking at her with blatant male interest. She withdrew her hand, suddenly conscious of her appearance, sans makeup and wedding ring. She wasn't sure which made her feel more naked.

"Do you live here alone?"

She knew what he was asking—if she was single… available. According to the papers she'd just received, she was indeed single, but was she available?

The sounds of summer imploded on them. The buzz of

the honeybees drawing on the neglected ginger plants, the caw of birds perched in the fan palm trees overhead. "Yes, I live here alone," she said finally.

Another nod. "If the construction noise disturbs you, let me know."

"I will."

"Guess I'd better get back to work." He half turned and descended her porch steps.

"So…you're in real estate?"

His smile was unexpected, white teeth against brown skin. "No. I'm a carpenter, but I sometimes flip houses. How about you?"

An expert wife. "Unemployed art historian, which is why I fell in love with your house."

"Maybe you'd like a tour sometime." He was backing away, but still looking at her—all of her.

"Maybe," she said, hedging. Now that he was out of arm's reach, she was regaining her composure. There was something dangerously magnetic about the man. In a matter of minutes, he'd demonstrated an uncanny knack for extracting the truth from her.

He lifted his hand in a wave and walked away, his long legs eating up the ground. From the safety of her shade-darkened porch, Gemma watched him cross her yard to his, drawn to the way he moved with athletic purpose. His broad back fell away to lean hips encased in dusty jeans with a missing back pocket. He stopped next to a silver pickup truck parked in the broken-tile driveway and from the bed lifted a table saw, stirring the muscles beneath his sweat-stained T-shirt. He carried the unwieldy tool to the front door of his house and disappeared inside.

Gemma wet her lips, conscious of a foreign stir in her midsection—arousal?

Then she scoffed. That was impossible.

Stepping back inside, she closed the door and turned the dead bolt lock for good measure. Her reaction was mere curiosity…and pleasure that the house next door seemed to have acquired a good caretaker for the time being.

She liked the way he'd referred to the house in the feminine sense, as if he were restoring honor to a once-grand lady. The affection in his voice for something that he'd been willing to wait for left Gemma warm and wondering. Between his benevolence and his…bigness, the man was an intriguing addition to the local scenery.

Not that she knew many of her neighbors. Even though she and Jason had lived in the neighborhood for two years, their social circle had remained with Jason's law cronies and state government associates. Gemma had made a few acquaintances while working in her flower beds, but nothing past small talk and vague promises to get together sometime for a cookout. She'd known that if Jason won his bid for attorney general, they would be relocating anyway.

Now it looked as if she'd be living alone at 131 Petal Lagoon for the foreseeable future.

She sighed and glanced at the envelope her neighbor had handed her. Her maiden name and the street address were typed neatly in the dark font of a laser printer. The return address was a post office box in Jacksonville—no doubt a mailing from Covington Women's College.

Gemma gave a wry smile and tossed the envelope onto the table with the rest of the mail. She'd have to defer her annual donation to her alma mater until after she found a job and paid down her bills. With that goal in mind, she retrieved the bundled newspapers. While the logistics of finding a job seemed overwhelming at the moment, the idea of having her own career sent a flutter of nervous anticipation through her chest. How long had it been since she'd given her own ambitions more than a passing thought?

Since before Jason...since college.

Squinting, she tried to remember her goals before she had allowed herself to be absorbed into Jason's life plans. They must have been flimsy, she acknowledged ruefully, if she had been so willing to cast them aside. There had been many trips to art museums, she recalled, to make notes on traveling exhibits that she might never get to see again. Where were her journals? And she'd volunteered her services to catalog tedious bits of obscure collections that might or might not prove valuable someday, such as hand-drawn elevator door designs from the late 1800s and the tools used by mason workers to cobble the streets of Saint Augustine. Being around old things comforted her—the permanence, or at least the history, of objects made her feel as if everything in the world had some significance, herself included.

But the last time she'd been to an art museum had been for a political fund-raiser, where bleached smiles and glad-handing had overridden the more meaningful backdrop.

She opened a week-old newspaper and, after glancing over the headlines that she'd missed, turned to the Help Wanted ads.

"Art, art, art," she murmured, skimming the columns with her finger, thinking that a curatorial position would be nice, or something in art preservation. Or maybe teaching. Her finger stopped on an ad for an executive assistant for the director of a local museum. She smiled—maybe this wouldn't be so hard after all. The job description sounded

interesting and challenging. Then she skimmed the requirements and pushed her tongue into her cheek. A master's
degree, two to four years experience, and proficiency in
computer programs she'd never heard of.

Still, it was worth a phone call. She dialed the number
listed and after a series of automated selections was finally
connected to a live person in human resources who informed Gemma that the job had been filled through an employment agency the same day it had been listed.

After browsing the ads of other, less appealing jobs
available in the "arts" field and realizing that she was
woefully underqualified for all of them, Gemma pushed
to her feet. Crossing the kitchen, she fought a panicky
feeling that was becoming all too familiar lately—the
feeling that the exit she'd chosen in life had no reentry back
onto the freeway.

In a word, she felt...*stupid*. And angry with herself.
Thirty-two years old and she was suddenly ill equipped to
live her own life.

Hoping that a pot of java would improve her outlook,
she filled the coffeemaker and listened to it gurgle as she
stared out the window at the house next door. With its
shutters, doors and windows thrown open, the house
looked vulnerable. Indeed, it seemed to be sagging in self-
consciousness, as if the old girl were resigned to the idea
that before she could be restored, she first had to be
stripped of her pride.

And from the dust clouds buffeting out of the second-
story windows, Chev Martinez appeared to be the man for
the job. She craned for a glimpse of him, but the rude beep
of the coffeemaker interrupted her idle musings.

Which was just as well.

CHEV MARTINEZ PAUSED and leaned on a push broom to allow the dust in the room—and in his head—to settle. He'd been anticipating this day for months, since he'd first spotted the Spanish-style house sitting abandoned, a fading exotic bloom in an otherwise bland but upscale neighborhood. Since that time, he'd driven by countless times, just to reassure himself that the place was still standing, still waiting for him.

And he'd become accustomed to seeing the fresh-faced blonde next door tending to her flower beds. He'd seen the husband's name on the mailbox, knew the man's title and position, and had tried to put her out of his mind. But there was something about the woman that spoke to him—the grace of her lithe body, the big hats and colorful gloves she wore gardening, the fact that she always looked as if she were humming.

She was…*happy*. Chev had envied the man who came home to her sunny smile every day, had imagined that she possessed a wicked sense of humor and was a great lover. The kind of woman who presented a proper appearance for the political scene and her suburban neighbors, but came undone in the privacy of her own bedroom.

When he'd pulled up today, he'd known something had changed. Her yard was untended and newspapers were piled on the porch. Her house was dark and quiet. His first thought was that she and her husband had taken an extended vacation, but then he'd seen a light go on in an upstairs room, had seen her solitary figure moving around. Knowing she was there had left him feeling antsy all morning. Finding the stray letter in his yard had given him a legitimate reason to knock on her door, but he'd paced around like a kid before working up his nerve.

With good reason.

Seeing her up close had sent his vital signs galloping. Her red-rimmed eyes and damp cheeks had confirmed his suspicion that something was wrong, and the tan line on her ring finger had given him a clue as to what. Her response that she lived alone cinched his suspicion that the woman's happiness had been brought to a halt by a sudden end to her marriage.

The knowledge both saddened and unnerved him. He'd met plenty of women for whom he'd felt a physical attraction, but there was something so...*appealing* about this woman that it disarmed him. He could see in her eyes how broken, how vulnerable she was, and while his first instinct was to get close to her, he didn't want to get involved with a woman who lived only a few steps away from his work site...and who was still holding a torch for her ex. Besides, he was only responding to the wild fantasies he'd spun about the woman. She was probably nothing like he'd imagined.

Gemma.

Of course her name would be unique, special. Of course she would recognize the neglected charm of this house. Of course her legs would be long and her breasts full. Of course she would have a brown beauty mark next to her shapely mouth that completely stole his concentration.

He pulled a handkerchief from his pocket and mopped at the sweaty grit on his neck. He had to get his libido under control and his mind back on the job. It wasn't as if Gemma Jacobs was looking to start up something with him. Her husband's policies hadn't been particularly friendly to Americans of Puerto Rican descent—for all he knew, she might share her ex's views. It was, he acknowledged, a flimsy attempt to distance himself from the woman in his mind, but he had a full plate at the moment and he couldn't afford the distraction.

This would be the third house he'd flipped in the past year. For someone who didn't own a house of his own—and didn't plan to ever settle down—he seemed to have a knack for knowing what home buyers looked for. He had one month to finish this renovation before he had to be in Miami for a lucrative commercial job. His goal was to put the For Sale sign back in the yard within that time frame and have a fat check in his hand before he left town. The auction was already scheduled. If he missed the deadline, he was screwed. Which meant there was no time to waste on a flirtation, no matter how tempting.

No. Matter. How. Tempting.

Forcing aside the thought of his neighbor's lush body, Chev walked to the window and ran a hand over the carved woodwork of the frame, some of it flaking paint, some of it rotted. This one repair alone would take hours, but in the end, it would be worth the hard work. People buying in this neighborhood would expect attention to detail. The place reminded him of pictures of his grandparents' colorful home in Puerto Rico. He took in the wide plank floors of the large room, the cracked plaster walls and ceiling, the tall rounded door openings, all of the finishes compromised from neglect and exposure to extreme temperatures. But the house would be grand once she was restored to her former self.

He stared across at the picture window where he'd seen his new neighbor this morning. Considering she'd been scantily clad and her hair tousled, it seemed likely that it was her bedroom window. A filmy white curtain moved with a light breeze, as if in confirmation.

Her window was larger and slightly lower than the one where he stood. At the thought of having a clear view of her bedroom, his sex hardened and pushed against his fly. Did she have flowery sheets? Did she like to sleep late? Did she ever sleep in the nude?

Chev turned away and shook his head to dislodge the image from his mind. He went back to sweeping, putting more muscle in it than necessary. He was losing his mind, playing with fire by indulging these dangerous fantasies. He made his living on the road, moving wherever the best jobs took him, satisfying his sexual urges with the occasional pretty barfly or waitress, partners who were as transient as he was. Not suburban divorcées who tended flower beds.

Besides, if Gemma Jacobs knew what he was thinking, she'd probably have him arrested.

3

AFTER POURING HERSELF a tall mug of coffee and adding milk, Gemma returned to the Help Wanted ads armed with a red pen. Several frustrating phone calls later, she had learned two things: jobs in the immediate Tampa area generally didn't remain open for more than forty-eight hours, and the majority of positions were filled through employment agencies. So when she spotted an ad for one such agency, she made another phone call.

A chipper sounding woman answered the phone and invited Gemma to come in the next morning for an "assessment of her skill set." Gemma made an appointment and hung up slowly, feeling as if she were back at the placement office on campus looking for work-study programs that would mete out enough to pay for toaster-oven meals and discount dresses.

When angry tears threatened to undo the progress she'd made, she turned her attention to the cleaning she'd told Sue she'd get to today. The house was musty and dusty and the laundry could no longer be ignored. Gathering cleaning supplies, she threw herself into the task, only to be derailed every time her feather duster encountered a photo of her and Jason, or when the vacuum cleaner unearthed relics of their relationship—a valentine that had fallen behind a table, a cuff link. The yawning emptiness of the house made it feel like someone had died. She considered making paper carnations out of the crumpled tissues littering the floor, but she had to admit, it felt good stuffing the tear-stained clumps into a trash bag.

The stack of things that Jason had inadvertently left behind continued to grow—a pair of golf shoes here, a wife there. Gemma made slow but steady progress, although she was hanging on to her emotions by a thread when the phone rang late in the afternoon. Seeing her mother's number on the caller ID screen did nothing to improve the day's direction.

But considering that her final divorce papers were on the table next to her *Real Simple* magazine, it seemed the moment to come clean with Phyllipa Jacobs was at hand.

"Hi, Mom."

"Gemma," came the wounded reply. "Is there something you want to tell me and your father?"

Gemma bit down on the inside of her cheek. "I guess you heard."

"You mean about my own daughter's *divorce?* A complete stranger at the local paper called to get my comment. I've never been so mortified in my entire life."

If the newspaper in the tiny town of Peterman had heard about the state attorney general's divorce, then it had to be on the wire services. Had Jason's office released a statement? "I didn't know how to tell you. I'm sorry you found out from someone else."

"Then it's true?"

"Yes."

"I don't believe I'm hearing this. What happened?"

Gemma dropped into a chair and gave a choked little laugh. "I really don't know."

"You're laughing?"

She closed her eyes. "No, I'm not laughing, Mother. I'm telling the truth. It was Jason's…idea. He wanted the divorce."

"*Jason* wanted the divorce? What did you do?"

Gemma flinched. "Why would you think I did something?"

"Because Jason loved you. He gave you a wonderful life."

"Mom, I—"

"Did you even *try* to work things out?"

The unexpected attack took her breath away. "Mom, Jason didn't want to work things out."

"That doesn't sound like the Jason I know."

Meaning Gemma didn't know her own husband—a direct hit. And true. He had fooled them all. Jason's parents were deceased, and her parents had welcomed him into the family like the son they never had. They had been delighted and proud that their daughter was married to such a powerful man.

"I know that you and Dad are disappointed, and I'm sorry."

"But what are you going to *do,* Gemma? How will you make it?"

She blinked at the utter certainty in her mother's voice that she couldn't survive on her own. "I'm going to get a job."

"Doing what?"

"I do have a college degree."

"That you've never used."

Gemma put her hand to her temple. "I'm sure I'll find something."

A baritone voice sounded in the background, then her mother said, "Your father wants to know if you need money."

"Tell him no, but thanks."

"Gemma," her mother said, lowering her voice, "if things were unsatisfactory in the bedroom between you and Jason—"

"Mom, don't—"

"I'm just saying that if he looked elsewhere for companionship, it doesn't necessarily mean that things are over."

"What's over is this conversation, Mother. I have to go. I'll call you soon."

She disconnected the call and dropped the handset as if it were on fire, still trying to process the surreal conversation. Her mother—the woman who had draped a kitchen tea towel over Gemma's face while she explained the birds and bees so she wouldn't have to make eye contact—was giving her advice on how to deal with a sexually unfulfilled husband?

Would everyone automatically assume that she was lousy in bed?

Probably, since she had jumped to the same conclusion herself.

Even in the beginning she and Jason had never lit up the sheets, but their lackluster sex life hadn't been an issue between them because they were compatible in so many other ways. They made time for each other...usually. His schedule had grown more demanding as the election had drawn near. But he'd sworn to her that no one else was involved in their breakup, and she wanted to believe him.

Two frantic days of tearing apart his desk, closet and credit card statements hadn't yielded any suspicious purchases or activities. After which she'd lain awake agonizing over what was worse—being dumped for another woman, or being dumped for no discernible reason.

A low buzzing noise sounded from next door. She stood and glanced out the kitchen window to see Chev Martinez wielding the pressure washer on the stucco exterior of the house. He had removed his shirt in deference to the late afternoon heat, providing a heart-stuttering view of his powerful chest, glistening from sweat and mist. A red bandanna covered his head, giving him a roguish appearance. His jeans were soaked up to his knees, and water dripped from his elbow as he moved the wand, removing years of grime from the house one swath at a time. The dark outline of the tattoo encompassed the muscle of his thick upper arm.

Gemma's body warmed in forgotten areas. The man was exotic and out of place in this sleepy neighborhood, like an animal who had wandered in from the wilds. The tip of her tongue emerged and whisked away the sheen of perspiration on the rim of her lip. But when he turned his head in her direction, she shrank back from the window, feeling foolish, like a sex-starved housewife ogling the pool boy.

She gave herself a mental shake—this wasn't like her. She wasn't the woman at the cocktail party glancing across the room to catch the eye of a handsome man, the kind of woman who flirted with waiters and shoe salesmen. She had been physically committed to her husband, had closed her mind to the idea of touching another man, or having another man touch her.

She didn't know how to behave like a single woman, couldn't remember the vocabulary, the body language.

Suddenly she felt tired, her lazy muscles taxed from cleaning. She needed to take a shower and start thinking about tomorrow's appointment at the employment office. She pitched the old newspapers and sorted the rest of the mail, tossing Jason's magazines and catalogs into a basket, her fingers hesitating over the divorce decree.

Where did one keep their divorce papers? In a box with

their defunct wedding photos and marriage license? In a file with other routine documents like tax forms and canceled checks? In a frame, mounted on the wall?

She sighed, postponing yet another decision. When her hand touched the white envelope—presumably from Covington Women's College—that Chev Martinez had delivered, a nostalgic pang struck her. She had savored her time at the school, had been ecstatic to escape the suffocation of her parents' close supervision. The young women she'd met there had seemed so much more worldly and more mature than she'd been. Gemma had been content to hover on the periphery of their candid opinions and heated debates about the human condition, trying to soak up their moxie.

She tore open the flap with her thumb and removed the contents, another envelope tucked inside a cover letter. The yellow flowered envelope plucked at a memory chord. On it was written a series of numbers and letters that made up a code of sorts—she frowned—in her own handwriting?

Unfolding the crisp cover letter, she scanned the letterhead. *Dr. Michelle Alexander* elicited another tug on her memory, compelling her to read on to determine why.

Dear Ms. Jacobs,
You were a student in my senior-level class titled Sexual Psyche at Covington Women's College. You may or may not recall that one of the optional assignments in the class was for each student to record her sexual fantasies and seal them in an envelope, to be mailed to the student in ten years' time. Enclosed you will find the envelope you submitted, which was carefully catalogued by a numbered code for the sake of anonymity and has remained sealed. It is my hope

that the contents will prove to be emotionally con-
structive in whatever place and situation you find
yourself ten years later. If you have any questions,
concerns or feedback, do not hesitate to contact me.
With warm regards,
Dr. Michelle Alexander

Wonder flowered in Gemma's chest as memories came rushing back in a torrent of disjointed images. The Sexual Psyche class had been legendary at Covington. Jokingly dubbed "Sex for Beginners" by the female students, Gemma had felt naughty simply signing up for it. She recalled how nervous and self-conscious she'd been the first time she'd slid into a seat in the rear of the class, eyes lowered.

Dr. Michelle Alexander had been a lush-hipped woman with long, dark wavy hair and a wide, warm smile. She had made sex seem like a glorious gift rather than the obliga- tion that Gemma's mother had conveyed. Gemma had been mesmerized, wondering as the woman lectured on the virtues of self-gratification and multiple orgasms, how many lovers she had at her beck and call. The class had been an awakening for Gemma, an outlet for all the pent-up questions she had about a topic that had long mystified her.

She fingered the flowered envelope, oddly embarrassed at the prospect of reading things she'd written as a virgin, before she'd even met Jason, now that she thought about the timing.

Gemma bit into her lip. Why was the prospect of having insight into the woman she'd been before Jason so unset- tling? After all, she had come full circle.

4

GEMMA CARRIED the envelope upstairs along with a half bottle of wine, deciding to take a shower and relax before delving into the past. The air on the second floor was warm and moist. She glanced at the clock and groaned—she'd forgotten to call a service company to come fix the air conditioner. Tonight was going to be a hot one.

But the water in the shower was cool. She slipped beneath the stream and leaned her head back, capturing a mouthful of water, then expelling it straight up. She smiled, realizing she hadn't done that in a while. It was such a silly thing to encourage her, but it did. A unwitting moment of pleasure, a few seconds of forgetfulness.

Then she spotted one of Jason's razors in the shower caddy, and the awful feeling, which she imagined as similar to being in a car accident, returned. No warning, no control and no mercy. And the numbness afterward, the deep denial that something that happened countless times a day to other people could happen to her. She and Jason—they had been special…different…happy.

Wrong, wrong, wrong.

She soaped and rinsed her skin hurriedly, suddenly eager to get out of the shower, to stop her mind from wandering to unhealthy places. When she turned off the water, she picked up Jason's razor and tossed it in the garbage can. Then she pulled a towel from the rack to blot her hair and pat her skin dry. She caught a glimpse of herself in the mirror and stopped for a candid appraisal.

Out of neglect, her hair was a little longer than she normally kept it, but it made her look younger, softer. She had always taken care of her body through Pilates and regular outdoor activity, and although she might have lost some definition over the past few weeks of apathy, she still looked as good naked as she ever had.

She ran her hands over her breasts and down her flat stomach.

Had Jason simply grown bored with her? She turned to look at her behind, wryly checking for an expiration date she might have missed. She was no longer a coed, but she refused to believe she was past her prime.

Gemma wrapped a towel around her and tucked the ends between her breasts, then padded to the bedroom. After splashing a hefty portion of red zinfandel into a glass, she settled into an oversize chair and picked up the yellow flowered envelope. She held it for a moment, trying to remember the contents. She closed her eyes and visualized the dorm room she had shared with Sue and two other girls her senior year. She'd kept her stationery in a box under her bed. A memory flickered and she recalled that she'd sat up with a flashlight to work on the assignment— the act of writing down her sexual fantasies in the daylight had seemed unthinkable.

Two mouthfuls of the wine made a mellow path down her throat. She carefully worked loose the old, dry adhesive on the envelope, her heart quickening behind her breast-bone. Removing several neatly folded stationery sheets, she recognized her girlish handwriting—more timid back then, tighter, smaller.

The subject matter probably had something to do with that, she conceded.

The date was January, the last semester of her senior year.

I don't know how to start this letter, really. The instructor of our Sex for Beginners class says we're supposed to write down our sexual fantasies. Dr. Alexander says that we'll learn a lot about ourselves by understanding our deepest desires. In ten years, she's supposed to find us and send us our letters. In ten years I'll be thirty-two and it seems so far away I can't imagine what I'll be like then.

Gemma released a dry laugh. Ten years had evaporated, and she still didn't have a clue as to who she was.

And as far as the sexual fantasies go, I'm not sure I know enough about sex to know what excites me. You see, I'm a virgin, so I don't know what it feels like to make love. I've never even seen a naked man, except for pictures. And I watched a couple of X-rated videos with Sue that she got from some guy. Sue says that sex is more fun for the man than the woman and that doesn't seem fair. The women on the porn video seemed to be having fun, though.

I touched a penis once, at a party. The guy was kissing me and shoved my hand down his pants. It was softer than I thought it would be, and hairy. Then he came in my hand and I had to go to the

*bathroom to wash it off. It smelled strange and not
at all like I thought it would. When I came out of the
bathroom, the guy acted like he didn't know me.*

Gemma grimaced. She didn't remember the guy, but she
remembered the incident. How naive she'd been.

*I didn't really care because I didn't like the guy. But
there was another time, another party, another guy.
He just looked at me from across the room. We never
talked and he didn't touch me, but there was something about the way he watched me that made me
tingle all over. It made me wish I was wearing something sexy. It made me want to touch myself in front
of him. It made me feel like I was someone else.*
   So I decided to become someone else.

Gemma stood abruptly, taking a deep drink from her
glass, unwilling to read further—at least for now. Her sex
vibrated on a low hum, her pulse hammered. Blocked
memories came flying back....

Dr. Alexander had not only encouraged her students
to write down their fantasies, but to act them out in a safe
way. The idea had captivated Gemma, who had always
kept her emotions bottled, ignoring an itch she couldn't
identify. The assignment was a permission slip to mis-
behave. For a week she had played the role of an exhibitionist, donning disguises and leaving campus to act
out her fantasies.

The things she'd done made her face burn even now. And
she'd come very close to getting into serious trouble. The experience had scared her straight, so to speak. And a few

weeks later, she'd met Jason, and her life had fallen into place. She'd been so grateful to have escaped that little detour unscathed. No wonder she hadn't been able to recall what she'd written—because it was better left unremembered.

Hastily refolding the letter, she returned it to the envelope. She paced, now restless, her mind racing. It was silly to rehash schoolgirl fantasies anyway. They had nothing to do with the current state of her life.

The phone rang, breaking into her erratic thoughts. She glanced at the caller ID screen, praying it wasn't her mother. It was Sue.

The lesser of the two evils.

Gemma picked up the receiver. "Hello."

"Hi, just thought I'd check in. How was your day?"

"I got the final divorce papers today."

"I'm so sorry, Gemma."

"As if it's your fault."

"Have you heard from Jason?"

She pushed her hand into her damp hair. "No. The doorbell rang this morning and, like a fool, I thought it was him."

"Who was it?"

"Some guy who's fixing up the house next door."

"Some guy? Is he cute?"

Gemma thought of Chev Martinez's sexy eyes and calendar body. "I really didn't notice."

"What did he want?"

"He was just delivering a piece of my mail that he found. Hey," she said to change the subject, "I have an interview tomorrow with an employment agency."

"That's great! Are you excited?"

"Yeah, I'm actually looking forward to it. Oh, and I talked to my mom today."

"How'd that go?"

"It was a disaster of monumental proportions. Basically, she assumes the divorce is my fault, that I didn't keep Jason happy in bed."

"Oh my God, your mother actually said that?"

"Yes. Hearing my mother talk about sex was like listening to a frequency not meant for humans. I think my eardrums might have burst."

Sue laughed. "Well, at least you're starting to sound like yourself again. Your mom will come around. They were just blindsided, that's all."

"Weren't we all?" Gemma said. "I also had two phone messages from reporters asking me to comment on the divorce."

"I'm not surprised. Did you call them back?"

"Of course not. One of them was that toad Lewis Wilcox who so blatantly opposed Jason's election."

"Nice of you to protect Jason, considering."

Gemma pressed her lips together—old habits were hard to break. "It's not just to protect Jason. I don't want the attention, either. Besides, it's not as if I have any sordid details to divulge."

"But it's just the kind of thing that Jason's political opponents would love to turn into a scandal if they could."

"The funny thing is, the truth is too boring for a headline: State Attorney General Tells Wife, 'I'm Just Not That Into You.'"

Sue laughed. "At least now that the divorce is official—and public—it'll be easier for you to move on."

"As if I have a choice."

"Things are going to be fine, I promise."

Gemma sighed. "I know. I just want it to be sooner rather than later."

"Call me tomorrow after your interview to let me know how it went."

"Okay, bye."

Gemma returned the phone to its cradle, feeling a surge of appreciation for Sue who had better things to do than make sure her newly divorced friend was treading water.

Sue was right...things were bound to get easier. A job would help Gemma find a center for her new life and leave her less time to dwell on her failed marriage. She glanced at her closet and frowned. She knew how to dress for a fund-raiser, for a luncheon and for a political rally, but what did one wear to a job interview these days? Some companies encouraged their employees to dress casually, while others policed toe cleavage.

When she opened the folding doors of the closet, she nursed a fleeting pang for the empty side Jason's clothes and shoes had once occupied. A few odd hangers, a plastic collar stay, and a dry cleaner's receipt were all that remained. How many times had she wished for more closet space? She had it now, she thought as she spread her clothes across the entire length of the rod.

Flipping through suits, jackets, pants and skirts, Gemma discarded one thing after another as being too staid, too dressy or too casual. Her fingers skimmed over an exquisite black beaded gown she'd worn to a state government function and she wondered wistfully if she'd ever have an opportunity to wear it again. Finally she withdrew a tailored shirtdress and turned toward the mirror, dropping her towel. Then she gasped.

She'd forgotten that she had a new neighbor and could no longer walk around nude in her bedroom.

But at the sight of the darkened window across from hers, she exhaled in relief. Considering the late hour, Chev Martinez had probably left to have dinner or perhaps had collapsed into whatever makeshift bed he'd set up in the house for himself.

Then Gemma pressed her lips together as a deliciously taboo thought, lubricated by the wine, slid into her mind. Just what would she have done if the hard-bodied carpenter *had* been standing at the window, watching?

CHEV STOOD frozen to the floor. He'd come back to the upstairs bedroom to close the window and collect a few tools. Then he'd glanced up in time to see Gemma Jacobs perfectly outlined in her bedroom window as she dropped her towel.

His throat contracted at the sight of her naked body, her breasts heavy, her waist narrow, her hips curved. Her skin was pale and translucent, her nipples pink and puffy. The triangle of hair at the juncture of her thighs was light brown. His cock began to throb, and he was afraid to move, afraid she would hear him or detect movement in the darkened room. He wasn't a Peeping Tom, yet he couldn't bring himself to look away. He'd fantasized about her too often…having the chance to observe her, unseen, was too much to resist. She was unaware he was watching. He was only hurting himself, he reasoned.

Gemma was looking into a mirror and holding up a blue dress, a nice color for her. She laid the dress on the bed and, from a drawer, withdrew bra and panties. When she leaned over to step into the panties, her breasts fell forward, sending blood rushing away from Chev's brain and to his erection. She pulled the pale pink panties high on her thighs, then reached for the lacy bra. Putting her arms through the straps, she fastened the bra with a front closure, then arranged her breasts in the cups.

Chev swallowed hard. He'd never dreamed that watching a woman put clothes *on* could be so erotic.

She lifted the dress over her head, arching high. He could almost hear the rustle of the fabric as it shimmied down over her body. She buttoned the dress slowly, turning this way and that, then fetched a pair of high-heeled shoes to step into, rendering her long legs even longer, emphasizing the curve of her calves. He thought she looked beautiful, but she made a face, apparently dissatisfied, then proceeded to unbutton the dress with maddening slowness and lift it over her head.

He let out a small groan. Bra, panties, and high heels— God help him.

Next came a slim skirt and prim button-up blouse. "Nice," he murmured, although she wasn't showing enough leg for his taste.

She pirouetted in front of the mirror, then shook her head and, to his delight and despair, undressed again. Her breasts threatened to spill out of the bra as she moved her arms. He squirmed to adjust his erection that now bordered on painful. A bead of sweat trickled down his tense back.

Next came another dress, this one a floral number with a swingy skirt and snug bodice. She changed shoes to strappy high heels and as she turned in the mirror, he grunted in affirmation, then whispered, "Lady, you are gorgeous."

He shifted and accidentally nudged the wet/dry vacuum, which hit a ladder, which fell and took down several boards leaning against the wall, all of it crashing to the floor next to the cot he'd set up to sleep on. If the racket alone wasn't enough to alert his neighbor, a fat flashlight came on when it hit the floor, rolling and sending beams of light around the room like a strobe.

Chev dove on the flashlight, but the switch was broken and it wouldn't turn off. As he scrambled to remove the batteries, he glanced up to find Gemma staring at his window—staring at him. Chev realized with dismay that he was shining a light on his own face.

Busted.

5

AT THE SIGHT of Chev Martinez's face illuminated in the window across from hers, Gemma froze. From the guilty look on his face, it was clear he'd been there for a while, watching her. Watching her dress…and *undress*. The pale pink lace bra and bikini panties she wore left more skin uncovered than not. Several outfits were strewn over the bed.

A hot flush spread over her face and arms as she realized just how much of a show she'd inadvertently given him. And while her mind screamed for her to cry out in alarm, to cover herself and yank the curtain closed, her body seemed unable to comply. Slowly she realized that the inability to move was actually the *unwillingness* to move.

It was as if her wanton thoughts of him watching her had conjured up his image, had drawn him to the window. How could she shriek and flail about when she was the one who'd secretly wanted him to be there, and he was the one who looked stunned and…*trapped?*

It would be less embarrassing for both of them, she decided, if she pretended she didn't see him. So, with her skin warm and tingling, she turned her back and unfastened her bra, then retrieved a nightgown to slide over her head.

After the white filmy fabric fell into place, she turned back to the window and pretended to ignore him, although her nipples had hardened and warmth radiated from her sex. She gathered and rehung the clothes in the closet, all the while wondering if he was still there, and somehow knowing that he was. It occurred to her that even wearing the nightgown, silhouetted in the light and braless, she might as well be topless.

Did he like what he saw, she wondered. Feeling naughty, she turned sideways to give him a good view of her profile. Desire blazed through her body with an intensity that she hadn't felt in years…since college. She yearned to touch herself, but she had to remember that she and Chev Martinez would likely be crossing paths again soon. Performing for strangers as she had in college had been risky enough, but performing for a man who knew where she lived…

With slow reluctance, Gemma reached for the light switch and flipped off the bedroom light. Then she crawled into bed and lay there in the still, warm air, her body covered in a sheen of perspiration, pulsing with need. What had come over her? Was this the person she was without Jason? Libidinous? Out of control? Did she need his steadfastness to keep herself morally in check? Was she bound to slip back into the wickedness of her deviant sexual fantasies?

Several minutes later, the sound of an engine starting next door came through the open window, followed by the clatter of his truck leaving the property. She wondered what the dark-haired, dark-eyed man thought of her. Did he think she was depraved, or had she given him a hard-on? If the facilities in his house weren't yet functioning, he might be sleeping elsewhere. Was he fleeing to a girl-friend or wife nearby to share what had happened with a laugh before tumbling into bed? He hadn't been wearing a wedding ring, but that didn't necessarily mean anything, considering he worked with his hands all day.

Night sounds floated into the stillness of her room. Cicadas and other nocturnal insects emitted strident noises in rounds that swelled and ebbed. The perfume of fresh-cut grass and moon-blooming flowers rode the air. She felt utterly alone with her thoughts and nervous about this sense of restlessness her note to herself had reawakened. Knowing that sleep was long in coming, Gemma turned on the night-stand lamp and gingerly reached for the folded sheets of the abandoned letter.

With her heart pounding, she picked up reading where she'd left off, where the unknown boy at a party had watched her from across the room.

It made me feel like I was someone else. So I decided to become someone else. The next day I put on the sexiest pair of panties that I owned (pink with white lace), along with a short pleated plaid skirt and a white blouse. In the bathroom at the train station I put on a brown wig that my roommate had worn in a play, and large dark sunglasses. Then I got on a train going to a part of town where I knew no one. It was rush hour and the train was crowded, but I waited for just the right person. He got on a few stops later. He was cute and wore a gray pinstripe suit. He looked as if he was just out of college, probably working at his first job in an office somewhere. He sat a few feet away, facing me. He noticed my legs first. I was wearing white socks that came up to my knees, and black Mary Jane shoes. His gaze stopped again at my skirt, so I twisted in my seat to lift it a few more inches. And I parted my legs.

His eyes widened slightly and he glanced up to my face. But I kept my head slightly turned. With my dark glasses, he couldn't tell that I was looking at him out of the corner of my eye. He wiped his hand across his mouth and looked around to see if anyone else had noticed the panty show, but no one had.

His face turned as pink as my panties, but he kept watching, kept staring at me, sending tremors through my body. I knew he wanted me. I felt myself grow warm, then wet as I wiggled my skirt higher, my knees wider. I knew I was staining my panties, and wondered if he could tell. Apparently so, because he moved his newspaper over his crotch, then slid his hand beneath it. Knowing that he was secretly jerking off while staring at my pink panties made me feel powerful. I let him get his fill for several minutes, until his eyes went glassy. At the next stop, I got off the train. As the train pulled away, he was craning to see me through the window. I gave him a little wave to let him know that I had been in on it all along.

I could hardly wait to get back to my room. Thank goodness my roommates were gone. I went into the bathroom and closed my eyes, remembering the way that man had looked at me, and I made myself come over and over again.

Gemma set aside the letter, her ears pounding with the thrum of longing coursing through her. She sighed and pushed her sweat-dampened hair away from her face. Her mother's attempt at depicting sex as a necessary evil had backfired. By the time Gemma was finishing up college, she'd been burning up with a curiosity that Dr. Alexander's class had unleashed with a fury. What had been taboo had suddenly seemed accessible, only she hadn't been equipped to deal with the emotional and physical freedom. She'd been young and foolish, tempting fate with strangers in the pursuit of a sexual thrill. It had been liberating and exciting, but she had gone too far.

She was older now, wiser. She could control her fantasies, exercise restraint. She didn't have to act on them like before. The performance at the window had been accidental. She hadn't done anything that couldn't be innocently explained away.

Thank goodness.

Feeling relieved, Gemma turned over her pillow to find a cool spot and willed herself to go to sleep. She needed to be rested for her interview in the morning. Hopefully everything would go well and she would find a job quickly. Then she and Chev Martinez might not have the occasion to even see each other again before he moved on to another job. The incident would be forgotten. Perhaps, it had *already* been forgotten by him.

But her body still hummed with memory of his dark eyes on her, and for the first time since Jason's abrupt departure, Gemma fell asleep with the image of another man in her head.

CHEV PUSHED AWAY the remnants of a steak and baked potato and wrapped his hand around the fresh cold beer that the barkeep set in front of him. The any-town bar and grill was busy for a weeknight, with the jukebox blaring and the brews flowing freely between the men, some still garbed in work clothes, and the perpetually half-dressed coeds that populated every town in Florida he'd ever lived in, from Kissimmee to Miami.

"Lived in" was a stretch—more like visited. Moving from one commercial carpentry job to another, scouting for houses to flip in between. He couldn't remember being anywhere for longer than six months in the past five years, since his engagement to Brooke had ended so disastrously. At least he'd learned that his fiancée slept around—and upside down—before they'd said their vows. For the first two years afterward, he'd worked eighteen hours a day to keep the pain at bay, and by then, the frantic work pace simply became a habit. Lingering in one place too long would simply lead to…complications. His mantra was to keep his relationships light…portable…temporary.

And tangle-free. He didn't need to be arrested as a Peeping Tom for spying on the ex-wife of the state attorney general.

Chev shifted uncomfortably on the stool. He hadn't maintained a hard-on this long since high school, but even after a cold shower and a hot meal, he simply couldn't get the image of Gemma Jacobs out of his mind. He'd thought she caught him watching her, but then she had gone on as if nothing had happened, donning a nightgown that was as good as transparent, giving him a gut-clutching view of her full breasts tipping forward as she reached and leaned and stooped before finally turning off the bedroom light.

It was almost as if…

No. He scoffed. A woman like Gemma wouldn't…

Would she?

He pulled his hand down his face, wondering if it were possible that she *had* caught him watching her but hadn't minded. And, in fact, had extended the performance a little longer…

Then he expelled a harsh little laugh. Wishful thinking. Because the only thing hotter than watching her dress and undress in the window would be if she'd *known* he was watching her.

The moisture left his throat as his cock grew harder. He tipped up the beer and shifted again, troubled by the sudden thought that, after meeting Gemma and now having her nude body branded on his brain, there would be only one way to fully sate his appetite.

Unfortunately, that wasn't likely to happen anytime soon. The woman was way out of his league.

He turned his head and saw two pretty young brunettes staring at him over the tops of their drinks. They smiled and waved, twisting their tanned, nubile bodies to best advantage. Arms draped around each other's shoulders, they kissed full on the mouth for his benefit. He set his jaw at the lust that surged through him and considered the double-header diversion. A heartbeat later, he rejected the idea. Another time, he might have been interested, but tomorrow would be a long workday. It was best to call it a night. He gave the women a clipped nod, then tossed money on the bar and downed the rest of his beer before leaving.

He mentally kicked himself all the way back to Petal Lagoon Drive. Those two brunettes could've taken the edge off his libido and taken his mind off the blonde next door.

For a while.

The house next to his fixer-upper was dark when he pulled into the driveway, dimly illuminated by a dusk-to-dawn light on the street. His loud rumbling truck plowed through the quiet of the upscale neighborhood, reminding him that he didn't belong. He cut off the engine and sat listening to the silence of the suburbs, wondering what it would've been like to grow up in such an insular, privileged environment. A yard…trees…a pool…good schools for him and his siblings…good jobs for his parents. A world away from el Barrio where he'd spent his youth in Miami.

He climbed out of the truck and closed the door as quietly as possible, glancing up at the darkened window of Gemma's bedroom and feeling like a fool. The "performance" had been a fluke, and he'd have to put it out of his mind until the renovations on the Spanish house were done and he could sell it. Then, as far as Gemma Jacobs was concerned, out of sight was out of mind. In fact, starting tomorrow, he would do everything in his power to make sure that he and the blonde divorcée didn't cross paths again.

Staying away from her bedroom window would require a tad more willpower, but he'd put up a drop cloth, shutter the window, blindfold himself if necessary. Just because he hadn't been caught this time didn't mean he'd be so lucky next time.

And just like that, he was already fantasizing about next time….

6

DESPITE AN UNEXPECTEDLY good night's sleep, Gemma was jumpy as she sipped morning coffee standing at her kitchen window. She couldn't decipher if she was most nervous about the interview with the employment agency, or the possibility of running into Chev Martinez again after her unwitting peep show the night before.

His silver pickup sat next door in the early morning light, but all was quiet around the property as far as she could tell. She checked her watch—it was still early, but if she left now, she might be able to get away without even having to make eye contact with her neighbor.

She swung her bag to her shoulder and exited to the garage that seemed bare with Jason's car gone and his sports equipment missing from the walls. A black-and-gold monogrammed golf towel lay on the sealed concrete floor. Her heart squeezed as a fresh wave of loss swept over her. Gemma picked up the towel and ran her finger over the elegantly stitched letters, trying to remember who had gotten it for Jason. It didn't matter, she decided, laying it on a shelf. It was just a reminder of all the details in his life that were no longer her concern. She inhaled deeply and turned toward her car, thinking that if she couldn't rewind time to fix her marriage, she wished she could at least fast-forward to the day when things were okay again.

The pencil skirt she wore restricted her movement as she swung into the seat, but she told herself that she'd better get used to dressing up every day if she were going to rejoin the working world. Thank goodness that no one in Florida wore panty hose, but the rest of her outfit made her feel…proper. She was already eager to take it off. When the image of undressing with an audience of one flashed into her mind, she banished the thought. Squeezing the garage door opener on the visor, she started the car engine, poised for a quick escape. If she were lucky, she could postpone her next—undoubtedly awkward—conversation with Chev Martinez indefinitely.

Gemma put the car in Reverse and glanced in the rearview mirror, then slammed on the brakes.

Sitting behind her car, staring back at her was a large blue fowl, about three feet tall, with a sleek, pear-shaped body and elongated neck. He lifted his small, elegant head and emitted a loud, singsong call, then unfurled his tail plumage in an enormous, dazzling fan of iridescent greens, blues, aquas and golds, all sparkling in the morning sunshine.

She gasped in delight, having never seen a peacock at such close range. It was an extraordinary creature and rather intimidating in its full extension as it preened. It also appeared to be rooted to the spot.

Gemma backed the car out a few inches, hoping the movement would startle the bird into action, but he maintained his ground. She bit her lip and looked around. All was quiet. Nothing and no one around to distract the bird away from her driveway. She lightly tapped the car horn, but the cock merely bobbed his head, sending a plume of brilliantly colored feathers dancing. Gemma put the car into Park, and opened the door to step out.

"Shoo!" She waved her arms and walked toward it. "Go away!"

The creature seemed entirely unfazed.

"Move, birdie!" she shouted, flapping her arms. "I have to be somewhere important!"

The bird extended its neck and hissed at her. Gemma shrank back. She'd heard that peacocks could be aggressive and didn't relish being flogged.

Now what?

A low, rolling laugh reached her ears. She turned her head to see Chev standing at the edge of her yard, hands on lean hips, surveying the situation, a grin on his handsome dark face. Her midsection tightened, both at the sight of him in clean worn jeans and T-shirt, and at the knowledge that he'd seen enough of her last night to play connect the freckles. How would he react to her having ignored him? Would he assume she hadn't noticed she was being watched, or would he assume that she'd noticed and that she'd enjoyed it?

Gemma's face warmed. God help her, she *had* enjoyed it.

He walked closer, assaulting her senses. Her chest rose, pulling at the breast button of her starched white shirt. Her breath quickened and she couldn't tear her gaze from his dark, probing eyes.

"Trouble?" he asked mildly. The tiny gold earring in his left lobe glinted against his bronze skin.

She gestured toward the bird, feeling foolish. "I opened the garage door and he—it—was there. I don't suppose it's yours?"

His smile revealed white teeth and pushed his cheekbones higher. "No. It might have flown away from a zoo, but most peafowl are wild." He looked up into the trees. "Normally they don't travel alone. This fella must be lost from his bevy, or is looking for a new one."

Gemma relaxed a millimeter. "You seem to know a lot about peacocks."

He shrugged, displacing muscle under his T-shirt. "My grandparents used to have some on their property in Puerto Rico."

The exotic lineage suited him. "Does that mean you know how to get them to move?"

He laughed, a pleasing rumble, then strode toward the bird, waving his long brown arms. The bird, apparently more intimidated by someone larger and moving faster, startled, then moved away with a ruffle of bright feathers and a protesting yelp.

"Thank you," she murmured.

"Glad to help," he said with a slow nod.

Was it her imagination, or did his gaze pass over her? Had he remembered her outfit from the previous night's dress rehearsal? Her thighs tingled and she was glad to have the car between her and this enigmatic man who could set her skin on fire with his searing glance.

His mouth opened slightly and she sensed he wanted to say something, but his words fell silent on the heavy, humid air that hung between them. She knew how he felt—words would change everything. An apology would only multiply the awkwardness…a compliment could seem…unseemly.

"I'd better go," she said. "I'm late for a job interview."

His expression cleared and he stepped back with a little wave. "Good luck."

She swung back into the car and eased out of the driveway, glancing in the rearview mirror as she drove away. The man was striding back to his property, head up. Gemma shivered in the heat and exhaled a pent-up breath, trying to steer her mind away from her sexy—and temporary—neighbor and back to the task at hand: getting a job.

FROM THE OUTSIDE, the employment agency looked less than promising, wedged into a storefront in a shabby strip mall between a sandwich shop and a check-cashing joint. She hesitated before pushing open the door but forced herself to keep moving. The middle-aged woman behind the piled-high desk was on the phone, but waved for Gemma to come in. Her sharp, appraising glance left Gemma feeling as if she'd missed the mark with her prim outfit.

"You scare off everyone I send over there," the woman barked into the mouthpiece. "Up the hourly rate and I'll see what I can do." She banged down the phone, then turned toward Gemma. "What can I do for you?"

Gemma considered saying she was at the wrong address, but the image of the bills accumulating on her kitchen table was a stark reminder that she'd already put off this day for too long. "I'm Gemma Wh—er, Jacobs. I have an appointment."

The woman jammed on reading glasses and consulted a large wall calendar. "Yeah, there you are." She gave Gemma a flat smile. "I'm Jean Pruett. Have a seat, honey."

Gemma glanced at the mismatched chair opposite the desk that was filled with stacks of papers.

"Just set those on the floor."

She did, then lowered herself onto the edge of the chair.

"So, what kind of work are you looking for?" Jean asked without preamble.

"Preferably something in the art field. My degree is in art history."

Jean winced. "What's your work experience?"

Gemma shifted in the stiff chair. "In college I was in work-study programs with local museums—cataloguing and preservation."

"I meant lately."

"Oh. Lately I've been involved in charity work mostly, fund-raising, that sort of thing."

"I see. Do you have computer skills?"

Gemma brightened. "I have a computer at home." A castoff from Jason, which she'd never turned on.

"Do you know how to work with spreadsheets, databases or Web design programs?"

"Er…no."

"Do you have a teaching certificate?"

"No."

"Speak a second language?"

"I took a Spanish class…in high school." Which only made her think of Chev Martinez. *Por dios,* the man had a body. But for the life of her, she couldn't recall any other words in Spanish.

Jean sighed. "I'm sorry, Miss Jacobs, but unless you can give me something more concrete, I'm afraid I don't have anything for you."

Gemma felt the flutter of panic in her stomach. She didn't want to rely on Sue or Jason's contacts to find employment. "Surely there must be something."

"Most of the jobs I fill are temporary, either short-term or a few days here and there. They require either specific qualifications, or no qualifications at all, meaning the jobs aren't very desirable. And I can see from your appearance—"

"Try me," Gemma said.

Jean looked dubious, but turned to her computer and clicked on the keyboard for several long minutes. "Something in the art field, you say?"

"Do you have an opening?"

Jean named the art museum that Gemma had called the previous day about the executive assistant position. "They're looking for tour guides—"

"I'll take it."

Jean pursed her mouth. "It does pay pretty well for a part-time position. And it says chances are good it will become full-time. Can you start today?"

"Absolutely."

"Good. Um, there's only one catch...."

7

"A SEX EXHIBIT?" Sue asked with a laugh.

"The History of Sex," Gemma corrected into her cell phone. She checked her side mirrors, feeling self-conscious, as if someone might have witnessed her debut tour and be following her home. Thank goodness the employment agency had promised that her personal information would remain confidential, and she didn't have to wear a name tag.

"Do I even want to know what's on display?" Sue asked.

"Let's just say that no one under the age of twenty-one is admitted. And the tours are by reservation only."

"Ooh, sounds intriguing. Do you get to play show-and-tell?"

"Uh...that's one way to put it, I suppose."

"What aren't you telling me?"

Gemma sighed. "There are...costumes."

"Costumes? You mean uniforms, like flight attendants?"

"Only if the flight attendants work for Incognito Playboy Airlines."

"Oh? Do tell."

Gemma squirmed. "The guides have to wear sexy costumes."

Silence. Then, "Well, you certainly have the figure for it."

"And Lone Ranger masks."

Silence again, followed by, "But that could be a good thing, yes?"

"Considering that I'd rather not be recognized as the ex-wife of the state attorney general, yeah. Jason would be mortified if this got out. The press would crucify him."

"I don't plan to tell anyone," Sue said. "Do you?"

"No." Gemma worked to keep her voice casual. "Have you talked to him?"

"As a matter of fact, I ran into him today in the lobby of the capitol building."

Gemma closed her eyes, hating herself for caring but unable to resist asking, "How is he?"

"Fine. He's fine, Gemma."

In the awkward pause that followed, Gemma sensed that Sue wasn't being honest with her. Had Jason met someone else? Or had there been someone else all along?

"Have you seen your new neighbor lately?" Sue asked in a blatant attempt to change the subject.

Gemma's thighs warmed as the image of Chev slid into her mind. She spoke carefully. "I saw him this morning as I was leaving. He chased away a peacock that was blocking my driveway."

"A peacock? Where on earth did that come from?"

"I have no idea. Chev says they're wild."

"Chev?"

"Er, that's his name. Chev Martinez."

"Sounds exotic. Is he Mexican?"

"Puerto Rican, I believe he said."

"I had a Latin lover once," Sue said with a sigh. "He was heavenly in bed."

Gemma squirmed. "That's nice. And completely irrel-
evant to this conversation."

"I'm just saying."

"I'm not ready to move on," Gemma said. "You know
that Jason is the only man I've ever been with."

"All the more reason to have a fling," Sue insisted.
"Gemma, you and Jason are divorced. You don't owe him
any loyalty."

"I know. I just don't remember how to be single."

"Be indulgent. Try on new things…new men."

Just the thought of "trying on" a new man made Gemma
panic. She was better at performing at a distance than performing face-to-face.

Why else would her husband have left her?

"Right now I'm more worried about trying to pay the
bills," Gemma said, derailing the conversation.

"I can still make those phone calls on your behalf."

"I'm hoping this tour guide gig will lead to a full-time
job in the museum with a little more…coverage. If it
doesn't, I'll take you up on your offer."

"Okay. Gotta run. Talk to you soon."

Gemma disconnected the call and shifted in her seat,
staring at the long line of cars in front of her in the falling
dusk. She tapped her finger on the steering wheel to the
beat of the tune on the radio, frowning slightly when she
realized she was listening to a Latino pop music station.
She told herself it had nothing to do with the ethnicity of
her next-door neighbor and the attraction simmering
between them.

It was the job, that was all. The suggestive outfit that
she'd worn all day had her on a slow burn and sensitive to
the throb of the exotic music. Her dirty little secret was that

deep down, she'd experienced a thrill when she'd learned that flirty costumes were part of her new employment. She could feign consternation with Sue, but the only shameful part of being a tour guide for a naughty exhibit was how much she enjoyed it.

She had reveled in watching the eyes of men—and more than one woman—rove over her breasts and legs as she lectured from index cards about the history of erotica and pinups. Just talking about the taboo of nude photography over history had made her breasts heavy and sent moisture to the juncture of her thighs as she explained the lengths that the photographers and models had gone to—including breaking the law—in order to fulfill their own fantasies and the fantasies of people who would secretly view the shocking, illegal photos. The provocative nature of the exhibit hadn't been lost on the patrons. She had noticed couples touching more as the tour progressed and trading knowing looks as they left.

Gemma tugged at the short skirt that had crept up her thighs. The other tour guides had changed out of their costumes before leaving the museum, but she'd wanted to view herself in the getup at home, and at her leisure. She didn't plan to stop anywhere—she'd drive directly into the garage. No one would see her dressed in early fifties' "pinup girl" black miniskirt, fitted pink blouse, fishnet stockings, and peep-toe black high-heeled shoes. In her lap, she toyed with the crisp lace that added a feminine touch to the provocative black mask. The sensation sent erotic vibrations traveling up her arm.

When she drove by the Spanish-style home, she didn't turn her head, but in her peripheral vision she saw that the silver pickup was there. Willing herself not to react to the fact that Chev Martinez was nearby, she wheeled into her driveway.

But blocking her way was the pesky peacock.

He sat in the center of her driveway, head bobbing and tail sweeping the ground behind him.

"Not you again," she said with a groan. Then she rolled down the window and leaned out. "Shoo! Go away!"

When the bird didn't move, she set her jaw. She'd pull forward slowly. As soon as the bird sensed the heat from her car, surely it would move, simply out of self-preservation. She inched the car forward, wincing when the bird seemed determined to stand its ground. The bird disappeared from her sight beneath the front of her car, then appeared suddenly in front of her windshield in a flurry of flapping wings and honking noises, landing on the hood. Gemma cried out and accidentally sounded the horn, sending the bird into another round of hysterics, its claws gouging long marks into the paint of the blue Volvo.

"You're ruining my car," she screeched out the window. The agitated bird screeched back, then unleashed its tail fan on her, as if to scare her off with its dazzling plumage. Among the tail feathers were multicolored eye-shaped designs, a natural defense against predators, meant to confuse. Gemma's irritation gave way to wonderment—the creature truly was extraordinary.

"Quite a hood ornament you got there."

Gemma closed her eyes briefly in half-dread before turning her head to see Chev standing there, his dark head covered in a red bandanna, his skin and clothing coated with dust, his shirt sweat-stained and clinging to his broad shoulders. His dark eyes sparkled with suppressed laughter.

"Hello," she murmured, for lack of anything else to say.

"I think he likes you," he said with a grin. "Although I can't say that I blame him."

Her cheeks warmed as he walked up to the car. She cursed her decision to wear her costume home. What if she'd been in an accident? Or what if her sexy next-door neighbor happened to see her?

She shifted forward in her seat to hide the fact that she was scantily clad, hoping he couldn't see her in the waning light. "I hate to bother you again, but would you mind chasing him off my car?"

Chev waved his arms, grazing the big bird's feather enough to give it a start. It clambered off the car hood and strutted away, crossing her lawn. Her neighbor leaned over to inspect the scratches in the paint. "I think these can be buffed out."

"Thanks for your help," she said, then pressed the button on the garage door remote.

"Don't mention it."

Gemma pulled into the garage, thinking she'd dodged an embarrassing bullet, then realized that Chev was still standing next to her driveway, as if he wanted to talk to her. Lowering the garage door would be inexcusably rude, especially considering that he'd helped her not once, but twice today. So, swallowing her pride, Gemma opened her car door and stepped out. The black mask tumbled to the garage floor. She crouched to scoop it up. Although she was sure he'd seen it, she held it behind her back like a naughty child.

His gaze scraped her from head to toe, his eyes climbing in unasked questions. She had, after all, been wearing a rather prim outfit when she'd left the house this morning.

"Um, I can explain why I'm dressed like this," she said

as mortification bled through her. To her dismay, her nipples tightened in response to his appraising glance.

"It's really none of my business." He raised his hands, taking a step backward.

"It's for a job," she blurted, then realized that her explanation only made things worse. She smoothed a hand over her short skirt but, too late, realized it was with the hand holding the mask. "I'm a museum guide."

One side of his mouth climbed. "I don't remember seeing any guides dressed like that when I was dragged to museums as a kid."

"It's a, um, special exhibit," she said, crossing her arms across her chest in the glare of the overhead light that came on automatically. Admittedly the gesture seemed rather ridiculous considering how much of her he'd already seen. But being this close to him set her senses on tilt, left her feeling vulnerable as raw desire drummed through her limbs. "Thanks again for helping with the peacock," she said, nodding in the direction the bird had wandered.

"You're welcome. He shouldn't stay for long. He's looking for a mate, so once he realizes there isn't one here, he'll move on until he finds a bevy."

"That's comforting," she said, running her hands up and down her arms.

Silence followed, but electricity pulsed in the air between them.

Finally he broke the quiet with an awkward shift of his feet. "I just wanted to let you know that I'll be finishing some things in the house for a couple more hours."

"Okay."

"On the top floor."

She swallowed. "Okay."

"The electric in the house is spotty, so just because you don't see lights on doesn't mean I'm not there."

She realized what he was telling her—that at any time he might inadvertently see something through her bedroom window that she might not mean him to see. "O...kay." It was a gentlemanly way of letting her know that he'd seen her the night before.

"Not that everything I've seen in your direction isn't spectacular," he said in a low voice, wetting his lips.

Desire stabbed her low and hard. She didn't know how to respond, so she remained silent as heat rolled through her midsection, touching off little firestorms all over her body.

As if afraid he had crossed a line, he started backing away. "By the way, a tile crew is coming tomorrow, so there will be a wet saw operating outside. It might be, um, loud."

"I appreciate you letting me know."

"Hopefully the worst of the noise will be over by the time you come home from, um, work."

She felt humiliated all over again. "It's a temp job. I might get called in, I might not." Depending on how many reservations the museum received for the new, untried exhibit.

He nodded to cover what he must be thinking—how sad it was that the job she took not only required her to dress like a prostitute, but that she was basically on call...like a prostitute.

The automatic overhead garage light began to dim. "I should go in," she said.

"Of course. Good night."

"Good night." She waited until he was out of sight before lowering the garage door. She entered the house moving slowly, her underwear displaced and rubbing her in delicate places already tender with engorgement. An unattained orgasm sang low in her belly and she suddenly anticipated a self-stimulated release.

But where, she wondered, glancing around, her excitement mounting. The kitchen table? The shower? The bed? The blast of warm, stale air was a reminder that the air conditioner was still on the blink. She trudged up the stairs, flipping on lights as she went, her stomach growling from hunger. But a deeper hunger stirred in her pelvis.

She walked into her bedroom and turned on the light, then automatically went to open the window to welcome any breeze that might be stirring. As she slid aside the glass panel, her gaze went to the window across from hers. The room behind it was dark. Was he there?

Just because you don't see lights on doesn't mean I'm not there.

But was he the kind of man who would say that, then go upstairs to see what she would do? He'd made it clear that he hadn't looked away when he'd seen her undressing in the window, that he had enjoyed being the unintentional voyeur.

Her heartbeat increased to double time as blood rushed to her breasts and thighs.

Now that they both knew that he'd seen everything, would he scrupulously avoid the window? Or was he standing there, even now, waiting to see what would happen?

CHEV HELD HIS BREATH, hating himself for going straight to the window, but he'd been thinking of little else but Gemma all day, and his desire for her lay smoldering just under the surface. That provocative outfit of hers had been like a match thrown on the carefully banked coals, igniting an instant blaze in his belly.

She stood at the window, her face cast in shadow, her body outlined by the backlighting in her room. Her head was turned in his direction, although he felt certain he was hidden in the inky darkness. She stepped back from the window and he exhaled. She had understood his warning and would take steps to make sure it didn't happen again.

But instead of pulling the sheer curtain across the window, she simply started unbuttoning her blouse.

He stood riveted, because he knew this show was for him, purposely.

Facing him, she unbuttoned the low-cut pink blouse slowly, then shrugged out of it to reveal a black lacy bra that barely restrained her full breasts.

Chev sucked in a sharp breath as his cock hardened behind his zipper. He reached down to massage the length of his erection for some measure of relief. Where was this going, and how far would she take it?

Before the idea had slid out of his mind, he watched incredulously as she pulled the short skirt up around her waist, revealing the fishnet stockings—thigh-highs, Lord have mercy—and minuscule black panties. She lowered herself onto the edge of the bed.

Every muscle in his body tensed. Was she…? She wouldn't, he decided.

But she did.

She slipped her hand inside the black panties and as her fingers found their target, her head lolled backward, her mouth slightly open.

"Jesus," he muttered, dragging his hand across the back of his neck where perspiration had gathered. He knew he should leave for his own good, but he couldn't bring himself to look away. He told himself he would simply watch and not participate, refusing to relieve himself like a horny teenager. So he looked on, dry mouthed and overheated as Gemma's hand moved in a circular motion. He wondered idly how long it had been since she'd had a good orgasm, but he had his answer when, after only a few seconds, her body tensed, then spasmed with her release. His cock jumped in response and he thought he heard the sounds of her cries even through his closed window.

His breathing rasped higher in frustration as he was struck with the urge to ring her doorbell and give the woman a second orgasm the old-fashioned way. She withdrew her hand and leaned back on the bed for a moment, then pushed to her feet slowly and moved to the window. His cock throbbed for release, and he had the crazy thought that she would gesture for him to come over.

She lifted her hand…

And closed the sheer curtain.

8

GEMMA LOVED to make love in the morning…when the young sun suffused the bed with just enough light to see the expression on her lover's face as his body sank into hers. She slid her hand across the bed toward the man from her dreams, then blinked awake when her reach came up empty.

The erotic details of the dreams dissipated like fog, but she was left with the distinct impression of a dark-skinned man and a tiny gold earring. Her back was moist with perspiration, her body still vibrating from the intensity of the fantasies, no longer sated from her self-gratification episode of the night before.

A wicked thrill passed through her at the memory of her wanton behavior, and she wondered if and how her performance had been received. Had he turned away out of dismay, or had he, perhaps, exhausted himself along with her?

The idea of the big man watching her to achieve his own orgasm sent a shudder through her body. Then she bit into her lip—what if he was disgusted instead? What if he had reported her to the police or the neighborhood association as an exhibitionist? Last night when they were talking, she thought she'd sensed his arousal…but what if she'd misjudged mere politeness?

She went to the window and moved the curtain a millimeter. All was quiet next door, with no sign of the silver pickup truck. Perhaps he'd gone to eat, or to pick up supplies.

And then she noticed that the window across from hers was shuttered—the only one as far as she could tell.

Gemma swallowed hard. Was he sending her a message? It would seem so. A hot flush of humiliation scorched her skin as she turned away from the curtains. She'd pushed things too far, had exceeded the boundaries of good taste, or perhaps had trespassed on his obligation to another woman. Regardless, it appeared that he was putting an end to her watch-me games.

With a knot of anxiety in her stomach, Gemma dressed in shorts and T-shirt and descended to the first level. Feeling like a naughty child put in her place, she cursed her carnal weakness and chastised herself for not exhibiting more self-control. And she conceded that while she had considered and dismissed the danger in what she was doing (the risk was part of the thrill, after all), she was even less prepared to deal with outright rejection on the heels of Jason's departure.

Self-condemnation welled in her chest, choking her. God, she was lonely. She glanced at the basket holding Jason's accumulating mail and before she could change her mind, picked up the phone and dialed his cell number. While his phone rang, she reminded herself she had legitimate business to discuss with him and inhaled to compose herself. Should she try to sound perky, or detached? Which, she wondered, would best convey the notion that she'd moved on and was merely tending to the pesky loose ends of her marriage?

Jason answered before she could decide. "Gemma? What's up?" His voice was even and polite, as if he were talking to anyone...or no one.

A sharp pain struck behind her breastbone.

"Gemma? Are you okay?"

His thinly veiled irritation roused her from her wounded daze. "Sure," she said, sounding amazingly normal. "Sorry, I didn't expect you to answer. I was planning to leave you a voice message." She impressed herself with her improvisation.

"What about?"

"Your mail, and some other things you left. What should I do with them?"

"Is it anything important?" He sounded as if he was walking somewhere, juggling the phone.

She hardened her jaw. "Not to me. Some magazines, golf stuff."

"You can toss it as far as I'm concerned. I took everything that meant something to me."

Right between the eyes. She blinked, then nodded. "Okay, then."

"Did you tell your parents yet?" For the first time, she detected a note of sadness in his voice. It made her wonder if he'd prolonged the marriage for their sake.

"Mom called yesterday—she'd heard from another source. Did your office issue a statement?"

"No, we decided it was best just to ignore it and answer questions as they arise."

Ignore it. "I…" She almost faltered. "I have phone messages from several nonprofits asking me to help with their upcoming fund-raisers, on your behalf, of course."

"Divert them to my secretary. She'll take care of it, make appropriate excuses."

She wondered if kind old Margery knew that, after ten years, Jason still referred to her by her position instead of her name. Had he previously treated his wife with similar disrespect when talking to others?

"Is that all?" he asked, clearly already thinking about something else. "Do you need my help with something, Gemma?"

"No," she murmured. "I'm fine."

She hung up the phone quietly, in opposition to the fact that her heart was shattering all over again. She straightened her shoulders and exhaled. She wasn't fine yet, but she was going to work harder at it. Somehow she was going to find herself again, the woman she'd been before meeting Jason.

While she ate a bowl of cereal, she thumbed through the yellow pages for the names of companies to service her air conditioner. The first two she called were three weeks out on appointments, the third could come within a week at a price that took her breath away. She hung up the phone and decided that the sultry indoor temperatures were tolerable after all, at least until she achieved full-time gainful employment.

She checked her watch—8:15 a.m. Jean at the employment agency had said she'd call by eight o'clock if the museum needed Gemma, so it looked as if she needed to make alternate plans for her day. Hopefully by tomorrow, word of mouth about The History of Sex exhibit would have spread and the three newly hired guides would be booked solid.

She sipped the last of her coffee while standing over the sink, sneaking glances next door to see if Chev's truck had appeared. It hadn't. She decided she'd take advantage of the lower morning temps and work in her neglected yard.

She went to the garage and plucked her wide-brimmed straw sun hat from a hook, retrieving the floral garden gloves that she stored inside the crown. She hesitated before putting on the protective gear. The last time she'd worked with her flowers and plants, her life had been bumping along fine...at least, as far as she'd known. Jason had arrived home late, as usual, and she was still thinning the daylilies, having lost track of time. He had been irritated with her, she recalled, because she hadn't started dinner. And even after she'd reported spending most of the day volunteering at a local community center (representing his name and office), he had left her with the distinct feeling that she wasn't living up to her end of the bargain as a political wife, not contributing enough to his happiness.

She had been stunned and hurt, but had attributed it to postelection stress. In hindsight, it had been a warning of what was to come only a few days later.

She donned the hat and gloves, then pulled the lawn mower from the corner and gathered her bucket of gardening tools. A narrow door in the rear led to the backyard and patio. The wrought-iron table and chairs, with floral pillows and matching umbrella had been left by the previous owners and Gemma imagined a happy couple sitting there having an evening cocktail and winding down from the day. On occasion, she had brought reading materials out here to enjoy under the shade of the umbrella, but she couldn't recall Jason ever joining her.

As she picked up the festive pillows to rid them of leaves and debris, she wondered if Jason had decided to leave even before they'd bought this house...and then realized with jarring clarity that he probably had. He'd seemed detached throughout the buying and moving process, and other than setting up his office and staking claim to half the closet space and enough room in the garage for his golf equipment, he'd shown very little interest in either the house or the neighborhood. Because he'd known his days there were numbered?

From the patio she could see the back of the Spanish-mission-styled house next door. The tile walkways were broken and, in some places, missing altogether, and the yard and landscaping were overgrown. But other than a cracked and peeling oval-shaped pool, long since drained, the house itself looked to be in better shape from this side. She idly wondered what color Chev planned to paint the house and if he planned to restore architectural details. Probably not, since he'd made it clear he was flipping the house when it was finished.

The man would be gone within a month, and forgotten.

With a mental shake, she reminded herself that she had too much to do around her own house to be thinking about the goings-on of the man next door. Especially since he had likely dismissed her from his mind.

The grass was deep from neglect, necessitating two passes with the mower, one on a high setting, and one lower to the ground. But the physical exertion felt good, and the aroma of fresh-cut grass never failed to lift her mood. Before long, the tiny back and side yards were neatly shorn, and she had worked up both a sweat and a powerful thirst.

Retreating to the relatively cooler temperatures of the kitchen, she wet a paper towel and dabbed at her forehead and neck. From the refrigerator she retrieved a bottle of tea. Hearing a vehicle arriving next door, she glanced out the window over the sink to see a large flatbed truck back onto her neighbor's property. Its cargo appeared to be columns—many of them, in different shapes and sizes. The driver sounded his horn, then jumped down from the cab. When

Chev Martinez didn't appear, the driver gamboled to the door but still received no answer. He returned to the truck and appeared to check a clipboard against information stamped on the bottom of the columns. After much head-scratching, he looked utterly confused.

Finally, he set aside the clipboard and unloaded a column that caused Gemma to frown—it was clearly Corinthian, probably not the style that Chev had ordered to replace the ones that had once supported the arched entry porch. After a few seconds' hesitation, she went outside and walked next door, signaling the driver.

"Maybe I can help?"

"Are you the owner?"

"Uh, no. But I know something about the house, so if you're confused about which columns to leave, I might be able to offer some guidance."

He looked relieved. "That'd be great. If I leave the wrong ones, I can't come back until next week. The numbers are smudged, so it could be any of three different kinds I got here."

Gemma looked over the wood columns stacked on the flatbed like thick slabs of lumber and pointed out the pair that Chev had likely ordered. "The twisted ones."

The man unloaded the columns in a cleared spot along-side the driveway, then came back to where she stood and extended his clipboard. "Will you sign for these, lady?"

She hesitated, suddenly nervous at having made a deci-sion about something that was none of her business. She was saved from responding by the arrival of a silver pickup truck. "Here's the owner now."

Chev pulled up next to the bigger vehicle and swung down from the driver's seat. His gaze swept over Gemma and she was suddenly conscious of her sweat-soaked, stained work clothes. Remembering the shuttered window, her heart thudded in her chest.

"Is there a problem?" Chev asked.

The man pointed to the column he'd first taken off the truck. "Your neighbor here saw me unloading this column." Then he gestured to the pair he'd unloaded. "She said those were probably the ones you ordered instead."

Chev's gaze flitted back to her, molten in his appraisal. "She's right."

"Sign here," the guy said.

Gemma stood there until the driver pulled away, feeling awkward, her vital signs heightened. "I didn't mean to be nosy," she said in a rush. "But the driver looked confused and I was relatively sure you weren't going to install a pair of Corinthian columns on the front of a Mission-style house."

His slow grin melted her apprehension. "You're right. I owe you. That one mistake could've set back the entire project."

She shrugged, ridiculously pleased. "It was nothing. Besides, you've come to my rescue more than once the past couple of days."

He glanced around. "Any sign of our resident peacock?"

"Not today."

"Maybe he's moved on."

She nodded. "Well, I should be getting back to my yard work."

He nodded, but his gaze darkened and his lips parted, as if he wanted to say something…about last night? The tension in the air vibrated between them like a taut wire, but Gemma couldn't bring herself to look away.

"How about taking that tour we talked about?" he asked, nodding towards his place. "Actually, I could use your advice on a couple of other things inside the house since you know about the architecture."

"I'm no expert," she protested, shaking her head.

"Still," he said, coaxing her with a smile.

Between that smile and her burning curiosity to see the inside of the building, Gemma relented. "I'd like that."

He led the way, and she fell into step next to him, a tingle of anticipation in her stomach both at the prospect of seeing the interior of the house and at spending time with the vibrant, exotic man. He was dressed in work clothes that were, at this time of the day, relatively clean. She touched her hair self-consciously. "I must look a fright."

His sexy smile enveloped her in its radiating warmth. "You look great to me."

She blushed and chided herself for sounding coy when last night she'd climaxed in front of him, not caring—hoping, even—that he'd been watching.

He seemed to drag his gaze away from her. "The columns are meant for here, of course," he said, sweeping his arm toward the covered porch, whose roof was being held in place with several planks of wood that had been nailed together as a makeshift support system.

"They'll be perfect," she murmured.

He stopped at the front door. "I should've asked—have you ever been inside?"

"No. But I've peeked through the windows a few times." Then she blanched. Peeking through windows was becoming a theme where the two of them were concerned.

From the way he looked at her, she knew that he'd noticed her gaffe. Heat suffused her face, but his brown eyes glinted with the light of a banked fire. "It's even better when you can see things up close."

She swallowed hard, unable to maintain eye contact. He opened the door and motioned for her to precede him. When she brushed by him, a jolt of electricity shot up her arm where warm pink skin met warm brown skin. Warning bells sounded in her head. If the man could ignite her essence with an accidental touch, what kind of sensual assault could he perpetrate on her with full body-on-body contact?

Dismissing the thought with a mental shake, she walked into a once-grand foyer that even in its state of decay, served up a soaring welcome, from the wrought-iron chandelier to the curved staircase that led to the second floor. Terra-cotta tile at their feet, much of it now cracked and dull from dirt and age, stretched in both directions.

"Wonderful," she breathed.

"I'm going to have to replace most of the tile inside and out," he said ruefully, then led her to the left into a long kitchen/keeping room.

"It's huge," she observed. And it wasn't hard to imagine a family gathered here, laughing and passing heaping platters of food. Regret pinged through her chest. The holidays this year would be an awkward, lonely affair with only her and her frosty parents.

"I'd like to put in oversize appliances," he said. "What do you think?"

Gemma's eyebrows climbed. "About appliances?"

He shifted from foot to foot. "From a woman's point of view. It's been my experience that the kitchen usually makes or breaks the sale."

She hesitated. "Well, I'm not much of a cook…lately. But I'd say anyone who recognizes what a great kitchen this is will want appliances to measure up. Personally, I'd love a firebrick oven." She turned her head and smiled at the colorful picture that, with an inset wood frame, appeared to be built into the wall. "A mural, how lovely."

He made a mournful noise as he fingered the worn, moldy piece of canvas. "Unfortunately, it's so deteriorated I'm going to have to tear it out and fill in this area of the wall."

"That's too bad," she murmured, then turned to the end of the room. "Look at the fantastic natural light." She walked to the windows that faced out onto the dry, cracked pool in the backyard. "Are you going to restore the pool?"

He nodded. "I'm going to have it retiled."

He showed her two rooms that could be bedrooms, one of which he'd turned into a makeshift office with a card table and a folding chair. A box of files and a legal pad of paper sat on the table, with stacks of product brochures scattered all over. She noted the stark contrast of this man's workspace compared to Jason's home office, which had to be furnished with the best of everything before he could even inhabit the space.

"Do you have another home nearby?" she asked.

"Another home?"

"Do you…live in Tampa?"

"Oh. No. I move around a lot for commercial carpentry jobs. The reason I have so little time to flip this house is because I have a job lined up in Miami in a few weeks."

Why did the thought of him leaving plant a seed of worry in her stomach? She studied Chev's unyielding profile as he led her up the circular staircase. His strong nose, his high cheekbones, his chisled jaw. He exuded power…and sex appeal.

"Some of the woodwork is in bad shape," he said, shaking the wooden banister and watching splintered chunks fall to the floor below.

"Plaster ceilings," she exclaimed, glancing up at the fissures around the iron light fixture.

"Expensive to repair, but worth it, I think."

"Do you already have interested buyers?"

"An auction date is set, and several agents have said they'll have clients here. Assuming I can do justice to the original architecture, of course. She was a beauty."

Gemma murmured her agreement, especially when the second story opened into a master suite and bath that even in its state of disrepair, took her breath away. The wood moldings alone were a masterpiece. Her focus went to the cot set up in the corner of the room, then to the shuttered round window that was opposite her bedroom window.

"This is where I sleep," he said unnecessarily. "The bathroom up here is the only one working at the moment."

She nodded, hugging herself against the awkwardness that seemed to swamp the stuffy room. Wondering what was going through his head, she decided, was worse than knowing. "Awfully warm up here to have the window closed, don't you think?"

"I was just trying to give you some privacy," he said mildly. "This window looks into one of your upstairs rooms."

"My bedroom," she confirmed.

He nodded. "I, um, gathered that."

Feeling bold, she asked, "You don't like what you've seen?"

His mouth opened slightly, then his eyes turned smoky and he stepped in front of her. "On the contrary."

He was standing so close, they might as well have been

touching. His full, sensuous mouth was almost familiar to her. She could see the stubble of a patch of whiskers that he'd missed that morning shaving, could smell the lingering scent of his minty shaving cream. His powerful chest rose and fell quickly, his breathing as rapid as hers. He lowered his head and claimed her mouth in a motion so natural she didn't realize it was happening until she felt the shock of his warm tongue thrusting into her mouth.

Gemma moaned and opened her mouth to accommodate him. Her arms slid around his waist as if she were comfortable kissing a virtual stranger. The kiss went from hot to scorching as he pulled her roughly against him, his hands skimming up and down her back. Gemma gave up the kiss to let her head loll back in pure pleasure as his hands explored her body. He groaned in her ear as his erection pressed into her stomach, and he jammed his hand into the warm juncture of her thighs. She squeezed her legs against his fingers, her knees weakening as desire swelled in her midsection.

His hands felt so good on her body...too good—

Her eyes flew open as the reality of where they were headed crashed down around her. This was where touching led...to a dangerous, vulnerable place...much safer to watch, and to be watched...

She stiffened and withdrew from his embrace. "I...can't."

Chev's breath rasped out as he visibly tried to rein in his libido. "I guess I misunderstood."

Gemma started backing away, stumbled, and caught herself before he could get to her. "No, you didn't. But I need to keep things...at a distance."

Before the expression on his face could turn from puzzled to something worse, Gemma turned and fled.

9

CHEV PAUSED in the sweltering midday sun to shout instructions to one of the many tile workers who was replacing the hundreds of broken squares in the driveway. He pulled a bandanna from his back pocket and wiped his brow before tying it around his head. For the hundredth time that day, he glanced toward Gemma's house, wondering if he'd scared her off completely with his advances two days ago. He half hoped he had.

Then he lifted his gaze to his bedroom window that he'd unshuttered to let her know that he was interested in seeing her, even if it was only, as she'd put it, "at a distance." He scoffed at his hypocrisy—he missed seeing her to the point of distraction. Yet he didn't have time for a fling, and she didn't seem to have the heart for it.

Obviously she was still hung up on her ex-husband.

He grimaced, realizing he'd worked up yet another erection that would go wasted unless he went back to the bar tonight and looked for the conjoined brunettes. Gemma Jacobs had made it clear that she had no intention of getting involved with him…so why couldn't he get her and her performances off his mind?

"Chev!"

He turned his head to see a frustrated foreman trying to get his attention. Back to work.

Whatever Gemma was doing, he decided, she certainly wasn't thinking about him.

"ONE OF THE FIRST historically documented instances of a dildo," Gemma told her rapt audience, "is in Ancient Greece. The earliest dildos were made out of natural materials, such as wood or stone, and sold in public market-places. This particular example," she said, pointing to a crude yellowed phallus mounted on a pedestal under glass, "is made from human bone."

"Guess that's where the term 'boner' came from," a guy in the back cracked, eliciting laughs from the large group.

Gemma smiled obligingly and moved on to the next item on the tour. The museum's concerns about how the X-rated exhibit would be received had been laid to rest. Jean from the employment agency had informed her that the adult-only tours were booked solid for the next month.

Gemma had worked eight hours for the past two days and had the blisters on her feet to prove it. But she'd been glad for the work that pushed her body to exhaustion and her mind to distraction. It kept her from dwelling on the fact that Chev's bedroom window had been unshuttered since their encounter…an obvious invitation to resume her watch-me games.

She inhaled deeply, then exhaled slowly to calm her racing pulse. It was the charged air in the museum, she told herself, that had her thinking of Chev and his big, strong hand jammed between her thighs. Behind the mask that shielded her identity from the tour group, perspiration moistened her hairline. Today's crowd was more bawdy than most, tossing around jokes and innuendos that fueled the atmosphere to an almost palpable level. She'd lost a few couples already, slinking away to alcoves in the museum, she supposed, to indulge in a quickie before rejoining the tour.

Gemma used her tongue to whisk away a sheen of perspiration on her upper lip. She was beginning to feel like a fluffer on the set of a porn movie—the person who keeps everyone aroused between takes, but who never gets in on the action. The black corset she wore under a cropped jacket was chafing her nipples, and she ached to free them. But the costume of short shorts and jacket with stilettos was one of the most popular with the attendees—men and women alike were devouring her. Her sex and her breasts were heavy with awareness.

"This apparatus," she said, pointing to a metal device that resembled a bulky thong on a nude female mannequin, "is a chastity belt, which was padlocked to prevent access for sexual intercourse. They were common in the Middle Ages when crusading and wars were widespread. Some women wore them voluntarily to ward off rape, and some wore them to pledge fidelity to their husbands who might be away at war for years at a time. And some were installed by jealous husbands who wanted to ensure their wives would remain faithful during their long absences."

"Looks painful," a woman remarked.

"Which can be its own turn-on," another woman offered slyly.

A chorus of concurring murmurs met uncomfortable laughter as members of the crowd reacted. Gemma waited until the din had died before moving on to the room that housed furniture manufactured for the purpose of aiding sex—swings, contoured chairs, adjustable beds and benches.

Everywhere she looked, she saw Chev, making good use of the devices, his long, brown body poised for a session of Tantric sex. Although she had the feeling that a man like Chev didn't need props to shake a woman to her core. The sheer intensity of his kiss still plucked at her nerve endings.

She moved through the rest of the tour with the scent of his skin in her nostrils, the pressure of his mouth on her lips. By the time she bade the group farewell, she was ready to combust. She slipped into the employee ladies' room, lifted the mask to her forehead, and wet a paper towel to hold against her warm neck. The mirror reflected flushed cheeks, dilated eyes and swollen lips. Gemma felt ripe and moist.

"You'd think they could turn up the air," came a woman's voice from behind her.

Gemma looked up to see a woman with short jet-black hair with a pink streak wearing an outfit similar to her own. "Yes, it's…warm," Gemma murmured.

The woman lifted her mask, revealing sharp cheekbones and violet-colored eyes. "I'm Lillian," she said with a friendly smile.

"Gemma."

"Nice to know you, Gemma." Lillian adjusted the collar of her low-cut blouse. She was a fortyish petite woman with lush curves and trim, shapely legs. "How do you like working here?"

"It's interesting," Gemma said cautiously. It would be unseemly to say that she actually enjoyed the job, enjoyed injecting herself into the naughty museum exhibit.

"Are you married?" Lillian asked, fluffing her hair with well-manicured hands.

Gemma averted her glance. Eventually she would get

used to saying the word "divorced," but for now, it stuck in her throat.

"I just wondered what your husband thought of you taking this job," Lillian said into the pause.

"I'm not married."

"Oh, well, your boyfriend, then."

"I don't have a boyfriend…at the moment."

The woman looked dubious. "Really? Well, if you want one, this is the right job to find one."

Gemma shook her head. "I'd never date someone I met here."

"Smart girl." Lillian checked her lipstick. "It's probably just as well you don't have a boyfriend. My Joey is furious that I'm doing this—he doesn't like other men looking at me. And," she added lightly, "he doesn't understand why I'd want them to look."

Gemma met the woman's knowing gaze in the mirror and swallowed hard. Was her fixation so obvious that the woman could pick up on a kindred spirit? But then again, anyone guiding this particular tour had to enjoy being in the spotlight to some degree. Lillian blinked and whatever Gemma had sensed was gone.

"So, can you believe how popular this exhibit is?"

"It seems to have caught on in a big way."

Lillian laughed. "Guess someone underestimated just how starved people are for a little excitement in their lives."

Gemma tried to laugh in agreement, but she felt exposed, as if the woman was talking about *her,* and her life. Telling her that she was starved for something too, else why would she have taken this job? And why was she consumed, even now, with the thought of undressing for Chev Martinez? It was simple—she was a tease. She found more satisfaction in performing than in making love. Self-condemnation rolled through her chest. What would everyone think of her if they really knew what dark impulses drove her?

From the outside, she looked so normal, but on the inside, she was burning with her sordid secret.

"By the way," Lillian offered, "I heard that, since the museum denied the requests of local TV networks to tape the tour, it's possible a reporter might infiltrate one of the groups."

"Thanks for the heads-up. What are we supposed to do if we suspect someone is a reporter?"

"Watch for cameras and let the director know afterward." Lillian glanced at her watch, then lowered her mask into place. "We're up in two minutes. Ready?"

Nodding, Gemma settled her own mask in place and exited the bathroom, thinking she should have taken the time to adjust her underwear before the next group arrived, yet knowing why she hadn't—the chafing garment rubbing all the right places was keeping her in a heightened sense of arousal. It promised to be a long, stimulating day.

And—if Chev's window was still unshuttered when she arrived home—a long, stimulating night.

Her face burned with shame. What was wrong with her?

WHEN GEMMA PULLED onto her street, she steeled herself, ready to face either the cocky peacock or her hunky neighbor—or both. But all was quiet when she arrived home with dusk already setting on a blistering day. A few lights blazed in the Spanish house next door, so she assumed Chev would be once again burning the midnight oil. The fact that his bedroom window remained unshuttered sent a tremor through her womb. He still wanted to see her. Had he heard her arrive home? Was he waiting for her even now to appear at her window?

She sat in her car in the garage for a few minutes to postpone her decision, loath to go into the stifling house. When she cashed her first paycheck, she'd get the air conditioner repaired. But meanwhile, what was she going to do about the internal heat raging through her body?

Gemma dragged herself inside the house and listened to three messages—one from her mother to call her back, please, one from her credit card company to call them back, please, and one from the newspaper reporter, Lewis Wilcox, to call him back, please. Ignoring them all, she prepared a quick salad from bagged lettuce. All the while, she felt the pull to go upstairs and undress…and be seen. She fought the impulse, and when her attention landed upon the letter that she'd written of her sexual fantasies, she picked up the sheath of folded sheets. What better reminder of how her carnal compulsions had nearly led her to ruin before?

Her heartbeat picked up even as she skimmed the pages to find where she'd left off reading. Performing for the man on the bus in her schoolgirl costume…and loving it.

I was hooked. I learned from Dr. Alexander's lecture this week that I have a fetish called exhibitionism— I enjoy putting my body on exhibit. Which is very strange considering my personality. Most people would say that I'm a good girl, someone happy to remain anonymous and on the fringes of a group. My mother has pounded the idea of what a girl should be into my head: polite, quiet and accommodating. I was always taught that drawing attention to oneself was vulgar and conceited—better to blend in rather than risk ridicule.

But during twenty-two years of being good, nothing has felt as good as my one day of putting myself on display. I already wanted to do it again, couldn't sleep for thinking about it—what I'd wear, where I'd go, who I would entertain.

I kept my roommate's brown wig, and lied when she asked me if I'd seen it. An exhibitionist and a liar—I was getting good at being bad. I dressed in tight, sexy workout clothes underneath my regular clothes, then packed the wig in a gym bag. I took the train across town to a gym that I'd seen advertise free workouts, then pulled on the wig. I filled out the paperwork using a fake name and address, then went into the locker room and removed my street clothes. After adjusting my black short shorts (with no underwear, they felt very naughty) and white jogging bra, I grabbed a towel and walked out into the exercise area. I scanned the men working out for a potential target, and immediately found one in a twenty-something dark-haired guy in a gray sweat-stained T-shirt and blue running shorts.

The way he looked at me made me warm and moist. I walked past him close enough to smell the male scent of him, then got on the treadmill to run and work up a sweat of my own. The wig was hot, but its heaviness made me feel safe. In the mirror I could see the guy watching me while he made his way around the free weight circuit, adding iron plates to the barbells, then pushing his muscles to the limit. We made frequent eye contact in the mirror—his eyes were so sexy it was like he was devouring me. My shorts rode up from the friction, cutting into my privates and rubbing me in the most wonderful way. He couldn't take his eyes off me.

An older woman in sweats walked up to him and I realized that he was a trainer, and that she was his client. He pretended to be all business with the woman, but as soon as he got her situated on the stair climber, his eyes found me again. The tip of his tongue came out and curled upward. I knew exactly where he wanted to put that tongue. Tingling all over, I reached for my towel draped over the front of the treadmill, then purposely dropped it on the floor. He said something to the woman, then casually walked over to my treadmill. My heart raced even faster as he approached, his eyes smoldering.

When he crouched to pick up my towel, he lingered, at eye level with my crotch. My running shorts were more like a thong by this time, and my thighs were slick from sweat and my own personal lubrication. At his angle, I was sure he could see the lips of my sex squeezed out of my disappearing shorts. With every step I tightened my core muscles, and with the constant massage of chafing and his full attention on me, I could feel an orgasm rushing to the surface.

When I climaxed, the strain of not breaking stride only made it more powerful. My hip muscles contracted, and my breath gushed out in heaving pants. Only he and I knew what was happening. A shudder went through my body, but I managed to stay upright and moving. As I recovered, I slowed the treadmill to catch my breath. He straightened and slowly extended my towel. When I took it from him, I noticed the erection straining against his shorts. I used the towel to wipe my neck and chest. My white jogging bra had grown nearly transparent from my sweat, and my nipples were outlined clearly for him to see. His mouth opened slightly, but before he could initiate a conversation, I stopped the treadmill and stepped off.

"Thanks," I said, then turned and walked as quickly as I could toward the locker room. He started to follow me, but his client waved to get his attention. He hesitated, then went to her. I dressed hurriedly without showering and left without seeing him again. For days I fantasized about his reaction to me, wondering if he'd tried to find me and was disappointed or intrigued that the personal information I'd listed had led to a dead end. The thought that he might still be thinking about me, the mystery woman, made me feel so sexy and so powerful.

Gemma squeezed her eyes closed against the deluge of memories pouring over her. She had been young and flush with the excitement and newness of her own sex appeal. The world itself had seemed so…alive. And accessible. Even now, her heart beat faster at the memory of her thrilling adventure of experiencing a public orgasm with a private audience.

Her breath quickened and she felt the pull of the upstairs window like a magnet drawing her, a frame for her performance. And Chev wanted to watch…what better situation could she ask for? After all, the man would be there only temporarily. They could…play…and then he'd be gone. No harm done. She pushed to her feet and slowly walked upstairs, her muscles growing more languid with every step.

The upper floor was suffocating. She shed the cropped jacket and tossed it on the bed, then flipped on a ceiling fan to get some air moving. After a few seconds' hesitation, she walked over to slide open the picture window, allowing it to bang against the casing. The light was on in the opposite window, and a few seconds later, Chev appeared in jeans, shirtless.

His hair looked damp, as if he'd just emerged from the shower. His powerful shoulders and arms were outlined perfectly in the round window. She recalled how they had felt around her—dominant and insistent. A shudder went through her and she was glad for the distance. He leaned forward on the sill using both hands, as if to say that he wasn't going anywhere, that he wanted her to know he was watching this time.

A sweet haze of raw desire descended over Gemma. She acknowledged that she was sliding into a trancelike state. She wet her lips, then lifted her fingers to the front hooks of her black corset, and slowly began undoing them.

CHEV GRIPPED the windowsill harder as Gemma removed the corset, exposing inch after inch of luminous skin. Frustration and fascination warred within him as lust surged through his body. The little tease. She'd made it clear that she didn't want any hands-on interaction with him, but watching her through her window wasn't going to satisfy him.

Still, he couldn't bring himself to look away—he'd been

wound tight ever since the heated kiss they'd shared. He hadn't imagined her reaction...she'd enjoyed it as much as he had. But something was holding her back. Was she afraid of him? Considering his bulk and that she knew next to nothing about him, he wouldn't blame her if she was. But somehow, he didn't think that was the case. If she was afraid of him, she wouldn't tantalize him like this. Because if he wanted to be in her house, in her bed, he wouldn't let a few locked doors get in the way.

Chev gave himself a mental shake—he wasn't an animal, or a criminal. But this woman unleashed something primal in him. When the corset fell open to reveal the heavy globes of her breasts and budded pink nipples, he could actually feel his blood warming as it pumped through his body, thickening his cock.

Still wearing the gaping corset, she unzipped the black short shorts and shimmied them down her hips. At the sight of a tiny triangle of red panties, he groaned and leaned into the windowsill harder. The woman was killing him. His cock surged, the head pushing above the low waistline of his briefs. He could feel the sticky pre-cum oozing out, his balls tingling with the itch to relieve the tension that had been building for days. Damn, this little game of hers—look but don't touch—made him feel young again, back to the days when sex had been new and fun and taboo.

The best thing about maturing had been mastering control of his body, to make sure that his partner was as satisfied as he was. But growing up had also dimmed the sheer thrill of sex. For men and women alike, the erotic recklessness of youth seemed to give way to using sex to emotionally manipulate others. So while Gemma's actions were confounding, he had to admit that the woman had put a zing into his already healthy libido that had him distracted every waking hour and most sleeping hours, too.

He found himself smiling during the day for no good reason. Something akin to giddiness arose in him when he heard her car, signaling her arrival home. As Gemma's hand slid beneath the scrap of shiny red fabric, Chev studied her face as that strange sensation once again curled through his chest. The beautiful lines of her features softened as she began to sink into the rhythm of her fingers strumming her soft center. Her mouth opened slightly, her shoulders rolled languidly; her eyes fluttered and closed. Her cheeks were flushed with pure abandon, and a smile played on her lips. She was happy putting on this private show, and he felt flattered that she had singled him out.

Frustrated, he conceded as he smoothed a hand over his rigid erection—a tiny scratch applied to a raging itch—but flattered. And intrigued.

As Gemma's body convulsed in orgasm, Chev hardened his jaw against the urge to stroke himself to climax. Not yet. There was something going on with this woman, something that compelled her to experience such intimacy with such detachment. He was determined to find out what made her tick.

Face-to-face…hand-to-hand…and sex-to-sex.

10

Gemma loved to make love in the morning…when the sounds of the day were awakening: the soft tickle of tree branches brushing the roof…the vibrating hum of insects drinking from dewy grass…the rattling screech of something that sounded like a cross between a wet cat and a woman screaming "Help!"

Her eyes popped open. The inhuman noise seemed to be coming from her front yard. So much for a few extra z's on her day off.

She pulled on a robe and walked to the picture window, but didn't see anything from that vantage point. She did glance at the window opposite hers, but it was empty. Chev had probably been awake for hours, she decided, remembering the way he'd looked in the window last night, watching her…a zing went through her stomach and traveled down her thighs just thinking about it. How lucky to find a sexy man living next door—temporarily—who enjoyed watching her as much as she enjoyed performing.

The screeching noise sounded again, and she had a feeling she knew the source. She walked downstairs and into the living room for a view of the front yard. Then she gasped. Piles of new mulch and several clumps of flowers—roots and all—were scattered over the recently cut lawn. And the culprit stood in the middle of the mess holding a healthy marigold plant in his beak.

"Not my flowers!" Gemma shouted. As if the bird, or anyone else, could hear her. She nearly ran outside, then remembered her robe and pounded back upstairs for a pair of shorts, a T-shirt and sandals. Her mind whirled for some sort of weapon as she rushed downstairs. Desperate, she grabbed an umbrella on the way out the front door.

"Shoo!" she yelled, jogging down the front steps and into the yard, waving the umbrella at the peacock. It flinched, then squawked at her, dropping the mangled plant it had been holding.

"Go away!" she shouted.

The bird took a few steps backward, then shuddered and unfurled his tail in its magnificent fan in an apparent attempt to intimidate her.

Undeterred, Gemma opened the rainbow-colored umbrella and waved it at the destructive beast for a little intimidation of her own.

Low, rumbling laughter sounded. Her stomach tightened before she even turned around to see Chev standing at the edge of their property lines, leaning on a Weed Eater, his T-shirt already sweat-stained although the sun had barely begun its climb. His lopsided grin did funny things to her vital signs. She straightened and pushed a few strands of hair behind her ear, realizing how ridiculous she must look. Then she lifted her chin. "This isn't funny. This... *fowl* destroyed my flower beds!"

He held up his hand in an obvious attempt to stop laughing. "I'm sorry. But you're only making things worse."

Gemma frowned. "How?"

He walked closer and gestured to the colorful umbrella she held. "Now he probably thinks you're a potential mate."

Gemma squinted at the bird, who did indeed seem to be strutting his stuff versus scrambling to get away. She sighed. "Do you have any better ideas for getting rid of him?"

Chev pursed his mouth. "We males can be difficult to get rid of once we see something we like."

Her cheeks warmed as his meaning set in. A tickle of concern curled in her stomach. It was a good thing that Chev's days here were numbered. Otherwise, he might begin to expect more than she was willing to offer.

He lunged at the peacock, waving his arms, and succeeded in driving it into the air. Flying low, the large bird disappeared into a copse of trees several yards away.

"Thank you," Gemma said. "Again."

Chev's eyes twinkled. "You're welcome, but I don't think you've seen the last of him."

Gemma pushed one hand into her hair as she surveyed the damage to her flower beds. To her horror, tears filled her eyes. "I so don't need this hassle."

"Hey, hey," he said, sounding alarmed. He moved closer, touching her arm. "It's nothing that can't be fixed. I can give you a hand."

"That's not necessary," she said, wiping her cheeks hurriedly and pulling away from his disturbing touch. "I'm just feeling sorry for myself. Besides, you have your hands full with your own property."

"Actually, I was hoping I might negotiate some kind of trade."

Gemma swallowed hard. "What did you have in mind?"

A small smile played on his lips for a few seconds, as if he were considering all the pleasurable possibilities.

"Your expertise in return for any handyman work you have around here."

"My expertise in what?"

"My house," he said, jerking his thumb toward the Spanish structure. I want to stay as true to authentic Mission detail as possible, but I'm afraid I'm in over my head. I thought with your background in art history, you might be able to steer me in the right direction."

Gemma crossed her arms and considered his proposal. "For example?"

He shrugged. "Some guidance on the fireplace in the living room, the light fixtures in the bedrooms and things that I haven't even encountered yet."

"I have some reference books on the Mission style," Gemma said, her mind already sifting through options. She recognized a flowering sensation in her chest as pleasure. She couldn't remember the last time anyone had asked for her opinion on anything. Jason had been the resident expert on everything that mattered, she had simply been the attentive sidekick. "Would you like to come inside while I look for them?" she asked.

He nodded, and followed her. Her heart raced as they climbed the steps and crossed the porch. She turned the knob on the door and swung it open. As soon as he crossed the threshold, she regretted asking him inside. She felt guilty and skittish, as if someone might catch them, and found herself practicing explanations in her head. *He's the neighbor...a carpenter...temporary.*

"Nice place," he said, turning his head from side to side.

She saw the house as he might...clean, but dark and cluttered with little piles of Jason's stuff everywhere—the overflowing basket of mail, the milk crate of shoes and belts and crushed ball caps, the laundry basket of office equipment and thick volumes of books on Florida law. "I apologize for the mess—these are my husband's things." She put a hand to her head and gave a little laugh. "I mean my ex-husband. We recently divorced."

He nodded. "So I gathered."

She was embarrassed. She should've gotten rid of everything after her last phone conversation with Jason. The air seemed especially stifling.

"Sorry it's so stuffy in here. My air conditioner is on the blink. I've been keeping all the windows open, but it hasn't helped much."

"It's helped me a great deal," he said, his voice low and amused.

His candor shocked her—and pleased her. It was refreshing to speak honestly about a sexual experience instead of flirting around the edges. "I'm glad you think so," she murmured, and the air between them fairly crackled with static electricity. His dark eyes seemed to pierce her, and behind the blatant physical appreciation, she could sense his mind was racing, trying to figure out why a nice girl like her would be compelled to exhibit herself in such an intimate way. Gemma broke eye contact as a wave of anxiety washed over her. Honesty came with its own price.

"I could take a look at your air conditioner unit if you like," he offered, changing the subject easily.

"I couldn't bother you—"

"I might not even be able to fix it," he interrupted. "But I'd like to do something for you in exchange for your help with the details of the house."

There it was again, the look that said he wanted—*needed*—her help.

"Okay," she relented, then proceeded up the stairs. "The unit is up here in the hall closet if you want to take a look. I'll try to locate my reference books."

He strode to the closet with a casual authority that she admired, a man comfortable with houses and the things in them. Unlike Jason, she mused, who saw the yard work as a chore, the smallest repair around the house an inconvenient waste of time. He would often grumble that he had two college degrees, yet he was expected to know carpentry, too. He was too busy to be bothered, she'd always reasoned, hating to see him spend his precious few hours of free time on tedious tasks. Rather than bringing things to his attention, she would attempt the repair herself or call a repair service, with Jason none the wiser.

On the other hand, her mind whispered, Chev Martinez wasn't the most powerful attorney in Florida, with the ear of the governor, making decisions every day that affected the lives of everyone who lived in the state. If Jason knew what Gemma had been doing, exhibiting her body to a relative stranger, he'd be shocked and disgusted. He'd tell her that she'd gone slumming…that he was glad he had divorced her before he realized the extent of her perversions and perhaps ruined his career. A stone settled in her stomach. The men were too different to compare, she told herself. Besides, she'd had a ten-year relationship with Jason, and had known Chev barely ten days.

Yet his presence in her house had her on edge, his big body seeming to take up the entire hall as he scrutinized the unit and touched a tube here, a wire there. He seemed to fill the house, his male scent crowding the muggy rooms, his thoughtful hum soaking into empty corners, chasing away the loneliness that had pervaded the place since Jason's departure. Gemma allowed her heart to lift faintly and moved into her bedroom to consult her dusty bookshelves.

"I'm going to check your breakers," he called.

"Go ahead," she called back, struck by how domestic they seemed. Pleasure infused her chest—this little exhibitionist fling was exactly what she needed to help her push through the pain of Jason's rejection. She was suddenly very grateful for Chev's presence—and hoped that he didn't press her for…more.

CHEV WAS STRUCK by the domesticity of standing in Gemma's hallway, doing something her husband would've done if he'd been around. Would her ex object to him being here? Probably. He wondered if the guy had had an affair, if Gemma had thrown him out or if he'd left voluntarily. Chev couldn't imagine a woman more exciting than Gemma, but maybe the guy was a jerk…or gay. Or just a prude.

Chev flipped a breaker and glanced around to check that the section of power extinguished matched what was written on the switch's label. He moved through the motions of the routine repair, feeling relatively sure he could get the unit running again with a few replacement parts.

He heard Gemma moving around in her bedroom. Setting his jaw against the hunger that surged in his chest, he walked to the doorway and rapped lightly. His gaze swept past the picture window where she had undressed for him and over her unmade bed before coming to rest on the sight of her standing in front of a bookshelf, thumbing through a hefty volume.

She looked up, then flushed and gestured vaguely toward the tangled sheets. "Excuse the mess. I slept in this morning until the peacock woke me up."

He nodded, swallowing hard to control the reaction of his body to the image of Gemma undressed and lying beneath him on that bed. But his cock was having none of his stall tactics and began to swell against his zipper. She still looked tousled from sleep and he'd bet the sheets were still warm from her hot body. No wonder the air conditioner had blown. "The compressor is working. I think you need a new thermostat."

"That sounds serious," she murmured.

"Not really," he assured her, shifting slightly in an effort to reposition himself more comfortably. "I'll get everything you need on my next trip to the home center."

"I appreciate your help."

He nodded toward the book she held. "I appreciate yours."

She smiled and held up the book. "What do you want to talk about first?"

"The fireplace," he said randomly.

"Let's walk over so I can take a look."

"I'll follow you," he said, partly because he wanted to view her backside, and partly because he wanted to hide his growing erection. She picked up a sketch pad and swept by him in a cloud of feminine scent—fruity shampoo, heady womanliness and earthy sleep aromas. Downstairs he noticed blank spaces on walls and shelves where pictures had been removed and whatnots were missing. Containers of random men's things sat on the floor—her husband's leavings, no doubt. The rooms were clean, but appeared neglected and unused. She seemed eager to get outside, and he wondered if his presence made her nervous—more proof that she preferred distance between them.

They picked their way across her trashed yard. "I'll help you put things back in order," he offered.

"I'll do it later," she said with a wave. "I'm sure you have plenty of other things to keep you busy. Do you have a drop dead date for getting the house done?"

"Three weeks from now," he said. "This week is demolition and getting supplies. The serious work starts next week."

He led her inside the musty house and she went straight to the fireplace, all business. She touched the broken clay bricks as if they were old friends. She asked Chev what he was looking for in the restoration, but he was so distracted by her he could barely think. He loved the way her brow wrinkled when she concentrated, the way she angled her head as she sized up things. He fell back on what little he knew about the Mission style, describing the fireplaces in his grandparents' home. She made notes in her sketchbook, then some simple line drawings. He leaned in close and added his comments, getting caught up in her enthusiasm.

"All of this doesn't seem like much in return for fixing my air conditioner," she said. "So I'd like to offer to replace the mural in the kitchen."

He smiled. "You're an artist, too?"

Suddenly she seemed shy. "Not accomplished by any means, but I think I could paint a passable landscape, if you're willing to let me try."

"I accept," he said happily. A delivery truck pulled into the driveway, horn honking.

Gemma tucked a strand of shimmering blond hair behind her ear. "I guess I'd better get to my yard."

"I'll let you know when I get the thermostat for your HVAC unit," he offered as they walked back to the entrance. "Will you be around tomorrow?"

"I have to work tomorrow."

In yet another provocative outfit? He set his jaw against the images that exploded into his head. "I'll let you know."

She nodded, then turned and walked back to her own yard, seeming lost in thought. Chev spent the rest of the day finding excuses to look out the window or go outside to his truck so he could catch glimpses of her working in her yard, wearing her big hat and flowered gloves. It seemed incongruous that the woman was so…*normal* and yet so…titillating.

He had a feeling she wouldn't appear at her window that night, but it didn't stop him from looking. He gave up around midnight, lying on his cot with perspiration beading on his pent-up body as his mind played images of Gemma over and over. The woman confounded him, affected him like no other woman ever had. His body ached for her. He wanted to tell her that she didn't have to be tentative around him, that he would take whatever she had to offer for the short time he would be there.

But what if her erotic nighttime shows were all that she had to offer? The woman was still suffering from the breakup of her marriage. Maybe the window performances were her way of safely acting out.

Or maybe her behavior had led to the end of her marriage. Lots of couples had bedroom secrets, but the state attorney general's career probably would've been compromised if anyone knew that his wife was an exhibitionist.

On the other hand, Gemma didn't seem the type to…

He groaned in frustration. The woman didn't fit any "type" he'd ever known. Intelligent but unhappy, educated but badly employed, homey but sexy, bold but unsure of herself…complementary and contradictory.

Chev sighed, willing himself to put her out of his mind,

to find sleep. He'd just begun to relax when a honking, plaintive noise sounded outside his window, again…and again…and again.

The peacock was back, calling for a mate.

Chev put his pillow over his ears. It was going to be a long night.

11

"HOW'S THE JOB?" Sue asked.

Gemma held her cell phone between her ear and shoulder while she tied the belt on the lightweight black raincoat she wore over her costume. She unlocked her car door and swung inside, mulling her response. Her body was strung tight after a day of being on exhibit herself. She was looking forward to getting home and taking a long bubble bath. "Fine, I guess. I'm getting accustomed to the routine."

Sue gave a little laugh. "I might have to drive down there and check out your show."

Gemma hesitated, trying to adopt a casual tone. "Sue, do you remember the Sexual Psyche class in college?"

"Sex for Beginners? Sure, I remember. What about it?"

"Did you ever take it?"

"No. I thought I already knew everything—what a joke. But you took it, didn't you?"

"Yeah."

"And what made you think about the class after all these years?"

"I…received something in the mail the other day that… dredged up old memories."

"What?"

"An assignment that we had, to write down our fantasies. Dr. Alexander said she'd mail them to us ten years later."

"Wow, that's kind of cool…isn't it?"

"I guess, but a bit weird. I wrote them before I met Jason."

"Yeah, Gemma, you were an actual person before you met Jason. I was there, remember?"

Gemma blinked at her friend's sarcasm. "What's with the attitude? You introduced us."

A hesitant hum sounded over the line, then Sue said, "I thought you'd go out, have some fun. Honestly, I never dreamed the two of you would get married."

Gemma's mouth opened and closed. "So…you didn't… you don't think that we were a good match?"

"That wasn't for me to decide. But I admit I was surprised when you and Jason got serious."

"You didn't think I was good enough for him?"

"Don't be ridiculous. The two of you just seemed so… different. You were so earthy with your art, and he was already so judicial."

And judgmental, Gemma added silently. Jason had a way of making people feel they needed to be on their best behavior around him. He had been a lifesaver at the time, a reason to rein in her deviant sexual conduct and keep herself in check. She had needed him, and had worked so hard to be what he'd needed in return. "Well, since it didn't last," she said lightly, "I guess you get the prize."

"I didn't mean to hurt your feelings, Gemma." Sue sighed. "I'm just really happy for you that you're moving on."

Gemma leaned her head back on the headrest. "I don't feel like I'm moving on."

"You have a new job."

"It's temporary."

"And how about that neighbor of yours?"

"He's temporary, too. He's flipping the house by the end of the month."

"That old Spanish two-story? Isn't it kind of a wreck?"

Gemma lifted her head. "Yeah, but it's going to be spectacular. Chev is really paying attention to detail."

"Sounds like you are, too."

Gemma realized too late that her voice was elevated, her words rushed and excited. She backpedaled, adopting a casual tone. "He asked for my help on a couple of historical aspects of the house."

"Oh? Well, you know your stuff, so this Chev guy is showing good sense by asking your advice."

"I'm sure he wants to set as high an asking price as possible when it goes up for auction."

"Uh-huh. What kinds of things are you helping him with?"

"Architectural details. And I'm replacing a mural for him."

"You're painting again? That's wonderful! What's he paying you?"

Gemma swallowed. "Actually, it's a trade. He's going to fix my air conditioner."

"Is he now? Gotta love a man who's good with his hands."

"Sue, I'm not sleeping with the guy."

"Are you at least thinking about it?"

Gemma started her car engine. "Oh, look at that—my phone battery is dying, and I need to get home."

"Liar. At least tell me if he lives in Tampa."

"No. Like I said, he's temporary."

"No strings can be a good thing."

"Goodbye, Sue."

Sue sighed. "Goodbye."

Gemma disconnected the call and shook her head. Sue meant well by encouraging her to have a meaningless relationship to help move past Jason's rejection. But her friend would be shocked if she knew what had already transpired between her and her neighbor.

Just like she would've been shocked if Gemma's exhibitionism in college had been exposed. Shocked and ashamed.

On the drive home, Gemma reflected on Sue's comment that she and Jason hadn't been suited for each other. Had other people thought the same thing? Had people whispered that their marriage wouldn't last even as they were standing before the altar taking their vows? Had her desperation to marry Jason been so apparent?

Had Jason sensed it, too? Even though she'd never uttered a word of her subversive urges to exhibit herself, had being her safety chute worn on him?

By the time she pulled onto her street, both the sun and her mood were on the downslide. Chev's property was crowded with vehicles and equipment and workers, most of whom were loading up to leave. She saw him standing shoulders above them, looking like some kind of primitive chief in his bandanna, his torso bare and brown. He turned his head as she drove past and his dark gaze pierced her to the core, suffusing her chest with pleasure as she wheeled into her driveway.

But at the sight of the peacock in her yard, uprooting her newly replanted flowers, those warm, fuzzy feelings were obliterated, and high voltage anger whipped through her.

FROM HIS YARD, Chev saw the peacock and cringed. Considering the way Gemma had slammed her car into Park and come charging out, he wouldn't be surprised if she were about to wring the poor thing's neck.

The bird veered away, emitting its high-pitched mewling noise. Gemma chased it around the yard, windmilling her arms and stomping her feet. In her voluminous black coat, she looked ridiculous, but the peacock must have found her menacing. The bird lunged, flapping its wings and careening wildly to stay a few feet ahead of her.

The men standing around him laughed and made circular motions with their fingers indicating that Gemma was *loco*. Chev smiled and waved them on their way, then stood for a few minutes watching Gemma chase the squawking bird around her yard, laughing to himself.

It was therapeutic, he reasoned, for her to lash out at the bird. The woman had had her life torn apart and was clearly struggling to put the pieces back together. He couldn't blame her for snapping over a few unearthed flowers. The colorful animal was a handy target for her pent-up frustrations.

For the bird's sake, he decided to intervene.

As he walked up behind Gemma, she stopped and leaned over to grasp her knees. She narrowed her eyes at the cock, which had also stopped running and was eyeing her intently. "I wonder how you'd look on a platter," she muttered.

"The meat is supposed to be an aphrodisiac," Chev offered.

She turned and straightened, looking adorably sheepish, her cheeks pink from the exertion.

"Not that I can say firsthand," he added. "Peacocks are protected in most parts of the world, but some cultures still consider the meat a delicacy."

She glared at the bird. "We'd have to catch him first."

As if the bird had heard her, he extended his wings and

flew up into a nearby tree, then called down to them in triumph.

"I guess that's the reason they've been around for centuries," Chev said.

She stamped her foot clad in a chunky black high heel, then groaned when she realized what she'd stepped in.

Chev bent over laughing, then wiped his hand over his mouth. "Sorry."

"I called animal control," she said, indignant, "but they said they didn't have a place to take the bird even if they could capture it. They told me not to feed it, and if it hasn't left in two or three weeks, they would give me the name of a preserve to contact. They said that *I* was encroaching on the *peacock's* habitat."

"Unfortunately, that's true. We all are."

"But why did it pick *my* yard?"

He grinned. "I guess he just liked the look of your grass."

Her cheeks turned a deeper shade of pink. "Do you think he'll ever leave?"

"Eventually his instincts to mate will drive him to move on if he doesn't find what he's looking for."

The humidity in the air between them suddenly became sticky with mutual desire. His sex grew heavy as he imagined what lay beneath the belted raincoat. Considering the black mesh panty hose and high heels, he was sure it was something pretty damn fantastic. Her pale hair was tousled from the impromptu activity. Her mouth and eyes softened and her gaze traveled over his bare shoulders and arms. His chest expanded as he inhaled sharply. She wanted him...but enough to let him near her? He watched while she visibly struggled with her physical response to him. She looked away, and when she looked back, she had regained her composure.

"How's the house coming along?" she asked in a breezy tone.

Chev exhaled. "We made a lot of progress today. I wanted to show you a couple of things if you have time."

She glanced at her own house and he wondered if something had happened today to make her even more skittish of him.

Then she turned back to him and smiled. "Sure. I'm going to let this mess go for now."

"That's not a bad idea," Chev conceded. "Let it ride. You can clean up the yard once he's gone for good."

He said the words lightly, but as soon as they left his mouth he realized that Gemma might be drawing comparisons between him and the pesky peacock.

One delicate eyebrow arched, but otherwise Gemma didn't reveal what was going through that pretty head of hers. "Let me put the car in the garage."

Chev knew he should have offered to let her change clothes first, but honestly, he wanted to keep imagining what she was wearing under the coat. And he was hoping that when she undressed, she'd do it for him.

He bit back a smile as she dodged more bird deposits and sacrificial plants on her way back to the driveway. He glanced up at the peacock staring down from a tree branch and wondered if either one of them would have any luck finding female companionship at 131 Petal Lagoon Drive.

Not if Gemma's subconscious actions were any indication, he noted. Instead of pulling into the middle of the two-car garage, she carefully maneuvered into the rightmost space, leaving room for a phantom car. He wondered if she even realized she was still holding a place in her life for her ex's return.

They walked companionably to his house and she murmured appreciation at the obvious changes—the terra-cotta tiled walkway was newly restored and glistening with sealer. The arched entryway was repaired with the new columns in place and freshly painted. He stopped at an outside spigot to wash his gritty hands and face, then grabbed his work shirt from the handle of a wheelbarrow and shrugged into it, leaving it unbuttoned. He felt Gemma's gaze upon him and welcomed it. If he could affect her senses a fraction of the amount that she affected his, maybe she'd invite him into her bed instead of relegating him to the role of spectator at her erotic shows.

Especially since even her performances had ceased.

Inside, he helped her pick her way across plastic-covered floors. The tile work and wood planks underfoot would be one of the last installations, lest they be marred by machinery and heavy boots. The newly applied plaster on the ceiling in the foyer emanated a pungent but satisfying aroma. At Gemma's urging, Chev had sought out a metal salvage yard and purchased enough sections of wrought-iron railing to replace the crumbling wooden banisters.

"Gorgeous," she breathed.

"I couldn't be happier with the way it turned out," he admitted. "I'm going to replace the wood window shutters with iron detail, too."

At the mention of windows, he thought he detected a stiffening of her shoulders, but she didn't say anything. In the great room, Chev was pleased to see Gemma's face light up at the newly tiled fireplace.

"It's stunning."

"Thanks to you. I wouldn't have chosen these colors or design without your encouragement."

"I'm glad to help," she murmured, and he thought he detected a wistful note in her voice.

"You're good at this," he observed. "Have you considered consulting for a living?"

"Maybe someday," she said, nodding. "I hope I can put my degree to use for something more than being a tour guide."

"How's that going?"

"Um…fine." But he was alerted to the way her hand went to the vee of her coat to absently caress the bare skin there.

"I thought you said this was a part-time job. Haven't you been working almost every day?"

"The exhibit has been more popular than the museum anticipated." Her voice had dropped an octave and suddenly she fanned herself. "It's really warm in here."

"You can take off your coat."

"I…would rather leave it on."

Then it hit him. Gemma's job turned her on…allowed her to be an exhibitionist in plain sight, in the guise of a tour guide.

His cock jumped against his fly. Damn, the woman was killing him. But she seemed nervous, lifting her hair to fan her neck. He noticed that she had a tiny brown beauty mark on the nape of her neck that matched the one at the corner of her mouth. "I won't keep you much longer. I just want to show you the kitchen."

She followed him to the kitchen where a firebrick oven had been installed and mortared, next to shiny stainless steel appliances.

"It's magnificent," she said, clapping her hands like a child. Then her gaze landed on a long farmhouse wood table, the top of which was several inches thick. "Oh my— where did you get this?"

"Another find at the salvage yard. I don't intend to furnish the place, but it seemed perfect for this spot."

"It is," she said, running her hands over the scarred but smooth surface. She lowered herself to one of the two long weathered benches that matched the table, giving him a nice view of her legs in the black mesh hose.

He swallowed a groan.

She smiled up at him. "You could certainly seat a large family around this table."

"Funny you should say that," he said. "My parents and younger sister are coming to Tampa next week. They're visiting colleges. I have an aunt and an uncle who live nearby, and a young cousin. I thought I'd have them all come here for a little party since the kitchen is operational. It'll give my family a chance to see what I'm working on."

"That's nice." She gestured to the long empty wall behind the table. "I'll do my best to have the mural done before then."

"I wasn't worried about that," he said. "The house will still be a long way from being finished. Actually, I was wondering if you'd like to join us?"

Her eyes widened.

"It'll be casual," he assured her. "I'll have food and a cake delivered. Since the part for your air conditioner hasn't arrived, consider it a small thank-you to show my appreciation for all that you've done."

Gemma pushed to her feet. "Fixing my air conditioner will be plenty of thanks." His disappointment must have been evident because she added, "But...I'll think about it and let you know. I should be going."

He followed her to the front door and out onto the

covered entryway, stricken by the overwhelming urge to drag her into his arms. "Gemma."

She turned and looked up at him, her eyes questioning.

Chev stepped toward her and picked up a lock of her hair. "I've missed you at the window."

Her throat worked and her chest rose and fell rapidly. "I...it felt awkward since we've gotten to know each other."

"If I'd known that," he said with a smile, "I would've stayed on this side of my property line."

That made her smile and her tension was replaced with that matter-of-fact sexuality that made him wild for her. "Are you saying you don't want to be friends?"

He stepped closer and lowered his mouth to her ear. "I prefer friends with benefits."

A small sound of wanting came from her throat, but she pulled away. "Like I said, I prefer to keep things at a distance."

"But it's more fun up close." He slowly untied the belt of her coat, revealing a red satin bustier and black pleated short skirt. He groaned and his cock stiffened painfully as he slid his hands inside to caress her waist with his thumbs. "Gemma, don't you feel this...electricity between us?"

She bit her lip and nodded.

"Then why—"

"I can't," she cut in, looking away.

"But you want to."

"It wouldn't help," she said, sounding resigned to whatever demons were plaguing her.

He put his hand under her chin and forced her to look at him. "I want to get next to you, Gemma. Let me."

Her sigh caught in the moist air between them. Raw

longing emanated from her smoky green eyes. She was wavering. He lowered his mouth to hers and captured a moan.

A car horn blasted into the air, suspending the moment. A white Lexus sat in Gemma's driveway. A person alighted, frowning in their direction.

"Oh, dear God," Gemma murmured. "Mother."

12

AT THE SIGHT of her mother standing in her driveway next door, Gemma's knees turned to elastic. Her lips were still warm from Chev's, his hand still on her waist. And even at this distance, she could feel her mother's searing disapproval.

"I have to go," she said, pulling away, fumbling with her belt.

"But—"

"I'll talk to you later."

Without looking back, Gemma walked stiffly toward her mother. Phyllipa Jacobs stood holding a casserole caddy and leaning against her car as if she might need it to support her weight. Gemma waved in an attempt to diffuse the openmouthed expression on her mother's face.

"Mother…what a surprise." She reached forward for an embrace, but her mother remained immobile.

"Gemma, *who* is that man? Were you…*kissing* him?"

Gemma caught her mother's arm and guided her toward the front door. "His name is Chev, and he's fixing up the house next door. I'm…helping him."

Her mother allowed herself to be hauled up the stairs and onto the porch. "Helping him do what?"

"Choose architectural details for the renovation."

"I came to visit because I'm worried about you, and I find you—" she lowered her voice to a harsh whisper "—in the arms of a strange man?"

"We were just talking, Mother." Gemma worked the key in the lock furiously and pushed open the door.

"What on earth happened to your yard?"

"There's a rogue peacock in the neighborhood."

"A rogue...what? Gemma, have you been drinking?"

She sighed. "No, Mother." But she sure could use a tall one right about now.

After they entered the house, Gemma flipped on lights strategically, once again wishing she'd taken the time to throw out all the items that Jason had said he didn't want. Now they mocked her, proof of her reluctance to let him go long after he'd made it clear he wanted nothing from her.

"It's awfully stuffy in here," Phyllipa remarked.

"The air conditioner is on the blink."

"You should call someone."

Gemma tamped down the anger that flared in her chest at her mother's patronizing tone. "I have. The parts haven't arrived." She inhaled for strength and gestured to the casserole. "What did you bring?"

"Lasagna."

"Oh, nice. Can you stay and eat with me?"

Phyllipa nodded, then frowned at Gemma's coat suspiciously. "It's ninety degrees outside. Why on earth are you wearing a coat, dear?"

Gemma forced a shrug. "The weatherman predicted rain."

Phyllipa squinted. "What kind of panty hose are you wearing?"

"Uh, they're part of my work uniform."

"Doing what?"

"I'll explain over dinner," Gemma said, turning toward the stairs. "Let me change first." She bounded up the stairs as fast as the high heels would allow, then closed her bedroom door and exhaled. Her mother's sense of timing hadn't improved.

With her skin still tingling from being caught in a compromising position, she crossed to the picture window and glanced down. Chev was in the yard, hosing off the newly tiled walkway and watering large trees still in tubs, waiting to be planted. His work shirt gaped open and she shivered, remembering the smooth firmness of his skin as he pulled her body close to his. She reached out and touched her finger against the warm pane of glass, imagining the heat they could generate.

At that moment he glanced up and saw her. He wet his lips and stared blatantly, expectantly. The urge to expose herself to him seized her. Moving automatically, she untied her belt and allowed the thin coat to fall to the floor.

Chev's hand slipped and water surged from the hose he held. Her chest rose and fell rapidly, the edge of the red corset biting into the tender flesh of her breasts. She slowly unlaced the front of the corset, then peeled it off, allowing her breasts to fall free. Chev turned to face her, legs spread wide, the water hose hanging loose at this side. His brown skin glistened in the waning daylight, his jeans riding low enough to reveal the white waistband of his briefs. Her gaze went to the bulge there, and intense feminine satisfaction welled within her. She reached up to cup her aching breasts, longing for release.

A knock at the bedroom door sounded, crashing into her trancelike state. She gasped, crossed her arms over her breasts, and turned away from the window. "Yes?"

"Gemma," her mother said through the door, "how about a nice salad?"

"Sounds good, Mom. Thanks. I'll be right down."

She pushed her hands into her hair and let out a sigh. What had she been thinking? Was she so out of control that she couldn't even restrain herself when her own mother was in the house?

She practiced deep breathing, counting to ten. Then, somewhat calmer, she dressed in jeans and T-shirt, ignoring the pings of the sensitive areas of her body. The window was like a magnetic field, pulling at her. She avoided it and went downstairs to face her mother, a stone of dread in her stomach.

Phyllipa had donned an apron and was rinsing romaine lettuce at the sink while the microwave hummed away, warming the lasagna. Gemma stopped at the doorway of the kitchen and pursed her mouth, because her mother's attention wasn't on the salad. Instead, she was craning to look out the window, presumably for a glimpse of the "strange man" that Gemma had been adhered to.

"Dad didn't want to come?" Gemma asked, snagging a tomato slice from a plate.

Her mother turned and wiped her hands on the apron. "He had something he needed to do."

A big, fat lie. "The lasagna smells great."

Her mother crossed her arms and assumed her parental stance. "So…are you going to tell me what's going on?"

Gemma felt herself being pulled along on the force of her mother's not-so-subtle guilt trip. "I don't know what you mean."

"Jason is barely out of the house and you've already taken up with someone else? Or maybe that was the reason he left in the first place?"

"No, that's not the reason," Gemma said through gritted teeth. "And I'm not going to explain my personal life to you, Mother."

Her mother screwed up her mouth, which was too bad, because otherwise Phyllipa was a very attractive woman. But Gemma had a hard time imagining her cold, uptight mother being warm and intimate. No wonder her parents seemed so distant from each other.

"Have you talked to Jason lately?"

"As a matter of fact, I called to ask him what to do with the things he left behind, and he didn't even have time to talk to me."

"He's a very busy man."

"I know, Mother. I lived with him for ten years."

Her mother began ripping the lettuce into chunks. "A marriage requires sacrifice, Gemma, especially when your husband has a demanding job." Phyllipa nodded to the stack of rolled-up newspapers by the door. "Since you haven't been keeping up with the news, you should know that Jason is in the middle of a very important drug case right now. I'm sure his stress level is through the roof. He needs all the support he can get."

A lump of emotion lodged in Gemma's throat. "Why are you making this out to be my fault? Whose side are you on?"

Phyllipa turned a compassionate eye on Gemma. "I'm on your side, dear. I want to see you safe and secure. Do you realize that Jason might be the next governor?"

Gemma bit down on the inside of her cheek. "This isn't what I'd planned either, Mom, but Jason has made it clear that he doesn't want to be married to me."

"Do you still love him?"

She hugged herself. "I…guess so. I miss him. I was

blindsided, so I'm still getting used to the idea of not being married to him."

Her mother came over and ran her hands up and down Gemma's arms. "If you love him, you have to fight for him, dear. He's probably going through a little midlife crisis. He'll be back when he realizes that he can't live without you."

Phyllipa smiled, her eyes bright with concern and sincerity, and Gemma felt her mother's love wash over her. She made the scenario that Gemma had initially fantasized about—of Jason coming back—seem possible. And preferable. But so much water had passed under the bridge…she was growing stronger and more independent every day, looking forward to finding her own way. "Mom, I'm not sure that I would welcome Jason back."

"That's your anger talking," her mother said quietly, squeezing Gemma's shoulders. "And you're entitled to it. But don't let it harden you to the possibility of patching things up with Jason. The best thing you can do right now is to let him cool his heels. He'll come to his senses."

Her mother had a way of making things sound so simple. *If only.* Gemma decided not to respond, to merely let her mother think what she wanted. In time Phyllipa would have to accept reality.

Her mother pulled her into a rocking hug, then withdrew and angled her head. "In the meantime, don't do something that might make it even harder for the two of you to reconcile."

The reference to Chev was unmistakable. Warmth flooded her face, but Gemma was saved from responding when the microwave chimed, effectively distracting her mother. She made it through the meal with small talk about the weather and asking about her mother's book club. When the subject of her job came up, she said she was working for a local museum.

"From the looks of the panty hose you were wearing, they must have a strange dress code," Phyllipa observed.

Gemma simply nodded and complimented the food. Fortunately, her mother didn't like driving in the dark, so she left soon after they were finished eating. Gemma stood on the porch and waved as her mother pulled away. When the car was gone, she stole a glance next door and saw that a few lights were on. Chev was still working, probably on the yards of wood molding that still needed to be repaired. The man obviously enjoyed working with his hands, but he was intelligent, too. And oh, so sexy in an earthy way that appealed to her baser instincts.

In fact, she wondered if her exhibitionism would have been so quickly revived if he hadn't been such a willing participant, located so conveniently next door, with a bird's-eye view into her bedroom. Probably not, she decided with a little bubble of resentment that she allowed to grow. He was, at least partially, responsible for her wicked behavior.

Feeling marginally absolved, Gemma turned and walked back inside, scooping up the unread newspapers. Her mother's comments about Jason had piqued her interest. She had to admit that she missed being in the middle of state politics.

Poring over the pages of the papers, her heart caught at the pictures of Jason at a press conference, or striding into the capitol building, looking as if the weight of the world was on his shoulders. A gag order had been issued regarding the drug case.

No matter what had happened between them, she still

respected him for rising to such an impressive office. He was, as her mother had indicated, probably headed for the governor's mansion. To think that she might have been the first lady of the state....

The phone rang, piercing into her thoughts, jangling her nerves. She glanced at the caller ID and noted it was coming from a private source. Afraid it was that pesky reporter Wilcox again, she almost didn't answer. After the fourth ring, however, she changed her mind.

"Hello?"

"Hi, Gemma."

Her pulse spiked. "Jason...hi."

"Did I catch you at a bad time?"

Gemma glanced around at the dark emptiness of the house and almost laughed. "No."

"I just called to see how you were doing."

She frowned at the slight slur in his voice. "Have you been drinking?"

"A little. It's been a rough week." His voice sounded raspy and unexpectedly sexy. She pictured him still at his desk, pulling at his tie, loosening the precise knot. His light brown hair would be ruffled from running his fingers through it. He would be drinking scotch, neat.

"I know. I was just reading in the paper about the drug ring you're prosecuting. You look tired in the pictures."

"I am tired," he conceded. "I'm sorry if I was short with you the other day when you called. It was nice of you to offer to send the things I left. Actually, I did remember a favorite golf towel that I misplaced."

"The black one? I found it in the garage."

"Uh, yeah, that's the one." He gave a little laugh. "It's my lucky towel. Did you throw it out yet?"

She leaned over and fished it from a cardboard box near her feet. "I suppose I could dig it out of the garbage."

"I would appreciate it." He exhaled heavily. "I'm so sorry, Gemma."

His admission took her by surprise, and she wondered with a pang of anguish if he was on the verge of confessing adultery. "Sorry for what?"

"I'm sorry for everything. I didn't mean to hurt you."

Her eyes grew moist as a host of emotions galloped through her chest—love, hate, regret, remorse, frustration. "Okay," she said finally, surprised at how steady her voice sounded.

"I could drive down in a few days to pick up that golf towel."

Her heart lifted unexpectedly. It was a flimsy excuse to come to see her. She fought to maintain a certain nonchalance. "That would be fine. I'll hang on to it for you."

"Great," he said, his voice warm and melancholy. "I'll come down as soon as I get a break from this case. Take care."

She hung up the phone slowly, not sure what to make of Jason's phone call. It seemed as if he was offering some kind of olive branch. Or was he reconsidering the abrupt end to their marriage? Maybe her mother had been right—that he'd gone through a bit of a midlife crisis, had wanted his freedom only to learn that it wasn't what he'd expected. Maybe he was starting to realize that she had been more than just a political prop, and that success is empty without someone to share it with.

The thought of getting back together with Jason made her mind spin in confusion. In the first few days after he'd left, she had fantasized that he would come back on his knees. But in the weeks that followed, her hurt had turned into anger. And when she'd received the final papers, she realized now that the anger had turned into resolve. Her thoughts were no longer dominated by Jason, her actions no longer dependent on him. Getting back together now seemed…retroactive. Things would have to be different, at least as far as she was concerned.

Then she chided herself for worrying about it. Jason might have been simply feeling guilty about the way he'd ended things, wanting to ensure she wouldn't have something bad to say about him in a subsequent election.

Still, she had to admit that knowing he might be having second thoughts was salve to her wounded pride. And the knowledge that she wasn't holding her breath after one tentative call from him buoyed her spirits. She felt better than she'd felt in weeks.

Maybe in *years*.

She was humming as she climbed to the second floor. She opened windows and turned on fans to alleviate the stuffiness. When she got to her bedroom window, the sight of the open round one across from hers warmed her midsection. And yet…

The talk with her mother and the subsequent conversation with Jason made her pause. Not because she was afraid she would sabotage a chance at getting back together with Jason, but because, she suddenly realized, she liked the feeling of being unattached.

She touched her mouth, remembering Chev's kiss. It would be easy to become attached to him, and she couldn't afford to do that now when she was just starting to get her legs underneath her again.

Gemma caught sight of the folded sheets of her fantasy

letter lying on her nightstand and was struck with the urge to keep reading. It was, after all, a harmless way to relive her fantasies. She moistened her lips and acknowledged a stirring deep in her sex at the mere prospect. Then she slid a glance toward the window and changed her mind. Reading more of the letter would likely only increase her eagerness to put on a show for Chev, and he'd already made it clear he wanted more than a performance…more than she was willing to give.

She glanced around the room, looking for a distraction. At the sight of her sketchbook, she brightened. She'd promised Chev she'd have the mural finished before his little family gathering. It was the perfect diversion from all the jumbled thoughts in her head.

From a hallway closet she retrieved a folded easel, a dusty tube that held a roll of primed canvas, and a suitcase containing her stash of paints, linseed oil, turpentine and assorted brushes and palette knives. When she lifted the lid, a wave of nostalgia flooded her senses. The smell of the pungent linseed oil, the sight of curled tubes of paint, the comforting feel of a round wooden brush in her hand. She carried everything to Jason's office and set up an impromptu studio, her excitement growing as the room took shape.

Gemma used a utility knife to cut the canvas to the size she'd jotted down in her notebook, then used thumbtacks and clips to fasten it to the easel. There was something so optimistic about a piece of clean white canvas—she could make it anything she wanted. She took a few moments to picture in her mind a replica of the simple gestural landscape that had once adorned the kitchen wall of the Spanish house. With a vine of charcoal, she sketched the picture onto the canvas. When she was satisfied that it was a close rendering of the sketch she'd shown Chev, she wiped her stained fingers on a towel and stood back with a smile.

She missed the therapeutic power of creating art. Creating something where once there had been nothing, something that had never before existed, could be a magical, insular experience. It had a way of crowding out everything else.

Then the screech of the peacock cut into the night air.

Gemma grimaced. Well, almost everything.

As the bird continued its grating call, she remembered what Chev had said about the creature, that biology would drive it to leave if it didn't find what it was looking for—a hen with which to mate. And she got the feeling that Chev was hinting that he, too, couldn't wait forever for what he wanted—*her.*

The difference, she reminded herself, was that unlike the peacock, Chev Martinez would be leaving no matter what. No-strings sex would be the perfect solution, but she knew she couldn't sleep with her seductive neighbor and not feel something…and she didn't want to go there. From now on, she would be on her best behavior, which meant staying away from her window, no matter how desperate she was.

Gemma swallowed hard.

And no matter how tempting *he* was.

13

"SO HOW'S THE HUNKY NEIGHBOR?" Sue asked.

"Fine," Gemma answered cautiously into her cell phone. Over the past couple of days she and Chev had fallen into the role of…cheerful neighbors. He helped to chase the bothersome peacock from her yard, she answered any questions he had about the house and worked on the mural in her free time.

And she scrupulously avoided her bedroom window.

Meanwhile, he had respected the distance she'd put between them since her mother's visit, with no questions. Although when they'd discussed the mosaic for the pool renovation last evening, she had felt his hungry gaze on her.

And she'd reveled in it.

"I think you should go for it," Sue said, as if she could read her mind. "He sounds like the perfect prospect for a rebound affair. I say the sooner, the better."

Gemma stretched forward to glance at the steel-gray clouds hanging low that did not bode well for a quick commute to the museum. "What, is there a clock ticking on my sexuality?"

"You said he's not going to be around for long."

"And?"

"And Dr. Alexander would tell you to follow your instincts."

"Dr. Alexander isn't around," Gemma said. If she were, Gemma would be tempted to tell her that the little experiment in class ten years ago had nearly been her undoing—then and now.

"Are those letters of yours giving you any ideas?" Sue asked in a suggestive voice.

"They're the words of a naive schoolgirl," Gemma said, as if she were trying to convince herself. "Let's just say they have no basis in reality."

Sue laughed. "But then reality can be such a drag."

"Have you talked to Jason?" Gemma asked to change the thorny subject.

"Not for a while," Sue said, her voice cagey. "Has he called again?"

"No."

"Good. I hope he doesn't."

"Sue, for heaven's sake, don't you think that Jason and I should at least be friends?"

"I just don't want you to fall under his spell again."

Gemma laughed. "You make it sound like I have no power to resist him."

"Jason makes his living persuading people, Gemma. And he's the only man you've ever slept with—that's powerful stuff."

"You're jumping to conclusions. Jason didn't say anything about wanting to get back together. And I didn't say anything about wanting him to."

"But you do."

Gemma sighed. "Okay, maybe a tiny part of me would like the satisfaction of hearing him say he made a mistake. Is that so wrong?"

"No," Sue admitted. "I just think you're on the verge of having your own life, and I don't want to see you get folded back into Jason's."

Gemma didn't respond, fighting unexpected pangs of doubt. Having her own life was being dressed like a call girl, on her way to a job that would mortify her parents—and Jason. And looking forward to it, God help her. Especially since she hadn't been getting her fix at home, exhibiting for Chev.

Rain splattered on the windshield. "It's starting to rain, so I'll call you later, okay?"

"Okay, bye."

Gemma hung up just as the gray sky unleashed on the city. She flipped on her headlights and wipers and slowed to accommodate the low visibility. She wondered how the weather would affect attendance today at the museum.

She parked in the museum employee lot, then ran through the rain that was now coming down in sheets. Poor Chev—the pool excavation would be stalled in this soup.

In the lobby, she shook her umbrella and smiled at Lillian, who had also just arrived.

"Join me for a cup of coffee?" Lillian asked.

Gemma nodded, shivering. By mutual agreement, they kept their coats on to cover their risqué outfits when they went into the break room and poured steaming cups of coffee. Gemma added creamer to hers, Lillian took hers black. They sat at a table in the corner.

"Nasty day," Lillian offered.

Gemma nodded and sipped the scalding coffee.

"You look a little down," the woman offered. The pink streak in her hair matched her youthful attitude. "Want to talk about it?"

Gemma shrugged. "It's nothing specific. Did you ever feel as if your life hadn't turned out the way it was supposed to?"

Lillian's extraordinary violet-colored eyes danced with good cheer. "I guess I didn't plan that far ahead. I tend to take happiness as it comes, and other than my brokerage account for retirement, I try not to outthink tomorrow." She smiled into her coffee, then took a generous sip.

"Easier said than done," Gemma said wistfully.

"Not really. I'm a tad older than you, so maybe that gives me more perspective. But the only times in my life I've ever been unhappy were the times I was living to make someone else happy—my parents, a boyfriend, my husband."

"You were married?"

"For five glorious years…and two horrible ones." Lillian gave a little laugh.

"I'm divorced, too," Gemma said, and realized it was the first time she'd said the words aloud without flinching.

"Life is too short to be with someone who doesn't make you happy."

Two male employees came in and looked their way while they filled their coffee cups, devouring the women's legs, Lillian's in sheer black stockings, ending in black stilettos, Gemma's bare and tanned, ending in red peep-toe platforms. Gemma felt a little rush of adrenaline, and noticed that Lillian sat taller, too. The men smiled and waved, then left, exchanging regretful glances.

Gemma ran her finger around the top of her coffee cup. "But what if what makes you happy…isn't good for you?"

"You mean like drugs or alcohol?"

"No…this is a different kind of addiction."

Lillian nodded thoughtfully. "Does it hurt anyone else?"

"No…the participants are…willing."

"Does it expose you to harm?"

"Not if I'm discreet."

The woman smiled brightly. "Then what's the harm?"

"The guilt," Gemma whispered. "And I'm afraid it will keep me from growing close to someone."

Lillian took another drink of her coffee. "Did your ex go along with it?"

Gemma wet her lips. It was strange—and liberating—to talk to another admitted exhibitionist. "No. He knew nothing about it."

"And were you close to him?"

"As it turns out, no."

"So depriving yourself didn't bring you the closeness you crave either, did it?"

Gemma shook her head, realizing the woman spoke from experience.

Lillian patted her hand and lowered her voice to a whisper. "So why deprive yourself? The right man will accept you and all your delicious inclinations." She glanced at her watch. "We're up in fifteen minutes, and I'd like to stop by the ladies' room. See you later?"

Gemma smiled and nodded, then sat at the table a little while longer looking for answers in the depths of her coffee. She wished she had Lillian's fearless outlook, could be so comfortable with her *inclinations*. She took a drink from her cup, remembering that for a few weeks during her senior year in college, she *had* been fearless.

But her fearlessness had also nearly ruined her life.

She turned her mind away from the disturbing murky memories, then emptied her cup. Still nursing more questions than answers, Gemma walked toward the cloakroom. The woman at the counter smirked when Gemma shrugged out of her coat, revealing her short red skirt and white bustier. Gemma ignored the woman's slight because her midsection was already tingling at the anticipation of leading the first tour of the day. When she walked up to the meeting place, she saw that the rain hadn't hurt today's reservations. If anything, the crowds were more swollen than usual.

The tours lasted anywhere from forty-five minutes to an hour, at the discretion of the guide, with a fifteen-minute break in between each tour. Gemma finished two tours before lunch, then ate with Lillian in the employee break room. It was becoming a habit, chatting away the hour. Lillian seemed to always know what to say, steering clear of talk about family and Gemma's ex, keeping the conversation light and breezy. The woman was well traveled and well read, with a wicked sense of humor.

Gemma laughed at something that Lillian said and realized with a start that she and Chev were the only people in her life who didn't know or weren't somehow connected to Jason.

Then bizarrely, she heard Jason's name on the television mounted high in a corner of the break room. She glanced up to see a clip showing Jason artfully dodging questions about the prosecution of the statewide drug ring that she'd read about in the papers. He sat behind a grand desk in what appeared to be his new office. His framed law degree hung on the wall behind him, and Gemma wondered idly what he had done with the photo of her that had once sat on his desk, wondered what the view was like from his office window. And was that a new suit? Her chest tightened unexpectedly at the proof that there was now a big chunk of his life that she'd been excluded from.

"He's handsome in a scholarly sort of way," Lillian offered, noting Gemma's sudden interest in the TV.

"Yes, he is," Gemma murmured. Her tongue watered to say the words that until recently she had been married to the handsome, powerful man. But she was mindful of the need for discretion in revealing her relationship to Jason to anyone she worked with. If word leaked out that she was giving tours for an X-rated exhibit, the press would have a field day...and her "delicious inclinations," as Lillian had called them, would be exposed.

"Funny," Lillian said, "but I pegged you for liking a different kind of man."

"What do you mean?"

Lillian shrugged her slender, toned shoulders. "I don't know, I just pictured you with someone a little more... free-spirited."

Gemma didn't respond, but the image of an exotic, brown-skinned man rose in her mind.

Lillian wadded up the paper wrapper from her sandwich and grinned. "Life is a smorgasbord. See you out there." She pushed to her feet and walked away.

Gemma finished eating lunch and took a few minutes to freshen up. Two more tours to go before calling it a day. Her step quickened as she neared the meeting place and slid her mask into place. Her body was already smoldering from the morning tours. Beneath the red skirt, she wore a white thong that bit into her skin with the insistence of a lover. Her clit was swollen and sensitive from the constant friction...just the way she liked it. She'd have to take it easy this afternoon or she might lose control and wind up giving the wide-eyed attendees a show they hadn't bargained for.

She extended a smile to the people already gathered for the first afternoon tour. "Welcome," she said warmly.

"We've been looking forward to this all week," a woman said, gesturing to a man next to her that Gemma assumed to be the woman's husband. "Our marriage counselor suggested that we come."

"That's nice," Gemma said. "It'll be fun."

"I'm having fun already," a guy standing nearby said, eyeing her bare legs. Everyone laughed, Gemma included, identifying the resident flirt of the group. There was always one guy who thought he could tease his way to getting Gemma's number at the end of the tour. What he didn't realize was that Gemma's "watch and learn" mantra extended to more than just the tour.

The area filled with more people, all slightly damp from the rain still falling outside. Warm, moist bodies, producing pungent odors, shifting from foot to foot in anticipation. Gemma silently counted heads, then squinted. The man in the back dressed in dark slacks and short-sleeve formfitting white shirt looked like...wait a minute—it couldn't be.

Chev?

He gave her a little nod of acknowledgment, then his gaze flicked over her costume. He must have abandoned his work site for the day due to the rain. A bolt of pure sexual electricity lit up her body at the realization that he would be watching her on the tour...and watching other people watch her. Pleasure coursed through her, but she was suddenly nervous, smoothing her hair behind her ear and fidgeting with her hands. Her thong suddenly seemed even more invasive.

After a deep breath to calm her nerves, she asked for the group's attention and announced they were about to begin. "A reminder that no pictures are allowed for this exhibit. Please keep your cameras stowed at all times."

As she scanned the faces in the crowd, she stopped abruptly. Lewis Wilcox—the reporter who had tried to thwart Jason's election and who had left her voice messages since the divorce. Alarm washed over her. Did he somehow know her identity? At the moment he was staring at her legs. She held her breath, but when his gaze reached her face, he gave the mask no more than a cursory glance. She relaxed a little, conceding it was just bad luck that he would be the reporter the TV station would send to check out the tour *and* that he'd wound up in her group. At least she had the mask to protect her identity. She was grateful she'd never talked to the man on the phone, so there was no way he'd recognize her voice.

Chev was frowning at her and mouthed *Are you okay?* She nodded and gave him a singular smile, grateful for his concern, even if he didn't know the source. She started the tour and, within a couple of minutes, became immersed in her lecture. She tried not to seek out Chev's face, but she couldn't help it. If the man cut a sexy figure in his faded work clothes, he was devastating in dress clothes. Not surprisingly, he was garnering a few looks of his own from women in the group, but he seemed unaware. He seemed, she realized happily, to have eyes only for her.

CHEV HADN'T BEEN SURE what to expect, wasn't even sure he'd be able to get in Gemma's group. In fact, he'd first landed in a group led by a petite, curvy woman with a pink streak in her black hair. When she'd noticed him craning, hoping for a glimpse of Gemma, the woman had quietly asked him if he was looking for another guide. When he'd nodded, she had covertly pointed him through another door where he found Gemma corralling a crowd of about twenty-five people.

The sight of her in the sexy red-and-white getup made his mouth water and his cock twitch. Her legs were long and bare and tanned. And that black mask of hers made him feel…proprietary. It was as if they shared a secret over the heads of the other people standing between her and him.

As she welcomed the group and gave them a brief overview of the exhibit, his chest warmed with admiration. She was engaging, her voice low and husky. A natural performer, and these people hadn't even seen her best show.

She led the group into the first area that housed nude photography that dated practically as far back as the time when photography was first invented. She moved like a cat, her limbs lithe and limber, her curves straining against the confines of the snug red skirt and white bustier. He stayed in the back of the crowd, felt the temperature of the group's collective libido rise as she explained the risks taken by the models and the photographers to capture the provocative images.

His own fire was stoked higher, not by the pictures of the white-thighed women in the photos who hid their faces from the camera, but by the heightened color in Gemma's cheeks as she caught his eye. Her mouth curved into the most sexy smile, setting off the beauty mark near the corner of her mouth.

"Blondie's hot, isn't she?" a man next to him whispered.

Anger sparked in Chev's belly watching the man salivate. Protective feelings crowded his chest. He wanted to pick Gemma up and carry her out of there, but he knew she enjoyed this part of the job…being watched.

And who was he to get between her and her fetish? Nobody, just a guy passing through. One of the many drooling guys who enjoyed looking at her, except he couldn't get enough, was starting to feel compulsively… *attached.*

As the tour progressed, she exchanged frequent glances with him, her body language becoming more animated. His body responded in kind until his erection throbbed against the fly of his dress slacks, his balls full and achy. From the photography exhibit, she led the group into a room of sexual devices. She donned a pair of white gloves and removed a couple of the primitive dildos from their containers. He saw the man who had made the comment about Gemma being hot stealthily lift a cell phone and snap a couple of photos. Chev nudged the man's arm, then shook his head meaning-fully. The jerk looked sheepish and put away the phone.

A slow burn was consuming Chev by the time Gemma led the group into the room housing sex furniture. Perspi-ration trickled down his back, and his hands fairly shook from wanting to touch her. She lectured on the surprising number of beds, swings, benches and chairs built through the ages especially to aid in having sex or having sex in more interesting ways.

Behind the black mask, Gemma's eyes were bright and her hands languid as she touched the sometimes humorous-looking contraptions. But some of the more modern pieces of formed maple and leather upholstery were beautifully crafted and sent his mind spiraling in carnal directions, picturing Gemma draped over the contours, positioning her supple body perfectly to receive his.

Chev gave himself a mental shake and exhaled slowly. His body was like a furnace and every glance from Gemma in her red-and-white peep-show outfit added fuel to his fire. Worse, he suspected every man in the group was on the verge of incineration. He didn't like the idea of other men looking at Gemma, sporting hard-ons for her, but he could tolerate it if he knew he'd be in her bed tonight.

In truth, he'd settle for watching her undress and pleasure herself.

But at the end of the tour, despite the fact that he was burning up for her, Chev didn't seek her out. He sensed that the more he behaved like a stranger, the more intrigued she would be. It was a tactic he didn't like, but if it gave him a chance to get closer to Gemma in the long run, then it was worth pretending. So when she bade the group good-bye and caught his eye, he nodded curtly and beat a hasty exit out of the museum.

The rain was still slashing down, but Chev skipped an umbrella. He jogged through the downpour to his truck and climbed inside, drenched. Driving his fingers into his damp hair, he exhaled loudly. He'd hoped the wetness would cool his desire for Gemma, but it hadn't.

And it was time to face the fact that his longing for her had moved from something physical to something essential.

14

AT THE SIGHT of Chev's receding back, unexpected disappointment billowed in Gemma's chest, leaving her breathless with confusion. Her watch-me games had never before included this element of...*loss*. Part of the thrill had been the fact that it was a stranger watching her, a person she would probably never see again. Performing for Chev had seemed safe because he was moving on in a couple of weeks. She hadn't anticipated missing him after he was gone. If this achy sensation was any indication of how she would feel when he was out of her life, she might be in trouble.

Gemma put her hand to her throat, felt the heat there. Having his eyes on her during the tour had heightened her excitement to nearly unbearable levels. It was as if he were next to her, stroking her, whispering in her ear. For the first time, she'd wanted the crowd to disappear and leave her alone with one man, this man who could bring her body to the brink of orgasm simply by raking his dark brown eyes over her. If Chev could do such amazing things to her erogenous zones with only a glance, what kind of havoc could he wreak with his hands...his cock? A shiver raised gooseflesh on her scorching skin.

After letting management know she'd had a reporter in her group, she moved through the last tour of the day like an automaton. The rain had diminished but the soggy drive home seemed so interminable she thought she might break through her skin. She couldn't wait to get home, but was half-afraid of what might happen when she did.

Chev's truck sat near the curb, empty, but lights were on throughout the Spanish house. Puddles of muddy water sat in his construction-torn yard. Her yard looked almost as bad from the rain and the mess that the peacock had left her with. She leaned forward and looked up into the bird's favorite tree but didn't see the telltale swoop of tail hanging down. Perhaps the weather had driven him on to fairer skies.

She pulled the car into the garage and walked inside, her heartbeat thumping wildly. Still wearing her thin raincoat, she climbed the steps to the second floor, barely registering the stuffiness of the still air. The rain falling on the roof of the house lent an insular, cozy feel to her bedroom. She donned the black mask and walked directly to the picture window, wondering if Chev would show up at his to watch her. When she pushed aside the filmy curtain, she inhaled sharply.

He was there, waiting for her.

The light in the room behind him silhouetted his wide shoulders and broad chest. Still in his dress clothes, he stood with hands braced on either side of the rain-streaked pane, his gaze dark and hungry.

For her.

Gemma shrugged out of her coat, let it fall to the floor. She loved the fact that the rain had fogged the edges of the glass, had softened her frame. The white bustier had constricted her all day, pushing her breasts up and out. Now her increased breathing threatened to spill them over the top of the garment. Her nipples were showing, hard and extended. She pressed them against the window, gasping at the shock of the coolness on the sensitive tips. Her eyes closed involuntarily against the sensations spiraling through her body. She wished she could make the session last but knew she was too wound up to draw it out.

When her eyes fluttered open, though, Chev was gone.

Gemma pressed a hand against the frame in distress. Rejection and shame washed over her. She turned away, panicked by the emotions bombarding her. She couldn't need this man…she couldn't. Tears of frustration welled in her eyes.

Then the sound of the doorbell pealed into the house.

CHEV WAITED in front of Gemma's door, water streaming off his hair and fingertips. Enough was enough. Watching her would no longer satisfy his lust for her. If she didn't answer the door, he'd leave her alone. Because as much as she obviously loved being an exhibitionist, he couldn't take it anymore.

He held his breath and listened for noise inside the house, any indication that she was going to answer the door. Several seconds went by…then a minute…then two.

Chev pulled his hand down his face in frustration and turned to go. So be it.

And then the door scraped open.

He turned back to see Gemma standing there, still wearing the mask and holding the black raincoat in front of her. Her eyes were questioning but unwavering.

He reached her in two strides and gathered her in his arms, lowering a savage kiss on her mouth. She came alive, responding with the intensity he'd known she possessed, her movements frantic and a little desperate. He backed her into the house and kicked the door closed. Her raincoat slid to the floor. Chev deepened the kiss, exploring her sweet mouth, the prospect of experiencing all of her making his hands quake.

Gemma moved toward the staircase and pulled him with her. She half reclined, half pulled herself up the steps backward with him on top of her, crawling over her to keep up with her, snatching a kiss here, dropping a bite there. She smelled of an enticing mix of earthy perfume and rain.

"I'm getting you wet," he murmured, licking the moisture from her collarbone.

"Yes, you are," she whispered in a husky tone that sent another surge of lust ripping through his body. With both hands, he nudged the red skirt higher to reveal the miniscule white thong underneath. The knowledge that she'd been wearing it all day while he watched her at the museum sent a jolt to his balls. Taking advantage of the leverage the stairs provided, he knelt between her knees and lowered his head to capture the thin fabric in his teeth. When she moaned and thrust her hips up, he buried his head between her thighs and tongued her heated folds through the thin barrier, inhaling her rich, womanly scent.

She drove her fingers into his hair, urging him on. It was all the encouragement he needed to roll the thong down her legs for full access to the nest of light brown hair that at this moment held the answer to every question pummeling his body. He clasped her bare thighs and opened her legs wider to him, then lowered his mouth to her glistening sex, kissing, licking and sucking her engorged clit. Her musky nectar filled his mouth, fueling his desire for her to unbearable heights.

From her frustrated noises, he sensed that she, too, was close to the edge. "Please, Chev...please."

He stabbed his tongue inside her and moaned against

her sensitive pink flesh to send vibrations to her pleasure centers. Concentrating on her enjoyment helped to keep his own arousal in check. She came with a great anguished cry of satisfaction, her clit pulsing against his tongue, her knees squeezing his shoulders. Masculine pride filled his chest that he could deliver her to a place where only physical joy mattered. He allowed her to recover for a few seconds, but he knew his own body well enough to know that he couldn't hold out much longer.

He picked her up and carried her the rest of the way up the stairs to her bedroom. When he released her, she slid down his body with her arms looped around his neck, a sleepy, sexy smile on her face beneath the mask. He kissed her beauty mark, then claimed her mouth. He reached under the skirt to cup her bare ass in both hands, feeling her wetness on his fingers.

She pulled his damp shirt over his head, then unfastened the waistband of his slacks and lowered the zipper. Chev stepped out of them, shucking his waterlogged shoes and socks in the process. His briefs clung to him, his desire for her unrepressed. He reached for her, wanting to rid her of her clothes, but Gemma pushed him toward the bed and urged him to sit. Then she walked out of arm's reach.

When she began to unlace the white bustier, Chev leaned back on his elbows to enjoy the show. With the skirt rucked up, hugging her thighs, her bare, tanned legs looked a mile long in those red high heels. His cock surged. Clear liquid oozed out of the head that protruded from the waistband of his briefs, pooling on his stomach. She slowly unlaced the bustier and allowed her breasts to fall free. He groaned to see the magnificent globes up close, his hands itched to touch the distended pink nipples.

She turned away from him and gave him a coy smile over her shoulder, then shimmied the skirt down to her ankles. Her tight ass made his mouth water, but when she bent over to step out of the garment, the view made the moisture on his tongue evaporate.

"Come to me," he commanded, his voice hoarse.

She turned and walked to the bed, her breasts bouncing, her thighs still shimmering with wetness.

"Take off the mask."

She shook her head. "I like it better this way."

Not in a position to argue, Chev pushed off his underwear, releasing his raging erection. She climbed on top of him and wrapped her fingers around his dick. The sensation made him buck. He clasped her hand. "I have to have you now. Let me get a condom before I explode."

Gemma stopped and for several agonizing heartbeats, Chev feared she would say that she didn't want to have sex. She seemed to be balancing on some sort of precipice and for an angry split second, he thought it was good that she could trust him. If she said no, he would find a less pleasurable way to achieve his release, but another man who had been tantalized by her watch-me games might not be so accommodating.

"I have a condom," she said finally, then leaned over to a nightstand and removed one from the drawer.

Her ex-husband's condoms, he realized in a haze. With her hands on him, rolling on the thin sheath, he frankly didn't care where it had come from.

Chev flipped her onto her back and settled his body over hers. He feasted on her breasts, sucking and biting on her nipples until they were hardened and scarlet.

"Yes," she murmured. "Oh, yes."

Chev had always prided himself on taking it slow with his lovers, but with Gemma, he felt feverish. And suddenly, he couldn't wait any longer. He kissed her mouth and her neck, then entered her silky channel in one deep thrust. Her body clenched around his like an exquisite spring—he set his jaw against the tornadic pull of her core.

Even as his body found a rhythm with hers, something akin to fear reared in his chest...it had never been like this before. This...*force* that seemed to be drawing the life fluid out of him. She lifted her hips to meet him stroke for stroke, her nails digging into his shoulders. Behind the mask her eyes were glazed with passion.

He tried to maintain control, but within a few seconds, he felt his body racing toward paradise. Her cries escalated and she climaxed again, contracting around the length of him in waves. Chev surrendered to the power of her and shot rope after rope of his essence, shuddering at the sheer intensity of being emptied so completely.

When their moans had subsided, he lowered his body gingerly, careful not to crush her, and rolled to the side. Gasping for breath, he lay staring at Gemma's still-masked profile, reeling from the emotions plowing through him. When had this happened? When had he fallen for her? And what could possibly come of it?

As if by mutual consent, they didn't speak. The rain falling on the roof was hypnotic, prolonging their fantasy state. Dusk was giving way to darkness quickly, casting shadows across the bedroom. The scent of their lovemaking filled the air and incredibly, Chev wanted her again. He reached for her hand, twined their fingers. "Gemma—"

"Shh," she whispered, putting a finger to his lips. Then she pushed herself up to straddle him. Her magnificent breasts swung heavily, the large peaks within easy reach of his lips. "Let's think of something to do with our mouths other than talk."

The woman was nothing if not persuasive. Chev opened his mouth to receive an engorged nipple and sucked hungrily, determined to grant every sexual wish Gemma had, hoping that she would allow him to stay in her bed… and perhaps, in her life.

15

GEMMA LOVED to make love in the morning. She stretched her arms tall and her legs long until her muscles sang, then she smiled and rolled over.

But at the sight of Chev Martinez slumbering on Jason's side of the bed—his black hair stark against the white pillowcase, his gold earring glinting against his skin, his tattoo of a leafless tree vivid on his muscled shoulder—she panicked. His being here seemed so…wrong. She sat and pulled up a sheet to cover her breasts, still tender from Chev's skillful hands and tongue.

Sometime during the night the rain had stopped. The morning sun slanted in the picture window, casting harsh light on the aftermath of their night of unbridled sex. The air was ripe with the aroma of body fluids, with at least three spent condoms in view. The sheets on the bed were tangled and warm, the bedspread and decorative pillows flung to the far corners of the room. The black mask dangled around her neck. Her costume from yesterday lay in one pile, his clothes in another. The sight of another man's dress shoes on the area rug made her heart race. What had she done?

"Hey."

She jumped, then looked over at Chev's lazy morning smile. His impressive erection tented the sheet. His long bronzed limbs were sprawled across the bed, taking up an inordinate amount of space, crowding her.

"Hey," she said, wondering how to delicately diffuse the situation…erase the previous night…go back to the way things had been—safe.

He reached forward, turned her hand over in his and ran his thumb over her palm, sending vibrations up her arm. "Since you don't have to work today and I'm not expecting my crew for a couple of hours, how do you feel about making love in the morning?"

An alarm sounded in her head. This was too much, too soon…it couldn't go any further. She pulled back, careful to keep herself covered. "Chev, we need to talk."

His expression clouded. "Uh-oh, I know that tone."

The ring of the phone cut through the air like a knife. Knowing it was rude, but grateful for the distraction, she dove for the receiver. In the back of her mind, despite the bad timing, she wondered perversely if it was Jason calling.

She was officially losing her mind.

"Hello?"

Sue's voice came over the line. "Hey, there. Did I catch you at a bad time?"

Gemma shot a glance at Chev, who was watching her closely, his dark eyes too perceptive. "No, you didn't catch me at a bad time. What's up?"

"I feel bad about some of the things I said yesterday morning," Sue said. "I shouldn't have encouraged you to have a fling with your neighbor. It's none of my business."

Chev swung his legs over the side of the bed and pushed to his feet. Gemma watched him under her lashes, conceding a thrill at the sight of his lean buttocks and broad, muscled back.

"Are you there?" Sue asked.

"Yes, I'm here," Gemma said, yanking her attention back to the phone call. "And that's okay, you don't have to apologize."

With his back to her, Chev picked up his pile of clothes and walked across the hall to the bathroom. The door closed with a dull thud.

"Do you have company?" Sue asked, her tone suspicious.

"What? No, of course not." But Gemma heard the false, tinny ring to her own voice.

"Oh, my God, you do have company! It's the neighbor, isn't it?"

In her confusion, Gemma waited too long to respond.

Sue whooped. "Yes! Was it fantastic?"

Gemma stood and reached for a robe, eager to be covered when Chev reemerged. "Um...can we talk about this later?"

"Only if you promise me the play-by-play."

"Goodbye, Sue."

She was tying the belt on her robe when Chev came out of the bathroom, fully dressed. She finger-combed her hair self-consciously, hating the awkwardness that reverberated between them, hating that she was the cause. She sensed that with one signal from her, he'd carry her back to bed. Her nipples hardened and he noticed, but she crossed her arms over them.

"Do you want to talk about last night?" he asked.

"Not really," she said, being honest. She inhaled deeply, then exhaled. "I told you I'm better at keeping things at a distance."

"Really? Then you faked it pretty convincingly."

Her traitorous body started humming in remembrance. "Chev, we both know this can't go anywhere."

His dark eyes bored into hers for several long seconds, then he nodded. "You're right. I guess that's my cue to leave."

But when he turned to go, she experienced that same horrible empty feeling she'd experienced when he'd left the museum. She realized with a sinking heart that while her mind knew what was best, her body knew what *felt* best.

"Would you like to see the mural before you go?" she asked, gesturing to the room she'd turned into a studio.

He pursed his mouth. "Sure."

She led him inside the room, feeling a little lift at the sight of the simple but colorful landscape that had emerged on the piece of canvas.

He looked at it thoughtfully for a few seconds, so silent that she began to feel nervous.

"If you don't like it," she said hurriedly, "don't feel compelled to hang it."

"I think it's wonderful," he said solemnly. "You're very talented, Gemma."

A flush warmed her cheeks. "I haven't painted anything in years. I enjoyed doing it. It should be dry enough to install soon."

"Okay. I'll let you decide when," he said, his gaze level.

She realized he was referring to more than the painting. Gemma swallowed and nodded, following him downstairs. But she needn't have. After a glance at Jason's things still cluttering the living room, he was out the front door and had closed it behind him before she reached the bottom step. She glanced guiltily through the front window, wondering if any of her neighbors had noticed the strange man leaving her house at the unseemly hour. After deeming that Petal Lagoon was deserted, she heaved a sigh of relief, feeling as if she'd dodged a bullet.

Déjà vu. Like years before…a close call.

But on the heels of relief came that nagging feeling of watching Chev walk away…and not liking it. Still, she couldn't have it both ways, and this was how things had to be. She couldn't undo last night, but it would be foolish to let her relationship with Chev become more complicated.

She climbed the stairs and stepped into the shower brimming with self-recrimination. Leaning her forehead against the cool tile, she groaned. She should've maintained distance between them, like she'd planned. Then she wouldn't be haunted by the memories of making love with the man all night long. Her body sang with latent longing. Unbidden, delicious chills ran over her shoulders and down her arms.

The chemistry between them was undeniable, unbelievable. For the first time, she understood what Dr. Alexander had been trying to tell her female students about the almost magical occurrence of having sex with a partner who was physically compatible in every respect.

Gemma leaned back to let the warm water fall over her breasts and find a natural trail down to the juncture of her thighs. At one point last night, she had felt as if she were having an out-of-body experience. Dr. Alexander would definitely approve.

She had to admit that sex with Chev had been more satisfying than performing for him. On the other hand, performing for him had stoked them both to the fever pitch that had catapulted them into bed. And kept them there for hours and hours…and hours.

And while it probably wasn't fair, it was impossible not to compare his lovemaking to Jason's. They were, after all, the only two men she'd ever slept with.

Where Jason had been tentative, Chev was fearless.

Where Jason had been reserved, Chev was expressive. Where Jason had been missionary, Chev was acrobatic.

But you can't stay in bed twenty-four hours a day, her mind whispered. And what happens after the spontaneous fire burns itself out?

Loneliness…

Sobered, Gemma climbed from the shower and forced herself to matters at hand. The museum was closed today, so she didn't have to work. She spent the morning paying bills and balancing her checkbook, a task that took twice as long as it should have because her mind kept straying to the noise of the equipment and activity next door. Then she reasoned that since the weather had improved, she might as well clean up the mess the peacock had created in her yard before the neighborhood association left a threatening note in her mailbox.

The mailbox…changing her name was one more thing she'd been stalling on.

She wondered if some small part of her thought that if Jason did return, seeing the mailbox unchanged would be a sign that their marriage could be repaired.

Adding to her mental to-do list, she gathered her yard tools, hat and gloves.

It was a glorious day in the neighborhood. The rain had given summer a nudge, turning pale greens to deep emerald and dark greens to teal. The bird-of-paradise plants had bloomed riotously, with vivid orange petals and arrow-shaped blue-and-white "tongues." From the thickened grass, Gemma picked up a vibrant peacock feather and stroked the fringed edges, admiring the iridescent colors of green and teal and gold. She shaded her eyes and looked up into the trees that the peacock had favored, but the flamboyant pest was nowhere in sight. After creating upheaval in her life, it looked like he had finally moved on.

As she raked the yard and filled lawn trash bags with debris, she found herself stealing glances next door. More trucks and bodies than she'd ever seen before rambled over the property, apparently trying to make up for the day lost to rain. She saw Chev moving among the men in his work clothes, a red bandanna tied over his jet-black hair. Just watching him interact with the other men made her midsection pulse and her breathing accelerate. He looked in her direction once, but she couldn't tell if it was accidental or if he was seeking her out.

But why would he? She'd made it clear that she didn't want to sleep with him again. She should be relieved that he had indicated he would respect her wishes.

Wait for her to make the next move.

Her body felt heavy and stiff with tension, feeling at war with herself. Part of her ached to feel Chev's touch, part of her was convinced it would only lead to heartache. She should have insisted that they keep things at a distance. Now things were complicated. Now her heart was involved, and it made her feel exposed in a way that performing for him at the window never had.

She dragged the bags of lawn debris to the curb. Gemma removed her hat and used a glove to wipe away the perspiration on her hairline. She stared at her mailbox, wavering. *Jason and Gemma White.*

A shadow appeared overhead, then a loud yelp sounded. Gemma cried out and covered her head with her arms. The wide-winged peacock landed gracefully on the mailbox with a sound like a heavy blanket being shaken over a bed. The blue bird tucked in his wings and stared at her, his long train of tail feathers hanging to the ground, his head bobbing. The precise crown of feathers on its head gave the appearance of a Medieval war helmet topped with a colorful brush. Indeed, he didn't look particularly friendly at the moment. He thrust his regal head forward and unleashed a series of high-pitched cries.

Gemma stumbled backward and fell hard on her tailbone, then put up her arm to ward off the bird in case he decided she looked…mountable. "Go away!" she shouted, flailing to get to her feet.

A strong arm hauled her up. "Are you okay?" Chev asked, his face creased in concern.

"I'm fine," she said, feeling foolish. And feeling something else at the familiarity of his touch.

He waved his arms at the bird until it flew up in the trees.

"I was hoping I'd seen the last of him," she muttered.

"He's stubborn," Chev admitted. "It might take more to get rid of him than you planned."

His words resonated with double meaning, but if his words sounded menacing, the mischievous twinkle in his dark eyes took the sting out of them.

"Thank you for rescuing me," she said. "Again."

"You're welcome. I also came over to tell you that the thermostat for your HVAC unit arrived. I have my hands full right now, but I was thinking I could come over tomorrow and install it for you."

She knew that his simply being in her house again would be a dangerous temptation. Gemma moistened her dry lips. "I have to work. Could you come over when I get home?"

His regard swept over her, grazing every nerve ending. "I'll be watching." Then he turned and walked away.

16

GEMMA'S PHONE RANG as she slid behind the wheel of her car for the commute home from the museum. It was Sue—again. Since yesterday morning her friend had left two messages to call, but Gemma hadn't yet because she didn't want to be grilled about Chev.

Yet at the third insistent ring she conceded with a sigh that she was only putting off the inevitable.

"Hello?"

"Well, it's about freaking time. I was ready to come see you in person to make sure you were okay."

"I've been busy," Gemma hedged, starting her car.

"Good. With the neighbor?"

Damn…just the mention of Chev made her heart beat faster. "Sue, you're making way too much out of this."

"Humor me, okay? There's nothing this juicy going on in my life."

"He's coming over to fix my air conditioner tonight. I wouldn't call that juicy."

"That depends on which tool he pulls out of his belt."

Gemma couldn't help but laugh at her friend's silliness. "When did you get so bawdy?"

"I'm envious. You have a sexy job and a hot new boyfriend."

"He's not my boyfriend."

"So you don't deny that he's hot?"

"No comment."

Sue laughed. "You don't have to tell me. I can hear it. When you talk about this guy, your voice gets all low and husky. You never sounded that way when you talked about Jason."

Gemma swallowed. The last thing she needed to be told was that her lust for Chev was so obvious. If Sue could pick it up over a phone line, Chev would certainly be able to tell when he came over tonight. After all, the man was so observant. The perfect audience…

"Congratulations, Gemma. I think you've officially turned the page."

Her friend's words conjured up an image of the fantasies letter folded on the dresser in her bedroom, the one she still hadn't been able to finish reading. But she felt its presence, waiting for her.

"Thanks for the support. I'm getting ready to head home, so I'll call you later, okay?"

They said goodbye and Gemma pulled out of the museum parking lot while digesting her friend's words. After a day of tours, her body was primed for passion. She'd thought of little more than Chev all day, and the intensity with which he'd made love to her. It was a safe bet that if Chev was in her house this evening, proximity alone would set carnal things in motion.

By the time she arrived home, the bikini panties she wore underneath a pair of black short shorts were soaked. One crew was leaving Chev's property, and another one seemed to be packing up. He turned his head as she drove by and she felt his gaze on her skin like a full-body caress.

A shiver skittered over her shoulders as she pulled her Volvo into the garage.

She entered the house and had barely set her purse and black mask on the kitchen counter when the doorbell rang. She tightened the belt of the thin coat that covered the costume of shorts and sleeveless white tuxedo blouse and made her way to the entrance, her pulse going haywire. When she opened the door, she was taken back to the first time she saw Chev standing on her threshold. Was it possible that it had been little more than a week ago?

His clothes were dusty, but his big brown hands and muscular arms were clean. His expression was friendly but guarded, his eyes slightly hooded as he glanced at her legs, clad in fishnet stockings. The bandanna covering his head and the tiny gold earring in his ear made him look like a pirate bent on plundering. His sheer maleness nearly took her breath away.

"Hi," he said, holding a toolbox in one hand, lifting a small cardboard box in the other. "One thermostat."

Considering how stifling the air had suddenly become, it had apparently arrived just in time.

"Are you ready for me?" he prompted.

"Oh…yes," she managed to answer past a tight throat. She stepped aside to allow him entry, but she nearly tripped over a box of Jason's things that she still hadn't gotten around to moving to the garage. The sight of the golf towel that he had asked about gave her pause.

Chev cleared his throat and pointed to the stairs. "Why don't I go ahead and get started?"

She nodded. "Can I get you something to drink?"

"No, thanks. It shouldn't take too long to make the repair."

He was already walking up the stairs, his broad body

nearly spanning the entire width of the staircase. She followed him and squeezed past him in the hallway, then headed to her bedroom to change. Being so close to him conjured up visions of being even closer to him. "How's the house coming along?"

"Ahead of schedule," he said, concentrating on the HVAC unit exposed by the folding door. "The electric and plumbing is finished, and most of the woodwork is ready to stain."

He went to the breaker box and flipped switches to cut the power. Without the white hum of appliances, the house was hushed and echoey. Chev turned a flashlight on the work area and began to install the new thermostat. Beneath his gray T-shirt, the muscles in his shoulders bunched as he worked, giving her snatches of the tree tattoo that she had traced with her tongue between bouts of making love.

"Wh-what about the pool?" Gemma asked, struck by the awkward juxtaposition of the domesticity of the situation and the underlying sexual current sizzling in the thick, warm air.

"I'm still trying to settle on a design for the mosaic, but I'm close. I'd like to finish it before my family gets here in—what?" He squinted. "Three days. I thought my sister and cousin might like to break it in with a swim."

Warmth spread through her. He was obviously an adoring brother and cousin. "The mural is almost dry."

"Great." He removed a wrench from the toolbox and glanced over his shoulder. "You're still welcome to come to the party."

She smiled and nodded, but didn't commit. She barely knew him. Meeting his family was too…familiar. There was no point. All that existed between them was physical. And fleeting.

From the way Chev's jaw tightened, she had a feeling

he had read her mind. He looked as if he might say some-thing, but changed his mind and turned back to the job.

"I'm going to change," Gemma murmured, and stepped into the bedroom. Although when she crossed the thresh-old, it was hard not to remember the way her bed had looked with Chev's big bronze body sprawled across its width. She closed her eyes against the erotic images and untied the belt on her coat.

"Can I watch?" he asked from directly behind her.

When she turned, he was standing in the doorway, one hand braced on either side. The hunger in his eyes ignited a fire in her midsection that threatened to consume her. She slowly unbuttoned her coat, then allowed it to fall and puddle around her feet.

A guttural noise sounded from his throat and his hands tightened around the door facing.

He wanted to touch her, but she appreciated his re-straint. He knew how much pleasure she derived from him watching her. The anticipation was such a rush, Gemma felt lightheaded.

She unhooked the top button on her blouse to reveal a glimpse of cleavage and a lacy see-through bra. She was rewarded with his slow exhalation and the growing bulge behind the zipper of his jeans.

Then a foreign noise cut through the haze. Chev turned his head and straightened, a frown passing over his face. And before she could ask what was wrong, another man appeared in the doorway, his body language explosive, his eyes wide and bewildered.

Gemma's heart nearly stopped. *"Jason?"*

17

GEMMA'S MIND CHUGGED to process the surreal scene. Her ex-husband stood in the doorway of her bedroom in a dark, elegant suit, frowning back and forth between her and Chev. In his hand he gripped a bouquet of white lilies—her favorite, she registered vaguely.

"Gemma, what's going on?" Jason gestured to her outfit in dismay. "What are you wearing? And who the hell is this man?"

She opened her mouth, but no words seemed forthcoming.

Chev stepped forward. "Wait a minute, buddy. You're the one who just waltzed in as if this was your house."

Jason's head snapped back. "This *is* my house, *buddy.*" Then he looked at Gemma. "The doorbell isn't working."

"The electricity is off," she murmured. Not exactly the first words she thought she'd utter when she saw Jason again. She glanced down and realized her bra was showing, then hastily refastened the button. "This is Chev. He's... fixing the air conditioner."

The men sized each other up. They were about the same height. Chev had twice the bulk, and Jason, twice the attitude. Testosterone bounced around the confined space like rounds fired from a weapon. Gemma felt claustrophobic and sick, unsure of what was about to transpire.

"Are you almost finished here?" Jason asked Chev, nodding toward the open mechanical closet.

Chev's jaw hardened. "Yeah, I'm almost finished."

"Good," Jason said, eyeing the man suspiciously. Then he looked at Gemma. "I'm sure you'd like to change. I'll wait for you downstairs."

She exchanged an unreadable glance with Chev, then closed the bedroom door and hurriedly changed into jeans and a T-shirt. Her stomach was knotted with nerves, and her hands shook. The shock of seeing Jason again, seeing him toe to toe with Chev, left her breathless and confused. Why was Jason here? And how did she feel about him being here?

She breathed deeply to calm her racing pulse, but when she emerged, she still felt flustered. Chev was standing in front of the breaker box, flipping switches, his expression stony. Zone by zone, the electricity came back on, lights and appliances buzzed to life. Then he went to the wall thermostat and adjusted the temperature until the air conditioner clicked on. He reached up to hold his hand over a vent and grunted. "Cool air."

She wrapped her arms around her waist and made herself smile. "Thank you."

He leveled his dark gaze on her, then nodded curtly. "You're welcome. Now you don't have to worry about opening your windows."

Humiliation stained her cheeks. She swallowed past a tight throat but couldn't respond.

He leaned over and picked up the toolbox, the tattoo on his arm jumping. "I'll see you around."

She followed him downstairs where Jason stood like a sentinel watching Chev. Jason reached into his inside jacket pocket and withdrew his wallet. "What do I owe you?"

Mortification bled through her. "Jason—"

Chev glanced at the wad of cash her ex held. "It's already been taken care of." He looked back at Gemma and pursed his mouth, then opened the front door and walked out, leaving it open. When Gemma went to close it, she caught sight of his back receding, his shoulders taut. And she got the same empty feeling in her stomach that she'd felt before.

"Is that the neighbor guy your mother saw you with?"

Gemma closed the door and turned to face Jason. His pale blue eyes burned with...*jealousy?* The injustice of the situation sent anger galloping through her. "That's none of your business, Jason. And for the record, this is *my* house, remember? And why are you talking to my mother behind my back?"

"She called me. She was concerned about you."

"She doesn't need to be."

"Really? What's with the skimpy outfit you were wearing?"

Gemma frowned. "It's a costume. For a legitimate job."

He picked up the black mask from the counter next to where he'd laid the sheath of flowers. "What kind of a legitimate job requires a disguise?"

A flush climbed her neck. "It's only temporary."

"You got that right." He held up his cell phone. "Lewis Wilcox, the news reporter who dogged me during my entire campaign, sent a couple of photos to my phone this morning."

The tone of his voice alone was enough to cause her heartbeat to accelerate. When she glanced at the small screen, her worst fears were confirmed. It was her, leading a museum tour in the red skirt and white bustier, holding one of the primitive dildos. She was masked, of course, but the next photo was a close-up that clearly showed the beauty mark next to her mouth.

"I took a job as a tour guide at the museum."

"For an X-rated exhibit? What were you thinking?"

She moistened her lips, trying to keep the panic at bay. "I was thinking that I needed to take what I could get and work my way up. I was careful to use my maiden name on the application. I was told that the identity of all of the tour guides would be kept confidential for security reasons."

One side of his mouth slid back. "If Wilcox thought it was you, all he had to do was look for your car in the parking lot and run the plates."

Alarms sounded in her head. "Why would he send these photos to you?"

"Blackmail. He said he'd go public with the fact that you work the exhibit unless I gave him details of the drug case I'm prosecuting."

"I thought a gag order was in place."

"That's right."

Her eyes filled with sudden tears, realizing the precarious situation she had put him in. Full-blown panic flooded her limbs. "I'm sorry, Jason. I never meant for this to happen."

To her surprise, he put his arms around her and made soothing noises. "Don't cry. Everything's going to be okay."

She leaned into him and inhaled his familiar scent, recognized the familiar planes of his lean body. He lowered a kiss on her hair and tightened his grip.

"I'm the one who's sorry," he said, his voice breaking. Gemma pulled back cautiously. "What do you mean?"

His expression was contrite and she was astonished to see tears in his eyes, as well. She had never seen Jason moved. "I made a mistake. I want us to try again."

Gemma saw stars. "What?"

He loosened his tie—one that she'd lovingly selected for his last campaign. "I'm an idiot. I had the world's greatest, most beautiful wife, and I messed it up."

Salve to her wounds, to be sure, but she was wary of his apology. "You said our marriage wasn't working for you anymore."

Jason shook his head and paced a few steps. "I mistook comfortable for monotony. I realize now that we were just going through a slump after the craziness of the election." He stopped pacing and pulled her into his arms. "I want you back, Gemma." He lowered his mouth to hers for the kind of kiss that she'd yearned for from her husband for as long as she could remember…a hot, intense meeting of tongues and teeth, with body language to match. He ran his hands down her back and pulled her hips against his, making the little grunting noises that she knew meant he was getting turned-on.

Gemma's mind reeled, but the seriousness of the situation kept her senses in check. She pulled back and walked away from him to lean against the breakfast bar and regain her composure. "Jason, I don't know what to think. This is just…so sudden." She crossed her arms over her chest. "I'm just now getting past the hurt. Starting over."

"With that guy?" Jason asked, jerking his head in the direction Chev had gone.

"Chev has been a gentleman. A good friend, who helped me when I needed it most." Helped her feel desirable again.

Jason pulled his hand down his face and suddenly looked tired. "It's my fault. I should've never moved to Tallahassee without you."

"But you did," she murmured, and the pain felt fresh,

slicing her heart open again, the same way it had when he'd first told her he wanted a divorce.

"Come with me now," he said, clasping her hands. "*We* can start over. Get married again, take a honeymoon. We'll tell everyone it was just a misunderstanding. Your parents will be so happy. And I'll make you happy, too, Gemma, if you'll just give me another chance."

Emotions assailed her from all directions—guilt, regret, remorse. Feeling under attack, she stiffened and pulled her hands from his. "I don't know, Jason. You blindsided me… again. I need time to think."

"Of course you do." He touched her cheek in a way that dredged up memories of good times together. "But the sooner you decide, the sooner we can get back to the way things were meant to be. I love you, Gemma, I realize that now. We can still have the wonderful life we planned." He nodded toward the cell phone that he'd set on the counter. "Dressing like a call girl, giving sex tours. That's not you, Gemma."

She swallowed hard.

"Let's try again," he said earnestly. "I can protect you from Wilcox if we get married again, if we're together."

Just the mention of the reporter's name made her stomach clench with dread. If he splashed her picture across the news, everyone would know—Jason's colleagues, the people with whom she used to raise money for charity, her parents. The shame, the scandal would humiliate her family and friends, and it would haunt Jason's political pursuits. What had she done?

Jason kissed her tenderly, and when she closed her eyes, she could almost forget that they had ever been apart.

"I'm going to be governor one day," he whispered fiercely, "and I want you by my side, Gemma. But it's up to you."

A panicky voice inside clamored for her to say yes on the spot. *Leave with him...before he changes his mind. Before* you *change your mind.*

The last thought shook her to her center. She gently broke free of his embrace and exhaled. "I'll think about everything you said."

He smiled the hopeful, boyish smile that reminded her of the way he had been when they'd first met, full of optimistic ambition that no one questioned, including her. She'd felt so lucky simply to be included in his plans. She walked with him to the door.

"I won't sleep until I hear from you," he said, with one hand on the doorknob.

She smiled, then her eye landed on the golf towel he'd asked about. She scooped it up and handed it to him. He took it, but glanced at it with an odd expression, as if it wasn't nearly as important as he used to think.

"If Wilcox tries to contact you, call me ASAP." He kissed her again and this time she tasted his desperation. He was worried...and it scared her.

She stood at the window and watched his car lights back down the driveway. When he pulled up next to the mailbox, the car paused. Was he checking to see if she'd removed his name? Then he pulled away from the curb and his taillights disappeared.

Gemma released a pent-up breath and massaged the sudden ache at her temples. With no appetite for dinner, she extinguished the lights and climbed the stairs, reveling in the cool air circulating once again. Her mind and body felt battered from sensory overload...the decision at her feet felt more weighty than she would've thought possible.

She considered calling Sue, but she already knew that her

friend would tell her to get on with her life—*without* Jason. Her friend's loyalty was touching but probably a tad biased.

Her mother, on the other hand, would tell her she'd be a fool not to go back with Jason and live a life of some celebrity and relative ease.

Regardless, she was glad she hadn't responded immediately, that she had held on to her pride by not jumping on his proposal to get back together, but also that she hadn't allowed her anger to cause her to reject him outright. She owed it to herself to consider his offer, if only out of respect for the years they'd been together. After all, she had invested a lot of time in Jason's success.

Gemma downed aspirin for the headache, then took a warm shower and poured herself a glass of chilled wine. Wrapped in a lightweight robe, she settled in an overstuffed chair in her bedroom and nursed this strange new sensation regarding her relationship with Jason—*power.* He had never been abusive, but there had never been any doubt who had been in the driver's seat in their marriage.

Because she had cared more about him than he'd cared about her. And the person in the relationship who cared less always had more power.

She could picture Dr. Alexander standing in front of the class saying those words, explaining the dynamics of any relationship, but especially between lovers.

The folded fantasies letter on the dresser called to her. Gemma retrieved it and, after another mouthful of wine, unfolded the flowered pages. She skimmed the slanted script, noticing that when she described her bouts of exhibitionism, her writing became less legible and more frenetic. She picked up reading where she'd left off, after the scene in the workout facility where she had performed for the young personal trainer while everyone else in the gym had been oblivious.

After leaving the gym, my urges were satisfied for a while. I went about my schedule as usual, and had decided that it was some kind of kinky phase I'd gone through. But two days ago I woke up with the familiar tingle of anticipation between my legs. In class, my mind wondered to scandalous places, like what the male instructors would think if I opened my legs to flash the color of my panties...or loosened the top button on my blouse and bent over to pick up a dropped pencil to give them a good view of my cleavage.

I met up with Sue for lunch and she told me about a guy she wanted me to meet, a friend of hers in law school who was in town for a few days. She said he was straitlaced, just my type, and I laughed to myself—she has no idea what my "type" is. I told her thanks, but no thanks. I had other plans.

While traveling around the city on the train system, I've noticed handbills for a "gentlemen's club" advertising amateur night. I'd decided that's where I was going last night.

Gemma inhaled a sharp breath and poured herself another glass of wine. The anxiety building in her chest was crushing, but she forced herself to read on. Her handwriting changed yet again, now nearly a scrawl, as if she hadn't wanted to document what had happened next.

The strip club was easy enough to find, but I confess I had reservations before going inside. I'd never been to a strip club before—I was a nervous wreck. I wore the brown wig and big sunglasses, and beneath a tailored trench coat, a bikini and high heels. I walked in behind two tall blond girls who seemed to know where they were going. When we were inside, one of them turned to me and asked if I was new. I held up the handbill advertising amateur night and they told me to follow them.

Once inside, some beefy guy asked if I was twenty-one and I said yes. But since he didn't ask for ID, I'm not sure he cared. I signed up as "Jewel" and was sent backstage for more instructions. There were a half-dozen other women, most of them young, who were listening to a woman named Breeze give advice on how to make an entrance, how to work the stage, and how to exit once our routine was finished. We could take off as much or as little clothing as we wanted to. We were allowed to keep our tips, and were promised that a bouncer would always be between us and customers who might try to manhandle us.

When the music started blaring, everyone seemed nervous—except me. I was breathless with anticipation as I watched other women go out and dance. Some of them were bad, but a couple of them were trained dancers and got the crowd going. I was last and when I stepped out on that stage still wearing wig, sunglasses and coat, something happened to me—it was like I was a different person.

It was a full house and the air was charged with sex. I've never been much of a dancer, but the music seized me and, running on adrenaline alone, I strutted up and down the stage, losing the coat to reveal my teeny bikini. I had told myself I wouldn't get completely bare, but the excitement of the crowd, the excitement of being watched, buoyed me and instinctively, I unhooked the bikini top and the crowd went wild. I've never been so turned-on and next thing I knew, I was wearing only the stilettos, wig and sunglasses. I hadn't thought to wear a garter to hold tips, and frankly, I didn't care about the money that was tossed at my feet. I was in heaven with the eyes of everyone in the room on me.

I was making my last trip back up the stage when the sirens sounded and the club lights came on. A man with a bullhorn announced this was a police raid and told everyone to freeze.

Instead, everyone ran. My life flashed before me: arrested, expelled from college, disowned by my parents. I somehow found my coat and was swept along with the crowd. It was pandemonium. I was terrified I would fall and be trampled. Breeze, who had been instructing the amateurs, grabbed my arm and pushed me out a fire exit door. When the police stopped us outside, she whispered for me to run, and I did...as if my life depended on it.

I managed to escape and ran until the crowd thinned. By that time I had twisted an ankle and was hopelessly lost. I threw up on the side of a deserted street. I was close to full-out panic when I realized my wallet was in my coat pocket. I hailed a cab, but it was after midnight when I got back to the dorm, carrying my shoes, still naked under the coat and wildly disheveled. I had tossed the wig and the sunglasses, but I still garnered some strange looks from *my roommates. Sue, in particular, gave me the third degree, but I begged a headache and went to bed.*

I didn't sleep a wink. I kept thinking about how disastrously the night could have ended. For me, acting out my fantasy nearly led to my ruin.

And the worst part of it all? It's been only two days and I want to do it again.

Gemma pushed to her feet and paced, feeling flushed. The bad memories from that night came back to her in snatches of pure emotion—the shock of the raid, the horror of trying to outrun the police, the fear that had lingered for days that they would somehow discover she had been at the club and come to arrest her. As it turned out, the club had been a front for a drug operation. She had simply been in the wrong place at the wrong time.

But at the time, it had seemed like retribution...karma for doing something so wicked. The incident had, so to speak, scared her straight. She'd told Sue she wanted to meet her straitlaced friend and had latched on to Jason like a lifeline. He had saved her from herself.

Gemma stared at the letter in her hand with disdain. Its timely appearance had reawakened dormant impulses, had sent her to the window to undress for Chev, had pushed her into taking a sordid job at the museum. Once again, she was on the verge of being revealed...and once again Jason was in a position to save her. These subversive impulses of hers could lead nowhere—nowhere good, that is.

She glanced at the picture window but forced herself not to go there—literally and figuratively.

Gemma found a book of matches and lit one. With a shaking hand, she held up the fantasies letter and lit one corner. The pages began to char and curl, destroying the words and, she hoped, the urges they described. She dropped the letter into a metal trash can and drained her glass of wine while watching the flowered sheets of stationery disintegrate into a little pile of white ashes.

She had gotten another reprieve. She and Jason could marry again, quietly, maybe in Belize or Hawaii, and start a new phase of their life. She would slip back into her role as Jason's assistant, head hostess and all-around helpmate. He would appreciate her this time. They would be partners. He would be governor someday, then probably head for Congress or the U.S. Attorney's office. They would once again be the golden couple.

And she could put this naughty little exhibitionist phase behind her. Again.

18

GEMMA LOVED to make love in the morning. She rolled over and palmed the area of the mattress that, with a single phone call, would once again be occupied by Jason. He wasn't a morning person when it came to sex, but in the scheme of things, it was a very small price to pay. Marriage was more than great, earth-shattering, mind-bending sex.

The hum of the air conditioner filled the air. And even through the closed windows, she could hear the construction noises from next door.

Since Jason's visit yesterday, she had forced herself not to think of Chev, told herself that he couldn't figure into her decision to go back to Jason. He would, after all, be leaving soon. Their time together had been simply a pleasurable diversion, nothing more.

She reached for the phone to call Jean at the employment agency, planning to tell her that she was quitting her job with the museum. But at the last second, she instead dialed Lillian's cell phone number.

"Hello?" The woman's voice trilled over the line, low and honeyed.

"Lillian, it's Gemma."

"Hi, doll. What's up?"

"I…" Why did the prospect of telling Lillian that she

was quitting her job make her feel as if she was denying something they both knew to be true? "I'm not feeling well today."

"Oh, that's too bad. I can cover for you if you like."

She exhaled in relief. "I would appreciate it."

"No problem. I hope whatever's wrong will run its course soon."

The woman was nothing if not perceptive. "I think it will," Gemma murmured. "Thanks again for covering for me."

She hung up the phone, feeling torn. Why was she stalling on what seemed to be an obvious answer to her dilemma? Was she postponing her decision to prolong Jason's agony? Her attention traveled to the picture window. Or was she simply giving herself time to tie up loose ends?

"CHEV?"

He turned his head to see his foreman's face creased in frustration. "Sorry, what?"

"Man, where is your head today?" Then the man looked past him to Gemma's house, and he scoffed. "Dude, you're worse than that lovesick peacock strutting around in her yard."

Chev straightened. "I don't know what you're talking about."

"Yeah, right." He clapped Chev on the shoulder. "We're ready to unveil the pool."

Reluctantly, Chev dragged his gaze away from Gemma's house. The peacock was back, parading around her yard, its tail unfurled, calling like some kind of horny lawn ornament.

He knew how the bird felt. He kept hoping Gemma would

emerge so he could rescue her from the nuisance again. A pathetic ruse, like thinking he could rescue her from her ex-husband last night. It was obvious she hadn't wanted to be rescued. She was still hung up on the guy. And why not? He was successful and powerful, not a jack-of-all-trades carpenter who moved around like a Gypsy.

But the man had also broken her heart. He couldn't love her if he had put her through that kind of torment.

"Whoops, here she comes," the foreman said. "The pool can wait until later."

Chev turned to see Gemma walking down her front steps wearing jeans and a sunny T-shirt, carrying what appeared to be a rolled-up canvas. To his dismay, just the sight of her made his big, stupid heart swell.

He had it bad for this woman.

He moved toward her at the same time as the peacock, who thrust its head forward and unleashed a torrent of calls. At her expression of half irritation, half fear, a pang of remorse struck his chest. She didn't need the extra aggravation of him or the bird in her life.

She hurried toward him, and the bird followed her as fast as its cumbersome tail would allow. He couldn't help laughing, though, and happily positioned himself between her and the peacock, stomping his foot to send it scrambling back to her yard, yelping.

"Hi," he said, smothering a smile.

"Hi," she said, her color high, her voice exasperated. "I'll be so glad to be rid of that bird!"

He arched an eyebrow. "Oh? Are you hoping it will leave, or are you planning to leave first?"

She averted her eyes and cleared her throat. "I'm sorry about last night. I...wasn't expecting Jason to drop by." She fidgeted. "He's a powerful man...he's accustomed to getting his way."

"I know who he is," Chev said. "I watch the news."

A flush climbed her face. "I didn't mean to imply otherwise."

"Does he want to get back together?" he blurted. As soon as the words left his mouth, though, he raised his hands. "I'm sorry, that's none of my business." But he could tell from her body language that he had guessed correctly.

She held up the canvas with a smile. "The mural is dry."

"Great. I have the frame ready, but I could use a hand installing it, if you have a few minutes." A thinly veiled excuse to keep her within arm's length.

"Glad to help," she said cheerfully, but her nervousness was apparent in the stiffness of her shoulders, her quick hand movements.

He wanted to say something to put her at ease, but it felt hypocritical when his unsolicited cock was swelling in his pants.

He led her into the house, which reeked of fresh paint and sawdust, and echoed with the sound of hammers in distant rooms finding their mark.

"Everything is coming together so beautifully," she said, running a shapely hand along the woodwork of the new chair rail that ran throughout the house.

He remembered exactly what it had felt like to have her hand running along the indentation of his spine. "Thank you. Your opinion means a lot to me. You've been so helpful, Gemma."

She smiled. "Speaking of helpful, the air conditioner is working perfectly."

"Good. So you slept well last night?"

She hesitated. "Reasonably well."

He held her gaze for a few seconds, trying to telegraph his hopeless feelings for her. Finally he smiled in concession. "I can't wait to see the mural on the wall."

Once in the kitchen, he held the end of the stiff canvas and allowed her to carefully unroll it, revealing the colorful, gestural landscape. Together they positioned it on the wall where the deteriorated canvas had been removed. Once the painting was centered, he tacked the corners with penny nails, then stood back to admire it. "It's perfect," he said. "It'll be a nice selling point, and I'm sure the new owners will enjoy it every day."

"I'm glad you like it," Gemma said, clearly pleased.

From the long farmhouse table, he selected the four pieces of mitered seasoned oak he'd carefully measured and cut. Using a drill, he put tiny pilot holes in the frame, then screwed them in place around the canvas. The effect was an old-fashioned built-in mural that might have been in the house for generations.

"Nice," he said, giving her a grateful smile.

"I guess this means we're...even," she said.

Chev knew a brush-off when he heard it. "I guess that means you won't be coming to the party tomorrow night."

"I don't think so. I might have to work late anyway."

He didn't believe her excuse, but he nodded.

"By the way, when you were at the museum the other day, did you happen to see anyone taking pictures?"

Chev frowned. "As a matter of fact, there was a guy with a camera phone. I let him know I saw him and he put it away."

"Not soon enough," she murmured.

"Is something wrong?"

"His name is Lewis Wilcox and he's a reporter. He

knows who I am—or rather, that I used to be married to the state attorney general. He sent the photos to Jason and is threatening to reveal everything."

Chev shrugged. "So?"

"So…it will be bad for Jason that I'm doing something so…controversial."

"But it's not illegal, and besides, you're good at it. And I know you enjoy it."

She gave him a tight smile. "Too much for my own good."

"Ah. Your ex doesn't know that you're…"

"An exhibitionist?" she said bluntly. "No. And I wasn't one when he and I were together."

"So this is something recent?" he probed, his balls throbbing just talking about it.

"No." She looked up, down, all around. "My first experiences were in college."

"And it started up again after your divorce?"

She nodded. "When you moved in."

He stepped closer and picked up her hand. "Look, Gemma, I'm no expert. But it doesn't take a psychiatrist to see that you're using this fetish to keep from getting close to someone."

"Maybe," she admitted.

"All I'm saying," he said gently, stroking his thumb over her palm. "Is that the two don't have to be mutually exclusive."

Her chest rose and fell as her breathing became more labored. The hardened points of her nipples showed through her T-shirt. Her lips parted and her eyes dilated. She wanted him, he could feel it. She was thinking about the night they'd spent together burning up the sheets, barely speaking because they hadn't needed words to communicate. They were communicating now, he realized as the air became thick with need.

"Gemma—"

She abruptly pulled her hand from his. "I have to go."

Chev didn't try to stop her. He had no right to.

SHAKEN, Gemma practically ran back to her house, dodging the peacock, which seemed determined to block her path. "Get out of the way!" she shouted, shooing the bird, thinking if it hadn't been for the pesky creature, she and Chev might not have interacted so much, and she wouldn't be...

Confused.

She closed the front door and leaned against it. It was the man's bottomless dark eyes, damn it. The way he looked at her...as if she were the only thing in the world that mattered. It was, she realized, why they seemed to have such a deep sexual chemistry. They connected through meaningful and purposeful eye contact.

It occurred to her suddenly that she and Jason had moved through their entire marriage making as little eye contact as possible. Was it because they each didn't like what they saw? Didn't feel the connection, so they'd found it easier and better to just stop looking?

Her cheeks were wet when she walked to the phone. She dialed Jason's number and he answered on the second ring, his voice pleased. "Gemma? I saw your name on the display."

"Yes, it's me."

"How are you?"

"Fine. Is this a bad time?"

"No worse than usual." He gave a tight little laugh. "Have you given some thought to what I proposed?"

To what I proposed. As if it were a business deal to be settled. As she listened to papers rattling in the background amidst keys clicking on a keyboard, her heart sank. He couldn't set aside work long enough even to talk about rebuilding their marriage. Was he so sure that she'd come running back to him that he'd already crossed it off his to-do list? Tears clogged her throat, but at least it confirmed her instincts.

And her decision.

"Gem, are you there? I don't mean to rush you, but I have to be somewhere in fifteen minutes."

"Of course," she said. "This won't take long. I've thought about what you said, Jason, and I've decided that I prefer to leave things the way they are."

Silence resonated over the line as the paper rattling and key clicking stopped. "I'm sorry—what did you say?"

She inhaled. "I don't want us to get back together."

Disbelieving noises sounded in her ear. "But…you're making a mistake. If we don't get back together, Gemma, I can't control Wilcox. You won't have the protection of my name or my office."

She pressed her lips together, biting down. It was so like Jason to try to exert pressure to get his way. "I hope he doesn't use those pictures to embarrass you or your office, Jason, but if he goes public with them, I'll be fine. I happen to like my job and frankly, I'm good at it." And she was no longer going to be ashamed of her "inclinations," as Lillian had so aptly put it.

"Gemma, why are you doing this?"

"Because I love you, Jason, but not enough."

"Not enough to what?" he asked, incredulous.

Gemma closed her eyes at his inability to grasp the

emotional gravity of the situation. "Exactly," she murmured, then hung up the phone.

She took a few moments to breathe deeply and to mourn the time lost. They both deserved better. She pushed to her feet and, eager to rid herself of all the artifacts of her marriage, carried the boxes and baskets of Jason's things to her trash bin in the garage. The divorce papers went in the file cabinet. Then she tackled the photos.

While she sorted through pictures of their life together, making a stack for herself and one to box and send to her mother, she slipped their wedding DVD in the player and let it run in the background. She'd watched it countless times during the divorce proceedings, but this time it was different. This time, she was dry-eyed and philosophical, wishing she could talk to the young bride in the film and tell her to run and find someone who knew everything about her—including her fetishes—and still wanted to be with her.

She smiled at the picture in her hand, one of her and Sue at a charity golf scramble from a few years back, their arms around each other's shoulders. But it was something in the background that caught her eye—Sue's golf towel... black with a gold letter monogram. Exactly like the one that Jason had seemed to prize, a gift from someone...

An awful seed of dread took root in Gemma's stomach. She picked up the remote control and went back to the beginning of the DVD, this time watching the interaction between Sue, her maid of honor, and Jason.

They'd stared at each other when Sue walked down the aisle, escorted by Jason's best man. After Sue took her place at the altar, there was an exchanged glance...then another...and another, each more lingering than the last. Even while Gemma walked down the aisle. Sue was nervous, fidgeting. Jason looked…uncertain. When he wasn't looking at her or Sue, he was looking straight up, as if he were struggling with a decision. And when the minister asked if anyone knew of any reason she and Jason shouldn't marry, Sue had opened her mouth…then closed it. Then *there*.

Gemma froze the tape. Jason had pivoted his head and looked at Sue, a pleading expression in his eyes. An expression of *love*.

She covered her mouth with her hand. Jason and Sue… how had she missed it? Snatches of conversation came back to her.

I never dreamed the two of you would get married… I'm just really happy that you're moving on…I don't want to see you get folded back into Jason's life.

Sue had scoffed at the idea of her getting back together with Jason…because she wanted him for herself? How convenient that she was in Tallahassee and so was Jason. And that he had left Gemma in Tampa.

With the frame of Jason looking at Sue over her head frozen in the background, Gemma picked up the phone and dialed Sue's number, her fingers shaking.

"Hi, Gemma," Sue sang cheerfully. "What's up with you?"

She gripped the phone, bile backing up in her throat. "How long?" Her voice quaked.

Sue gave a little laugh. "How long what?"

"How long have you and Jason been fooling around behind my back?" At the silence on the other end, tears filled Gemma's eyes. "Oh, God, it's true."

"Gemma, let me explain—"

Gemma disconnected the call and unplugged the phone, then hugged herself, every part of her aching. Her marriage had been a lie…Jason had never loved her. Her friendship with Sue, another lie. Their late-night gabfests in college, sharing hopes and dreams, long-distance phone calls when they'd landed in different cities after she'd married Jason, making it a point to never miss a birthday or anniversary of some special occasion. To think that she had relied on Sue's advice to get through the divorce. And to top it all off, she had slept with Chev at Sue's repeated encouragement to "go for it."

A few minutes ago, she had felt like an independent woman reclaiming her life, only to discover that she had been manipulated every step of the way. She had to be the world's biggest fool.

She put her head down on her knees. And the loneliest.

Outside the peacock emitted its high-pitched call. She was struck again by how similar it was to a person screeching, *Help! Help!*

Help was right. She longed to go to Chev, to escape in his arms tonight, but she didn't dare invest any more in a man who would be leaving in a few days. She couldn't afford to lose any more of herself.

19

GEMMA EXPECTED it to be a sleepless night, and she was right. Knowing that Jason and Sue were involved was like getting divorced all over again. The peacock, as if sensing her mood, wailed plaintively most of the night, keeping her company. She cried until she was sick for the wasted years with Jason, then lay awake dry-eyed as the sun came up and light crept across the room. The peacock had grown either tired or philosophical, since its cries also quieted at daybreak.

She didn't feel like going to the museum and she knew she was wearing her distress on her face, but she needed something to occupy her time. And frankly, she was once again in the situation of needing the money. So she showered, gulped down a cup of coffee and carefully applied makeup to hide the plum-colored circles under her eyes. Then she dressed in a fitted short black sheath and black pumps—demure compared to her other costumes.

As she made up her bed, she listened to the work site next door come alive with vehicles arriving, supplies being moved, and equipment starting. She would miss it, she decided, the comforting noises of the bustling activity. And she would miss Chev.

The doorbell rang and her spirits lifted instantly at the prospect of seeing him. She hurried down the stairs and swung open the door, but at the sight of Sue standing on the threshold, she balked. "What are you doing here?"

Sue had been crying, too, her dark eyes red rimmed. "Please...just hear me out."

Gemma didn't say anything, but stepped aside to allow her entry. Sue was taller, curvier, with flaming red hair that was always cut in the latest style. She swept by Gemma, then turned with a pained look on her face after the door was closed. "Can we sit down?"

Gemma nodded and waited for Sue to sit, then lowered herself in the opposite chair.

Sue's chest rose with a deep breath. "Gemma, I know you're hurting, and I'm sorry. I have a lot of things to apologize for, but I'm *not* having an affair with Jason."

Gemma crossed her arms. "There was a golf towel that was special to Jason, a gift from someone. I saw a picture where you have one that's identical. And I watched our wedding DVD—the way the two of you were looking at each other." She stopped, her voice choked.

Sue nodded slowly. "Jason was in love with me back then, but I never felt the same way about him. The golf towel was a gift from him, something he had made for us. When I introduced the two of you, I was hoping his feelings for me would go away. And I think they did...for a while. But I had my reservations about the two of you getting married."

Gemma swallowed past the lump in her throat. "But why didn't you tell me?"

"Tell you that you shouldn't marry Jason because he was in love with me?" Sue gave a dry laugh. "How would that have gone over? The way you fell for him, so fast, it was like you just *needed* him so much."

She had, Gemma conceded miserably. After the terrifying episode at the strip club, she had latched on to Jason for his strength—his feelings for her had been secondary. She had convinced herself that she cared enough for both of them.

"I just couldn't do that to you," Sue said with a teary smile. "So I moved to Tallahassee and hoped that Jason would realize what a catch you were."

"But he never stopped loving you."

Sue leaned forward. "I know he cares deeply about you, Gemma. He's told me so many times."

"But at the prospect of moving to Tallahassee, where he knew he'd be crossing paths with you, he couldn't take it anymore and asked me for a divorce."

Sue hesitated, then nodded. "I told him it was pointless, Gemma, but he did it anyway. He hated to hurt you, and didn't tell you why because he knew it would only hurt you more."

Gemma nodded. The divorce had devastated her, but knowing that he was in love with her best friend would have broken her. "You must have made it clear that you weren't going to marry him after all. Because he came back two nights ago, asking me to forgive him and to give our marriage another try."

Sue's mouth tightened. "I thought he might. What did you say?"

"I considered it," Gemma admitted. "But in the end, I couldn't do it."

A relieved smile lifted the corners of Sue's mouth. She leaned forward and grasped Gemma's hands. "I'm so glad. Jason is a great guy, but you deserve someone who adores you."

"That's why you kept encouraging me to have a fling, to get on with my life," Gemma murmured.

"It helped, didn't it?"

She laughed. "Yes. It did."

Sue squeezed Gemma's hands. "And how do you feel about this guy Chev?"

Gemma sighed and glanced in the direction of the Spanish house. From this angle she could see a portion of the pool, covered with a large blue tarp. "He's...fantastic. Sexy, intelligent, warm...sexy." They both laughed. "I think it could be special...but he's leaving in a couple of weeks, as soon as the house is renovated and auctioned off."

"Maybe he would consider staying."

Gemma shook her head. "The auction date is already set. And I don't think I'm ready to make that kind of commitment anyway. I jumped into a relationship with Jason. I don't want to do that again."

"Smart," Sue said, standing. "But you're older, and wiser. You know your own mind—and body—much better. Trust your instincts. You'll know if it's worth the risk."

"How about you?" Gemma asked. "When are you going to get someone special in your life?"

"Still looking," Sue quipped. "And always hopeful. If I could go back, I'd take that Sexual Psyche class with you in college. Maybe it would've helped me figure out a few things about myself."

"It helped me," Gemma admitted, then smiled a secret smile.

They embraced and Sue walked to her car after extracting promises to call. While Gemma stood at the top of the steps, waving, the peacock waddled up to the bottom of the steps and unfurled his tail in a spectacular iridescent fan.

The morning sun reflected a thousand brilliant colors in his magnificent plumage, shimmering against the dew-laden grass. The sight of him took her breath away, and in that moment, Gemma felt blessed.

Sue rolled down the window, her expression wondrous. "Looks like you have a pet."

Gemma laughed. "Since I can't seem to get rid of him, I might have to keep him."

Sue waved and drove away. Gemma looked down at the blue bird, who angled his head at her. "Looks like it's just me and you."

Her gaze wandered to the site next door, but she didn't see Chev among the workers. He would be busy today, putting finishing touches inside and out to get ready for his family's visit that evening.

There was that funny feeling in her stomach again…the "missing him" sensation. If only…

She glanced at her watch and gasped when she realized she was going to be late for work. She grabbed her coat and purse and backed out of the garage without incident— the peacock had found something to eat at the base of one of her trees.

On the way to the museum, she realized that she was actually humming, that she felt better than she would've imagined possible a few weeks ago. When she arrived at the museum, she looked for Lillian to thank her for covering for her the previous day. She found her in the ladies' lounge, adjusting the back seams on her sheer black stockings.

"How did women deal with these seams?" she asked, exasperated.

Gemma laughed. "They were just happy to have panty hose back then, I think."

Lillian narrowed her eyes with good humor. "You seem to have recovered well. What's with the good mood?"

"I didn't realize I was so morose," Gemma said dryly.

"Not morose, just....injured."

"I guess that's true," she murmured.

Lillian angled her head. "But you're better?"

Gemma did a gut check and was happy to find her heart at peace with the past. "Yes."

"And that lovely dark-haired man friend of yours, does he figure into it?"

"How did you know about him?"

Lillian waved her off. "That's not important. Do you love this guy?"

Gemma blinked. "Our relationship is just…physical."

"The importance of which is never to be underestimated," the older woman said. "But does your soul smile when he walks into the room?"

"I…I don't know. He makes me happy."

"Good. I'm glad I could see you happy before I leave."

Gemma frowned. "You're leaving?"

"They announced the exhibit will end in a couple of weeks, so I'm moving on to another temp job."

"The woman at my employment agency told me this could lead to another job in the museum."

"Maybe for someone with your background, but not mine. No, I'm off to my next adventure. But it has been a pleasure getting to know you." Lillian winked. "It's always nice to meet someone who shares particular interests. Good luck, Gemma. Always be true to yourself."

The woman's words stayed with her throughout the day. It was difficult to pinpoint the change in her, but as the tours progressed, she felt her mind expand to accept new possibilities for her future…and none of the options included compromise. She only hoped that it didn't mean she'd be lonely for the rest of her life.

When she arrived home, she marveled at the changes in the Spanish home just since the morning—the yard was newly sodded, with tree plantings and landscaping. The stucco walls of the house had been painted with an aged ochre that was a striking contrast to the red-tiled roof. Even though it was still daylight, the structure was illuminated inside and out. A caterer's truck sat next to the curb, along with a van from Party Balloons. Gemma smiled at the indulgences that reflected Chev's affection for his family and acknowledged a pang of regret for turning down his invitation to join them. But considering her last conversation with him, things would be way too awkward between them, and she didn't want to intrude on his family time.

Setting aside her disappointment, she hit the remote control and opened the garage door. The peacock wasn't around, but he had uprooted several clumps of daylilies. She sighed, then cut her wheel to pull into the right side of the garage. A split-second later, she frowned. Why was she still leaving room for Jason's car? Feeling magnanimous toward herself, she pulled into the center of the garage, leaving lots of breathing room on either side.

As the garage door was going down, she spotted the mailbox that still read Jason and Gemma White. "You're next," she announced.

She went inside, changed into casual clothes and grabbed the old suitcase containing her paints, then stopped in the garage for her hat and a garden trowel to replant the uprooted lilies. Outside, she inhaled the rich scent of an early summer evening. The sharp sweetness of new soil and grass rode the air from Chev's yard, tickling her senses.

Not Chev's yard, she reminded herself. The yard of whoever would buy the house in a couple of weeks. Most likely, a couple with children to enjoy the pool and the large family kitchen. Chev would pocket the money and move on to his next project—Miami, hadn't he said? And on to his next woman?

Of course he'd have another woman, and another after that. He was, after all, a hot-blooded, great-looking man with a healthy sexual appetite.

Who accepted her exhibitionism.

Who didn't judge her.

She exhaled, then plopped the hat on her head and walked to the mailbox at the curb. The honeysuckle bush she'd planted around the post was covered with fat buds that would soon burst with little cream-colored flowers and the most beautiful fragrance imaginable.

She remembered the day she'd painted their names on the mailbox. They had been in the house for less than a week. Jason seemed uninterested in anything having to do with the house and yard. She, on the other hand, had been eager to put their stamp on it, to make it theirs. He was working long hours, and she was in a nesting phase. She had bought a small can of black paint for metal surfaces and painstakingly painted on their names. Jason hadn't noticed and when she'd brought it to his attention, he had told her she could hire someone to do that kind of thing.

She took a deep breath and with a few strokes of a spray can, she obliterated their names with white primer, reducing the mailbox back to a clean, blank surface. She stared at it for a couple of minutes, then nodded. It felt right.

While she waited for it the primer to dry, she replanted the lilies, muttering under her breath about the peacock who seemed to be enamored with her yard. It had left behind two exquisite feathers. She set them on the porch to add to the others she had collected—they were simply too fine to throw away. A keepsake for the time after the bird had flown away.

Then she went back to the mailbox and, using a small brush and black paint, hand-lettered "Gemma Jacobs" on the side. She didn't realize she was holding her breath until the sight of it made her exhale in satisfaction.

She was putting the finishing touches on the paint job when two cars pulled into Chev's driveway. Doors opened and out came several people who obviously knew one another. When Chev came out to greet them, dressed in slacks and a collared shirt, there were shouts of joy and hugs all around. He shepherded them all into the house, then glanced in her direction.

Gemma couldn't look away. Even at this distance, she could feel the intensity of his regard.

He lifted his hand in a casual wave.

She waved back.

He hesitated a few seconds, then disappeared into the house.

And there it was...that achy emptiness in her stomach. And she realized in a blinding split second that she was letting something that could be incredible slip through her fingers. Sue was right—she was older now, and wiser. Old enough to recognize a good thing when it crossed her path. Wise enough not to pass up a chance to see a different side of this man she was falling in love with.

Having made up her mind, she couldn't shower and dress fast enough. For a hospitality gift, she settled on a vase of yellow and gold flowers cut from her garden. At the last minute, she added a peacock feather to the arrangement.

As she crossed her yard to Chev's, she was racked with nerves over seeing him again and meeting his family.

Funny how she was more comfortable performing as a stranger than as herself.

"ARE YOU OKAY, son?"

Chev looked up to see his mother walking toward him where he stood by the kitchen window overlooking the newly unveiled pool. Seeing his family again had lifted his spirits considerably, but it also had sharpened his awareness of missing Gemma. It shouldn't matter so much when he was leaving soon. But seeing her changing the name on her mailbox had left him feeling torn. If she wasn't going back to her ex…

The concern on his mother's sweet face made him smile. "I'm fine, Mama."

"You look sad."

"I'm just tired."

"It was nice of you to have this party for Maria, and to invite Juan and his family."

"I thought it would make you happy."

"It has. The house is beautiful. It will make someone a lovely home."

"I'm glad you like it, Mama."

"It reminds me of the house I grew up in."

"There's still plenty to do before the auction, but I think it's turned out well."

"So when will I see you settling down in a home of your own?"

He put his arm around his mother's shoulder and gave

her a squeeze. "Someday. Why don't we cut the cake? I know that Maria and Jeffrey are dying to get into the pool."

The sound of the doorbell cut through the air.

"Are you expecting someone else?" his mother asked slyly.

"Maybe," he said, perplexed. He excused himself and, as he walked toward the entrance, he allowed himself to hope that Gemma had changed her mind.

When he opened the door, her back was to him and she was scolding the peacock, which had apparently followed her over. Her efforts to shoo him away seemed only to provoke the blue bird because it unleashed a torrent of calls and unfurled his tail with a full-body shudder.

She turned back to the door, startled to see him standing there. "Hi."

"Hi," he said over the noise of the peacock, unable to mask an amused smile.

"Is there still room for one more? I promise to leave my friend outside."

"Absolutely," he said with a happy grin.

"We heard the noise," his mother said. "Oh, look!"

Everyone in his family came outside, exclaiming over the peacock, which seemed to know he had an audience and strutted like royalty around the colorful tiled walkway. Chev managed to introduce Gemma as the artist of the kitchen mural, and almost felt sorry for her under the onslaught of his boisterous parents, sister, aunt, uncle and cousin. His mother complimented the vase of flowers, then linked arms with Gemma and walked back inside.

His heart expanded in his chest, but he reminded himself that he couldn't get used to the idea of loving her. She had issues and at least one powerful reason to go back to her ex-husband, if she was afraid of what that reporter might reveal. And there was the little matter that in two weeks, he would be selling this house and leaving for Miami...

Determined to enjoy the day, he rejoined the party in the kitchen where the cake for his sister Maria who had graduated high school was being cut among choruses of cheers and singing. Chev glanced down the table where Gemma sat wedged between his mother and his aunt, and winked at her. She looked a little unsure of herself, but after a few minutes, she was laughing with everyone else.

After the cake had been devoured, his sister and cousin raced to change into their bathing suits. Chev watched for Gemma's reaction to the pool mosaic. She turned from the window with a look of wonder. "A peacock?"

He joined her there in the warmth of the sun and looked down at the sparkling blue water of the pool, dazzling against the design of a riotous peacock in the tile work of the bottom and sides. "It seemed fitting."

"It's beautiful. I wish I had brought my suit." Her green eyes danced mischievously.

Desire flooded his midsection. He leaned near her ear and whispered, "Why don't we have a private swim when everyone's gone?" He waited for her answer, needing to know if she had come to the party out of kindness, or for some other reason. "Unless you have other plans tonight," he added.

"No," she murmured. "I'm...free."

"What about your ex?"

"Still my ex."

"And the pictures the reporter took?"

She shrugged. "The guy's a jerk, but what can I do? I don't think it's anyone's business what I do for a living, but I've decided that I won't be ashamed if it gets out."

She was changed, he realized. She seemed stronger...
braver. And if possible, sexier. Had the exhibitionism em-
powered her to make the decision not to go back to her ex?
Or had something else figured into her decision?

Chev loved his family and enjoyed seeing Gemma
interact with them, but as the hours passed, he grew more
eager to be alone with her. When his family took their
leave, he waved until the taillights of their cars disappeared, then turned and pulled her into his arms for a deep,
thorough kiss. He wanted to have her now, against the
wall, or in the grass. With a groan, he tore his mouth from
hers. "Hold that thought. I need to run an errand."

A little frown marred her forehead. "Now?"

"Trust me—it can't wait."

"What about our swim?"

"Get your suit and wait for me at your house. I won't
be gone long."

She sighed, then angled her head. "Okay. I'll be watching."

20

GEMMA DRESSED in a half-dozen different outfits waiting for Chev to return. Nothing seemed right...nothing seemed special. After an hour of indecision, she was struck with a panicky feeling that sex with Chev wouldn't be the same if she couldn't strip for him, or wear some sort of disguise.

If she couldn't pretend to be someone else.

Chev had accused her of using the exhibitionism as a way of avoiding emotional intimacy, and she couldn't deny it. He also said the two didn't have to be mutually exclusive. But she didn't see any way the two conditions could be reconciled.

Instead, she would simply enjoy the time she had left with Chev. He didn't have to know that she was falling for him.

So she settled on a skimpy black bikini with a short cover-up and high-heeled mules. And the mask...always the mask. She poured herself a glass of wine and drank deeply, feeding the languorous vibration that was already humming in her sex at the thought of performing for Chev. She had to admit that no stranger had ever fueled her lust to such heights. Knowing what lay in store for her in his arms made her feel loose limbed and expansive.

But how long would that feeling last? How long until

she yearned to perform for strangers again? She paced, alternately wanting answers and wanting options. Neither seemed clear or obvious…or satisfying.

It was getting late when Gemma heard his truck return. Mellow on wine, she lowered the mask in place and met him at the front door. With the light from the street behind him, she couldn't see his expression. But his low whistle got his point across. He reached for her hand and she allowed him to lead her outside to the glorious lit pool in his backyard. The going was precarious in the dark, especially with her wearing a mask and heels, but they laughed and stumbled their way through the grass.

The neighborhood was quiet and dark, with cicadas chanting in the background. Their sole attendant by the pool was the peacock, which seemed to enjoy watching the dappled surface. His head bobbed in time with the gentle slap of the water and he occasionally called out to a yet undiscovered mate.

Chev lowered himself to the edge of the pool next to a feather the bird had shed, removed his shoes and socks, and leaned back…to watch. Gemma obliged, shedding the cover-up first and walking around him suggestively. He reached for her, but she ducked away, then unhooked her bikini top and tossed it toward him. She crossed her arms over her breasts and turned back to face him, thrilled to see the bulge in his dark slacks. He pulled his shirt over his head and consumed her with his eyes.

The headiness of the wine and the sight of Chev's brown, bare torso sent ripples of excitement through her. She lifted her arms overhead, allowing her breasts to swing free, heavy and hard with need. She leaned over and shimmied off the bikini bottoms and threw those to him, too. He caught them neatly and brought them to his face, his eyes hooded. Then he picked up the peacock feather and pushed to his feet to stand before her.

Gemma stood perfectly still except for the rise and fall of her breasts. This man affected her body like a drug—she could hardly breathe, and her limbs seemed limp. His body was an inch from hers, his slacks and underwear the only clothes between them. Even barefoot he towered over her in heels. The dark springy hair on his chest tickled her erect nipples, his warm breath fanned her face. He lifted the feather and brushed it across her collarbone, over her breasts, down her stomach…and lower.

The velvety fringe was an erotic whisper over her sensitive folds, sending the most delicious sensations to her core. Behind the mask, she opened her mouth and sighed, looping her arms around his neck for support. He captured her mouth in a probing kiss and stroked her with the feather until she felt the moisture of her own lubrication on her thighs.

"Chev," she pleaded, fumbling with the fastener on his waistband. "Take me…now."

He helped her with his pants, stopping long enough to retrieve a condom from the pocket to sheath his rigid erection. Then he lifted her, wrapping her legs around his waist, and impaled her on his cock. Gemma gasped at the sensation of being filled with him, clawing at his back. He buried his head in her neck, grunting with every fierce stroke that joined their bodies more intimately, more savagely.

Her climax staggered her, crashed over her with a force that triggered every muscle in her body to contract involuntarily. She cried out his name and clung to him, disoriented because she felt as if she were falling.

"I've got you," he murmured, then grunted his own release, pumping into her while holding her against his chest. His strength alone was an aphrodisiac to her.

Afterward, he lowered her to the sweet, damp grass fringing the pool and eased his body from hers. "That was incredible," he murmured.

She moaned her agreement, thinking she'd love to lie here with him forever. He made her feel so alive, so feminine. She lifted his hand to her mouth for a kiss, then frowned at the torn skin on his knuckles. "Did you hurt your hand?"

He flexed it. "No. Just scraped it when I was loading some supplies earlier."

Her eyes had adjusted to the semidarkness, allowing her to study his body. "Does your tattoo have significance?" she asked, tracing her finger over the expansive branches and root system of the leafless tree.

He shrugged and craned to look at it. "What do you see?"

"Strength. And solitude."

"I guess that works," he agreed.

"Do you like your solitude?"

"Most of the time. But this is pretty nice."

She smiled in agreement.

"Although," he whispered, fingering the mask she still wore, "I wouldn't mind finding out more about the woman behind the mask."

Gemma swallowed hard.

She'd never met a man she felt so deeply connected to. But she also knew she couldn't—didn't want to—live without exhibitionism. Between her fetish and the fact that he was leaving soon, it was better to leave some things unsaid and unexplored.

CHEV FELT Gemma stiffen in his arms at the mention of losing the mask. She obviously wasn't comfortable enough with him to drop the pretense of the costume. Maybe she would never allow herself to be close to one man again.

Maybe it was best for him that he was leaving soon.

"How about that swim?" he suggested.

21

GEMMA LOVED to make love in the morning. She rolled over, and when she saw Chev lying next to her, she waited for lust to seize her.

Instead, love washed over her like a cleansing wave. She adored this man. He gave her joy...and hope. She reached out to touch the tattoo that spanned his deltoid muscle, reveling in the sensation of warm, smooth skin under her fingertips.

His eyes opened and he smiled at her, then clasped her hand, intertwining their fingers. She fought the sensation of shyness that descended in the daylight, without her mask and naked before him. Not an exotic, mysterious per-former. Just Gemma.

"Last night was amazing," he murmured.

She could only nod, now nearly panicked by her bur-geoning feelings for him. The phone rang and she moved to answer it, but he pulled her back.

"Stay with me," he urged.

She wanted to, but morning intimacy was so raw, so... *honest*. She was terrified it would break the spell. And then in a split second, she realized that breaking the spell might solve all her problems.

The machine kicked on. When she heard Jason's voice, she froze.

"Gemma, hey, it's me. Listen, I'm sorry if I was unkind on the phone the other day. I just had my hopes up, that's all. But you're right —we shouldn't get back together." He sighed heavily. "I also talked to Sue. She said she told you everything, and I'm sorry about that, too. More sorry than you'll ever know. I wanted to let you know that I called Wilcox to work out a deal on the photos. Funny thing is, he must have had a change of heart. He assured me that he'd destroyed the photos, said he didn't want to cause any trouble for you. Anyway, stay in touch. And Gemma…be happy."

Gemma smiled, abject relief flowering in her chest. "That's odd."

Chev rolled over and captured one soft nipple in his mouth. "What?" he murmured against her awakened skin.

"That Wilcox would have a change of heart about the photos. Why?"

"Who knows?" Chev murmured, traveling up to nuzzle her neck and covering her body with his. His thick erection pressed against her thigh.

A rogue thought popped into her mind. She frowned and lifted his right hand, the one with the scrapes across the knuckles. "Chev, did you go see Lewis Wilcox?"

"Maybe," he said, then kissed her ear.

Gemma gasped. "You beat him up?"

He ran his tongue along the sensitive cord of her neck. "I didn't have to. One punch and the guy was willing to negotiate."

"Negotiate what?"

Chev sighed and scratched his temple. "His cell phone and the promise that he wouldn't go public with the photos in return for his pretty TV face."

Shocked and flattered that Chev would stand up for her, she cupped his face in her hands. "You did that for me?"

"Yeah. I told him if he had a beef with your ex, he should take it up with him and keep you out of it."

Gemma smiled and whispered in his ear, "And what can I do for you?"

He nudged her sex with his. "You're doing it. No mask, no costumes. It's you that I want."

He entered her body to the tune of their mingled groans and made love to her slowly, his eyes locked with hers throughout. Watching his expression change with every nuance of heightened sensation opened her mind and body, magnified every touch, left her feeling out of control and hopelessly lost in him. This recklessness was like being disconnected from her physical self. She was powerless to do anything except go where his body took hers.

When her orgasm began to claim her, he urged her to the highest pinnacle she'd ever reached physically and emotionally. She came in a shattering clash, and carried him over the edge with her as he shuddered his release with full-body spasms. He cried her name over and over, pulsing inside her. Then he collapsed and rolled over, pulling her to his chest.

"I'm glad you're a morning person," he said, between re-covering breaths. "It's the best time of the day to have sex."

Gemma closed her eyes. She knew a sign when she saw one. "I love you," she blurted.

In the ensuing silence, she died a hundred deaths, wishing back her words. His hand traveled down her spine, over the curve of her hip. "I love you, too."

She lifted her head and stared at him, at his amazing eyes that spoke to her.

He sighed. "I feel a *but* coming on."

"The auction is in two weeks. You're leaving. And I have to be honest with you, Chev. Even though the job at the museum is ending soon, I don't know if I can ever let go of the watch-me games. It's…part of me."

He twined a strand of her hair around his finger. "So we have two weeks to see where this goes."

She nodded. An experimental period for them both to assess their options. This intense blaze they felt for each other might burn out. Or one of them could change their mind. They were both quiet, both lost in their own thoughts.

The two weeks stretched before Gemma like a big question mark.

22

"ARE YOU SURE you want me to do this?"

Gemma bit into her lower lip and nodded at Chev. "It's for the best."

His expression was pensive as he held the Auction Today sign with one hand and drove it into the ground with several whacks of the mallet. She stood back and looked at the sign, content with their decision.

A sedan pulled up next to the curb in front of the Spanish house. A suited man stepped out, along with a couple. "We're here for the auction?" he shouted.

"Change of plans," Chev said, waving them over. "This house is on the market instead—131 Petal Lagoon." He settled his arm around Gemma's shoulder. "Last chance to change your mind about moving in with me."

"Nice try," she said with a laugh. "As soon as my house sells, you're stuck with me."

Another car pulled up behind the first, then another. And it was still an hour before the auction. "What beautiful birds!" a woman exclaimed, obviously enchanted by the two peacocks strutting across Gemma's lawn. A peahen had arrived out of the blue, much to the cock's delight. They had become a celebrated pair in the neighborhood.

"Guess both of us cocks got lucky," Chev murmured to

her as he carried the mallet back to his pickup parked near her mailbox.

She elbowed him, but laughed. Then she spied a brown sack in the back of his truck and frowned. "What's that?"

Chev seemed flustered and tried to move the sack out of sight. "Nothing. Grass seed, I think."

She put her hands on her hips. "Let me see it."

He hesitated, then lifted the bag that read "Wild bird seed—for turkeys, pheasants and peacocks." The bag was almost empty.

Her eyes widened. "You were feeding it? *In* my yard?"

Chev gave her a sheepish smile and nodded.

"That's why I couldn't get rid of it!"

He shrugged. "A man's gotta do what a man's gotta do."

She punched him playfully, but he countered with a kiss. "Now that you're going to be a bigwig executive assistant to the director of the museum instead of a tour guide, if you get the urge to…you know, it's okay…as long as you come home to me."

"Always," she murmured, brimming with love for this sexy, sexy man.

"What's the letter?" he asked, pointing to the envelope she'd brought out with her.

She turned it over and smiled at the address. *Dr. Michelle Alexander.* "A thank-you to an old friend."

Gemma walked to the mailbox, wondering about the other young women in her Sex for Beginners class, where they were and if, like her, they'd received their fantasy letters at a pivotal point in their lives. And if, like her, they would use their letters to reclaim a part of themselves.

She hoped so. Because of her letter, the future lay before her, no longer a question mark, but a bold exclamation point.

Gemma placed the thank-you note in the mailbox, raised the flag and turned back to Chev, her heart full of him. She'd finally learned who she was. And she'd found a man who knew it—and loved it—too.

* * * * *

UNDER HIS SKIN

Jeanie LONDON

Jeanie London has always loved to read and write. School years were spent sneaking romance novels into school when she should have been learning algebra and biology. College years were spent taking electives such as journalism and creative writing classes when she should have been taking algebra and biology.

Nowadays, she's still reading and writing. She writes romances because she believes in happily-ever-afters. Not the "love conquers all" kind, but the "two people love each other, so they can conquer anything" kind. The commitment and monogamy of romance are strong values she's passing along to her daughters, who'll search for their own heroes someday. Jeanie's own romance hero is a very supportive guy, who reads fantasy and watches football and doesn't mind eating the same meal three nights in a row while she's writing. As far as Jeanie's concerned, she's blessed with the very best job in the world.

To the best sister in the world, my sister,
Kimberly Yodzis. You'll know why. I honestly
can't imagine my life without you, and
I wouldn't want to. ;-)

And special thanks to Tara Randel and
her hero – *The Randy*.
Appreciated your help steering me past the flag!

1

"I WANT TESS HARDAWAY."

The statement came out sounding more like a demand than a request so Anthony DiLeo forced a smile at the guy behind the registration desk and tried again. "Is she around yet?"

"She was, but she left again."

"That's what you told me an hour ago."

"I know." The guy gave a lame shrug. "Sorry. You just keep missing her."

Anthony hoped like hell his bum timing didn't foreshadow the weekend ahead. Meeting Tess Hardaway was the only reason he'd come to Nostalgic Car Club's annual convention. He hadn't set eyes on her yet and already she'd given him the slip. Twice.

He tried not to look impatient. "You told me she'd be greeting people during registration."

"She has been. But she's also on the club's board—vice president of programming. She's been getting her presenters settled, too."

Okay, Tess Hardaway was a busy lady. He got that part. Anthony also got that this guy was nothing more than a volunteer. Wearing a vintage leather flying cap and goggles, he looked ready to take off in an old barnstormer. Obviously no one close to the elusive Tess Hardaway.

But he seemed to take his job seriously. He wore a T-shirt with the convention logo—a cartoon of an oversize, powerful engine plunked down in the middle of the French Quarter. The catch phrase read: Big Banger and Bourbon Street.

Anthony glanced down at the volunteer's name badge. Timmy Martin, Montgomery, Alabama.

"All right, Timmy from Montgomery. Maybe you can tell me where to find Ms. Hardaway since I'm not doing such a hot job tracking her down on my own."

"How about the AutoCarTex Foundation's hospitality suite? Have you tried there yet?"

"Didn't know AutoCarTex had a hospitality suite."

Timmy from Montgomery frowned. "Let me make a suggestion."

"Go."

"I know you wanted to register with Tess, but why don't you let me do the honors? I'll give you the registration packet and you can check out everything that's happening. Not only does AutoCarTex have a hospitality suite, but also they're hosting an event. Tess will be at both. If you want, I'll leave her a message. If she knows you're looking for her, I'm sure she'll contact you."

"Yes register. No message."

No forewarning. He couldn't risk losing the slight advantage he had in her not knowing she was being pursued. There might be a picture of her in the program. If he knew what the woman who held the titles of AutoCarTex Foundation's managing director and Nostalgic Car Club's vice president of programming looked like, he could locate his target sooner.

The guy nodded and got down to business. "Name?"

"Anthony DiLeo."

The Nostalgic Car Club apparently favored nostalgia in more than just cars. There wasn't a computer in sight, so Timmy from Montgomery searched through good old-fashioned file boxes filled with alphabetized folders.

He withdrew one and skimmed through it.

"Everything's in order, Mr. DiLeo." He offered the folder. "This has your name badge, meal tickets, driving passes, room assignment and itinerary. Let me get your bag."

Disappearing beneath the desk, he came up with a bag imprinted with the convention logo. "This has your shirt, a commemorative plaque and a booklet with all the requirements for the weekend's events. That's important if you plan to participate in any of the races. You've got paperwork to turn in."

"Got it." And Anthony did. He'd wanted Tess Hardaway and he'd gotten a convention bag instead.

He *really* hoped this wasn't an omen.

After a pit stop at the front desk, he collected his garment bag from his car and headed to his room to stow his gear.

The room was standard trendy. The hotel was standard trendy. The Chase Convention Center sat on the outskirts of Metairie, a stone's throw from New Orleans. Catering to traffic from the airport and Dixie Downs Speedway, the place was so close to Anthony's house he could have driven here nearly as fast as finding a free elevator to get down to the first floor.

But Tess Hardaway was somewhere in this hotel, and he'd waste valuable hunting time if he had to drive back and forth every day. He planned to make the most of every chance to cross her path this weekend.

Once he finally caught her.

Grabbing the convention program, Anthony sat on the edge of the bed and studied the hotel map to get a lay of the land. All the hospitality suites were located on the second floor, promoting sponsors who'd paid big bucks to have their names appear in the brochure that would go to twenty-six hundred conventioneers and car enthusiasts from all over the world.

Anthony knew every one of the advertisers. Automotive suppliers. Major manufacturers. Classic car restorers. He'd even heard of the new car dealerships. Only the biggest and best could afford to host events and advertise in Nostalgic Car Club's slick promotional program.

Turning the booklet over, he wondered what an ad in here would cost. Hell, what about the price of hosting a weekend hospitality suite for twenty-six hundred guests?

Ten, twenty grand?

While he could have afforded to spend that kind of money on advertising, this wasn't his market. His business might have grown into New Orleans's most reputable service and maintenance center in the years since he'd opened the doors, but vehicle owners wouldn't travel from Maine or Washington state to have their car tuned up at Anthony DiLeo Automotive.

This sort of promotion only benefited the big boys.

Over the past few years, Anthony had watched Auto-CarTex become a big boy. The used-car dealership had expanded its operation by opening new service centers all over the nation, growing slowly, steadily, *successfully.* If he hooked up with Tess Hardaway, he'd take a step toward becoming a big boy, too.

With that thought, he rolled up the program, stuffed it into his back pocket and headed downstairs.

He found AutoCarTex's hospitality suite easily enough. People had already begun milling through, glancing at the full-color advertising spreads detailing AutoCarTex's unique philosophy on used vehicles as they worked their way toward the buffet.

Anthony wasn't interested in food. He was interested in the woman dressed in a dark blue business suit working the crowd.

Tess Hardaway?

He couldn't catch her name badge from this distance but in that getup, she had to be with the company. He'd already had his fill of dealing with the AutoCarTex corporate types in his quest to get to the man who'd founded the company—Big Tex Hardaway.

Now those fruitless dealings had brought him to this convention to track down the man's only daughter.

But as he neared the woman, Anthony second-guessed himself. From what he'd read about Tess Hardaway, he'd expected someone less...*suit,* precisely the reason he'd chosen her.

He waited. The woman didn't take long to direct her guests to the buffet, and when she had, she extended her hand to him.

"Penny Parker of AutoCartex." Her name badge read Marketing Director.

A *serious* suit.

"Anthony DiLeo of Anthony DiLeo Automotive."

She had an easy smile and a sharp gaze that took him in all at once. "A business owner. Local?"

He inclined his head.

"Please tell me you're not worried that AutoCarTex's Louisiana expansion will cut into your bottom line."

Anthony laughed. "I happen to respect smart business strategy, and Big Tex's makes sense. He has made reliable used transportation more accessible. I think that's a good thing."

"Even when we open an auto showroom in your backyard?

"My service center is well established in town. I don't have anything to worry about."

Her expression suggested she approved his answer, and he continued, not above showing at least one of AutoCarTex's suits that this auto mechanic was made of more than they seemed to think. "Too many people treat cars as if they're disposable. Consumers pay through the nose to drive a new car out of the showroom when an older one only needs a little TLC."

"You sound like a spokesperson for AutoCarTex, Mr. DiLeo."

That made him smile. "Anthony."

"All right, Anthony," she said with just enough drawl to tell him she was Southern. "If you didn't come to pick my brain about our new showroom, then what can I do for you? Interested in our mission statement? Our involvement with the Nostalgic Car Club? How about our service warranty contract?"

"I'm looking for Tess Hardaway. I heard she'd be around."

"Really? Do you know Tess?"

"Not personally."

"I'm afraid you just missed her."

"I seem to be doing that a lot today."

That sharp gaze cut across him again, seemed to notice there was more here than met the eye. And she clearly hadn't decided if *that* was good.

"You don't happen to know where she went, do you?"

Penny leaned back on her stylish pumps and folded her arms across her chest. "Normally, I wouldn't dream of asking, but something about your interest is smacking of more personal than professional. Why do you want to see Tess?"

"I'm sorry if I gave you that impression, Ms. Parker."

"Penny, please."

"Penny. My interest is strictly business. I came to this convention to network with Ms. Hardaway."

"Are you interested in the AutoCarTex Foundation?"

"So to speak." That wasn't entirely true, but close enough. "I'd rather keep my business between me and Ms. Hardaway."

"Now I'm intrigued. Not even a hint?"

He spread his hands in entreaty. "Nothing mysterious. Just business."

She eyed him again. He got the impression she couldn't quite make out what a local service center owner might want with the director of the AutoCarTex Foundation, which dealt with the public relations and charitable donations parts of the corporation. He also got the impression *her* interest was more than professional.

"She went to the speedway for the race."

"What race?" he asked. "I thought the convention didn't start until the welcome reception tonight."

"It doesn't *officially* start, but we always kick off with a low-speed race. Gets everyone in the mood. Tess wouldn't miss it for the world. Didn't you read your itinerary?"

"Not closely enough." He extended his hand. "A pleasure meeting you, Penny. Looks like I'm off to the races. I'm sure I'll run into you again."

She shook with a firm grip. "If you don't catch up with her, try back here later. She'll be in and out all weekend."

"Thanks."

Anthony left the hotel optimistic that he might finally catch the woman who'd been eluding him all day. His optimism lasted until he reached the speedway ticket booth.

"Gates closed to the public," a grizzled man wearing a Dixie Downs uniform told him.

"I'm attending the convention."

"Name badge? Driving pass?"

Damn it. "In my hotel room. I didn't know I needed them."

"Can't let you through without your name badge and your driving pass."

A car stopped at the nearby booth, flashed some papers and drove through the gates.

"I won't be driving, just watching."

The gate didn't budge.

"When does the race start?"

The ticket-taker glanced at his watch. "Ten minutes."

Not enough time to get to and from the hotel and still search the crowds for Tess Hardaway before the race began. He didn't think she'd be hard to find, though. Probably in the stands with the event hosts. "Can you call someone with the convention to verify I'm registered?"

"Call who?" the man asked gruffly, clearly not thrilled that Anthony intended to give him a hard time. Cocking his grizzled head toward the parking lot beyond the gate, he said, "The whole car club is inside for the race."

Anthony thought about dropping Penny Parker's name, but decided against it. The woman had been skeptical enough about his interest in Tess. "The volunteer working the registration desk will confirm I'm with the convention—"

"I got my orders."

"What about the hotel? They have me checked in with the car club's room block."

"Name badge and driving pass. It says so in the rules." He flourished a copy of Big Banger and Bourbon Street's program.

"But I—"

"Name badge and driving pass," the ticket-taker repeated stubbornly. "Or I call security."

First impressions were everything and being labeled a gate-crasher by speedway security was *not* the first impression Anthony wanted to make with Big Tex's daughter. The success of his new career path now depended on her.

Scowling, he shifted his car into Reverse and backed out of the ticket booth. It wasn't until he'd almost reached the road that a sign caught his eye.

Drivers.

Anthony was New Orleans born and bred. He might not have belonged to a fancy car club like Nostalgic until he'd wanted to meet Tess Hardaway, but he'd been around cars since he could sit up straight enough to be strapped into his dad's vintage GTO.

Even more importantly, he'd been hanging around Dixie Downs for nearly as long. His first paying job had been in the pit working for a locally sponsored team. He knew his way around.

Without another thought, Anthony bypassed the gate

and wheeled his car down the road leading to the track. He slid into the queue as if he belonged there.

When he reached the crewman in charge of registering the racers, he cranked down his window and said, "I'm looking for Tess Hardaway."

The guy didn't even look up over his clipboard. "The pole."

Well, well, well. He'd been wrong. Tess Hardaway wasn't in the stands, after all. She was lined up to race.

Leaning out his open window, he craned to see around the queue to the course and spotted her immediately. One look and every bit of his inner car enthusiast cringed.

A *Gremlin?* A *purple* Gremlin.

He couldn't miss the florid paint, the custom parts or the jacked-up rear tires turning the classic that had inspired the phrase "What happened to the rest of your car?" into a hot rod to shake the streets. The driver wore a matching purple helmet.

He smiled. Here he'd been worried about first impressions. Anthony had to wonder if Tess Hardaway would want to know his first impression of her. He doubted it.

"Where's your gear?" The crewman had finally glanced up from his clipboard. "Can't give you a number without your gear."

"In the trunk." He'd expected to race sometime this weekend and now seemed as good a time as any to start. Hopping out, he circled his car, hoping he didn't need anything more than a helmet and gloves.

The crewman gave a nod. "We're running with the National Racing Council rule book. Helmet will work today, but if you want to race in Saturday's high-speed autocross, you'll need a fire suit."

"Got it."

The crewman must have assumed Anthony had shown his name badge and driving pass at the gate because he slapped a number twenty-one inside the windshield and waved him through. The next thing Anthony knew, he slipped into the third row of the grid to wait for the pace car.

He finally had Tess Hardaway in sight.

Pulling on his helmet, he revved the engine to drown out the low-slung Corvette showing off in the slot beside him.

Classic car owners could be a competitive bunch, and he easily admitted that he was no different. But in Anthony's experience Corvette owners were the worst. Elitists.

A past president of the local Corvette club had officially endorsed Anthony's service center as the place to cater to the classic crowd. Ever since, he had been servicing the bulk of their members, most of whom thought they were doing him a favor by letting his staff touch their showy wheels. Some even tried to make him see the error of his Pontiac-driving ways.

This Corvette looked mint, but his own first-generation Firebird had a 400-cubic-inch V-8. He'd personally disabled the manufacturer's device that kept the engine from reaching full throttle. His Firebird would dominate that black Corvette before they'd pulled through the second lap.

Anthony might not have raced in a while, but his foot slipped onto the gas pedal instinctively when the pace car appeared to lead them around the track for a parade lap. One by one the cars pulled out to give the spectators a good look at the lineup.

Then came a pace lap before the official start of the

race. The drivers traveled in formation, steadily increasing speed until they hit the ceiling before the starting line.

Then came the flag.

Anthony's adrenaline shot into gear with his engine. The Dixie Downs Speedway was his course. He knew the groove by heart—when to shut off to negotiate banked turns, what turns to ride the rails. He knew when to lean into the accelerator to gain distance through the chutes.

His Firebird took to the track as if he'd just raced her yesterday, and when the black Corvette tried to shut him out, Anthony diced a little, forcing the Corvette to back off.

He blew past with a laugh, his fingers easily gripping the steering wheel. He sailed past a mint-condition Camaro. No contest. The Firebird had been designed to outrun the Chevy. It had been too long since he'd done anything that had gotten his blood pumping like this.

Too damned long.

His fellow contestants didn't stand a chance. Anthony had a Gremlin to catch, and a driver leading the pack.

The feel of the track beneath his wheels and the silky way his car handled each turn brought back memories of the innumerable times he'd raced here. With his dad when he'd been alive. With his brother Marc, who had such a serious need for speed that their mother swore he'd given her every gray hair she kept meticulously dyed. When Anthony had worked in the pit, making passes around this track in his employers' cars to clock some wickedly fast times.

Now each lap brought him closer to that purple hot rod.

Finally, he slipped into place behind her. After a few laps on her tail, Anthony admitted that not only did her funky little Gremlin pack more rpm grunt than he'd expected, but Tess Hardaway was one damned skilled driver. A little ruthless even.

She clearly enjoyed the thrill of the chase because she kept blipping to make him adjust his speed. Anthony let her play him for a bit. He intended to ride her bumper straight to the finish line. This woman would *not* get away again.

But the more she toyed with him, the harder he found it not to toy back.

Instinct finally took over. Slipping into her draft, he followed closely enough to take advantage of the decreased air resistance, so close that the chrome Gremlin character on her hatch grinned wickedly like a dare.

The race was on.

He sped up.

She slowed down.

He maneuvered the track.

She shut him out so he couldn't pass.

While Anthony might not have Tess Hardaway's maneuvers, he had the better car. And he put his Firebird to work when she fishtailed out of a hairy turn. She controlled the motion instantly—testimony to her skill—but skill was the only thing carrying her right now.

Instinct told him her hot rod was full out while his V-8 still had more to give. With a little more grunt and a lot of luck, he could maneuver past, well before that checkered flag came down to signal the end of the race.

Anthony had a split second to decide.

Whipping this woman's butt on the track hardly seemed a better introduction than being dragged in by security for crashing the gate.

But even more important than making a good first impression was the question: could Anthony live with himself if he let that prissy purple Gremlin whip *his* butt?

THE FIREBIRD DRAFTED Tess all the way down the chute. She couldn't shake him. Although she drove with her pedal to the metal, this muscle car clung to her bumper as though it had been painted on. And the second she misjudged a banked turn, it broke out of her draft to slingshot around and take the lead.

Now it was Tess's turn to ride a bumper. But what a bumper it was. The shiny chrome and gleaming taillights blurred as the Firebird drifted into the chute, a neat, controlled slide that sealed the deal about who would win this race.

The distance between them lengthened as they neared the checkered flag. Her five-liter engine might give her lightweight Gremlin a lively performance, but it couldn't touch what this driver had growling beneath his hood.

And she had to give him credit for not stroking all the way to the finish line. He could have rubbed her loss in her face by slowing down when he knew she couldn't catch up, but once he took the lead, he ran with it.

As long as he was winning, he would win big. As far as Tess was concerned that sort of confidence said something about a driver. And by the time she wheeled into the pit lane, she wanted to know who he was.

She didn't recognize the red Firebird with the white hardtop and gleaming chrome side pipes. Removing her helmet, she handed it to the volunteer who had been assigned to her pit and treated herself to a deep breath of fuel-tinged summer air. *Mmm-mmm.* There was nothing like it.

"Well now," a familiar voice drawled. "There's a sight you don't see every day. Tess Hardaway in the number two spot."

She turned to find a coworker strolling toward her on grossly expensive Italian pumps. "What are you doing in my pit? Your hair will smell like exhaust fumes."

Penny ran a manicured hand over her smooth black bob and patted it in place. "Can't be helped."

"Why's that? And aren't you supposed to be working the hospitality suite?"

She nodded. "I passed the ball to our resident over-achiever. He was happy to do his bit for the cause."

This overachiever was the AutoCarTex Foundation's newest employee, and Tess's personal assistant, Hal. The new graduate could make typing a letter seem worthy of his business degree from a prestigious northeastern university. That knack had won him the job. His enthusiasm felt contagious, and she appreciated anyone who could spread it like butter around her office.

"I'll bet," she said. "Just don't take advantage of my assistant. I need him this weekend. All I've been doing is putting out fires. Nothing's coming together."

"I'll say." Penny laughed. "We'll be able to hear your Uncle Ray hooting from Texas when he finds out you lost a race. So who did the honors?"

Tess glanced to where the driver of the Firebird had pulled before the stand to accept his trophy. "Whoever's driving that Firebird. My money's on a local. He knew the track."

But Penny didn't respond. She was too busy staring at the man who emerged from the winning car. Even from this distance, Tess could make him out as a tall, very well-built man who filled out his jeans nicely. He pulled off his helmet to reveal tawny blond hair that waved back from his face, long enough that he'd tied it in a small ponytail.

"That's Anthony DiLeo. You're right. He's a local."

No surprise there. "Who is he?"

"A service shop owner who's apparently so well established, he's not in the least bit worried about us cutting into his business when we open our new showroom in town."

No surprise there, either. The man drove confident, which meant he must be confident.

Penny shot her one of *those* expressions, one that declared something was up. "He came to the hospitality suite looking for you. Said he'd been missing you all day."

"What does he want?"

"Business. Wouldn't say what kind. Thought I'd give you the heads-up."

Tess would have to be deaf to miss the innuendo in that statement. "Are you worried?"

"About this man? No. I liked him, but I did promise your father I'd stay on red alert so the wack job du jour doesn't get anywhere near his precious baby."

"Give it a rest, Penny."

"Your father's worried, Tess. He doesn't want you driving the rally alone, and I can't say I blame him. So don't shoot the messenger. I'm just doing my job."

This was a tired excuse Tess had heard all too often. "Last I heard you were a marketing director, not a babysitter."

"With any other company the roles would be mutually exclusive. Not at *your* company, though. According to your father part of my job is watching your back, as you well know."

Boy, did she ever. Shielding the late-afternoon sun from her eyes, Tess watched Anthony DiLeo toss his helmet inside his car. Nope, she'd never seen him before. She wouldn't have forgotten a man who walked like that, long legs chewing up the track with possessive strides. And his car…that was one well-kept muscle car. She wondered if he'd restored it himself.

"No clue what he wants?"

Penny shook her head. "None. But I'll be disappointed if he turns out to be the latest wack job. He is one handsome man."

"Wouldn't know," Tess said dryly. "I've only seen him with his helmet on when he passed me on the track."

"Then take my word for it. This one's yummy."

"You said the same thing about Daryl Keene."

"That one's yummy, too."

Tess rubbed her temples. If she could just rub away Penny as easily. But no matter where she turned lately, she ran smack into someone her daddy had sent to watch her back.

"You know, it's not so bad having people look out for you," Penny admonished.

Spoken by someone whose back wasn't being watched. Tess leaned against the railing and met Penny's scowl. "Do you know how many people work at AutoCarTex headquarters? That's *a lot* of back watchers. My daddy is on the wrong side of overprotective on a good day, and he's gone off the deep end lately."

Penny's scowl faded fast. "I had no idea the commercials would turn into a trail of bread crumbs for the crazies."

"You couldn't have foreseen the problem. None of us

could. Most of Johnny Q. Public thinks Daddy is their best friend. And look at all the good the commercials have done. Not only for corporate but for the Foundation."

"I still feel responsible. I dreamed up the promotional campaign. And these letters your father's been getting lately have him really worried. This latest one is threatening family and friends along with the accusations of gross capitalism."

Boy, did Tess know all about that. Daddy hadn't been this worked up since she'd gone to the movies on her first date with that cute hand from the Critchley ranch.

"Do you think this one's trouble?" She glanced at Anthony DiLeo as he exchanged greetings with the car club's president.

"He didn't strike me as a crazy, but he wants something."

"Who doesn't? Another side effect of Daddy's success, and one you're not responsible for."

Penny gave a low whistle. "If you don't mind my saying, Tess, every drop of blood in your veins will turn to prairie dust if you don't have some fun. *Soon.*"

How much fun could she have when all of AutoCar-Tex's employees kept their eyes on her at work? Daddy and Uncle Ray tag-teamed at home, and dropping by her apartment unexpectedly and checking out her friends were both time-consuming jobs. She knew they had more important things to do than babysit her, so by necessity, Tess limited her activities.

This hadn't proven much of a problem lately. Except for the convention, her schedule had been keeping her pretty close to home. And she hadn't met any man who seemed worthy of checking out in a while.

"Penny, I'll date again just as soon as I come across a man who isn't more interested in Daddy than me."

"What could Daryl Keene possibly want?" Penny sidled up to her and peered down the track to where the man himself directed the pit crew's efforts with his black Corvette. "His daddy is richer than your daddy."

Tess grudgingly followed her gaze. All right, she couldn't argue finances. Or appearance, either. Daryl Keene had been cut from a very handsome mold. Tall, polished looking with his neat black hair and slick smiles.

"I don't know. But he wants something or else he wouldn't still be hounding me for a date. He's even started e-mailing me through my corporate account. And now he's checking out a dealership in Lubbock. He told me he's heading up the project so he can spend more time in town."

"Sure you're not paranoid? Sounds like he doesn't want more than to get inside your size-four jeans. You should go to dinner or a movie. Something *fun.*"

Tess rolled her eyes. "Not interested."

"But why? Your daddy knows his daddy, so he probably doesn't even need to run a background check on the guy. Not to mention he's downright yummy."

"He's a trailer queen."

"Who cares if he hauls his car or drives it? He's cute, and rich to boot."

Tess bit back a smile at Penny's criteria. "Honestly, I can't take Daryl up on his offer."

"Why not? I'm talking dinner here, not marriage and two-point-five kids. Give me a reason that's based in reality."

"No sparks. Not a one."

Penny considered that for a minute then pushed away from the rail with a heavy sigh. "Damn shame that."

Although Tess didn't consider Daryl much of a loss, it had been so long since she'd felt sparks for any man she'd begun to wonder if it wasn't a hormonal thing. Did the libido die down the closer one got to thirty?

She couldn't bring herself to ask Penny, who was around her age. While they were friendly, Penny was a career gal well aware of who approved her every step up the corporate ladder. The last thing Tess needed was her daddy getting wind of any medical concerns. Maybe she'd do some Internet research. This might be something a few herbal supplements could cure.

Or maybe Penny was right, and she was paranoid. But Tess had a right to be cautious. Most men weren't interested *in* her, but in *using* her, a problem she'd first encountered long ago, while dating a man from upper management at AutoCarTex Corporate.

Everyone seemed to want to get close to her daddy.

"The winner of Big Banger and Bourbon Street's first race is new car club member Anthony DiLeo." The car club's president rescued her from more self-analysis when he spoke over the microphone. "To celebrate his win, Mr. DiLeo is making a generous ten-thousand-dollar cash contribution to the Children's Hope League in the name of his service center, Anthony DiLeo Automotive of New Orleans, Louisiana."

The crowd roared approval and Penny said, "Well, well, well. Looks like my instincts are on target. Anthony DiLeo isn't striking me as your run-of-the-mill wacko."

"That remains to be seen."

"Sour grapes. You can't win every race. At least hear what the man has to say."

Tess didn't have to hear him speak a word—she already knew what he was up to. "He's sucking up."

"What makes you say that?"

"We're sponsoring the Children's Hope League this year."

"And AutoCarTex is the only corporation contributing to this charity?"

"Of course not," she huffed. "But I'm guessing he's contributing to this charity because we are. The man definitely wants something. I want to know what it is."

2

APPARENTLY ANTHONY DILEO wanted her. He glanced Tess's way as soon as he left the stand, and after tossing his grand-prize trophy carelessly into the back seat, he hopped into his idling car and headed toward them.

Tess watched as he backed across the track in a quick, clean move, and she had to admit that while his driving skill clearly wasn't a result of formal training, he had a natural ability that impressed her.

Pulling to a sharp stop, he left exactly enough room to open his door and clear the rail separating them. Another smooth move probably meant to impress. She had to admit—at least to herself—that it did. But not nearly as much as the man who stepped out of the car.

He unfolded a lean, mean body in an energetic burst of strength that made her stare, starting at the butter-soft-looking leather slip-ons he wore with no socks. Nicely muscled thighs did even better things to his jeans up close, and his neat cotton shirt hinted at some serious definition below. And when she finally made it to his face…

Tess had already guessed by the name that something about this man would be Italian. But one glimpse into his handsome face confirmed that not something, but *everything* screamed his heritage. Deep olive skin. Strong, carved features that contrasted strikingly with golden-brown bedroom eyes that checked her out as thoroughly as she did him.

His gaze swept across her like a warm breeze, a physical sensation, and the *only* thing to remind her to breathe again.

His hair was too long to be considered anything but rebellious, yet it was a tawny touchable blond. And his smile… This man had a kissing mouth, plain and simple, because there was no way Tess could look at that wide mouth and not think about kissing.

She had to shake her head to clear *that* thought away.

Whoa! Anthony DiLeo had chemistry with a capital *C* and he blasted it all over her. And that knowing smile assured her she wasn't the only one thinking about kissing right now, either.

Then he reached over the railing and took her hand.

His handshake should have been perfectly professional, but the instant their fingers met, Tess knew she wouldn't need any herbs to jump-start her libido. Touching this man did the trick nicely. He had working hands. Rough skin here and there. And danged if she didn't vibrate a little when his warm, strong fingers finally slipped away.

"Ms. Hardaway, I've been hoping to meet you." His voice was all whiskey smooth and lazy bayou, a sound that strummed her insides like a guitar under a starry sky.

"So I've heard." The crazily breathless sound of her voice came as another surprise.

And made Penny snort with laughter behind her.

Tess had forgotten Penny was even there, but a glance over her shoulder proved she was still watching Tess's back. The look on her face screamed smug amusement, which did a lot to help Tess get a grip on her brushfire reaction to this man.

"What can I do for you?" She took a step back, amazed by what a little distance did to slow her racing pulse.

After nodding in greeting to Penny, Anthony slid his warm gaze back to her. "I hoped for some of your time this weekend. I have some business to discuss."

"See what I mean about this cryptic stuff?" Penny might have sounded wary, but she eyed the man as if he were the last finger-licking-good drumstick.

"Is that why you made such a generous contribution to the charity I'm sponsoring this year, Mr. DiLeo? Were you hoping to score points so I'd make time for you?"

Hooking an arm over his car door, Anthony DiLeo looked at her evenly, and his expression suggested he didn't mind her candor. "I wanted to make a good first impression."

"You could have stayed behind her on the track," Penny said. "That would have worked."

He laughed, a rich rolling sound that sent another shock wave through Tess. "If I could have, I would have."

"Why couldn't you?" Tess asked, curious.

"I've got this thing about looking myself in the mirror and respecting what I see. I couldn't let you win when I knew I could. I hoped my contribution would make up for the slight."

Tess backed away, needing more distance between them to reason this through. "You didn't want to lose to a woman?"

"No. I have zero problem with you being a woman." That gaze of his raked along her body, proving his point louder than words ever could. "I didn't want to lose to a *purple Gremlin*."

Penny hooted with laughter. "Calling Tess's baby ugly is *not* the way to make friends."

He lifted those broad shoulders in an apologetic shrug. "I didn't say ugly. But I'd be lying if I said that maniacal grinning Gremlin didn't provoke me a little."

"Another man who's attached to his car," Penny said. "But this one's no trailer queen, I'll bet."

Anthony DiLeo let his grimace speak for him, drawing her attention back to his striking features, and the way her stomach swooped every time she met his bedroom gaze.

She couldn't be *this* attracted to a nutter, could she?

No. This man might have a big car and an ego to match, but she had an internal alarm that was even bigger. She could spot a sidewinder from a mile off—had certainly honed her skills—and while Anthony DiLeo might want something from her, he'd been shooting straight so far.

"What sort of business did you want to discuss? Penny told me that you're a service center owner here in town. You do realize I'm with the AutoCarTex Foundation, don't you?"

"I did my research, Ms. Hardaway."

"Is that how you knew I'd be racing today?"

He shook his head, and she couldn't help but notice the way his hair glinted. Thick, silky hair that was the most incredible color, like a sun-washed echo of his golden-brown eyes. "Penny was kind enough to give me that information. She took pity on me because I've been chasing you all afternoon."

"The hotel was the only place you couldn't catch her," Penny said. "Another hint, Anthony. Tess isn't used to losing on the race track."

He waved a hand dismissively, and she noticed he wore

no ring on his third finger. "Not with her skill, but I had the edge. I've been racing this track since I learned to drive."

"So you don't think you're a better driver?"

"Penny!"

Anthony laughed. "Like I said, I had the edge. My car's bigger, too."

"I'm warming to him, Tess. He didn't come right out and say you're a better driver, but he knows it."

"What does this have to do with anything?" she asked.

Penny elbowed Tess playfully, but her eyes swept over the man as if she wanted to lick her fingers. "Shows a man's character, I think. His ego's not so fragile that he has to lie, but he's no pushover, either."

"I don't have any problems with my ego," he said.

No doubt. But Tess didn't miss how diplomatic he was, which she thought said a lot about him, too.

She wished she could see inside that handsome head to know what he was thinking. He'd tracked her down to discuss some sort of business and wound up with Penny inspecting him like a breeder. She wondered what Anthony DiLeo thought of all the innuendo pouring off her companion right now.

Tess knew what she thought—that this was the grossest display of unprofessionalism she'd ever seen. And Penny would hear about it as soon as they were alone again.

But until she could voice that opinion, she would run interference, which meant ending this interview. "I enjoyed the competition. I'll make some time to talk this weekend."

"I'm at your convenience, Ms. Hardaway. Just name the time and the place."

"I'm afraid tonight's a bust. The board is throwing a dinner for the presenters."

"What about tomorrow morning?" Penny suggested.

"No go." Tess shook her head. "I'm moderating the panel discussion during breakfast."

Anthony waited patiently while she mentally worked through her schedule.

Penny wasn't so patient. "Why don't you give me Hal to set up at the park? I doubt the hospitality suite will have much traffic with everyone getting ready for the caravan. You can slip away and meet Anthony for coffee."

"That'll work. Hotel coffee shop around eleven?"

Anthony nodded. "I'll be there."

With bells on, if Tess read the smile right.

ANTHONY TOOK ONE LOOK at the babe sprawled on the classic car's hood and knew he'd been plunked into the mother of all fantasies. He also understood why *Auto Coupe Magazine* had featured a purple AMC Gremlin in its annual calendar. This babe could make any car look good. Even this one.

She had a mane of glossy brown hair that tumbled sexily around her shoulders. She leaned back on her hands, which thrust her breasts proudly forward, and hiked one of her long bare legs on the hood. The other draped down in front of a headlight, dangling an ultrafeminine sandal from her foot. Her neat toenails were painted a pale pink that strangely complimented the garish purple paint.

Then again, with this babe showcasing the car, who really cared what color the car was?

Not Anthony. Not when the calendar babe wore a matching pink muscle shirt in some clingy fabric that

hugged her full breasts so close that he could see the outline of her nipples.

She wasn't wearing a bra.

The silky shorts didn't leave much to the imagination,
either—except to inspire thoughts of how he could peel
them down her legs....

With his hands while stroking her soft thighs.

With his teeth while nibbling her creamy skin.

With *her* hands while she performed a fantasy striptease.

Yeah. He liked the idea of Calendar Babe stripping for
him.

But when had *Auto Coupe Magazine* turned his garage
into a photo set?

Sure enough when Anthony looked around, the purple
Gremlin with its lovely model was parked smack in the
middle of his twenty bays, and he didn't have a clue how
they'd gotten there. His head couldn't fit the pieces together, and his body didn't care. Not when Calendar Babe
had come to life.

Propping herself up on one hand, she brought a manicured finger to her lips, drawing his attention to how ripe
her glossy mouth was for kissing.

Oh, yeah!

Then she trailed that finger down her throat...down...
down. Hooking it inside the scooped neck of her muscle
shirt, she drew his gaze like a magnet to the creamy swell
of her cleavage, the rise of luscious breasts on an excited
breath.

Then she dragged the shirt down.

Full swells of pale skin spilled out in a tumble, riding
high over the straining collar. The sight stole the breath

from his lungs. His dick shot to about one degree below a crippling erection. He clutched the doorjamb tighter.

Her rose-colored nipples were darker than he'd imagined, the tips harder than he'd hoped.

Anthony *had* died and gone to heaven.

Calendar Babe heaven.

Suddenly, her foot stopped in middangle, dragging his gaze from those lush breasts to the sandal suspended from her toes. She let it fall to the floor. He knew the wooden heel must have made some sound on the concrete, but he couldn't hear a thing past the blood throbbing in his ears.

Then she drew her long legs underneath her and spun around, an erotic display of motion that turned the car hood into a dance floor. Her arms lifted gracefully. Her breasts bounced sexily. She rose up on her knees so he could admire her in profile. Then she began rocking her hips back and forth.

And working those pink shorts down, down, down.

Anthony watched, his breath stalling as the curve of a slim hip appeared. Inch by inch, more creamy skin became visible…the tight curve of her butt…the sleek line of her thigh…and Anthony realized…Calendar Babe went commando.

"Will you pull it out for me, Anthony?"

It?

In some dim part of his brain, Anthony knew Calendar Babe's Texas twang should have been familiar. But for the life of him, he couldn't remember why. How in hell was he supposed to think when she dropped that emerald gaze to his crotch?

It.

He was game. Hell, it seemed only fair to return the favor when she performed so eagerly for him. Unzipping his fly, he slid his pants down on his hips, carefully maneuvering his erection away from the zipper.

"Will you stroke it for me? I want to see you get hard."

Get hard? He was as stiff as a steering column.

But he wouldn't deny her anything. Wrapping his fingers around himself, he gave a slow tug. Then another.

She pursed her lips and blew him a kiss. "Mmm, you are hard, big boy. Come here."

Sliding the shorts over her knees, she kicked them off her feet. Then she slithered off the hood and stood in all her barely clad glory.

For a minute, Anthony could do nothing but stare. She posed in front of the car, bare bottomed, breasts still popping over her collar in a stunning display of nipple and skin.

Then she flashed him an inviting smile. The eagerness he saw in her face, in those deep green eyes that were almost too green to be real, was enough to propel him into motion.

He wouldn't miss this fantasy.

She extended her hand to him as he approached, and the feel of her fingertips slipping around his erection, drawing him to her, was the last proof Anthony needed to know he'd indeed died and gone to heaven.

He went to pull her into his arms, but she tightened her grip on his dick, used it as a handle to steer him to the car. Then she pushed him toward the hood.

"Sit."

He could barely think let alone argue. So he hoisted himself onto the hood, watching in amazement as she bent low over him, her mouth replacing her hand....

She swirled her tongue over him in a warm velvet stroke. His dick jumped, bumping against her shiny pink lips.

She laughed, a delightful silvery sound. "Oh, Anthony."

She moved in for the kill.

Her mouth became a suck zone, drawing him in, one long pull that made him tingle from his toes to the roots of his hair. A growl spilled from his mouth, a sound that echoed off the garage walls, the sound of appreciation.

Spearing his fingers into her hair, Anthony hung on while she took him for a ride, head bobbing, tongue swirling, those glossy pink lips in a liplock that could have sucked the chrome off his bumper.

Somewhere in the rational part of his brain, Anthony knew her lipstick should have long ago smeared. But those enticing lips remained as glossy and perfect as they had when this fantasy began, and he couldn't spare even a brain cell to reason through the phenomenon.

Not when he couldn't keep his fingers from threading deeper into her hair, urging her to quicken the pace. Not when he couldn't stop arching his hips to press back inside her warm mouth.

He hovered in that twilight moment—about to explode but unable to let himself go because the fantasy would be over.

Calendar Babe must have read his mind because she slipped her hand under his balls and fondled him. Her shiny lips parted, and she twirled a hot wet lick around the head of his dick.

She slipped her fingers between his legs and whispered, "I hear this is the male G-spot."

Slithering a moist finger backward...

Anthony opened his eyes and stared blindly at the bed-side clock. It took forever to make sense of what he was seeing—a digital display that read 3:14 a.m.

Still eight hours before he met with the woman who'd just made an appearance in the most erotic dream he'd ever had. And as he lay on the hard hotel bed with every nerve in his body firing like a new spark plug, Anthony got the sinking feeling that eight hours and an icy shower weren't going to take the edge off the effects of *that* dream any time soon.

ANTHONY ARRIVED at the hotel's coffee shop early enough to locate a table reasonably removed from the traffic. After ordering a big cup of joe with a few extra shots of espresso thrown in to clear his head, he booted his laptop, organized his spreadsheets for easy access and took a few gulps of the supercharged brew.

He needed the extra caffeine after spending the remainder of his night too keyed up to sleep. His brain had replayed that incredible dream, and when Tess strolled through the door a few minutes after eleven, Anthony knew he was in trouble. *Big* trouble. The sight of her hit him every place it counted.

She moved with a light, purposeful grace. She wasn't exactly tall, but she was willowy and slim, which made her appear that way. He hadn't gotten close enough yet to tell for sure, but he thought the top of her head might reach his chin if they stood close.

The effect Tess was having on him came as a shock.

She might be one damn fine-looking woman, but Anthony knew many fine-looking women. There was something about her that made him think about sex in a way he hadn't in forever. Interested. Excited. And the feeling was about more than her glossy hair waving prettily around her face or those big eyes that were so deep a green they didn't seem real.

It wasn't the insane elf getup, either.

She'd dressed head to toe in red-and-green stripes for the Christmas in July caravan event. The short-shorts made him ogle her legs. Suspenders with blinking lights drew his gaze to her lean curves and left him wondering how he would conduct business when she looked like a Christmas present he wanted to unwrap.

Anthony had no good answer. He was completely aware of this woman and completely sandbagged by the feeling. He hadn't felt this sort of awareness for a woman since…hell, he'd only felt this punch-to-the-gut sort of awareness about *one woman.*

The woman he'd lost a long time ago.

"Good morning, Mr. DiLeo." Tess approached the table, all smooth moves and sultry Texas twang. "Please excuse the costume. AutoCarTex Foundation is sponsoring today's caravan. I'm headed there right after I meet with you."

He managed to pull his thoughts together in time to stand and slide out the chair for her. "Anthony, please. I appreciate you making the time to talk to me."

He appreciated another chance to get close. It had been so long since his body had shot into overdrive that he barely recognized the feeling.

Slipping into the chair, she sat down and eyed the table filled with his presentation gear. "I'll admit to being as curious as Penny about your business."

There was a breathless quality about her voice that had a similar effect on him. Chemistry. He'd been so caught up in his own yesterday that he hadn't been sure it worked both ways.

Today he was sure.

Motioning to the table between them, he said, "I

brought everything to show you but, first, can I get you coffee? Or something to eat? You worked through break-fast this morning."

"Yes, I did." She shot a glance at a glass case display-ing high-calorie goodies and a tiny frown creased her brows.

"How about something to hold you over until lunch later?"

Anthony might not have belonged to any car enthusi-ast organization before this one, but he learned fast. When he hadn't been able to fall back asleep, he'd taken Timmy from Montgomery's advice and studied the itinerary. Now he was armed with enough information to know the cara-van event would parade a long route through the city be-fore arriving at a park for lunch. It would be hours yet before Tess's next meal.

She nodded. "Okay, thanks. A beignet and café au lait."

"Got it."

He headed toward the counter to place the order, pleased she'd taken him up on his suggestion. Now he'd have her undivided attention for at least as long as it took to eat.

He would play his hand straight with Tess. He'd pre-pared for months and wasn't about to let chemistry detour him from his course. He'd already learned the life lesson about letting his hormones rule his actions, and he'd learned it the hard way.

When Anthony returned to the table, he set the cup and plate in front of her and got straight to business. He had one shot to impress this woman with his business pro-posal, and spinning his laptop toward her, he maneuvered through windows to begin his PowerPoint presentation.

It was just a flashy overview of his business question,

but an impressive one, he thought. With photos taken in his own garage combined with stock photos of scenes from various AutoCarTex locations, he detailed facts about AutoCarTex's current service department situation and the numbers the company had reported for the past six quarters.

The situation in a nutshell: AutoCarTex sold used cars with service plans at affordable prices then maintained the cars to keep them running like new. Big Tex Hardaway's philosophy made reliable transportation available to the masses and his commitment to his customers had made AutoCarTex a houschold name.

The only flaw in Big Tex's smart business strategy was subcontracting his service centers, which made it hit-or-miss from dealership to dealership. The man's expertise clearly served him with sales and customer satisfaction, not in car maintenance.

That's where Anthony DiLeo Automotive came in.

He watched Tess sip her coffee as his proposed program—AutoTexCare—flashed across the screen. She looked politely interested but neutral as his presentation outlined what the plan would cover and how Anthony would standardize service in all AutoCarTex locations.

He could turn them into authorized service facilities and assets to the corporation—light-years stronger than the program currently in effect.

When the last slide concluded, he opened the folder. "I've brought along the numbers that support my projections."

Tess darted her tongue out to lick powdered sugar from her lips, and her gaze drifted to the spreadsheets. "Auto-TexCare, Anthony? You said you did your research. The

AutoCarTex Foundation handles public relations for my father's corporation, not automotive service. Why are you presenting your idea to me?"

"I've taken the conventional route through corporate channels," he said. "I haven't been able to get my proposal on the right desks. Your father's management staff doesn't seem interested in any ideas except those generated in-house."

Anthony knew that for a fact after spending five months being shuffled from desk to desk only to be told "Thanks but no thanks" in a form letter.

"I see. So Daddy's staff isn't interested in your idea."

"Afraid not."

"But you don't think he should subcontract his service work."

"I don't." Anthony slid the spreadsheet toward her for a better look. "It's all here in black and white. Subcontracting is the reason for these disparities in his year-to-date numbers. Of course I only had access to public record, but it's still easy to see that his service departments operate like wild cards, and he's using certain dealerships to carry others.

"It's ineffective. Your father breaks even on service, but give him a year or two when service dips into the red in too many locations, and his service plan becomes a liability. He'll be forced to divert profits from sales to balance the difference. Or to reconsider his service plan."

"But that plan is what makes AutoCarTex unique."

He nodded. As an industry insider, she knew the ups and downs of the car business and made his job easier with her knowledge. "With AutoTexCare, your father can standardize service and bring it consistently into the black. Like you said, his plan makes AutoCarTex unique. Reliable service should be a given in all his locations."

Tess toyed idly with her napkin and considered him for a moment. "Don't you think my daddy's staff is aware of all this?"

Anthony ignored the way she glanced up from beneath her lashes with those sultry green eyes and forced a diplomatic reply. "They're approaching the problem like corporate managers, not people who understand automotive service."

"They *are* corporate managers. And if that's a problem then whose desk do you think is the one to put your proposal on?"

"Your father's."

She inhaled deeply, visibly withdrawing into full professional mode, and while he didn't understand why she'd shut him down, he knew she had. "Well, I'm impressed with your research. You've obviously put a great deal of thought and effort into your proposal."

He'd worked on this proposal for six months before ever making the first overture toward AutoCarTex Corporate. His AutoTexCare plan represented his next career step.

And while gratified that Tess appreciated his effort, he'd also received enough polite dismissals to recognize another one coming. He cut her off at the pass. "I know coming to you is unconventional, but I've taken the normal route without success. Your public relations work for the AutoCarTex Foundation and your connection to Big Tex made you my best chance of success."

"You think you know what AutoCarTex needs better than the people Daddy pays?" Her Texas twang grew sharp around the edges. Her expression flared with challenge. Her green eyes gleamed.

"In this instance, yes. If your father would only take a look at my proposal, he'd agree."

She twirled a fingertip around the rim of her cup, drawing his gaze to the manicured pink tip no matter how hard he tried to stick to business. "You're very confident, Anthony. What makes you so sure Daddy will see your way on this?"

"Your father's employees might be capable corporate managers, but they don't have experience in running an automotive business. Your father does, and so do I. His expertise is in sales, mine's in service."

He'd plunked the situation squarely in her lap, forcing her to make a choice.

To help or not to help, that was the question.

One she wasn't sure how to answer. Her mood mirrored the sudden silence that became almost alive between them, an odd mixture of awareness and challenge.

"Wouldn't it just be simpler to sell franchises for your service center?" she finally asked. "Your name won't be in lights if you redesign Daddy's service departments. All your work will fall under the AutoCarTex umbrella."

"Seeing my name in lights isn't the point," he said, seizing the opportunity to prove he was focused strictly on business. "Reliable service is. My AutoTexCare plan offers that."

"Well, I certainly understand why Daddy's managers are having a problem with your proposal."

"Why's that?"

A smile tugged at the corners of her mouth. His question had clearly amused her, and something about that pricked his pride, made him feel as if *he'd* amused her.

"In order to implement your AutoTexCare plan, Daddy would have to create a new department to handle service. You're bypassing the corporate ladder, don't you think?"

"I'm qualified for the job. I have a degree in business."

"Perhaps, but the people on my daddy's team have climbed the rungs to their current positions in their careers."

"So have I. In my own corporation. I brought my company's prospectus along. You just have to take a look to see that I'm not bypassing anything. I've put in my time in the trenches. My experience servicing cars and running a business is what gives me the edge in pinpointing your father's needs."

"But why, Anthony? Why are you looking for a spot in my daddy's organization?"

"I believe in what he's doing." This was the *only* career move to spark his interest in a long time. "Your father is revolutionizing the automotive industry. I want to be a part."

"Revolutionizing, hmm? Interesting word choice. Are you looking for a thrill here?"

Ouch.

Damned if she didn't nail him on the story of his life. And after yesterday's race, he could have asked Tess Hardaway the same question. But the fact that she decided whether or not he was worth a recommendation made him keep his opinion to himself. He would be professional if it killed him. And when his gaze drifted to the red-and-green stripes stretching across her full breasts, Anthony knew it just might.

"My track record speaks for itself," he said instead. In business, and his personal life, which might explain the incredible awareness of this woman, everything from the way a tiny frown rode between her brows to the way she shifted slightly to hook her ankles beneath the table.

Why he felt *challenged* to convince her that his plan was worthy of a recommendation to her father.

"If you don't mind my asking, what's concerning you? You're a businesswoman. If you didn't see some potential in my proposal, you'd have already told me to take a hike."

"Do you have any idea how often I'm asked for introductions to my daddy?"

Ah, now they were getting somewhere.

"My idea is worth an introduction. If your father doesn't agree, I'm gone. No harm no foul. He stands to benefit, *a lot.*"

"So you say." Glancing at the spreadsheets between them, she left him to admire the silky black lashes that formed starbursts on her cheeks. "Not everyone is worth an introduction to my daddy. Ever since he started starring in the television promotional campaign, we've had all sorts of…*people* trying to contact him. Not all of them good."

He couldn't miss the subtext in that statement. "I'm not a stalker, Ms. Hardaway. Take a look at my credentials. I'm just a businessman who's out of options."

The tips of her mouth tucked up again, and she was fighting a smile, *amused* by him again. "I'll have to think about it, Anthony. That's the best I can do."

"It's not a no. And that means I have a chance to convince you I'm worth an introduction."

That challenge flared in those green depths again, unmistakable, but she effectively ended the conversation by glancing at her watch. "I'm not entirely sure what I'm setting myself up for, but I'm afraid I don't have any more time to discuss it. I've got to get to the lineup to talk with the police about any last-minute changes to the caravan route."

"I'll head over with you, if you don't mind." He quickly shoveled papers inside the folder and powered down his laptop.

"You're registered? I don't recall your name on the list."

Shoving his laptop inside the case, he tossed the spreadsheets on top. "I registered this morning."

"If you're driving in a Christmas in July caravan, don't you think you should dress the part? And your car, too."

"The paint's red. Does that count?"

"Hmm." Her mouth pursed in a contemplative moue. "I might have something that'll work."

"I'd appreciate it." Gathering up his things, Anthony followed her out of the coffee shop.

The Gremlin was a bizarre-looking car on a good day— he would have never called a lady's car ugly—but decorated with red-and-green garland and ropes of twinkling lights pushed it past bizarre into something downright alien.

And despite his decision not to let chemistry interfere with his plans for this woman, he found his resolve under attack every time she disappeared into the hatch, treating him to prime shots of her bottom in those striped shortshorts.

Anthony's pulse rate spiked accordingly, and he marveled at the speed and strength of his reaction. There'd only been one woman who'd ever possessed the ability to throw him onto red alert like this, one woman who'd dared him to reach beyond himself and strive to accomplish his goals.

And that had been so long ago he'd thought his ability to feel this sort of awareness dead and gone. Figured that it would crop back up exactly when it shouldn't.

"Here we go," Tess said. "Green garland to go with

your red paint. I used up all my lights, but I have this for the driver."

Draping green garland over her shoulder, she emerged from the car with a pair of brown felt antlers decorated with golden jingle bells. With a flip of a tiny switch, she showed him the best feature—blinking lights.

"You expect me to wear that." Not a question.

Leaning up on tiptoe, she dragged him from professional to personal in one liquid move. Suddenly she was so close he could smell her hair, fresh with an underlying hint of something sultry like vanilla or almond. Close enough to realize that the top of her head did indeed brush his chin. She slipped the antlers onto his head then stepped back to survey her handiwork.

He didn't need a mirror. Her facial contortions reflected his appearance better than a mirror could.

She was trying not to laugh.

"This is a character test, isn't it?"

Plucking the box from his arms, she deposited it back in her trunk. "We'll see how serious you are about impressing me."

"I can handle whatever you dish out, Ms. Hardaway."

She glanced back over her shoulder, a silky dark brow arched in question. "You're that sure?"

"Yes." The word came out sounding impressive, but inside Anthony didn't feel sure at all.

He didn't know how much longer he'd be able to resist slipping his arms around her, pulling her close and kissing that daring smile from her face.

3

TESS FROWNED INTO her rearview mirror at the man driving the parade route behind her. Anthony DiLeo maneuvered through the French Quarter streets keeping easy pace at this butt-numbing speed. The green garland streamers they'd wrapped around his car shimmered. He'd added a pair of stylish sunglasses to his costume, but even with a car length between them, she couldn't miss his antlered silhouette through the windshield.

So Anthony wanted to prove himself enough to let her dress him up like the Christmas goose?

That much determination said a lot about what he would do to gain her support for his cause, but this shouldn't come as a surprise. Been here, done this all before.

With one important difference—Anthony hadn't tried to put anything over on her.

He'd pursued her openly, stated his goal and how he intended to win her support. He hadn't finessed his way into her graces or manipulated an introduction. He'd been straightforward.

What wasn't so straightforward was her reaction to the man. Since the TV commercials had turned her smiling daddy into everyone's best friend, the rats had started crawling out of the woodwork with alarming frequency.

She'd met her fair share of men who wanted something from her, so this disappointment she was feeling didn't exactly make sense.

Why did she even care about Anthony DiLeo? Because he'd sparked life signs in her vacationing libido?

Maybe. Maybe not.

Mulling the question, Tess smiled at the police officer who'd blocked yet another intersection with his patrol car before she wheeled into the city park. She followed the parking attendants to rows reserved for the parade drivers.

Relieved for the chance to stretch, she parked and got out, waving to the crowd that had gathered along the sidelines to see the classic autos. She picked out Penny instantly, dressed smartly in a red-and-green pants suit that was bright enough to do justice to a Christmas in July event.

In her periphery, she saw Anthony emerge from his car and resisted the impulse to wait for him to catch up. She headed toward Penny instead. "I hope you don't melt in that getup. Didn't anyone tell you New Orleans gets hot in July?"

Penny smoothed the collar of her blouse, a poinsettia print number that complemented her slacks. "I represent AutoCarTex Corporate. I have to dress the part."

"And I don't?"

"You're the owner's daughter. You can get away with looking like one of Santa's elves."

"Good for me. I don't know how you stand there with this sun and not sweat."

"Good genes." She issued a low whistle. "And guess who's coming up the rear. The meeting go okay?"

Tess had only a chance to nod before Anthony appeared

behind her, his tall, broad self sucking up all the summery air with his maleness. Then came the blinding smile—clearly meant for her—and the responding flip-flop deep in her stomach that proved she was aware of him on a cellular level.

"Great antlers," Penny said.

"Christmas New Orleans style."

Tess wasn't sure what reindeer had to do with New Orleans, but before she had a chance to comment, her assistant showed up, looking frayed around the edges in his red-and-green attempt to dress for success and still fit in with the picnic crowd.

"Crisis, Hal?"

"The Children's Hope League representative is giving a statement to the press. I thought you'd want to be there."

"I do. If you'll both excuse me."

She followed Hal, not unhappy to give Anthony the slip. Somehow their arrival together had lent the situation a proprietary feel, which was completely irrational.

Tess didn't know why her suddenly reawakened hormones were going haywire now, but she wouldn't let them lead her around by the nose. Especially not with a man who hadn't expressed any interest in her beyond what she could do for him.

After allowing Hal to lead her into the crowd, she spent the next hour playing meet and greet with VIPs from the various organizations who'd contributed to her caravan, a charity event to benefit the Children's Hope League.

She liked this organization. They solicited donations all through the year to grant wishes to children suffering from serious illnesses. As a result, today's event required a great

deal of schmoozing to get other convention sponsors to do-
nate as generously to the cause.

But despite the hard work, the heat growing steadily
more oppressive as the sun climbed in the sky and the fact
that her stomach grumbled louder every time someone
walked by with food, Tess surveyed the park with a great
sense of satisfaction.

She'd coerced the city of New Orleans into lending her
decorations from their annual French Quarter Christmas
Festival and had recreated the holiday in this park. A
twenty-feet-tall tree. Street lamps turned into candy canes
dripping with red-and-white garland. Huge plastic poinset-
tias bordered every walkway.

Even the carnival rides she'd rented reflected the holiday. The moon bounce was red. The giant sack slide was
white. The Tilt-A-Whirl blazed red-and-green lights. Santa
Clauses and elves milled through the crowds dispensing
candy canes, and she'd even hired local singers to spend
the day caroling.

In Tess's mind, no Christmas celebration would be
complete without gifts, so she'd solicited businesses to
load up the tree then invited the local chapter of Big Buddies to attend.

This program paired children with caring mentors, and
now big and little buddies milled around, enjoying music,
food and fun while awaiting the gift giveaway at the end
of the day.

With all the activity and the endless rounds of introductions to keep her busy, Tess couldn't help but notice how
Anthony never seemed far from sight. Perhaps it was his
height and the blinking antlers, but she picked him out of
the crowd no matter where she was. She noticed him giv-

ing people a tour of his Firebird then saw him in line at a beverage booth.

Perhaps some sort of hormonal radar had kicked in but when she saw him chatting with the Big Buddies' representative, Tess finally accepted that she simply couldn't ignore the man.

Especially when he stood laughing with a dark-haired woman as if they were two old friends. Tess wondered if they knew each other, *hoped* they did, or he had just lost points for picking up a date during a company function. The man might not be a part of AutoCarTex, but that's exactly what he'd proposed, so she'd hold him to the standard.

Breaking away from a group of conventioneers from Seattle, Tess headed toward the food tent. She needed a meal before her crankiness leaked out all over folks she wanted to impress.

"Not so fast, gorgeous," a male voice called out.

Tess winced at the familiar voice but managed to school her expression by the time she'd turned around to greet the approaching man. "Hello, Daryl. Having a good time today?"

"You look like the perfect Christmas present." He'd dressed in black jeans and a muscle shirt that made him look as bad as his matching Corvette.

"Did you enjoy the tour through town?"

"I would have if I could have seen you around the souped-up Firebird that took my slot."

Tess didn't point out that his vantage was a direct result of his low-riding car. "That was my fault. I insisted on dressing up that Firebird for the parade, so we ran late. The police had to slide us in after the lineup."

"Who's the driver? I saw you talking with him at the speedway yesterday."

"A local business owner."

"Dealer?"

"Service."

A satisfied expression replaced Daryl's frown, and had Tess been a betting woman, she'd have wagered big money that he'd just dismissed Anthony DiLeo as beneath his notice.

"So, Tess, are we on for the rally? We'll have a good time in my 'vette."

"I appreciate the invite, but I told you, Penny flew in specifically to ride with me for the event."

"The rally is supposed to be fun. Not work. Wouldn't you rather make the trip with me?"

No. The upcoming rally was a competitive run over public roads under ordinary traffic rules. For four days, the drivers would head west, stopping at prearranged checkpoints. The thought of being trapped inside the Corvette's tiny interior with Daryl Keene nearly cost her the appetite currently gnawing its way toward her spine.

"I'm sure it would be fun, but—"

"Don't rule it out yet. We've still got a few days. Who knows what will happen. Hal told me Penny had trouble getting away from the office. He said everyone's been working hard on the launch of your new locations."

Hal would never have passed out that information unless Daryl had pressed him, and she suppressed a wave of irritation that this man seemed determined to strong-arm her into a date. "Penny has been working hard. She'll enjoy a break."

He ignored her and peered around her hat, his gaze narrowing. "I haven't heard word one about where we're headed."

"The committee's hush-hush. You know that. Only the car club president has final approval, so no one should know our destination until the start of the race."

"Yeah, but something usually leaks out. I don't think that's all bad, either. It builds the suspense."

Before Tess could reply, she discovered exactly what— or *who* in this case—had put the scowl on Daryl's face.

Anthony DiLeo—carrying a tray of food.

"I brought you something to eat." Extending a hand to Daryl, he introduced himself.

"Daryl Keene."

"The black Corvette."

Daryl only nodded, apparently not needing to ask what Anthony drove after riding the Firebird's bumper through town. Who could miss those antlers?

"Tess said you owned a garage," Daryl said, and the way he said it made it sound like a disease.

"Anthony DiLeo Automotive. New Orleans. You're with Keene Motors out of Tulsa?"

"I'm Keene Motors."

The crown prince of the empire. And while Tess had to admit dealerships in major cities spanning three states made the Keene empire an impressive one, she thought Daryl sounded as though he had something to prove.

Maybe he did. To her mind, Anthony DiLeo's easy pride shone a lot brighter by comparison.

"Well, Keene Motors," Anthony said. "Hate to interrupt, but Tess has been on the run all day. She needs to eat."

That caught *her* off guard. She wasn't sure whether his statement—as if it was any of his business when she ate— or hearing her name in that whiskey-rich voice surprised her most. He made a simple, one-syllable name sound personal.

Too personal, apparently. Testosterone surged between these men so fast she expected it to knock them backward. Had Tess not been so surprised, she might have assumed control quicker, or laughed. Something about these two squaring off in the middle of a park reminded her of bullies sparring during school recess.

Dressed in black, Daryl looked like Billy Badass. And while Anthony DiLeo might look like one of Santa's finest, even the antlers couldn't hide the rugged street-savvy male beneath the casual expression. The man had too much unleashed tension simmering below the surface, visible in an attitude that said, "Want to push? Go on. Try me."

Despite the biceps, Daryl was all polished manners and private schools. The prince of his daddy's domain, defending his turf because he'd decided she was a potential princess.

The kicker—neither of these men was interested in *her*, only in what she could do for *them*. She might not have figured out what Daryl wanted yet, but from the depths of her soul, she knew he wanted more than to get inside her jeans.

Plucking a small tart from a plate, Tess popped it into her mouth. The flaky pastry melted around some heavenly spicy filling. She swallowed and heaved a sigh. "Thanks so much, Anthony. I am starved. So if you gents will excuse me…" She reached for the tray, but Anthony clung to it with a death grip.

"Lead the way." He inclined his blinking antlers toward the picnic table area, making his bells jingle wildly. Then he said to Daryl, "If you'll excuse *us*."

Daryl's scowl said everything—the crown prince didn't like being dismissed by a local garage owner.

"Gentlemen, the only thing I'm interested in right now is food. So if you'll excuse *me*."

Tess wouldn't touch this situation with her daddy's cattle prod. She didn't want to spend time with either man right now, and didn't have to. Not when there was a whole tent nearby filled with food… She didn't wait around to find out what Anthony would do but let her nose lead her away.

The tasty meat pie did nothing but jump-start her appetite, and she groaned when she saw the line leading to the buffet. She debated whether her VIP status would justify a cut to the front when a familiar voice said, "No sense waiting in that line when I've got all this here."

That whiskey voice ruffled through her like a warm breeze, and she spun around to find Anthony, holding up the tray as a peace offering. "Sorry I chased off your friend."

His grin suggested he wasn't sorry at all. Neither was she, for that matter, but she wouldn't tell him.

"You didn't make Daryl *your* friend." She slid onto an empty bench at a nearby picnic table.

"Probably a good thing I didn't come to this convention to make friends."

He'd come to pitch his AutoTexCare plan. She'd gotten that part loud and clear.

Setting down the tray, Anthony sat across from her. Tess ignored him, spread a napkin across her lap and dug in.

"This beats the hell out of hot dogs," he said. "Did you choose the Réveillon feast?"

She nodded, her mouth too occupied with a bite of chicken and oyster gumbo to answer. Divine.

He occupied himself arranging plates then slid the tray out of reach, clearing her path to all the tasty dishes. Looked as if he'd brought her a few bites of everything, and she gave Anthony DiLeo a few points back for thoughtfulness and practicality.

"The restaurant I used to cater suggested the menu," she told him. "Supposedly this is New Orleans's Christmas feast."

"You did good for an out-of-towner. This restaurant actually does justice to the menu."

She resisted another bite and swirled the spoon around the bowl. "Since we're on the subject, what exactly is a Réveillon feast? I was never clear on the point. I think I insulted the restaurant manager when I told him to fax the menu to avoid a blow-by-blow account of how the chef prepared each dish."

Anthony laughed, a rich sound that managed to drag her attention from the gumbo. She could feel his knees pressed close beneath the table. Knew that if he stretched out a hand, their fingers would meet right beside the cake plate.

He was just so…*male.* The thoroughly unnoticeable act of sitting suddenly became noticeable, and her chest constricted enough so breathing required conscious effort.

"Le Réveillon is the awakening," he explained in a smooth-a-hand-over-velvet voice. "It's what families do after midnight mass on Christmas Eve."

"And the chefs around here take their feasts seriously."

"*Chère,* this is New Orleans." He drawled the name into one long word that sounded like N'awlins.

She couldn't help but smile. "I might have heard somewhere that people around here take their food seriously."

"*Very* seriously." He grabbed one of the two bottled

waters and twisted the lid before explaining how Louisiana Cajuns and Creoles inherited the custom from their European ancestors.

His story ended when the representative of the local Big Buddies' chapter showed up.

Anthony made space for her on his bench. "Tess, do you—"

"We've met," she said.

Courtney Gerard shifted a crystal-gray gaze her way. "I know I already thanked you for inviting our chapter to your event, Tess, but let me say it again. This day is turning out to be really great. Every one of the Big Buddies I talked to has told me how much the kids are enjoying themselves. Not only the rides, but they love the cars."

"I'm glad."

Tess shouldn't want to know how these two were acquainted. For all she knew, Anthony serviced Courtney's car. But there was something personal in their body language—this wasn't the first time they'd sat close. "So how do you two know each other?"

"Courtney is my…" He hesitated, frowning down at the beautiful woman. "What exactly are you?"

"I'm like a sister-in-law." She sounded offended he'd even asked. "I don't have a drop of Italian in me, Tess. But once you've been adopted by the DiLeo family, you're family for life. Today I'm Anthony's character reference."

"She's going to tell you how wonderful I am."

Courtney slung her arm around his neck. "This man is *beyond* wonderful. Locals call him Mr. Noble-enough-to-be-a-saint. Kids and dogs follow him wherever he goes. Need I say more?"

Anthony gleamed smug approval, and Tess sank her

spoon back into the bowl. In his fitted jeans and mesh tank that hinted at the golden hairs sprinkling the sculpted chest below, about the last thing to come to mind about this man was sainthood.

But steamy, sweaty sex definitely made the list.

4

THE PICNIC WOUND DOWN late in the day, and Anthony found himself back in the parking lot to show off his car. He'd just said goodbye to a couple from Kenner when he spotted Keene Motors, bypassing his Corvette and heading straight for him.

"Damn," Anthony muttered.

"Why are you getting in my way with Tess?"

As this jerk had been popping up around her all day, Anthony could have asked the same thing. But he refused to get sucked into a pissing contest and shot for diplomacy instead. "She and I have business to discuss."

"Didn't look like business, DiLeo. Looked like lunch."

Anthony circled his car, fitted the key in the trunk lock and tried to look casual. "How does this concern you?"

"I'm interested in her."

"Is she interested in you?"

"We're getting to know each other," he said. "I plan to continue. Take the hint."

That sounded like more of an order than a hint. It turned out to be a winning combination with the guy's attitude, which screamed Anthony should be the one to step aside.

"You dating her?" he asked flatly.

A hard scowl answered that question.

"Then there's no reason why I can't get to know her, too."

"Except that she's out of your league, DiLeo. *Way* out."

Anthony had zero patience for this argument. He might have decided to keep things professional with Tess, but he was just cranky enough about that decision to go head-to-head with this overindulged rich boy. "Maybe that'll work in my favor. Tess doesn't seem too impressed by your league."

The lady herself cut off further reply when she strolled toward them with a group of people. Big Buddies, Anthony guessed, by the mixed ages.

Because of the caravan lineup, she'd parked her Gremlin in the spot beside his, and he had to bite back a smile when Keene Motors scowled even harder. Tess inclined her head in polite greeting as she passed, then entertained her audience with facts about her unique car.

Anthony watched her, and a rush of awareness sucker punched him. She moved around her car with fluid strides, all sleek motion and liquid grace.

He couldn't help but stare when she leaned over to open her door. Those holiday short-shorts left miles of long leg bare. Stylish platform sandals showed off polished red toenails.

It was no wonder he'd had a dream about this woman last night. Sexy babes showcasing high-ticket cars during the months of the year was tradition with car enthusiasts—much like *Sports Illustrated* and their annual swimsuit issue. He'd grown up with those sexy calendars gracing the garage wall, and he'd spent more than his fair share of time sneaking peeks at his favorites whenever his dad and older brothers weren't around.

Tess was the real deal, and while he intended to keep things on the up-and-up with her, he was on fire inside. He hadn't been this attracted to a woman since he'd had his one shot at true love and blown it.

And he'd blown it with Harley big.

It might have taken time, but he'd finally accepted that he wouldn't get a second shot at that kind of love again. No man could be so lucky. He'd had everything in his life, and in his bed, but had been too wrapped up in career ambitions and the thrill of the chase to make it his. As a result, a special woman had gotten away.

He had no one but himself to blame for getting to watch Harley live a head-over-heels love with someone else while he blew through one quick-to-burn, just-as-quick-to-burn-out relationship after another. And with each passing year, even the satisfaction of his career and thrill of the chase wore thinner.

Until now.

He found the idea of chasing Tess a thrill in the extreme. She was hands-down gorgeous, and the combination of her fast answers and Texas twang made his gut clench like a fist.

Unfortunately, he was a day late and a dollar short.

With approximately twenty-four hours before this convention ended, he barely had enough time to prove he was worthy of an introduction to her father, let alone a date after they concluded their business.

And then there was a significant logistical problem. Louisiana and Texas might share a border, but he couldn't easily show up on her doorstep in Lubbock with an invite for dinner.

Before he had the chance to consider that, Anthony

found himself jerked from his thoughts by the sight of a familiar face in the crowd. He didn't know this man personally, but after a lifetime spent around cars, he couldn't have missed him.

Number 7. The Maverick.

Everyone even remotely interested in racing, and likely many who weren't, had heard of Ray Macy, a racing legend. Anthony had more than a passing interest and had seen the Maverick race numerous times on New Orleans's very speedway. A big cowboy wearing hand-tooled boots and a flashy silver belt buckle, he was as large in person as he was on TV.

Anthony watched with growing amazement as he cut a path through the cars straight toward them.

Tess was just saying goodbye to her group and glanced up with a look of pleased surprise. "Hey, hey, Uncle Ray."

"Hello, sweet thing." The Maverick scooped her into his arms for a hug.

Anthony claimed to have done his homework, but he'd obviously fallen short on the job. He'd had no clue Ray Macy was Tess's uncle. Suddenly her skill on the racetrack made sense.

He wasn't about to let this opportunity pass, so when Ray Macy let his niece go, Anthony moved toward them and extended his hand. "Anthony DiLeo, sir. Pleased to meet you."

The man shook with a firm grip, looking unsure why he should be interested.

"Anthony is the owner of a local service center, Uncle Ray. We've been discussing service in this market."

This wasn't exactly the truth, but it was enough of a connection to Tess and AutoCarTex to spark Ray Macy's interest.

"Pleased to meet you, Anthony. We're putting a lot of emphasis on our expansion into Louisiana."

"I didn't realize you were affiliated with AutoCarTex."

"Technically, he's not," Tess explained. "He's Daddy's right-hand man."

"And sweet thing's, too." Ray shot her a fond smile.

Which would explain why Anthony hadn't come across the man's name during his research.

"So what are you doing here, Uncle Ray?"

"I've come to swap places with Penny."

One glimpse at Tess and Anthony knew this wasn't news she wanted to hear.

Obviously Uncle Ray recognized the same thing because he held up his hands and said, "Now before you start bucking, let me tell you that I already promised your daddy."

"There's no need for this." She sounded exasperated. "If Penny has to head back to Lubbock, fine. I'll drive the rally on my own. I never invited her in the first place."

"Your daddy wants to sleep at night."

Anthony grasped an idea of what was happening here. Tess had said she was scheduled to drive in the rally tomorrow and it looked as if her driving buddy had a sudden change of plans.

He didn't understand why Tess's father wouldn't sleep at night if she drove alone but couldn't think of a way to ask without sounding as though he was butting into family business.

"I disagree." Keene Motors strolled toward them. "Hey, Ray. Good to see you again. My father mentioned something about threatening letters. He said Big Tex is worried about Tess."

Judging by her narrowing gaze, this wasn't anything Tess wanted to hear, either. "Daddy's gotten letters before."

"What letters?" Anthony seized his opportunity.

Tess waved a dismissive hand. "With the TV promotional campaign, Daddy gets lots of viewer mail. Not all of it good."

"He's gotten some correspondence lately that has him worried," Ray Macy said, "Rightfully so, in my opinion. Especially after the one that arrived yesterday."

"My father told me these letters mention family members." Keene Motors looked appropriately concerned for the occasion, but Anthony couldn't shake the feeling that he was pleased with himself for having inside information.

"What did this one say?" Tess asked, looking worried.

"This one took your daddy down for the TV ads. Said he should stop trying to be everybody's friend and pay more attention to his daughter." Ray Macy slipped his arm around her and gave a fond squeeze. "Now you see why he doesn't want you on the road alone, sweet thing?"

"I do understand, but I thought you were putting your new car in the Phoenix 1000. You said you were pressed getting her ready. You can't take time to drive the rally with me."

"Of course I can. Anything for my favorite niece."

"I'm your only niece."

"If you don't want to rally with your uncle, Tess, my offer still stands," Keene Motors said. "Drive with me."

Did Keene Motors really think he could bully Tess? He might be *getting to know* her, but he obviously didn't know enough yet. Anthony had only been around a few days, but he already understood that this woman did not like to be pushed.

Uncle Ray didn't say a word. Neither did Anthony. He held his breath instead, waiting to see which way Tess went.

"I appreciate the offer, Daryl," she said. "But I'm thinking it might be smarter to use the time to work."

Keene Motors looked irritated. "You'll back out *now?*"

"I said *work.*" She narrowed her gaze. "Anthony and I are in the middle of discussing some business. He offered to drive the rally with me, but I turned him down because Penny was here."

Anthony saw right through her attempt to use him to sidestep this situation, and since Tess had just given him the mother of all chances to impress her, he'd damn sure make good.

"Obviously I understood that Tess had previous plans," he said. "So I offered to make a trip to Lubbock. But driving the rally together would give us the time we need to cover all our business a lot sooner—"

"And save you the trouble of the drive, Uncle Ray."

"What business?" Keene Motors demanded, drawing all their surprised gazes.

"Business between Anthony and me," Tess said coolly.

Keene Motors shot Ray a disbelieving look. "I don't like this one bit, Ray. We don't know a damn thing about this guy."

Silence fell as hard as the humidity in a New Orleans summer. Keene Motors' comment hit home, and Anthony could see the effect. Ray Macy grew worried. Tess and Keene Motors looked outraged, although likely for different reasons.

"I appreciate your concern, Daryl," Tess said with effort. "But I don't need a babysitter. And I really don't need you telling me how to do my job."

"If it's any help—" Anthony addressed Ray Macy, hoping to smooth through the tense moment "—Tess has been working with my sister-in-law for this convention. My older brother is a lieutenant with the NOPD, and I'm a well-established business owner in this town. You have my word I'll keep her safe."

Ray Macy still looked dubious, and Tess must have realized that, because she sidled close enough to raise a question about whether their business might be mixed with pleasure.

Linking her arm through his, she gazed up at him, her green eyes sparkling with challenge. "Anthony's trustworthy, Uncle Ray, and he's been dying for a ride in my Gremlin."

ANTHONY DILEO switched gears so fast that even Tess was impressed. He didn't blink when she dragged him into the fray, and smoothly assumed control of the situation.

"I can't say I've been *dying* for a ride in her car," he told Uncle Ray, "but I am looking forward to it."

"How long have you known my niece?"

Uh-oh. "Do you want Anthony to sign something in blood to take back to Daddy?"

"You're all chuckles today, sweet thing." In a lightning-fast move, he had his Stetson off his head and on hers, flipping the brim down so she couldn't see. "I don't need blood, but your new friend here has to be clear that if anything happens to you, he'll be answering to me."

"I understand, sir," Anthony said, very respectfully. "My intentions toward your niece are honorable."

Tess flipped the hat from her head and shot him a look. *Honorable?* She'd see how *honorable* he'd still be when

they were alone. She had a hankering to pull out that rebellious ponytail and see what that tawny hair looked like
after she'd run her fingers through it.

"I'll keep my cell phone on, so you can check in with
me whenever you feel the need, Uncle Ray. Tell Daddy."

"You tell him yourself."

She should have known she'd get no help on this. Not
with the way Daryl had gotten his hackles up about Anthony.

"I'll give you my cell number just in case." Anthony
whipped his wallet from a back pocket and withdrew a
business card before wandering off to his car for a pen.

He jotted down a few numbers, and she watched Uncle
Ray put on his imposing look, a surprisingly grim face for
a normally good-natured man.

Anthony handed him the card. "My service center number is on the front and my home and cell numbers are on
the back. I also wrote down my brother Nic's number at
the police station. Call anytime. The duty sergeant can always get through to him. And this—" he pointed to the bottom of the card "—is my mother's number. Call her
anytime, too. She's someone else I'll be answering to if I
don't take good care of your niece."

Tess burst out laughing, and Uncle Ray's frown melted
in a look that suggested he appreciated not only the numbers but the humor. Good for Anthony.

Daryl looked incredulous. "You're going to check this
guy out, Ray, aren't you?"

Not that it was any of his business, Tess thought, folding her arms across her chest. "You're kidding, right?"

"The rally doesn't start until tomorrow," Uncle Ray
said. "I'll have your daddy run the drill."

"The drill?" Anthony asked.

"The drill." She rolled her eyes. "If a guy smiles and says hello, Daddy has his security chief run a background check."

"By the way, sweet thing, I'll be bunking with you tonight. There's not a room to be had at the Chase."

The way Uncle Ray was eyeing Anthony, he probably wanted to make sure she didn't get too close to the man before he saw the results of that background check.

She had plans for Anthony DiLeo all right, but they'd wait until they were on the road and well away from her babysitters.

"So, is everyone finally satisfied with my plans for the rally?" she asked, earning a curious glance from Anthony who clearly hadn't missed her sarcasm.

"Good to see you again, Ray." Daryl extended his hand then stalked off with barely a nod.

He ignored Anthony completely.

Withdrawing her hotel key card from the convention badge she wore around her neck, she handed it to her uncle. "I won't be leaving here for a while yet, so you can get settled in."

"Trying to get rid of me?"

She leaned up on tiptoe and kissed his cheek. "Yes."

He laughed. "What's on the agenda tonight?"

Tess invited him to join her for the awards banquet, and he agreed to come—so he wouldn't miss a chance to interrogate Anthony, no doubt. She saw him off to the hotel, and when she returned to her car, she found Anthony waiting.

"Am I a convenient escape from your overprotective family?"

"Would it bother you if you were?"

"A little."

"Yet you're willing to come anyway. Even if it means driving in my Gremlin." She eyed him curiously. "So you're willing to get involved with me to get your introduction?"

"No, Tess, I'm not." His gaze flashed golden fire. "I won't try to manipulate you. That's not how I operate."

"Glad to hear it." Not that she thought he *could* manipulate her. She'd cut her teeth on men who were a lot less noble and straightforward than this one.

"Then, Anthony, the answer to your question is yes and no. Yes, I used you to sidestep my babysitters and, no, that wasn't the only reason. I'd like to spend some time alone with you."

That fire in his eyes flared hotter now, not indignation but desire, a look that made the bottom of her stomach swoop wildly like a ride on the back of a bucking bronco.

But she sobered up quick enough when she caught Daryl watching them from his car. She didn't like the look on his face one bit. Anthony hadn't made him a friend, and now she'd publicly rejected him on top of it.

Then again, who was Daryl to use her uncle's concern to strong-arm her into driving the rally together? She'd been polite, but clear she wasn't interested. Just as she'd been polite but clear when rebuffing every one of his advances.

The man refused to let her off the hook. Still, in hindsight, she shouldn't have let her irritation get the better of her. There were much more effective ways to handle someone like Daryl. Flaunting another man in his face wasn't one.

"Here's the deal," she said, eager to cut to the chase. "How about four days on the open road. You, me. No babysitters. No strings. Just some fun. What do you say?"

He didn't answer right away. Tess knew he wanted her—she hadn't misread those signals—but something was holding him back, and that surprised her.

"What is it?"

He reached up and suddenly his thumb glanced the length of her jaw, a whisper-soft touch of calloused skin that galvanized her to the spot. It took a moment to realize he'd only brushed away a strand of hair.

"I was hell-bent on staying professional." A soft smile touched his lips, lips that were just perfect for kissing. "I didn't want to get business tangled up with personal."

"Oh, well." She flipped her hair back haughtily and spun on her heels. "If your introduction to my daddy is more important than having fun with me then your loss."

He snagged his arm around her waist, stopping her short so suddenly she let out a gasp.

"That's not what I said, Tess." He steadied her against him, his face pressed close to hers. "I'm willing to give up my business with your father for a chance to know you."

His words got lost somewhere in her hair, a promise that filtered through her like a warm caress.

Well, that was more along the lines of what she'd been looking for. "Lucky for you, business and pleasure aren't mutually exclusive. Why don't we agree to keep them separate? It'll be a nice break from reality, don't you think?"

"Providing my background check meets with approval."

Tess laughed. "There is that, of course."

But she knew by the heat in his eyes that they were going to have a good time on the open road and *honorable* would only play a small part.

5

HAD IT ONLY BEEN a few days since he'd arrived in the hotel looking for a lady named Tess? In his wildest dreams, Anthony couldn't have imagined what he'd find.

The lady in question had dressed for comfortable driving in a yellow T-shirt and shorts that hinted at all her inviting curves. Her sleek legs drew his gaze down to the strappy slide-ons that left her toes bare.

"You, me. No babysitters. No strings. Just some fun. What do you say?"

Anthony said he wouldn't have missed this trip for anything. He wanted more time with Tess—not only to prove he was worth that introduction to her father, but so he could figure out exactly what was happening between them.

Whatever it was, it felt good.

He watched her maneuver through the Sunday-morning traffic, which would have been light but for the jam of classic cars now crowding I-10's lanes. Thirty-seven rally contestants had left the hotel to fanfare from the conventioneers, and the excitement continued well beyond the speedway.

He extended his arm out the open window and waved yet again when a motorist honked and raced to keep up with them. "Is this going to happen all the way to San Francisco?"

"It won't be so bad once we get underway and the drivers head off on their own routes. Right now we look like a parade."

They were surrounded on all sides by mint-condition classics, ranging from those with their original parts to ones like Tess's that had been souped up into impressive-looking hot rods. "Damn straight."

She smiled, the morning sun washing her profile in light. She looked excited to be on the road, even a little breathless.

He leaned back in the seat, contented by a physical awareness he hadn't felt in so long he'd forgotten the feeling. "Explain to me how this parade is supposed to be a race. I missed that part at the send-off this morning."

The car club had sponsored a farewell breakfast where the rally contestants received their travel instructions in a ceremony that combined sealed envelopes and a video presentation to rival the Academy Awards.

"It's more of a symbolic race," she said. "We don't put our foot to the floor and make a straight run. We drive our own routes, stopping at checkpoints every night."

"With our checkpoints in Dallas, Santa Fe and Las Vegas it won't be hard to come up with alternate highways."

"That's the point. It's no fun if everyone travels the same roads. We all pick what we think will be the most interesting route and bring in a souvenir when we pit stop at night."

"So whoever makes the checkpoint first each night wins?"

She shook her head, sending glossy waves tumbling around her shoulders in a sexy spill that made him think of what she'd look like wearing nothing but that hair and a smile. "We compare rankings, but there are no winners in the conventional sense. Except for the Women's Cancer League, of course. Earning money for them is the whole point. Whoever ranks first on the final day will have the privilege of presenting the check to the Cancer League representative."

Anthony still didn't get the *race* part, but he wasn't about to complain.

"Trust me, Anthony. You're in for a treat," she said. "The rally committee does something special at each checkpoint to pamper us after a long day on the road. We'll get a good bit of promotion for our businesses, too. But most importantly, we just want to have a good time."

She seemed so focused on having fun that he could only guess that she'd been as bored with life as he'd been lately. Not so surprising given the protective people in her life.

"Y'know, Tess, I told you I'd done my research, but I had no idea you were related to Ray Macy. I suppose I should have figured something was up with the way you drive."

"I'll take that as a compliment."

"It is."

"There's no reason you should have known about Uncle Ray. He's not technically with AutoCarTex, even if he does do more work for Daddy than the VIPs."

"He's your mother's brother?"

She nodded, shifting her gaze up to the rearview mirror for a quick peek. "Her older and *only* brother."

"I can't speak to the only part, but as an older brother, I can understand why he'd be so protective of his niece."

She grimaced. "When he's not worrying about me, he's worrying about my daddy."

"When does he find the time? He races hard. I follow his career."

"Daddy and I are his only family. He never married, so he takes his wonderful nurturing soul and points it our way. He promised my mom before she died that he'd look after us the same way he looked after her. He's never stopped."

"When did you lose your mom?"

She smiled softly. "A long time ago. I was ten."

"Accident?"

"Cancer."

"That's rough."

She only inclined her head, but knowing Big Tex had reared his only daughter with his brother-in-law's help fitted another piece into the puzzle about this woman.

"I lost my father when I was eight," he said, sharing the sense of loss that years didn't diminish. "A massive heart attack. It happened so fast I always wished we'd had a warning, some more time before he died."

"I'm sorry for you and your family. There were some good things about knowing my mom was dying. We got to blow off the rest of life and make the most of the time we had left together. We said things we might not have said if we hadn't known we wouldn't get another chance." Tess shook her head, a tiny gesture that convinced Anthony no matter how much time had passed, some memories still hurt. "But she got so sick. It would have been easier on her if she'd gone quicker."

"Losing a parent sucks no matter what."

"Yeah." The conversation faded off into a thoughtful silence, broken only by the steady hum of the engine and the miles rolling under their tires.

"Are you sorry you brought the subject up?" she asked.

"Just sorry I made you sad."

"Memories are a part of who I am." She shifted her gaze off the road and gave him a smile. "I assume that's what this is all about. You want to know about me."

"I do." He fingered a soft brown curl that trailed along the back of the seat. "Don't you want to know about me?"

"It'll be a long couple of days if we don't talk."

"That's the truth."

She didn't seem to mind the intimacy of him touching her hair, so he thumbed the sleek texture, liked the connection between them, no matter how small.

"So your father never remarried?"

"Nope. What about your mom?"

"Nope. She just works a lot and dotes on all of us."

"Sounds exactly like my daddy. He's got AutoCarTex, and he's got me. Toss Uncle Ray into the mix, and I've got two doting men with nothing better to do than mother-hen me."

"I hear a *to death* in there." He tugged the curl just enough so she could feel it, smiled when he noticed the color rise in her cheeks.

"You got that right."

And he did. The tiny frown riding between her brows told him this gorgeous woman risked drowning in good intentions. And while Anthony's pride might have stung that she'd used him to sidestep a babysitter on this trip, he wouldn't have missed this chance to explore this chemistry happening between them.

"I'm glad your father and uncle were satisfied with their background check," he said. "We'll have fun this week."

"I'm counting on it." Shifting her gaze off the road, she glanced over the rims of her stylish sunglasses in a sultry look that made his blood throb hard, and Anthony recognized what he saw in her face.

She was chafing against the restraints of her life.

He knew because Tess wasn't the first woman he'd known to feel this way. There was another woman near and dear to his heart who'd felt smothered beneath the love and concern of her five older brothers.

His baby sister, Frankie.

She'd needed to spread her wings so much that she'd taken off from New Orleans without a backward glance. Except for Christmas and birthday gifts to their mother, not a one of the DiLeo family had heard from her since the day she'd left town.

There was no missing those symptoms in Tess, and Anthony decided right then and there that he wasn't going to make that mistake with her. He met her gaze with a smile and thought…*Tess Hardaway, get ready for the ride of your life.*

TESS SHOULD HAVE BEEN exhausted after a long day on the road. She wouldn't have traded her Gremlin for the world, but even she admitted the ride left a lot to be desired. Late model cars took the miles with smooth aerodynamics, not to mention important amenities like body-hugging seats.

Still, excitement started her pulse speeding as Anthony maneuvered her car through the outskirts of Dallas. Her mood had nothing to do with physical exhaustion and everything to do with physical awareness. A day spent in close quarters with this laughing, handsome man had definitely taken its toll.

And her libido needed no herbal supplements, thanks.

Things hadn't been so bad when she'd been behind the wheel, but sitting in the passenger's seat with nothing to do but notice things about him proved sheer torture.

Mile after mile of that fast smile and deep-throated laugh. Broad, broad shoulders that took up more space than his due. Long fingers poised easily on her steering wheel. That nubby ponytail teasing the headrest of the driver's seat.

Although Tess guessed he'd rather drive than *be* driven, she hadn't had to fight for equal time. They'd made the trip north through Louisiana at a decent clip, stopping every few hours to walk and switch places, making up for those stops by opting for a drive-through lunch.

They'd discussed everything from family to careers, and he'd entertained her with stories from his service center—a huge establishment with employees that sounded like the comedians from *Whose Line Is It Anyway?*

She'd told him about her office inside AutoCarTex Corporate. Not nearly as slapstick as Anthony DiLeo Automotive, perhaps, but she was proud of her work in public relations, liked supporting Daddy's business by spreading around his goodwill.

Not once did Tess feel as if she was getting the third degree. She was, of course, but he'd been so easy to talk to she'd almost forgotten.

They'd even had their first argument about what souvenir from their trip to bring to the checkpoint. But Anthony had managed to be witty and charming, and when he wheeled into the parking lot of the Grand Vista Hotel, she felt a crazy mixture of regret to see the day end and excitement for the night ahead.

"We made it." Slipping the car into gear, he paused with his hand over the ignition. "I know you want to gas up tonight so we can start fresh in the morning, but do you mind if we wait until after check-in? I want to look under the hood to see how she's burning oil."

"Do you think there's a problem?"

"No, this long haul is probably the best thing in the world for her engine, but these old gals need extra special care. I want to get a read on how she's running, and I can't do that until she cools off."

Made sense to Tess. "The sooner we check in the better. Just bring our souvenir. We won't need our luggage yet."

Anthony grimaced, reminding her exactly what he thought about their souvenir—*she'd* won that argument. But he didn't say a word while getting out. "I'll get your door."

Tess reached for her purse and waited as he circled the car, amused by the gesture when she could have been halfway across the parking lot already. But she knew he wanted to impress her. So far he hadn't missed a trick.

The rally committee had set up a banquet room as a pit stop for the contestants, with food and refreshments and a map to chart the day's miles. They bypassed the hotel's front desk and followed signs through the lobby to a marquis that read Rambling Rally Pit Stop.

Anthony sidled around her and grabbed this door, too, and they stepped inside a room that had been decorated with a flashy racetrack theme. Pennants hung from the ceilings bearing names of popular racers. She caught sight of her uncle's and smiled. A buffet and a beverage bar had been set up, and the servers wore coveralls that made them look like part of a pit crew.

"Wow," Anthony said at her side.

"Gotta love this car club. When they host an event, they host it right."

"They? *You.* You're a board member."

"But I'm not on the rally committee." Tess gazed up at him, struck by the sight of him from this vantage point. She'd gotten used to seeing him in profile with his stylish sunglasses shielding those potent dark eyes.

Now he gazed down at her with an amused expression, and she was treated to the full force of his smile—the flash of white teeth, the creases around his mouth that made one smile spread across his whole face.

He was new enough in her life that she wasn't familiar with his striking looks yet. Definitely hadn't grown accustomed to this crazy flutter whenever she glanced his way and found herself surprised by how handsome he was, by her reaction to the chemistry between them.

She had to consciously draw another breath, so she didn't get dizzy.

"Just getting in now, Tess?" a familiar voice asked, stealing away the moment and jerking her back to reality. "Decided to work instead of compete?"

She and Anthony turned in unison to find Daryl sitting at a nearby table with a blonde. Since they'd just walked through the door and were still carrying a souvenir bag, she thought the answer should have been obvious.

"Good drive today?" she asked politely.

"Never better." Daryl shot his companion a cheesy smile

that made her giggle. "Glad you made it safe. But keep my cell number handy in case something comes up. I'd hate to think of you stranded on the open road."

"Daryl—"

"Appreciate the concern." Anthony cut her off. "You don't need to worry about Tess. She's in good hands."

The innuendo in *that* statement wiped the smile from Daryl's face fast, but Anthony didn't give him a chance to reply before leading her to the check-in table.

"Hello, pretty lady." Ralph, the round-cheeked cochair of the rally committee, stood and leaned across the table to kiss her. "Good run today?"

She nodded. "Where are we?"

"Twelfth in the lineup."

"Twelfth? Ugh."

"That's not too shabby, Tess. Twenty-five contestants still haven't made it in yet." Anthony grabbed the clipboard and signed his name before handing it to her.

"True, true," Ralph agreed. "The first day always starts a little slow. You know that."

"True, true." And she was surprised to realize that she protested more out of habit than anything else. She'd enjoyed the ride today, and her companion.

Anthony introduced himself and asked, "So what's next? Souvenirs?"

He held up the bag containing the book of folklore from Melrose Plantation, a Louisiana property whose history revolved around two liberated-before-their-time women. He'd wanted a model of a 1913 steam locomotive, complete with coal car and caboose, from the DeQuincy Railroad Museum. She'd insisted and, after a valiant fight, he'd given in.

To impress her, no doubt.

"Over there." Ralph pointed to a table setup where the few odd packages sat. "But, Tess, before you go, we've got to talk."

"What's up?"

"The hotel messed up the room block."

"You're kidding?"

"It's not tragic, but it isn't good. We're shuffling all the rally committee members around. Tripling up so we can give our rooms to our contestants. We were wondering if you'd stay with Margaret and Janie. Your friend can stay in my room."

Now that wasn't at all what she'd had in mind for her first night on the road with Anthony. And one look at him assured her a slumber party wasn't on his mind, either. "Why don't we just get rooms in the overflow hotel?"

Ralph shook his head and did the closest thing to a scowl that Tess could imagine on a jolly-cheeked man. "No good. The political convention is in town this week along with those makeup ladies who wear the pink jackets. Did you know there are so many of them that their annual conference runs for four weeks? I had *nine* on my plane from New Orleans this morning."

Now it was her turn to frown. "This is Dallas, Ralph. There have got to be rooms somewhere."

"Let me know if you find them. We've been making calls all day. Five would wrap things up nicely."

As a car club board member, Tess couldn't exactly refuse to give up her room while the rest of the committee did. And even if they could find a room elsewhere, she'd look like a problem child by not cooperating, which would reflect poorly on AutoCarTex.

She shot an appealing glance at Anthony, who only nodded. "No problem, Ralph. We'll do our bit for the cause."

"Thanks, Tess. Now go mark today's route on the map. And make sure you eat." He cast a longing glance at the plate piled high at his elbow. "At least they got the barbecue right."

Tess managed a smile. "I won't ask who picked the menu."

"Not impressed, hmm?" Anthony asked as he led her across the room to the map.

"I'm from Lubbock, remember? You sure you're okay with our change of plans?"

"We'll make do. Besides, we've still got some time before we have to hit the sack."

"Are you being *honorable?*"

"Trying."

She chuckled.

"Should I be surprised they assigned us purple?" Anthony asked dryly when they reached the map.

"My car is legend wherever I go."

Reaching for a nearby basket, he began picking out tiny purple pushpins. "Here you go. Start marking."

Tess traced their route off I-10 and noticed that so far they'd been the only ones to travel these roads through Louisiana. "We'll have to look at the maps before splitting up tonight. We have to declare tomorrow's route with the rally committee before we leave in the morning."

"The rally committee knows our route but the other drivers don't, is that it?"

"Right. Liability issue. The committee needs to know which way we're headed in case we have a problem. At night we mark our routes to see how we matched up against everyone else." She frowned at the purple pushpins dotting the map. "We didn't do so hot today. I thought you said this would be the best route off the main highway."

"Depends on your interpretation of *best*. You said you wanted the most interesting, not the quickest."

She huffed. "I've never had such a poor showing, even on the first day of a rally."

Anthony dropped another few pushpins into her palm. "Got more than your fair share of the Maverick's competitive blood, hmm? What was all that you said about getting off the highway to see the countryside and have fun?"

"It's fun to compete even if we can't win. After the way you beat me at the speedway, I shouldn't need to explain that."

"You want to have fun, see the sights and rank number one, too. So you basically want everything."

"Is that really so much for a girl to ask?"

"Not with me, it's not." He shot her a totally roguish look, and Tess laughed, drawing the attention of several folks around them. Including Daryl, who narrowed his gaze.

"You are such a bad influence."

"Me, *chère?*" That roguish grin faded into a look of pure innocence. "What makes you say that?"

"Oh, please. Let's get out of here."

"No barbecue? Don't tell me you're not hungry." Now it was Anthony shooting the longing look at Ralph's buffet.

"I don't want to eat here."

She didn't have to say another word. Anthony led her out of the room and even went so far as to get directions to a Chinese place within walking distance. It wasn't long until they were back at the hotel, strolling a path around a lake, discussing tomorrow's route and munching from a meal in cardboard boxes.

"You seem awfully familiar with takeout," she said.

"I'm a healthy boy, and since I don't live at home…"

"Actually, I'm very impressed." She speared her chopsticks into her chow mein. "This was a great idea. I was dreading the thought of getting back into the car again."

"Just stick with me, and you can have it all."

She chuckled, and the sound faded in the twilight as they walked along, enjoying their meal in the golden spill of light from the lamps that marked the path and the black lake.

There was nothing like the Texas sky at sunset. The sky was bigger, the colors sharper and when darkness finally fell, it fell with a weight that seemed to cloak the whole world.

"So what's bugging you about Keene Motors?" Anthony asked.

Tess swallowed hastily and glanced at him in surprise. "Where did that come from?"

"You were willing to get back in the car just to get away from him. I didn't for a minute believe it was the barbecue. You're from Lubbock, remember?"

"Okay, it wasn't the barbecue," she admitted.

"Jealous?"

That made her laugh. "Hardly. Appreciative is more like it. That blonde seemed pretty caught up in him. I'm hoping this means he's found someone new to stalk."

"Harsh."

"Maybe, but he really had no right to be rude to you. We never dated, and I certainly never strung him along."

"He was trying to make himself feel better at my expense."

"That didn't bother you?"

He grimaced. "Of course it bothered me. But I'm all about what's going to impress you, which left me to choose between demonstrating my awesome self-restraint or letting Keene Motors drag me into a pissing contest."

"Point taken."

Loud and clear. A reminder of the reason Anthony wanted to impress her should have been enough to knock the edge off this feeling that they were the only two people on the planet.

It didn't. She was so aware of him, from his long-legged strides to the fingers maneuvering chopsticks in his carton. "I suppose I shouldn't be surprised after the way I handled him. I should have demonstrated as much self-restraint."

"Listen, Tess, I don't know what's been happening between you two before this convention, but I will say I'm not impressed with what I've seen. He should have backed off when you turned down his invitation to drive the rally. Using your uncle to try and get his way wasn't right."

"I only challenged him, and he was challenged enough."

Anthony stabbed his chopsticks inside his carton. He wrapped an arm around Tess's shoulder, a gesture that smacked more of reassurance than it did intimacy. But the instant her body came up against his, every nerve felt as though it suddenly ignited.

He possessed the kind of wiry strength that came from more than just working out. He lived a physically active life and she found his strength very appealing.

"Don't worry, *chère*. Keene Motors wasn't going to

like anyone who came near you. And while you might have made him unhappy, you made me *very* happy."

"You're making fun of me."

"I'd never make fun of you. If Keene Motors doesn't want to get burned, he shouldn't play with matches."

"Meaning I'm combustible?"

He squeezed her playfully. "Meaning the idiot shouldn't try to bully anyone unless he's willing to deal with the consequences. If the guy's been refusing to take *no* for an answer, you were within your rights to put him in his place. And witnesses never hurt. Especially when they're men who'll jump all over a chance to defend you."

She laughed, unable to help herself. No matter what Anthony said, Tess could have handled the situation with Daryl better, but he was very gallant to make excuses for her. And his excuses did make her feel better.

His nearness, too. He kept his arm around her as they walked back to the hotel, a sweet gesture that made her smile into the darkness. Penny was right—she hadn't been making enough time to have fun lately. One day of laughter drove home just how long it had been since she'd felt like laughing.

But between Daddy's letters and Daryl's hot pursuit, it was no wonder Tess had taken refuge in work. Yet now she had Anthony. For a few days at least. While she regretted that they'd lose tonight, she made the most of the moment by ogling his tight butt when he headed under her hood to check her fluids. Then she went a step further by snuggling close to him when he carried her garment bag upstairs to her room.

Tess's roommates were already there. Margaret and Janie were both nearing retirement age and owned different models of classic Mustangs, but that was where their similarities ended. Margaret was a grandmother who'd decided the garden club just wasn't her speed while Janie, who'd never married, had enjoyed the jet-setting life of a wealthy eccentric.

A car club event didn't go by without her sharing some story about a former lover from somewhere around the globe. This time it had been Ernst, who'd been of imperial Hapsburg descent and who had sequestered her inside an Austrian hotel room and made her miss an entire month-long tour of the Alps.

Janie watched Anthony appreciatively as he crossed the room to hang the garment bag in the closet, and Tess had to bite back a smile when he turned around, looking oblivious to the little old lady who was eyeing him as though he was a before-bed mint.

His gaze didn't miss the bed, though, and Tess's smile faded fast. Since deciding to proposition this man, she had to share her sleeping arrangements with Uncle Ray and now this duo of white-haired hot mamas. Things weren't going along anything like the way she'd intended.

But she did appreciate Anthony's ability to go with the flow. No doubt Daryl would have seen that bed as the land of opportunity and not gone down without a fight. Not Anthony, who just rolled with the punches, which had made things so much easier on everyone.

Leaning back against her door, Tess adopted a nicely casual pose, tipping her head back just enough to make her hair slither behind her shoulders. A kissing-perfect pose.

"Thanks, Anthony." She dropped her voice a throaty octave.

"My pleasure, Tess."

He pulled up in front of her, so close she could feel the heat radiating off his big body. He gazed down into her face, his expression just as warm, and the breath locked tight in her chest as she forgot everything but the sight of this oh-so-handsome man staring down at her with such longing in his eyes.

The moment was powerful. Even with Margaret and Janie watching. Awareness was all over him, a physical thing, and Tess stood there, lips parted, wanting a kiss more than she could ever remember wanting a kiss before.

For the space of a heartbeat, she saw arousal flare in his eyes then he lowered his face to hers and brushed that kissing mouth across her lips, the prelude to a real kiss, a promise.

"Sleep well, Tess, ladies." Then he disappeared into the hallway, and she stared after him, exhaling a sigh that made Margaret and Janie laugh.

6

ANTHONY YAWNED, unable to stop himself.

"You don't look like you slept much last night," Tess said. "Want me to pull over for coffee at the next Starbucks?"

"I spent the night imagining what you looked like in bed," he admitted.

She only laughed, and somehow it seemed preordained that he wouldn't get much sleep around her. Had it not been for her roommates, he'd never have been able to stop with one polite kiss. Not with his head filled with the memory of his sexy dream and the taste of her sweet lips. Not with his body honed to a fine edge after a day of driving together in close quarters. Not when he'd just walked through the starry Texas night with his arm wrapped around her, feeling as if she belonged tucked up against him, all warm and soft and sexy.

So he'd taken a cold shower then lain awake all night, thinking about Tess in the next room, imagining her stripping off the shorts outfit that had started the day so fresh and feminine and had ended no less attractive for the wrinkles.

He imagined her in the shower with her creamy skin all sleek and soapy beneath running water and scented lather.

He imagined what she would feel like naked against him, spread out under the covers, her long legs twined through his.

"Coffee isn't a bad idea," he said. "I need to get my blood flowing."

"Really?"

That statement dripped with innuendo, and before he had a clue what she was about, she'd swung the steering wheel a hard right. Gravel kicked up under the tires in a fierce complaint as she rode along the shoulder.

"Tess, what the hell—"

He cut off short as the car jerked to a stop and he grabbed the dash to brace himself. Dirt billowed up around the windows as she slammed the car into Park hard enough to make the steering column rattle.

"Kiss me, Anthony. Just kiss me."

He didn't get a chance to reply before she reached out, slipped her fingers into his hair and pulled him toward her.

Anthony had known from the second he'd met Tess that if he let go, he'd never be able to stop kissing her.

He let go.

His mouth came down on hers hard, and she made a small sound as her lips parted, all yielding softness and insistent need. The moment ground to a stop, and the world outside of the Gremlin fell away as if it never existed. The whiz of cars speeding past faded into the distance.

All Anthony could hear was their breaths colliding in greedy appreciation. He hadn't been the only one aching. He tasted Tess's impatience, an erotic mingling of sense and touch as her tongue swept boldly inside his mouth, another challenge, and every nerve ending in his body gathered in reply, so sharply in tune with this woman that he grabbed her to hang on.

His hands threaded around her neck, her soft skin yielding as she let him pull her deeper into their kiss. He inhaled the sultry vanilla-almond scent of her hair, tasted the coffee still lingering in her sweet mouth.

His body felt as if it had been honed in on a special frequency, and he could only think about the way she tasted, the way her skin felt beneath his fingers, the way her mouth demanded a response. And got one.

His whole body ached with a slow, potent burn. He wanted to drag her into his lap and wrap himself around her, test this sensation everywhere his naked skin could touch her naked skin.

But she was trapped behind the wheel, straining toward him, and he could only use his hands to explore, only make love to her mouth, only marvel at how she made love to his mouth back.

And it wasn't until a shrill horn screeched as a car sped past that they finally sprang apart.

A minute later or a day, Anthony couldn't say. He could only stare at the sight she made with her chocolate hair ruffled around her face, her cheeks flushed and green eyes alive with pleasure, and amusement.

"Blood flowing yet?"

He shook his head to clear it. "Damn."

She laughed, a silvery, satisfied sound, and he could only stare across the distance, at those kiss-swollen lips. "I knew I'd like kissing you."

And right then Anthony knew a need for this woman that transcended the physical ache pulling at every part of him, making him fight the urge to drag her back into his arms and lose himself inside this incredible heat they made together.

"I wanted to kiss you like that last night," she said.

God, what was it about hearing this woman admit she wanted him that struck a blow that almost felt physical?

Unable to resist, he reached up, dragged his thumb along her cheek. "Just wait until tonight, Tess. Just wait."

Threading his fingers along her jaw, he tilted her face up for another kiss to tide them over.

"WHAT DO YOU MEAN leave? Now?" Tess asked Anthony when he handed her the clipboard. "But we just got to Santa Fe."

"Let's check in with Ralph and then get out of here."

All her weariness from a long day on the road slipped away. Her muscles had been screaming with restlessness, but she suddenly forgot the spasms and twinges, forgot *everything* but the look on his handsome face.

His bedroom eyes swept over her, an intimate glance that reminded her of the way his mouth had felt on hers when they'd kissed, of the way she'd sighed and impatiently pressed against him. She'd wanted to feel her breasts against his chest.

"Where are we going?"

He tapped the clipboard, motioning for her to sign in, and said, "That's a surprise."

Tess backed away from the check-in table, out of earshot of Ralph, who was munching his way through a plate piled high with burritos and chicos while eavesdropping on every word they said. "Does this have something to do with spending half the day poring over the rally rule book?"

"I was looking for something."

"What?"

He shook his head, a slow smile drawing her gaze to his mouth and filling her head with the memory of what those lips felt like on hers. "If I tell you, I'll give away my surprise. How about you end the interrogation and trust me?"

She'd known he was up to something when he'd read the rule book cover to cover while she'd driven from Dallas to Wichita Falls. Well, she'd said she wanted to make the most of their time together... And there was something about him, something so confidently *male*, that assured her she was going to like his surprises. A little zip of anticipation shot through her, and she signed her name in an illegible scrawl.

"You rank first today, Tess. That should make you happy," Ralph informed her around a mouthful of burrito. "We've got no room problems and some serious New Mexican dishes, so eat up. The locals who catered the buffet cooked enough for an army."

"Thanks," she said absently.

She'd guessed they'd come in with decent standings as the food trays were full, the banquet room empty and it was still early yet. But she didn't get a chance to say anything else when Anthony slipped his hand around her waist and whisked her toward the buffet.

"Make a plate for the road." He grabbed two foam travel boxes provided for the eat-and-runners. She scanned the table of steaming goodies. Plates stacked with tortillas made from multicolored corn. Tureens filled with *calabacitos* and *frijoles refritos* and red chile sauce. Not to mention every garnish from cheese and olives to fresh veggies.

She ladled some colorful bean soup into a cup then

popped a few extra *chile rellenos* into Anthony's box. "Mind if I put these in yours? I don't want to take a box for just a couple."

He cast a sidelong glance at her cup then did a double take. "That's all you're taking? You haven't eaten since lunch."

"I haven't moved since breakfast. This is fine."

He frowned.

"What?"

"We won't have a chance to grab anything later."

She could have argued that a quick trip in the elevator and a few quarters would have made a meal in the hotel's vending machine in the middle of the night, but as she still didn't know what he had planned... "Is this an Italian thing, Anthony?"

"What?"

"Your obsession with what I eat?"

"Obsession? That's harsh..." His voice trailed off as his gaze riveted straight to the mouth in question. "All right. I admit I do think about what you put in your mouth."

Tess just rolled her eyes. "I thought we agreed I didn't need any more mother hens in my life."

"Food is different, *chère,*" he drawled. "It's important for you to keep up your strength."

"I haven't seen any reason why yet."

"You will," he whispered close to her ear. "Trust me."

That warm burst of lazy sound shimmered through her and started up the whole craziness inside again, the liquid heat that hadn't quite disappeared since their kiss hours earlier.

His open mouth brushed her ear, and to support his belief, she shivered, one of those full-bodied numbers that there was no way he could have missed.

He gave a throaty chuckle.

She waved goodbye to Ralph as they left the pit stop. "So where to now?"

"The car."

Tess came to a stop in the hallway and closed her eyes. "Oh, please tell me your surprise doesn't involve driving."

"'Fraid so. Can't be helped."

"I can't, Anthony. I just can't. I appreciate what you're doing here, but I'm going to crawl out of my skin if I have to sit in that car again tonight."

She opened her eyes to find him staring down at her, brow arched dispassionately, holding his food box one-handed like a seasoned waiter. "You said you'd trust me."

"But that was before I knew you wanted to get back in the car. I've got to swim or hit the treadmill, something...*anything* to move my muscles before they atrophy—"

"If you don't like road trips, why do you rally?"

That stopped her in midwhine, and she scowled at him. "I do like road trips. I just need to move."

"Then trust me. The sooner you get in the car, the sooner you'll get out."

"Oh, all right." She gave a huff then took off toward the front lobby and the exit without waiting for him.

When they reached the car, Anthony motioned her to the passenger's side.

"Why don't you let me drive, so you can eat?" she asked.

He popped the box lid to reveal a stack of neatly rolled burritos. "I made mine to go."

She laughed. "I'm impressed. You've really got take-out meals under control."

He slipped behind the wheel then drove out of the parking lot. Tess opened his box and spread a napkin over his lap while he merged with the highway traffic and headed north.

"Thanks." Grabbing a burrito, he skillfully brought it to his mouth without taking his eyes from the road.

"Totally under control," she repeated then sipped her dinner.

They drove in companionable silence for a while, and Tess finally put the lid on the remainder of her soup and fitted it into the cup holder on the utility tray. Anthony made quick work of his burritos, and she finally packed them up, too, watching curiously as he exited off the highway and headed down a one-lane road that looked as if it led to no place she wanted to go.

"Not even a hint?" she asked. "You're driving us into the sticks as if you've been here before."

"I have been here before, but only once. I still need some light to see the road signs."

"Which would explain why you were driving like a maniac today—to outrace the sunset?"

"It would."

She wasn't going to argue, or stress, either. They'd ranked first, after all. And Tess had grown up around cars—between her daddy's background in sales and Uncle Ray—she felt comfortable with the way Anthony handled himself on the road.

The sun set above the firs and juniper pines. Tess thought Texas had the biggest and best piece of sky anywhere she'd ever been, but way up high on New Mexico's plateau, she found this slice of sunset a breathtaking splash of colors.

"So when were you here before?"

"A few years back I took up road trips as a hobby," he said thoughtfully. "Decided I needed to get out of town more often. Long weekends and that sort of thing."

"Cool. So with whom do you take these long weekend trips?" The question was out of her mouth before Tess could consider how he might interpret it. She guessed it didn't really matter, though. She was interested in his love life, and couldn't see any sense pretending she wasn't.

He shifted his gaze off the road and eyed her searchingly. "I took this one with my brother."

"Oh. What's your brother's name?"

"Vinny." Anthony laughed. "He'd kill me if he knew I told a pretty girl his name was Vinny. Nowadays he goes by *Vince*. He has an image to maintain since he's doing his residency."

"Probably doesn't want to sound too young."

Anthony was obviously very fond of this brother, and she didn't think that should surprise her. The Anthony she'd seen during this past week might have been all swagger and cool business, but when she remembered how quickly he'd pointed Uncle Ray in his family's direction for credibility, she guessed they must be close.

"Well, I know you have an older brother in the police department, a younger brother who's a doctor, and a mother who reared you to behave like a gentleman around ladies. Anyone else in the family?"

"Two older brothers, two younger brothers and a baby sister."

"Whoa! *Six* DiLeos." She added a little mock horror for emphasis. "Your poor widowed mother. She had her hands full."

"Oh, yeah, but you'd have never known it. She kept us all in line. She might only be five feet tall, but she's tough."

"Is that an Italian thing, too?"

"Oh, yeah. No one messes with Mama. Marc tried once. " He gave another laugh. "And while she was cooking. The idiot."

"What happened?"

"She hurled a knife. Missed his ear by two inches."

"Bet that was the last time he messed with her."

He nodded. "You should hear him tell the story. Mama just says it was one of her defining moments as a parent. She needed to set an example for her boys. Without my father around, she knew if one challenged her authority, we all would. She's actually pretty funny about it. Especially when she launches into the part about how it doesn't matter how big we grow—she brought us into the world, she can take us back out."

An image of a tiny virago with blond hair and dark eyes and a knife sprang to mind, and she couldn't help but smile. "Sounds like a smart mother. And loving. Courtney sounded very okay with being adopted by your family."

"What's not to be okay with? You should taste my mama's cooking." He kissed his fingers with a juicy *mwah* sound. "She makes a red sauce that'll make you weep."

With a laugh, Tess sank back against the door to get a better look at him in the growing darkness. What was it about this man that felt so good? Here she'd placed him in a situation where most men would have shown their butts the first night, yet he'd entertained her and fretted over her and made her want him even more than she already did.

She was glad when he finally steered off the main road and pulled down the cutaway entrance of a wilderness preserve. A uniformed park ranger stepped out of the gatehouse.

Anthony exhaled heavily. "We made it."

"This is my surprise?" she asked, but didn't get an answer before Anthony rolled down the window to talk with the ranger.

While listening to their exchange, it didn't take long to piece together what was happening—Anthony had reserved spots on the wilderness preserve's popular "night walk," a silent, ranger-led hike through the dark ruins of Indian cliff houses and pueblo-style dwellings.

Tess knew a little about the area—not much, but enough to know the canyon was well over six thousand feet in elevation and the wilderness preserve encompassed a massive amount of northern New Mexico acreage. A hike through this trail would be the perfect way to loosen her muscles and work off restlessness.

And once Anthony pulled through the gate to park in the lighted lot in front of the visitor's center, she told him. He'd barely gotten the car into gear before she'd leaned across the seat and slipped her arms around his neck to kiss his cheek.

"This is a brilliant surprise."

Hiking through the darkness together, enjoying the activity, the clean high-elevation air, the peace and quiet of a starry night after two long days of sitting in the car. She couldn't think of anything better.

"This is only part of my surprise."

"What's the other part?"

"I checked the rule book. There's nothing that says we have to stay at the pit stop hotel."

She tipped her head back to meet his gaze. "I know. The hotel's just a convenience. Room block with a decent rate, and since we have to check in there anyway—"

"We'll spend the night out here in the campground."

The flood lamps outside spilled fractured light through the windshield to make his face a study of shadow and light. Yet still she could see the question in his gaze, knew that her reaction meant something.

"How did you arrange all this?"

"I made some calls when we stopped to pick up lunch."

"But we were together…" Then she remembered. "I thought you were in that bathroom a long time."

He grimaced.

"Are you still trying to impress me?" She scooted closer until she could—almost—press her chest against him.

Lowering his mouth to hers, he brushed his words against her lips like kisses. "I'm really going to impress you tonight."

Tess believed him.

7

OWNING A BUSINESS meant Anthony spent a good deal of time in his service center's office, but he'd never gotten out of the bays completely. He still worked on cars, mostly those of friends and family, not to mention keeping up his Firebird and the Harley-Davidson chopper he'd restored to mint condition over a decade ago. He preferred keeping physically active, so a hike through the ruins proved a perfect warm-up for the night ahead.

He and Tess had walked the trail with twenty other hikers then separated from the group at the visitor's center. Now they followed the ranger's Jeep to the campsite. Tess sat beside him as he drove, looking flushed and beautiful from the activity and curious about the night ahead.

"I haven't seen one campsite in this direction, Anthony. Isn't everything back on the other side of the visitor's center? That's where everyone else was headed."

"Nervous to be alone in the dark with me, *chère?*"

She rolled her eyes. "I've been *waiting* to get you alone in the dark."

Anthony liked how she'd formed her opinion of him then trusted her instincts even though they hadn't known each other long. She'd been on-target about Keene Motors, too, which told him Tess was a very good judge of character.

"There's another campsite on this part of the canyon, but a fire wiped out a portion of the forest a while back and some trails flooded from the rescue efforts. They've been rehabilitating the area."

"And they're letting us camp here? How'd you manage that?"

He chuckled. "It's not as impressive as it sounds, trust me. The rehab is basically over, so they'll be booking campers soon to catch what's left of the season. The other campsite is for conventional campers. Over here is where we yurt. I just talked the Preserve Director into letting us start things up early. We'll only be here for one night, and this is where Vinny and I stayed. I like the view."

"I'll bite. What's yurt?"

"You'll see soon."

She beamed a smile that made his blood start pumping warm and slow with awareness, made him glad he'd thought of this for what would be a first for them—a first night together. A night for seduction. He planned to make love to Tess out in this magnificent place.

When the ranger pulled to a stop and flashed his brights on a wooden sign that read: Piñon Campsite, Anthony pulled along beside him and turned off the ignition.

The ranger stepped out and shined his flashlight in the direction of the trees. "Your site's that way. Just follow the trail, and you can't miss it. It's the only yurt outfitted yet. There's a pit bathroom nearby."

"Great." He ignored the sight of Tess frowning in his periphery. "Tell Jay thanks again for letting me visit on such short notice."

"I'll tell him." The ranger extended his hand and they shook. "But you know Jay. He runs this place like summer camp. Having the yurts down all season has been killing him."

No doubt there. He and Vinny had camped here for a solid week, and during that time had shared some informative, and lively conversations with the preserve director. "Makes for happy return campers."

"Essential for continued funding." He touched the rim of his hat. "You folks have a good night. I left a radio, in case something comes up. This high up, the cell signals get sketchy."

"Thanks." Tess moved close as the ranger got into his Jeep and pulled out in a flash of red taillights. "Pit bathroom?"

"Okay, so it's more rustic than a normal campsite. How about I promise to make it up to you tomorrow night in Vegas?"

"Deal." The word came out on a little hitch of excitement, and Anthony found himself reaching up to touch her face, to trace the full curve of her lower lip.

Tipping her head back, she dragged her mouth against his thumb, a simple but intensely erotic move that made him eager to get to the seduction on the road. "Just bring my carry bag, please. I won't need anything but my toothbrush tonight."

Oh, yeah. He wouldn't even suggest a change of clothes for the trip tomorrow, didn't want the thought of clothes entering the picture now—not when he was picturing her without any.

Grabbing their carry bags, he led Tess into the forest with only the flashlight beam to slice along the dark trail. The wind rustled leaves and scuffles of wildlife broke the silence.

"If we hadn't just done that night walk, I might find this

place a little spooky," she whispered. "It feels like we're the only two people on the planet."

"That was the point, *chère.*"

She laughed, a silvery sound that made him smile, and then her eyes grew wide as the flashlight beam cut across the sizable dome that poised majestically overlooking the canyon.

"Oh, Anthony." She breathed his name on a whisper.

"A yurt." Dropping the bags, he touched their flashlight to direct the beam to the ground. "And look at this view. Worth a pit bathroom."

"It's perfect." She exhaled a long sigh—exactly the response he'd wanted. "I had no idea you were so romantic. You're usually all Mr. Macho Driver Man."

"Macho? Please. Romance is an Italian thing." Slipping his arms around her waist, he eased her close for a real kiss, one where he could finally feel her body pressed against him.

She melted into his arms with another soft sigh, fitting against him with almost magical precision. Her breasts molded his chest, her sleek curves pressed against all his right places, her long legs rested perfectly between his.

Grazing his hands along her back, he tested the supple lines of her spine, ran his palms along the curve of her waist. He wanted to discover Tess tonight, explore the way she made him feel, learn how to coax those little sighs from her lips.

To his pleasure, she arched backward and looped her arms around his neck. Her stomach cradled what was swiftly becoming an erection, and he pressed his mouth to hers, tasting the way sensation mingled a slow kiss with a rapid-fire surge of heat straight to his crotch.

Her sigh broke against his mouth. He slid his tongue inside, tangled it with hers. She snuggled against him, bombarding him with soft breasts against his chest, muscles gathering as her stomach rode his erection. She spread her legs just enough to keep her balance, and instinctively, he wedged his thigh between. The loose cotton shorts she wore left very little to the imagination. He could feel a warmth radiating outward, penetrating, promising.

Then she rode his thigh in one sleek stroke.

There was no missing the way she melted in his arms, no missing that she'd found a pleasure point. So he slipped his hand down to cup her bottom and helped her ride that next stroke, his erection surging almost painfully when she deepened their kiss and ground against him.

This woman was fire and he'd never guessed how much he'd thrill to the challenge of meeting her, dare for dare, of earning her interest and winning her trust and claiming her enthusiasm as the ultimate prize.

If he kissed her anymore right now, he'd lose it, and they'd be naked quicker than he could say, "Start your engines." And he wanted so much more for his first time with Tess. He couldn't keep running his hands over her body or get lost in the way she pressed against him in sexy invitation.

He needed to put on the brakes, so in a quick move, he scooped her into his arms.

She laughed against his mouth and hung on. Bending over, he held her tight so she could retrieve the flashlight and they stepped inside. She sliced the beam around to reveal a sparse interior and the most unique feature of a yurt—the acrylic skylight.

"All right, Jay." He scanned the air mattress covering enough of the floor to make a regular love nest, along with serviceable sheets, blankets and pillows.

"Wow," Tess said. "Much better than a night in a hotel. Especially after being cooped up inside a car for two days."

"My thoughts exactly." He rolled her out of his arms and onto the mattress, where she bounced with more silvery laughter. He flopped down beside her. "I was hoping a born and bred Texan would enjoy a night outdoors, since ya'll invented the concept of sleeping under the big sky."

"True, true. But I want to know who came up with this whole yurt thing. It's brilliant."

"If memory serves, Jay told us it was the Mongolians. Animal hides over wooden frames. Rustic and practical."

"Wow." She turned the flashlight off with a flick and cast their world into blackness. "No more light. I need my eyes to adjust. I've got some things I want to see in the dark."

"And what are they?" Anthony's night vision hadn't kicked in yet, but he didn't need sight. His body honed in on hers like a beacon. "The stars? The canyon? The trees?"

She flipped on top of him, and he pulled her into his arms, using touch to find his way, liking how the springy air mattress contoured to their bodies so they might have been wrapped around each other on a cloud.

"I want to see skin." Her body spread out against him, all sleek hollows and valleys of unfamiliar terrain he'd been dying to explore. "*Your* skin, Anthony. All of it."

Tess didn't ask permission but dragged her hands along his stomach until she found the hem of his shirt.

"Lean up," she urged, and Anthony propped himself up on his elbows, moving from side to side as she maneuvered the shirt over his head.

Her fingers glanced his skin and sparked fire in their wake. He tried to pull her back into his arms but she braced her hands on his chest and resisted.

"Not so fast. I'm not done looking yet."

"Your wish…" Hooking his hands behind his head, he stretched out. His night sight had adjusted enough so he could see her face and appreciate the pleasure he saw there.

And when she pushed herself up to straddle him, she made him thank whatever lucky star was shining on him that he'd pursued her. He didn't care whether his Auto-TexCare plan ever saw the light of day, not when Tess spread her legs over his erection and rode him a slow, hard stroke.

"This would be so perfect if we were naked." Her voice was an aching whisper in the darkness.

"That can be arranged."

She spread her thighs a little wider, pressing down on him in a sensual way that made him groan aloud. "All in good time."

She obviously wanted to play things her way, and as his crotch throbbed and his hands itched to grab her, Anthony would let her. He would try, at least. He couldn't promise anything as she dipped her fingers into the scoop between his neck and shoulders and massaged the muscles there, a firm motion that eased away tension and added to the languid way he felt.

Languid didn't last long.

Tess reared back and whipped her shirt over her head, taking her bra along with it. His heartbeat stalled in his chest as her pale breasts bounced free. Her nipples were smudges in the darkness, and the urge to reach out and cup their soft weight in his palms hit him hard. He wanted to drag those pouty nipples into his mouth, hear her moan in pleasure.

But Tess was the only one who moved.

She sank forward, a liquid motion that brought all that

smooth skin against his chest. He could feel the tips tighten as they traveled his skin, caught in his chest hairs, slow, tantalizing movements that nearly laid him low.

He groaned, unable to stop himself, fighting the urge to grab her, to press his crotch into her heat. She leaned a little closer, let her breasts swell against him, a soft fullness that brought skin against skin and made him clench his fingers together to resist touching her.

He buried his face in her hair instead, sucked in deep breaths of that sultry vanilla-almond mingled with the underlying scent of this woman who aroused him so completely.

She lifted up enough to skim her hands beneath her, threading her fingers through the hairs on his chest, tugging lightly as she went, evoking fire.

"I knew all this sexy gold hair would turn me on," she whispered.

He hadn't realized his mesh shirts, which were comfortable in the summer heat, were so see-through.

Or had Tess just been looking *that* closely?

Anthony didn't get a chance to enjoy the thought long because she chose that moment to slither her tongue inside his ear, and muscles all over his body contracted in response.

She gave a whispery laugh.

Against his ear, of course, which made all those muscles contract again.

"Oh, I like this, Anthony. We're fire together."

"Did you doubt it?" He sounded casual, in control, when he felt far from it.

"Not for a second. It's been forever since I've had any life signs. I thought something was wrong—until I met you."

That made him laugh, stoked some inner part of him that liked hearing how he'd done what no other man had lately. Especially Keene Motors.

Slipping his hands around her, he treated himself to the feel of her skin, skidding his fingers over her shoulders, along her arms, down her back. He teased himself by thumbing the sides of her breast, savored her reaction when she shivered. Not from cold because it was getting damn hot in this yurt.

She traced the shell of his ear with her tongue, exhaled a sigh, taunted him with her wispy breaths.

This was another game they played. Give and take. Control and submit. Thrill or be thrilled. And each part had its appeal. Touching Tess or letting Tess touch him.

Anthony liked it both ways.

So he dragged his hands down her rib cage into the scoop of her waist, over the swell of her hips, feeling, learning, savoring her smooth skin beneath his hands, the way she breathed against his ear.

He rounded the curve of her bottom, his fingers digging into cheeks enough to press her closer… Anthony couldn't resist. He ground his erection into the soft swell of her heat.

She let out a half moan, half sigh—or maybe he'd made the sound? He didn't know. He only knew that fire surged through him, and he could do nothing but anchor her close and grind against her once more, a hard thrust that mimicked the real thing.

His intensity seemed to spark Tess from her daze, and she dragged her open mouth down his neck, nipping his jaw along the way, making him vibrate with each playful bite.

He rode her again, stunned at the strength of his need. He'd always appreciated a good orgasm, but this brushfire heat was almost too hot to handle. When she slithered away from him, he groaned.

She raised her arms to sweep her hair back from her shoulders, giving him a shot of her naked upper body in all its glory. Her breasts thrust proudly. Her smile seemed both bold and thoughtful as she raked her gaze over him.

"One of us needs to lose more clothes," she said. "I think it's getting kind of warm in here."

He'd had that exact thought. To his profound pleasure, he watched her go for the button at her waist and shimmy out of her shorts in a series of moves that made her breasts sway. She dragged her panties along for the ride, and when the jumble of clothing caught at her knees, he asked, "Need my help?"

"Hmph." She rolled backward on the air mattress and drew her knees up, giving him a shot of her pale cheeks and making him wish for more light so he could enjoy everything the darkness hid.

He sat up, unable to resist touching her bottom, tracing the smooth curve of skin with his open hand, the line of firm muscle down her thigh. She kicked her clothes over the side then scooted out of reach.

"Hey," he protested. "I was enjoying myself."

"Me, too." Rolling off the mattress, she rose to her feet in a fluid move.

Anthony could only stare in dazed appreciation, momentarily blinded by the sight of this woman in all her naked glory.

She was exquisite. With the tumble of dark hair flowing over her shoulders and down her back and long shapely legs, she was gorgeous in an earthy, natural way he found so appealing.

"You're so beautiful, Tess."

It was trite. It was probably something she'd heard from every man she'd ever brought to his knees. But Anthony meant it. It was a simple truth that held a lot of power.

"Thank you."

No sassy comeback. No coyness, either, as far as he could tell. She had him by the balls and knew it, but respected him for being there. He liked her confidence. It radiated off her as she stood before him so at ease with her body in a way so many women would never be.

He liked that she eyed him so hungrily.

"Anthony, will you drag the mattress outside? I want to lay in your arms with the cool breeze running across my skin."

He extended his hand to her. "Help me up."

As soon as she slipped her fingers into his, Anthony levered his weight against hers and pulled her down beside him.

She landed against him in a tumble of laughter. Silky skin glanced against him, a thigh, a hip, a soft breast, and each galvanized the ache inside him. But he forced himself to stand.

He laughed to find his knees like rubber, but he didn't give her a chance to notice before skirting the mattress and kneeling down to give a push. "Hang on."

She rolled onto her stomach, spread her arms wide and grabbed the edges to brace herself.

"I'm going to dream about the sight of you like this every time I close my eyes for the rest of my life," he said.

"Glad you like the view." Then she spread her legs wide, hooking her toes on the mattress sides, teasing him with glimpses of places he couldn't fully see in the darkness.

He had everything he could do not to sink down on top of her, cover every inch of her sexy body with his. With another hearty push, he sent her jolting through the yurt flap.

He had to squeeze past the mattress to finish the job, but realized the benefits of being outside instantly. "You glow in silver out here, *chère*. You don't even look real."

She propped herself up on an elbow and looked surreal, spread out before him in the starlight, the wind whipping tendrils of hair around her face and neck.

"Cold?"

She raised her arms to him. "Come warm me."

He was beside her in an instant, savoring the way her body unfolded against him, all his fantasies realized when her legs twined through his and she threaded her arms around him, crushing her breasts to his chest.

He skimmed his hands down the length of her arms, around her back, felt the goose bumps on her skin. He brought his leg around her and anchored her close.

"Kiss me, Anthony."

"You say that a lot."

"I like the way you kiss."

"Lucky for me." Slipping his fingers around her jaw, he eased her face upward, a deliberate move that let him study her features in the starlight.

Thick lashes fringing eyes that seemed almost black in the shadows, the creamy skin, the pouty mouth so ready for his kisses. Then she let her eyes flutter shut and her lips parted on a sigh, a murmur carried off by a burst of wind.

He lowered his face to hers, savoring the anticipation as he closed in. Then his mouth touched hers, without the confinement of a cramped car to hinder movement, with the freedom to explore and the promise of the whole night ahead.

This kiss was the real deal.

This kiss allowed for roving hands and twined legs and thrusting hips. This kiss wound their tension tighter as the night wheeled around them, a heady combination of canyon wind and starlit shadow and loamy forest.

Of promise.

Of passion.

Anthony could smell desire, Tess's, his own. He could feel their hunger escalating in the way their hands traveled over each other in a frenzy.

And when she broke their kiss to trail her mouth along his jaw, down his throat, sucking gently on his pulse point, Anthony knew a need that went beyond the thrill of the moment, went beyond physical excitement… This kiss made him *want*.

He reached for the button that fastened his jeans, but Tess stopped him.

"No, let me. I've been wanting to see what you keep hidden in here since you nudged me out of first place on the track."

Her voice edged with excitement, her words bold and honest.

"Should I be worried?"

"Vengeance isn't my speed." She laughed. "This'll be a search-and-rescue operation."

He sucked in a hard breath as her fingers grazed his stomach. "Ah, man, Tess. Rescue away."

She unzipped his fly and slipped her fingers inside his briefs to maneuver the whole deal free. Her intimate touch made it impossible to hold back, and when she moved down his body, a vision better than any fantasy with all her pale skin gleaming, he couldn't keep his hands off her.

He stroked her breasts, her shoulders, her face, *everything* he could reach. But she wouldn't be sidetracked. She worked the tangle of clothes from his hips while he hiked his butt off the mattress to help her rescue his lower half.

He finally kicked his pants free. "It's damn cold out here without clothes, *chère*. I've got body parts shriveling up."

"Nothing we can't unshrivel with a little effort."

Very little effort, no doubt. But he didn't tell Tess. Let her work to please him. He couldn't think of a thing better.

"My wallet. Grab it from my pocket."

"Protection?"

He nodded.

She'd no sooner grabbed his wallet and tossed his jeans back into the yurt than he grabbed her.

"Anthony." She bounced down onto the mattress and tried to roll away.

She didn't stand a chance.

"I've wanted to feel you naked since the day we met."

"Really?"

"You're haunting my dreams, *chère*."

Apparently those were the magic words because she stopped resisting. But Tess had her own plan. Swinging her leg around, she straddled him again, sitting on his thighs, her woman's softness teasing him with her heat.

"I want to play Queen of the Mountain."

"How about Queen of the High Elevation? This is a canyon. Technically, there's a difference."

She laughed, the real woman far more gorgeous than

any dream. She had the sleek body of an active woman, all toned muscles and creamy skin that flashed and shone when she held up his wallet. "Do you mind? I want to do the honors."

"Be still my heart."

She met his gaze, eyes sparkling as she rummaged through his wallet to produce a foil square.

"Got it." She sent the wallet sailing behind her, through the open flap, where it clattered against…a lantern?

"Bull's eye," he said around a tight breath as she tore open the packet and honed in on his crotch.

But she wasn't ready to get straight to business. Slipping her fingers beneath his balls, she cupped him with a firm touch, weighing the guys in her warm palm to reawaken his body.

"Ah, Tess."

"Like that, do you?"

A rhetorical question because she couldn't possibly expect him to reply while she was dragging her fingers up his length. All he could do was hold himself brutally still. His dick swelled, and when she hooked her fingers beneath the head and gave a playful tug, his whole body jerked in reply.

"That's a hot spot." She did it again.

"You do realize if you keep doing that, I'm going to have to get you back, don't you?" He sounded a lot more controlled than he felt.

Another sharp tug.

Another full-bodied spasm that made her laugh.

"Vengeance, hmm? You're welcome to try, of course."

Anthony locked his hands around her waist and was about to show her a view of the sky from on her back, but she slid her fingers around his dick and hung on.

Pressing his head into the mattress, he let go fast enough.

"Now lie still." She worked the condom onto him in less than precise moves, and he smiled. He liked that for all her boldness he still had the ability to fluster her.

"A night outdoors was sheer brilliance," she said. "Now stop distracting me and let me thank you properly."

With a neat move she positioned herself and levered him against her heat. He skimmed along her body in a path of moisture, penetrating just enough to make him ache.

Her sigh and his groan collided in the night air.

She rose naked above him, her hair whipping out on the wind, her body gleaming silver. He reached up to cup her breasts in his hands, pinching her nipples, winning a response when she took aim and sank down.

She was hot and tight and stretched around him as though their bodies had been designed to fit together. She gave a full-bodied shiver and arched forward, the motion driving him inside even deeper. And the sight of her poised above him, her pale thighs straining as she rode up for another stroke...

The tumble of shiny hair in the darkness, strands whipping around her face and playing around her shoulders...

The warm breasts swelling against his palms...

The tightness of her wet heat clenching him in deliberate spasms that were making it impossible not to thrust upward, short driving strokes that made her gasp whimpery sounds, made his tension wind so tight he couldn't stop.

He tugged her nipples, as much to distract her as him, but evasive maneuvers were useless. Their bodies came together with no reference to how long he might want to make this moment last.

She rode him hard, again and again, and he locked his hands around her waist to lend speed to her efforts, unable to shut his eyes at the sight she made rocking sensually above him, breasts bouncing, bottom swaying to a rhythm he could feel through every nerve in his body.

He was on fire, his whole body consumed by her, and when she cried out, a sound of pure pleasure that disappeared on the wind, he went a little crazy, driving inside, wild with the way her sex spasmed around him, the way she gasped on each upstroke as if he forced the sound out with each thrust.

She didn't shy from him, but embraced the intensity of the moment, digging her fingers into his chest to steel herself and ride him as he growled out his pleasure, exploding.

Anthony didn't know when he'd closed his eyes. He had no idea when she'd collapsed on top of him. He only knew that she draped over him in a tangle of glorious woman, and he felt more contented, more *alive,* than he'd felt in so long.

He ran his hands along her to memorize the feel of each sleek curve, to capture everything about the way he felt.

She finally said, "Anthony, I'm freezing."

He laughed, a heartfelt sound that echoed down into the canyon and far off into the night.

8

TESS WAS STILL RIDING the weary glow from the night past, sipping her Starbucks coffee and contentedly watching the sky pale in streaks of a pastel sunrise. She would have loved to see the dawn over the canyon and decided she'd go back again to do just that—perhaps on the drive home, when they weren't crushed for time.

A smile tugged at her lips. She liked the sound of a sunrise in Anthony's arms. They deserved another special night together to make up for the one they'd lost.

She watched him as he drove, clipping along with the predawn traffic on the two-lane road they'd taken out of Santa Fe. For two days, they'd chatted constantly, getting to know each other, but this morning, they just drove along in companionable silence as the terrain rushed past in a blur of fading shadows.

Tess liked the quiet. It was filled with the warm familiarity of the night past, a lingering closeness that was somehow unexpected. She might not have dated in a while, but she'd had relationships before. Mornings after could be filled with a rush of new passion or tenderly awkward, almost too new. None had ever felt like this, breathless and...*inevitable.*

That surprised her the most. How satisfied she felt right

now, how comfortable she was sitting beside this man after all the intimacies they'd shared last night.

How eager she was to spend more time together.

He finally noticed her watching him. "What?"

"I was just thinking about last night."

A smile touched his mouth, too, and she liked the drowsy warmth that crept through her at the sight, liked having the power to please him.

Tess was still mulling her reaction to these unexpectedly warm and fuzzy feelings when the electronic jangle of her cell phone chimed over the hum of the car's engine.

She grabbed it from the utility tray, and glanced at the display. "Hi, Daddy."

"Good morning, sugar." His forceful voice seemed almost too big for the satellite signal. "Sleep well last night?"

"Never better."

"Pleased to hear it. Mind telling me *where* you slept that I couldn't reach you by cell."

Uh-oh. "At about six thousand feet. The ranger said the cell coverage might be sketchy."

That earned her a dubious glance from Anthony.

"You were camping?" Daddy asked, sounding as dubious as Anthony looked.

"We went for a night tour of the canyon. After two days in this car, we needed to get out and move around—it was gorgeous. That's why I forgot to check in. Sorry I worried you."

Anthony was frowning now, and Tess reached over to pat his knee. This was her fault, not his. She should have called to let her daddy know they'd decided to bypass the pit stop hotel.

"Another letter was waiting for me when I came in from

the office yesterday. I wanted you and that young man of yours to be on red alert."

"Oh no, Daddy. What did it say?"

"It asked me how I felt about my nearest and dearest heading out of town and leaving me alone."

That gave even her a chill. Whoever was sending these letters was watching their family a little too closely for comfort. She could just imagine her daddy finding this letter when he'd walked in the door from the office. He always came in late from his managers meeting on Monday nights, so he'd have tried to call her. No dice on her cell. Most likely he'd tried Anthony's cell, too. No dice there, either. He would have tried the scheduled pit stop hotel only to be told that she hadn't checked in....

"Didn't sleep last night, did you?" She already guessed the answer.

"'Fraid not. There's just something about knowing this crazy is watching my family close enough to know they are scattered like fleas on a dog's bath day that had me a bit unsettled."

A *bit* was putting it mildly. "Is Glen having any luck tracking down this one?" she asked, referring to Daddy's chief of security at AutoCarTex.

"He's working on it. This one came postmarked from Little Rock. Haven't had one from there before. So that's new."

Anthony must have gotten the gist of the conversation because suddenly he was motioning her to cover the mouthpiece so he could talk.

"Hang on a sec, Daddy," she said. "What?"

"Tell him that we won't be staying at the pit stop hotel tonight, either. Tell him we'll go five-star, and I'll explain the situation to security so they're on the lookout. We'll call and tell him where as soon as I book the reservation."

Tess relayed the message, knowing this was exactly what Daddy needed to hear right now. Anthony had just earned a few points with her. Probably with her daddy, too. And to her surprise, she really didn't mind.

Alerting security to a potential problem was a good idea, even if it did remind her that Anthony was all about winning her daddy's respect and approval for his Auto-TexCare plan. She hadn't wanted any reminders during their break from reality, but somehow it didn't rankle so much when she heard her daddy's sigh of relief on the other end of the connection.

"Let me know your plans as soon as you make them, sugar. I'll be waiting."

"I will."

"Have a good drive, and stay safe."

"Love you, Daddy."

"Love you, too, sugar." She blew kisses into the receiver then disconnected to find Anthony watching her as she set the phone back in the utility tray.

"Tell me all about these letters, Tess."

"Don't want anything to happen on your watch, hmm?"

His gaze narrowed, and that mouth she'd kissed so intimately last night straightened into a grim line. "I don't want anything happening to you at all."

"I AM SO READY for that shower," Anthony whispered to Tess when the hotel desk clerk moved toward the computer to pull up their reservation for their night in Las Vegas.

"You don't have to tell me," Tess said. "I've been stuck in a car with you all day, remember?"

Anthony blinked, and she had to struggle to keep hold of her deadpan expression. Fortunately, the uniformed desk clerk provided a distraction.

"There's been a change to your reservation."

"What change? I talked to your general manager and security chief making these arrangements."

Anthony got attentive fast. Probably worried about his shower. She hadn't been kidding. The man needed one. After a night spent making love under the stars and a day baking in the car, he smelled like a heady combination of ripe male and sex.

It had been all she could do to keep her hands off him during the long drowsy hours on the road. In fact, she hadn't been able to, Tess remembered with a mental sigh. Being together had driven away all thoughts of worrisome letters and concerned family members.

Even after Anthony had made the arrangements for tonight's stay, they'd tried to take turns napping to make up for an exhausting night, but sleep hadn't come to either of them. They'd both been suffering a serious case of *lust*sickness, and she remembered one particularly memorable stretch of desert road when she'd tested Anthony's driving skill by entertaining herself in his lap.

She hadn't been able to help herself, and decided his strong male smell wouldn't let her stop thinking about sex. Every time she'd stretch out on the bench seat, she'd find herself staring up at him, his chiseled jaw, the strong hands he rested easily on the steering wheel, and remembering how he'd felt inside her every time they'd made love last night.

"Let me double-check when this change was made and by whom." The clerk tapped out a rapid-fire burst of keystrokes.

Anthony glanced down at her, a brow arched in tenuous patience. A little thrill coursed through her as his golden-brown eyes trailed over her face, a gesture that assured her he was just as eager to get into their hotel room as she was.

He discreetly slipped his hand into hers, a gesture she found sweet. Then he bent low, so his mouth practically brushed her ear. "I'm looking forward to giving you a shower."

Her sex gave a needy little twinge in reply, and she smiled. "Me, too."

She hoped the trouble would be easily resolved. Anthony had been insistent about not staying in the pit stop hotel tonight, so he'd made this reservation from his cell phone en route. Everything had seemed pretty straightforward.

The clerk finally said, "I see what happened. The general manager upgraded your room to one of our presidential suites."

Anthony frowned. "You're sure?"

"Reservation for two under DiLeo?" There was a question in his voice as he shifted his gaze between them.

"That part's right," Tess said. "But why would your manager upgrade our room?"

The clerk opened his mouth to reply, but then a beautiful redheaded woman approached and said, "Security reasons, and he's sucking up to you."

She and Anthony exchanged glances, not sure what to make of the woman. She didn't seem alarming with her bright smile and professional blue silk suit.

"I understand the security reasons, but why would he suck up to us?" Anthony asked.

"Because his wife is a reporter with the *Vegas Times-Press*. She's been keeping track of all the rally contestants to see if any bypassed the pit stop hotel. When she heard contestants booked a reservation for tonight and needed additional security, she wanted an interview for an article. So he's doing his bit to make his wife happy."

"By putting us in a presidential suite?" Anthony asked.

"Gratis. They're the best suites in the house, and their floor has its own security monitoring station."

"I assume you're the wife," Tess said.

"Tori Grant." She extended her hand and launched into a cheery explanation. "My husband's sales director contacted the Rally Committee about hosting your pit stop. I have a daily column and want to feature the rally with something more than the typical spin the car club's giving the press. I thought it would be a good way to get the benefiting charity a little more promotion with readers who wouldn't otherwise be interested."

Good promotion for the AutoCarTex Foundation, too. Although Tess didn't think she needed to point that out to Tori Grant. This reporter didn't seem to miss a trick.

"While I'm not on the Rally Committee, I am a car club board member," Tess said. "I know there was concern at our general meeting about the casino. As rally hosts, the Nostalgic Car Club assumes a certain amount of liability. Our contestants sign on to drive a long haul in a short time, and we want them to be fresh when they're on the road, and safe, of course. We generally avoid hotels with nighttime entertainment. Avoiding temptation so to speak."

She hadn't avoided nighttime entertainment or temptation, though. She'd invited hers to make the drive with her.

"That's what I told Adam," Tori said. "But when I heard

you'd booked a room, I thought I'd give an interview an-other shot. So what do you say? Will you answer a few questions? The article won't run until long after you've left town if you're worried about security."

"We won't be around long enough to give an inter-view," Anthony said.

"We need to be on the road at the crack of dawn."

"My interview won't take long. I'll bring you up to your room, and we'll be done by the time you've gotten the grand tour and the bellman delivers your bags." She motioned to the desk clerk who immediately handed her their room key. "Sound good?"

Tess glanced up at Anthony, who shrugged, then said, "All right."

Tori Grant was as good as her word. She skillfully mas-queraded her interview behind a casual conversation about the rally while escorting them through the hotel.

While standard Las Vegas casino fare, the Parisian leaned more toward upscale than flash. The French ro-mance theme evidenced itself in everything from the five-star service to the stylized period decor.

Cherrywood, gilded decoration and rich colors hall-marked the Parisian's luxury interior, and Tess felt as though they'd stepped through a time warp into some elaborate European palace. She tried not to be distracted by her surroundings as they talked, but found herself glad Anthony, as a first-time contestant, provided a foil to her AutoCarTex Foundation public relations interpre-tation of the event.

Tori Grant seemed to appreciate the angle, too, because she skillfully zeroed in on their differing impressions of the rally, the contestants and the benefiting charity.

A little part of Tess couldn't help but be surprised by Anthony. Though the man wore a two-day stubble and smelled far from fresh, he segued into Mr. Charming Professional as fast as if he'd flipped a switch.

She'd met him in a casual convention setting and had only glimpsed his business persona when he'd presented his AutoTexCare plan. Otherwise, he'd been laid-back and very adaptable, and it surprised her to watch him slip into that professional role as easily as…well, as easily as *she* did.

Of course a lot of her surprise had to do with seeing his smile. Even though he sounded so contemplative and intelligent, whenever she looked at that dashing grin, she couldn't help but remember all the amazing things he could do with his mouth.

And those memories not only made her heart beat faster, but forced Tess to wonder why she had it so bad for this man.

The answer to that question was a no-brainer. One night alone together had *not* been enough. Not even close. She needed to get Anthony alone again to work off more of this excess lust that had been building since the moment she'd set eyes on him.

One glimpse inside the presidential suite, and Tess knew they'd come to the right place.

After their night in a yurt on a canyon top, this luxury suite seemed as different as a mustang from a mule. The foyer and sitting room continued the period glamour marking the rest of the hotel, but this suite had been furnished with costly antiques and fashionable porcelain pieces that lent to the impression of luxury.

The living room boasted French doors opening onto a

courtyard balcony that overlooked the sparkling terrain of Las Vegas at night. Curtains were fringed, swagged and decorated with tassels. Upholstered chairs and sofas were trimmed in similar fashion as the curtains. Bold-colored carpets covered polished wooden floors.

"Wow," was all Tess could say.

"French styles revived in the nineteenth century were identified by the kings' names who ruled when they were first used," Tori told them. "This is Louis XV. You can tell because he liked S- and C-shaped scrolls like these."

Tess gingerly touched one such scroll on a light that was part of a set flanking a gilded mirror. "I'm impressed. Is interior design a hobby of yours, Tori, or history?"

"Neither actually, but being married to the general manager of this hotel…"

"Got it." And Tess did. Whenever her father and Uncle Ray started talking cars or racing or AutoCarTex… She glanced around at Anthony, who was no slouch in this department, either. She'd learned enough about Anthony DiLeo Automotive in the past few days to get a job there.

They chatted with Tori about their plans for tomorrow's run, and when a knock sounded on the door, Anthony answered it to find the bellman with their bags.

"Okay, that's my cue." Tori extended her hand to Tess and thanked them both. "I'll leave a copy of my article for you when you check out in the morning. You'll have a chance to let me know what you think before it goes to print."

Then she left with the bellman, and they were alone.

Tess wasn't sure what she'd been expecting after she and Anthony finally made it to their hotel. And now that she thought about it, she realized that her sex-soaked brain hadn't been capable of thinking past her immediate need to get clean.

They needed to eat, too. And sleep definitely.

What she didn't expect was for Anthony to sneak up behind her and hoist her off her feet. Suddenly, she came smack up against strong arms, hard chest and sweaty neck.

"Argh, you big, stinky man. What are you doing?"

"Giving you a shower. You stink, too."

"Hmph." The sound only made him laugh as he maneuvered her through the doorway to the master bedroom.

The bedroom proved no less elaborate than the rest of the suite with more French doors and a tall antique bed with a cherrywood step.

"Now let's see what we have." He made another turn to head into the bathroom. "I'm gunning for a garden tub with jets."

"Be forewarned, stinky man. I will *not* get in any standing water with you until you've showered. A few hours ago you were sexy. Now you're on the bad side of ripe."

Without warning, he dragged his tongue up her cheek, a big slurpy lick that made her cringe. "You still taste sexy, *chère.*" Before she could reply, he stopped short in the doorway, forcing her to hang on tight. "Oh, yeah."

Oh, yeah was right.

The bathroom had all kinds of gold froufrou fixtures that gleamed against the white porcelain tile. And the double sink and separate lavatory were convenient, too. But the highlight of this room was the shower stall behind a glass wall large enough to host a party. Tiled with wall jets, a bench ran along two walls, turning the stall into a private sauna.

"No garden tub," she said.

"I'll live."

Given the expression on his handsome face, she guessed Anthony would do a lot more than live. He lowered her to her feet with a sigh and strode to the stall, whipped open the door and popped his head inside. "Twelve jets, Tess. This was definitely worth a fifteen-minute interview. We lucked out."

Tess was thinking along a similar vein as she admired his tight butt when he leaned forward to turn on the jets. A crazy zip of pleasure hummed through her, an almost giddy reaction to a man she'd enjoyed so completely last night.

"Do I need to grab our things?" she asked.

"Don't bother. Everything's in here."

Ah, the luxury of being pampered.

She wouldn't have traded one second of last night, but after their playful stripteases in the great outdoors, tonight's hasty disrobing seemed a joke by comparison. But they were eager. All right, *desperate*. Thirty-six hours was way too long to go without a shower as far as Tess was concerned, but as much as she'd enjoyed peeling off this man's clothes last night, she couldn't deny that watching Anthony tear off his clothes without preamble was downright sexy, too.

Especially when he disappeared beneath the near violent spray, all those muscles flashing, all that golden skin gleaming against the backdrop of tile.

The man literally stole her breath. Yes, he was gorgeous, but it was more than just gorgeous. It was the way looking at him affected her with those shivery feelings inside, a feeling that made her hold her breath to see what would happen next.

Stepping inside the shower, Tess lost herself beneath the

spray, ignoring the man who scrubbed vigorously only a foot away. The hot water pounded over her head and on muscles that felt the effects of too many cramped hours in a car, too many days at a convention running her sleep tank on fumes and a whole glorious night spent in her lover's arms.

The water pounded her into a daze and lather washed away the remnants of sex and sweat. She willed herself to revive so she could enjoy some of their night in this suite before collapsing on the plush bed and passing out. She was so deep into her internal pep talk that she jumped when a hard and thick male body part pressed squarely against her butt.

This body part needed no introduction, even if the rest of the man himself hadn't immediately followed, all strong, *clean* muscles surrounding her as he wrapped his arms around her.

"Mmm. You smell a lot better."

His chest heaved on a deep breath. "You, too."

Tess nestled her bottom against him, gratified when that hard erection surged. "Feeling more awake now, I take it?"

"Oh, yeah." To prove the point, he slithered his hand along her stomach, a glancing caress that made her muscles contract. Spearing his fingers into the hair between her thighs, he earned a shiver. "You, too, hmm?"

"Keep touching me like this, and the answer will be yes."

He chuckled, a throaty sound against her ear.

And he touched her again.

His calloused fingertip slipped between her sensitive folds to zero in on the nub of nerve endings hidden between, an exquisite friction that made her rock back against him and earn another chuckle.

He rolled that little hot spot around, and the pleasure came fast and furious. Tess let her eyes flutter shut and sank back, only vaguely aware of the way he rocked his hips to wedge that thickness between her cheeks and ride his own ache.

Trailing his mouth along her ear, he pressed kisses there, light touches that were as potent as the combined sensations of his skillful fingers and steamy water pounding over them.

She just stood there, allowing it all to wash over her with the water, amazed at the way her body leaped to life with an intensity she could honestly say she'd never felt before. Something about the way she and Anthony came together was so different, so easy. *Right.*

She could only marvel at the way her sex gathered in a slow squeeze as he lazily rolled her hot spot as if the only thing in the world he wanted to do was pleasure her.

And perhaps tonight he did.

He reached for the soap with his free hand then started at her neck, lathering her in lazy circles. Her knees turned to jelly as he massaged that bar around her breasts, more languid motion that made her nipples pucker beneath the spray.

Resting his cheek on the top of her head, he arched his hips to give his erection another slow push. She could feel the heat of his skin, the strength of his arousal, and she trembled at the erotic sensation.

Anthony didn't say a word as he swirled the soap over her ribs and along her stomach. He just cradled her close and touched her as if he wanted to learn her by heart.

And Tess was content to let him. Drowsy and replete, all this warm pleasure swirling inside, the heat building slowly. The reality of this handsome man stoking her passion seemed dreamily unreal right now. When he stopped the languid rolling motion, she tried to rally the energy to protest, but ever the gentleman, Anthony didn't abandon her. He lathered his hands, returned the soap and slipped his fingers between her legs.

"Oh!" she exhaled the sound on a gasp.

His fingers glided through her intimate folds, slick strokes that separated her skin and made her squirm. The memory of his sexy attention as he'd lain beneath her last night in the forest sharpened that ache to a fine edge.

Then he braced his arm around her waist and bent her forward enough so he could slide his hand between them. Suddenly, he probed her bottom with those soapy strokes, his broad hand parting her cheeks intimately. Rising up on tiptoes to manage his access, she didn't accomplish any more than to invite him to explore further…

"Anthony!" The man touched her in places he had no business touching, whether under the pretense of cleansing or not.

"Shh," he murmured thickly and hung on tight, not curbing his exploration with those soapy fingers one bit.

To Tess's amazement, she found herself not wanting to pull away as much as rock her hips to ride the sensation.

Who knew *that* would feel so good?

But feel good it did. So good, in fact, that she would have fallen on her face had he not held her so tight, each soapy stroke creating just enough pressure to make her start vibrating from the inside out.

Her sex clenched hotly, needily, and she wanted to swing around in his arms and hop on for a hard ride.

But Anthony had other plans.

He caught a nipple and gave a squeeze. The pleasure rode through her like a wave, hot and powerful and intense.

He laughed, and some dim part of her barely functioning brain recognized that he must have expected her reaction because he caught her easily when she swayed.

No one man should have such power over her.

No man ever had.

But these were thoughts that Tess couldn't reason through right now, not when she found herself held securely in his strong arms then led to the bench.

She stretched out, testing the strength of languid muscles, treating him to the sight of her spread out naked and clean. She had no idea what Anthony had planned next, but she sincerely hoped it involved his mouth.

Just the memory of the way he'd pleasured her with his mouth last night excited her. But he didn't even glance her way, instead heading to the valet on one of the shower walls to return with…

A razor?

She frowned when he handed her a small mirror.

"Will you hold this? I need to shave."

"I didn't mind your stubbly cheeks between my thighs last night. Hint, hint."

He flashed that lethal grin, and her insides melted.

"My turn tonight, Tess."

"Really?"

He nodded. "You had your way with me last night. It's only fair to return the favor."

She couldn't argue that. He had very graciously let her lead, even though she knew he'd been itching to impress her. And he *had* impressed her—by putting aside his wants for hers.

And taking her apart at the seams anyway.

She wouldn't admit *that,* though, so when he sank onto the floor beside her, she just positioned the mirror.

She found the sight of him dragging that razor over his stubbly cheeks arousing. Tess couldn't explain why. True, he was a beautiful man. His hair, wet and slick, clung to his neck and shoulders, a sexy look that made him seem bad boy in the extreme despite the green foam slathered along his jaw and neck.

He arched a brow. "Am I boring you, *chère?*"

"Not at all."

The companionable silence fell between them again, and Tess marveled at how easily they spent time together. Here they were butt naked with barely a week's acquaintance and one night of intimacy between them. Perhaps because they were spending around-the-clock time together. Three days in a car, and they had no choice but to get close. She couldn't make a ladies' room run without him knowing about it. Still, she couldn't recall this feeling with any other man she'd dated.

His cheeks had a slightly raw look to them when he finished, and he plucked away the mirror with a "thanks" and rinsed his face beneath a jet.

Then returned with the razor.

"Miss a spot?" she asked, trying to talk herself into rolling off this bench so she could rinse the conditioner from her hair and dry off.

That big cushy bed called to her. She wanted to slide between the sheets with a clean naked man.

"Mmm-hmm."

She peered curiously at his face, but couldn't see anything but kissable skin. "Looks good to me."

"The missing spot is on you."

"Where?" She lifted a leg in the air and ran a hand down her calf. Her skin felt baby-buns smooth.

"Not your legs. Here." He knelt beside her and smoothed his palm along her sex.

"You like bald women?" She wasn't sure what to make of this.

He grimaced. "Not *bald,* but I want you ultrasensitive. I want you to feel everything I plan to do to you tonight."

"Will it involve your mouth?"

"Mmm-hmm. You seemed to enjoy yourself last night."

Boy, had she ever. She wasn't about to admit that to Mr. I-Want-You-To-Feel-Everything over there, so she just spread her legs in an invitation.

If it involved his mouth, she'd be happy to oblige him.

Sinking onto the bench, he positioned himself between her spread legs in a breathtaking display of shifting muscle and squeaky-clean skin. "Sure you don't mind?"

"I'll let you know when it starts growing back."

With a laugh, he speared his fingers into the trimmed tuft of curls at the juncture of her thighs and gave a tug.

Tess swallowed back a moan. How much more sensitive could she possibly get?

When he shot a blob of shaving gel between her thighs, she knew she'd find out soon enough. And she didn't mind a bit. The sight of his dark hands working the gel to a lather made her sex give a slow squeeze. Especially when he started up all this perfunctory touching and tugging to manage a clean shave with a disposable razor. A very neat trick. And *arousing.*

"Wow. The razor has never felt like this the million or so times I've shaved my legs."

"That's because I'm doing the honors."

"And you do them very well. *Too* well. I don't think I believe what you told me about bald women."

He didn't answer right away, too occupied with working his way down that sensitive place where her thigh met all her private places. Slipping his fingers along her sex, he caught her curls and separated her sensitive folds so she could feel the steamy air everywhere.

Her stomach contracted. Her thighs quivered.

Anthony smiled, clearly liking her reaction.

"It's not about hair, *chère*. It's about touch. I want you to feel me when I touch you, with nothing in the way."

Pleasure turned his voice whiskey smooth, a sound that rippled through her senses, drugged her with its potency. He thumbed the tiny knot that made her pleasure simmer. "Just think about how good this'll feel when my mouth is on you."

That thought alone would have made her sigh, even if Anthony hadn't been idly thumbing her through the slick passage of shaving gel.

"Can't wait," she admitted.

"Me, either."

Tess liked that Anthony shared his passion so easily, liked how she felt so sexy and aroused and comfortable in the face of his passion.

"You know what I like about us?"

"What's that?" he asked absently.

"It's easy being together."

Her admission hadn't sounded nearly so intimate in her mind as it did aloud, and when Anthony stopped in midstroke to gaze at her curiously, Tess hoped she hadn't made one of the dating gaffes she'd read about in *Metropolitan,* the magazine for modern single women.

But Anthony didn't shy away from her honesty. He looked thoughtful when he met her gaze. "Me, too, *chère*. Me, too."

Somehow his admission sounded equally intimate, and Tess was amazed at how quickly she'd managed to take a casual, comfortable moment and turn it into something more.

Why had she felt the need to?

This question had no place between them. They were all about the here and now, about *fun,* about a break from reality. All too soon their little vacation would be over, and she'd be introducing him to her daddy for business.

She needed to remember that.

"Come with me," he finally said. "I want to clean you up."

Tess let him lead her back under the jets, glad for the distraction. She didn't want to think right now. Not when he worked his soapy hands over her body. Not when he helped her rinse the conditioner from her hair with that hungry gleam in his eyes.

"Stay under the water until I grab some towels."

Tess watched him slip out of the shower, wasn't entirely sure what to make of the way she felt right now.

She stubbornly shoved aside her thoughts, and when Anthony returned with warm towels, she moved into his arms, so their bodies met in a melding of wet skin and sensitive body parts.

To her pleasure, Anthony couldn't resist touching her at such close range, and for every part she managed to dry on him, she found herself dodging his caresses, being aroused by his laughter, being made love to with those bedroom glances.

To touch and be touched.

And then it was her turn.

He grazed the warm towel easily over her, polishing the water from her skin in almost gentle strokes. He massaged her shoulders, her arms, then carefully dried each finger before working his way down her front.

Anthony didn't talk, and she found she didn't have anything to say, either. That companionable silence had fallen again while the moment was charged with awareness, and promise.

When he sank to his knees before her, patting dry her newly shaved sex with soft touches, Tess realized that he hadn't been kidding when he'd said *ultra* sensitive. She wound up spearing her fingers into his wet hair to hang on, liking the way his wet waves felt beneath her fingers. His hair might look rebellious, but it felt decadent. This man was all about pleasure, and she enjoyed something as simple as his untrimmed hair.

After dropping the towels beside the sink, he grabbed her makeup bag. "Is your comb in here?"

She nodded, reaching out to dig through the bag when he opened it, their fingers brushing. Anthony slid his fingers through hers, an oh-so-simple handhold that somehow took on crazy new significance when he didn't let go.

After returning her bag to the vanity, he snagged a bottle of body lotion along with the comb, led her toward the bed then sat on the edge. He pulled her between his spread legs. She knew he only meant to comb her hair, but like holding hands, his attention suddenly felt like so much more.

Arousing. Exciting. *Overwhelming.*

What was it about his strong thighs anchoring her securely or the almost-erection pressed against her back that made her feel as if more than fun was happening between them? They were enjoying a thrill in an expensive hotel room while they raced to the coast. She shouldn't be wondering why he'd been so handy with the razor between her thighs.

But she was very interested in the women he'd honed his shaving skills on, which made no sense whatsoever. Tess had seen his résumé, knew he was several years older than she was. Had she honestly expected such an attractive, charming man to stay hidden in his New Orleans garage all the time?

Of course not. So why was she suddenly wondering where she ranked with the women he'd dated?

9

CLOSING HER EYES as he worked the comb through her hair, Tess shut out all stimuli and mentally cautioned herself against wandering thoughts. She'd signed on for a race to the coast.

She'd signed on for fun.

That's exactly what she planned to have.

Scooting forward, she escaped his warm embrace. He reached out to catch her, but she stepped away, shaking out her hair, letting the wet strands play over her shoulders, a chilly reminder that she needed to stay in control.

But Anthony wasn't having any part of her escape. Almost before she realized he'd moved, he'd slipped his foot between her legs and tossed her off balance. He stood before she could brace herself then, in a blur of motion, he spun her around and hoisted her up.

She barely had a chance to gasp before finding herself looking up at him from the middle of the bed.

For a breathless moment, Tess could only stare. By then he'd straddled her in another impossibly fast move.

"My way tonight, *chère*."

There was no doubt he meant what he said, but she didn't miss the amusement underlying his expression, just enough to spark her bravado.

"What was *that?*"

"Just making sure I get equal time."

Not much of a question anymore, as he had her pinned to the bed. "No, I meant what was *that?* It was some sort of move…or something. Do you work out?"

That was a stupid question. The man wouldn't have his body without working out. Add in his look of pure male satisfaction… He clearly liked that he'd surprised her.

"Martial arts."

"Oh." She should have guessed. No one moved as he had without lots of practice.

"Do you know what I like about you, Tess?"

"What's that?"

"You're a woman who knows what you want, and you're not afraid to take it."

"What do you think I want?"

"Me."

One word issued in that lazy bayou voice made goose bumps spray over her skin. One word that was oh-so true.

Tess did want him, so much that she liked how her world narrowed down to the sight of his dashing smile and broad shoulders when she lay underneath him. She liked the way he held her pinned to the bed with his strong thighs and very obvious proof of his desire.

She liked that he wanted her, liked it much more than she ever would have guessed.

"You know what I like about us?" he asked, his voice gentling, or maybe that was just the way his golden-brown eyes melted over her.

"What?"

"We're good together."

That intimacy thing was happening again, a feeling that

hinted more than fun was happening here. A feeling that made her want to slip her arms around his neck and hold him close.

Tess wasn't at all sure why she felt so tender and dreamy tonight, but sex seemed to make her wax romantic. She didn't bother resisting. Looping her arms around his neck, she pressed up against him, indulging the unfamiliar feeling, even though she wasn't a woman who usually looked for tender moments.

Anthony seemed to be a man who liked them, though. He nestled her close, blocked out her view of the world with his big warm body then rested his chin in the crook of her neck. He seemed content to hold her with his cheek pressed to hers, the silence filled with only the hush of their breathing and the awareness of how well their bodies fit together.

She had no idea how much time had passed before he said, "Hang on," and tightened his grip around her. With a series of small moves, he maneuvered them around on the bed.

"Anthony!" Tess couldn't help laughing. All his hard muscles rode her in all the right places—places that flared to life with desire, places that tickled. "What are you doing?"

"Getting you where I want you." He inched them forward until her head hit the pillows.

"I'd move if you asked."

"I don't want to let go. You feel too good."

So did he, but she felt a zip of pure feminine satisfaction to hear him admit it.

"You know what I like about you, Anthony?"

"What's that, *chère?*"

"You don't pull any punches. You're up-front about how you feel."

"I feel…" His voice trailed off as he braced himself one-handed and started propping pillows behind her. "How's that?"

"Comfy." She felt like a princess perched on a cushy throne and decided she liked the feeling. "You feel what?"

He raked a lazy gaze over her, a smile touching the corners of his mouth and making her feel so beautiful.

"I feel like touching you." He reached for the lotion, warmed a dollop in his hands.

"Oh, I think I'm going to like this."

He dragged his palm down her throat. "Oh, you will. I promise. It's my turn to impress you tonight, remember?"

Suddenly, his hands were everywhere, and Tess wasn't as much impressed as she was overwhelmed by sensation. His hands worked the lotion into her skin in firm strokes. Not so much a massage as an exploration of her body. Every touch designed to bring pleasure. Heat began to pour through her, a languid sensation that made her skin tingle and her blood simmer.

His strong fingers worked the muscles in her arms until she felt boneless. He pressed kisses to each of her fingertips, gentle grazes of his lips against skin she hadn't realized could be so sensitive. He'd told her romance was an Italian thing, and while lying propped against the pillows, feeling decadent and indulged, Tess agreed.

He was a very romantic man. Determined, too, because every time she reached for him, wanting to touch, to participate, to return some of the pleasure, she provoked another assault.

And when he scooted down the length of her body,

muscles trailing over skin he'd caressed into aching awareness, and settled himself between her legs, she knew what
was coming next...*his mouth.*

She sighed. Her body shot from drowsy to excited in a
heartbeat, some part of her not believing the way he'd
made her feel last night had been real. Surely all those exquisite orgasms had been some trick of her imagination.

But when he brushed his fingers over her newly shaved
sex, worked the lotion in with deliberate thoroughness,
Tess knew she hadn't imagined anything about last night.

Even the sight of him aroused her.

The lines of his long body stretched out before her, a
gorgeous display of golden skin and sculpted curves. Just
trailing her gaze over his broad back, trim waist and tight
butt felt like an indulgence, a gorging of her senses. He had
great legs, too, more hard muscle with that light sprinkling
of tawny hair. Even his feet were tanned and good-looking.

Who'd ever heard of good-looking *feet?*

Tess buried herself back against the pillows, deciding
she had it bad for this man. And it was no wonder, either.
Anthony DiLeo was too hot for her own good.

What woman could resist the way he slid his hands
down her thighs, coaxed her bended knees to cradle his
wide shoulders in an incredibly erotic pose? And when he
shot her a roguish smile while lowering his face between
her thighs... Her breath caught and held as he settled in,
and she felt the first warm drag of his tongue along her
most private places.

Pleasure seized every muscle between her knees and her
throat, and heat radiated outward from the point of contact. Her memory had been dead-on accurate.

Ohmigosh.

He knew exactly where to breathe those hot bursts of air to prolong the sensation. He nibbled his way into all her private places, tiny nips and bites that warmed her up for what was to come. He knew precisely where to spear his tongue and seek out all those receptive spots that quivered for his attention.

How could she not respond to such a skillful assault? Her breasts grew heavy and tight. It was all she could do to grab the pillows and hang on for the ride.

Anthony wasn't content to do just the mouth thing, either. He involved his hands in the game, calloused fingertips probing skin around that oh-so-sensitive knot of nerve endings, a touch that made her tremble.

And when he freed that tiny place, drew it inside his warm mouth in a slow wet pull...

"Oh!" She exhaled the sound on a sigh that echoed through the quiet room.

He was pleased with her response, pleased he had her hanging on to the pillows for dear life. She could feel his smile against all her skin when he raised his gaze, pleasure dancing in his eyes.

And when he used his fingers to test her moist opening...just enough pressure to make her want more...just enough to make her arch her hips and create more friction, she wished he had six hands so he could touch her everywhere. Her breasts ached so much....

Releasing the pillow, she reached for him, brushed her fingers over his shoulder, down that hunky bicep until she could catch a good hold.

"Anthony, up here." She barely recognized her own voice as it rasped through the quiet.

He let her guide his arm up, up, up…then he took things from there. He splayed his big hand over her breast, cupping her fullness as she arched up into his touch. He even did her one better. Slithering his other hand out from beneath her, he handled her other one, too, kneading, arousing.

He caught her nipples and rolled them hard, making her gasp out as sensation jammed through her. And through it all he just kept sucking at his maddeningly slow and steady pace. He sensed her pleasure building, but he wouldn't let her rush, even though she could feel him everywhere, couldn't stop rocking her hips.

And she wasn't the only one feeling. Anthony groaned, and he ground his erection into the mattress.

Suddenly Tess was done playing—she wanted to feel him inside her. Reaching for him, she sank her fingers into those broad shoulders, urged him to move up into her arms.

But he resisted and his earlier words echoed in her memory. *"My way tonight, chère."*

His way would likely kill her, but she knew their time together was too sweet to rush. He was right about that. But she wanted…oh, how she wanted. When he stopped sucking to tongue her with hot wet strokes, she almost bolted off the bed.

Those hands on her breasts stopped her, though, and he gave a breathy chuckle against her sex, another sensation that made her writhe. He lifted his face and met her gaze above the freshly shaved mound.

"See what I meant about ultrasensitive?" His sexy mouth gleamed with her body's moisture, and her sex gave a hard throb at the sight.

"Oh, yeah," was all she managed to get out in a gravelly voice that made him smile.

Then he brought one hand down and wriggled his finger into all her damp heat. "Like that?"

"Oh, Anthony." She couldn't stop rocking her hips and rode that stroke with a long, slow thrust.

Mmm, mmm, mmm, mmm, mmm.

"What about this?" Slipping another finger backward, he ventured off into places that awoke some naggy little part of her brain with a demand to stop. But for the life of her, Tess couldn't think why. Pleasure overruled naggy doubts and any ability to think anyway.

Especially when his palm hit her hot spot.

Then she was powerless to do anything but clutch his shoulders and ride that pressure.

When it broke, it broke *big,* overheating every nerve until she shook unceremoniously and collapsed against the pillows. She heaved broken breaths as though she'd just run a race and finally opened her eyes to the sight of utter satisfaction on Anthony's handsome face.

"Impressed yet?" he asked conversationally.

"That mouth of yours should be registered." She panted out the words. "You killed me. Happy now?"

"You're not dead, *chère.*"

And to prove it, he pressed his palm against her hot spot again, made her tremble as if she'd been struck by lightning.

"See. Everything's still working."

"Hmph." Flinging her arm over her head, she exhaled deeply, let her eyes drift closed again.

Anthony maneuvered around until he lay against her. She wanted to wrap herself around him, hold him close, but couldn't break through her lethargy long enough to lift an arm to flop it across him. But when he began idly thumbing her breast, she did manage to crack an eyelid to stare.

"What?" Laughter sparkled in those bedroom eyes. "You thought we were done?"

She couldn't have replied if she'd had the strength to open her mouth. She didn't. Turned out the man wasn't interested in talking anyway. He coaxed her onto her tummy. Then he started massaging warm lotion into her skin, along her thighs, her butt, her waist.

While working his way up her back, he nestled his erection cozily against her bottom. To Tess's amazement, she felt life signs in places that, by all rights, should have been dead. But there was something about the way she felt right now, something she couldn't put a name to, something that felt more than boneless and replete.

Her senses sharpened in on Anthony now, on the feel of his hands moving over her skin. Desire pooled low in her tummy, and her sex gave the odd clench, remnants of that incredible orgasm.

Her body had become a finely tuned instrument of pleasure, her every response honing in on his touches. It went beyond wanting him, beyond the incredible way he made her feel. She wanted to make him feel, too. To make him melt into a puddle of firing impulses the way she had.

To Tess's surprise, she wasn't as boneless as she'd thought. Either Anthony's hands had infused her with energy or he inspired her to new boldness because right now she knew exactly what she wanted.

Lifting her hips, she wedged that impressive erection snugly between her cheeks. Then she rode his length with a rather neat rolling motion that dragged warm skin against hot male heat. He groaned softly, and she rode him again, another slow deliberate stroke designed to get a response.

He responded. "Ah, *chère,* you feel so good."

His arms came around her. He slid his hands along the length of her arms, twined their fingers together. Pressing his cheek to hers, he covered her with his big body, such an intimate position as she mimed the act of lovemaking with her rocking hips. His erection swelled eagerly.

Tess felt eager, too. Excitement reawakened with a vengeance. A feeling so completely easy and natural that she'd never known the like. A feeling as if her pleasure hinged upon his, and the most important thing in the world she could do was coax another raw groan from his mouth.

She was back to his mouth again.

And there it was, close enough to kiss. She pressed her lips there, half kisses, just tastes really, because that's all she could reach. But even such simple touches were exquisitely erotic, supremely intimate. Their breaths twisted and lingered around each other. Their bodies swayed together sensually.

His throaty growl burst against her lips. A tremor ran through him, and she wasn't surprised when he lifted his hips, a huge move that freed his erection to slip between her thighs. All she had to do was arch her bottom in invitation.

He nipped her mouth with biting kisses. His fingers clung to hers, keeping her body stretched full beneath him as he shifted, took aim and slid inside her.

Tess stretched to accommodate him, her body slick, welcoming. Sighs tumbled from her lips, and she clung to his hands, an anchor as their bodies came together all white heat and desire. She felt surrounded by him, by the fingers that held her steady, by the solid heaviness of his beautiful body, by the overwhelming heat he pressed deep inside.

His thighs flexed, and he rode her with long, slow thrusts. She rose to meet each stroke, her hips the only part of her body she could move to create a sultry ebb and flow as they rocked together. A pace that blocked out the rest of the world, chased away all thoughts except the way pleasure built, intense, inevitable. A slow rise of tension that grew so great, so overwhelming, Tess let go completely.

She lost herself in the sounds of his quickened breaths as he reached the edge and his thrusts pushed her over, too, the pleasure shattering in another blinding orgasm that she knew instinctively she could only experience with this man.

Only Anthony.

10

"WHAT'S ON YOUR MIND?" Anthony reached for his sunglasses to shield his gaze from the glaring sun. "You've been staring out that window for twenty miles. Thinking about Tori Grant's article?"

Tess glanced his way, a smile on her lips. "No. Although I thought she did a nice job with it."

"Thinking about your father's phone call?"

"No, he sounded better since Glen was able to bump up the alert status with the Post Office."

"Were you thinking about how impressed you are with me, *chère?*"

She smiled. "As a matter of fact, I was. I'm not so ready to head back to the real world yet. I'd like to relax in San Francisco before we head home. If we stay in a hotel with decent security, I'm sure Daddy won't grouse. What do you think?"

Anthony thought he'd done exactly what he'd set out to do—impress Tess. It was all over her from the way she'd slept wrapped around him last night to the contented look on her face right now. He'd impressed her in a way he hadn't intended, of course, because seduction had been the last thing on his mind when he'd shown up at the convention.

Shifting his gaze back to Tess, he watched as she snuggled back into the corner between her door and seat, knees drawn up, silky dark head resting against the window, seat belt stretched impossibly across her. She wrapped her hands around her cup of Starbucks coffee and sipped contentedly.

Anthony wished he felt as content as she looked.

He'd held her close last night, and for the few hours they hadn't made love, he'd tried to sleep. He *should* have slept. He was beyond tired—the sex *should* have pushed him over the edge.

But the sex had pushed his *head* over the edge.

All night long his brain had been in overdrive. Reliving past mistakes. Tormenting himself with the way his life might have turned out if he hadn't been so caught up in proving himself. How he must not have learned much from his mistakes because here he was with a special woman who did things to him that hadn't been done in forever and his work was square in the middle of them.

Sometime during the past two nights of incredible sex, things had taken a turn he hadn't foreseen.

They'd gotten *complicated*.

Anthony had started this venture wanting an introduction, now he wanted more than a few extra days before they headed back to the real world.

He had no damn business wanting anything else. Tess had made it loud and clear from the start that she had no use for men who used her to get to her father. She thought of him as a fling with a capital *F* with no possibility of anything else.

Anthony found he wasn't content being her road rally entertainment, not one damn bit.

"I'm the Anthony DiLeo in Anthony DiLeo Automotive," he finally said. "Taking a few extra days isn't a problem, as long as I'm back in New Orleans by the sixteenth."

"You're sure?"

"Positive." He needed to figure out what he wanted from this woman and how to get it.

A few extra days together was at least a place to start.

"I DON'T KNOW WHY they bother calling this a race," Anthony said from the passenger's seat as he tried to read the San Francisco street map in the dark. "We didn't get on the road until noon."

Personally, Tess had enjoyed sleeping in and the break from the early-morning rally routine, but it had been a long day and they were on the final stretch to the last checkpoint. "I told you it's a symbolic race. Whoever comes in first gets the honor of turning over all the proceeds to the Women's Cancer League."

"If tonight's the punch line, then why did we sit through that boring-as-hell ceremony this morning?"

Tess smiled. "That boring-as-hell ceremony was supposed to be *fun*. Didn't you hear people laughing?"

"Oh, that's right. The souvenirs we've been picking up," he said dryly. "How could I have forgotten? Keene Motors' bobble-head cow from Amarillo had me in tears."

"Ha, ha. Everyone liked our slot machine from the Parisian, though. That was really sweet of Tori's husband to make it a gift." This cranky man needed some sleep. He didn't know it yet but they were going to find a hotel somewhere on the water tonight. He'd get all the sleep he needed, and then some. "That boring-as-hell ceremony breaks up the schedule. If you haven't figured it out yet, the checkpoints have been roughly six hundred miles apart. That makes for a decent driving day. But if we'd left at the normal time today, we'd have arrived in San Francisco during traffic hour. After four days on the road, no one wants to battle rush-hour traffic, so the committee lets us sleep late and start late on the last day so we don't get in until after dark."

Anthony just grunted, but Tess was pleased. They were making really decent time. It was just after nine o'clock and if their route through the city proved as easy as the rest of the day, they'd be in good shape.

They fell back into silence as Tess wound through the city streets with Anthony's direction. The night-dark city unfolded around them, and she enjoyed her rising excitement as they neared the end of the rally and a few more days together, *alone.*

It wasn't until they passed a gas station for the second time that Tess realized they must have driven in a circle.

"Are we lost, Anthony?"

"No."

"Are you sure? I think we drove past that gas station already." She shifted her gaze off the road, and one glance at Anthony was enough to make her cold. "What's wrong?"

"I don't want you to freak, *chère,* but we've got a little problem."

"What?"

"Someone's been following us for the past dozen blocks. An SUV filled with thugs. I can't tell how old they are, but they're not kids."

Lubbock might not be the biggest city in Texas, but Tess knew enough about big cities to know trouble happened a lot more often when the population got high and tight. She hoped trouble hadn't latched onto her and Anthony. "What should we do?"

"I had you make a turn back there so they'd think we were lost, but if you put those skills you learned with the Maverick to work, we might shake them."

Tess nodded and tightened her grip on the wheel.

They were silent as Anthony navigated her through a series of quick turns that took them off their declared route to the checkpoint still across the city. She resisted the urge to look in the rearview mirror and just kept her eyes on the dark streets. It was night, and a pedestrian could all too easily step out from between parked cars.

She could only go so fast without getting dangerous, and she pushed that limit to the max.

"No good," he finally said. "They know we're onto them. They're closing the distance."

"Is it a gang?"

"I thought so at first, but they're on us like glue. I don't get the feeling this is random."

She didn't like that *something* she heard in his voice, the inevitability, and when he unfastened his seat belt and twisted around to reach into the back seat, his intensity made adrenaline pump so fast she had to swallow a lump in her throat.

"Don't worry, *chère*. They've probably just taken a liking to your Gremlin."

She gave a short laugh despite herself, appreciated his effort to make her feel better. She watched in her periphery as he kneeled beside her to stretch all the way to the hatch.

"What are you doing?"

"Grabbing something from your trunk."

She would have asked what, but she had to do some fancy driving to miss a car pulling away from the curb. She needed to keep her attention on this road. Cruising along these narrow streets so far over the speed limit was begging for trouble.

Anthony settled back in beside her with a tire iron in hand, and Tess tried to stave off a rising sense of premonition as he flipped open his phone and made a call.

He summed up the situation, and she knew he'd called 9-1-1.

She finally glanced in the rearview mirror. "They're getting closer, Anthony. Do you want me to speed up?"

He shook his head. His voice was calm when he said, "Did you notice that last street sign by any chance?"

"No."

"We're from out of town." He spoke into the phone. "We got off our route trying to shake these guys, so I don't have a cross street yet."

He listed a few landmarks as they drove past them, then Tess's headlights reflected off a street sign as she eased up on the pedal to cruise through an intersection.

"That sign says Tavist Avenue."

Anthony repeated the information. "We'll try to keep heading west, but we're driving a purple Gremlin with a white racing stripe and Texas tags. Tell the patrol they couldn't miss us if they tried."

Tess gave a huff, a crazy sound that had only the barest trace of bravado.

The traffic light ahead switched to yellow.

"Run it," Anthony said coolly, with the phone still poised at his ear.

Tess hit the gas and leaned on the horn to signal traffic, but just as she hit the intersection, the car idling on the north side of the street jumped the light.

"Damn it." She swerved hard to avoid a collision, forced to brake as her trajectory changed, and she was suddenly facing a line of parked cars.

Wheeling the car around, she narrowly cleared an old sedan's fender.

But those seconds cost her big.

She came out of the spin to find the SUV screeching toward her, cutting off her escape. Tess had to brake to renegotiate her direction before she gunned the engine again.

The SUV looked like a monster bearing down on them, and when it nailed her quarter panel, she had to brake again.

This time the SUV's doors swung wide and men jumped out.

Six men wearing ski masks.

Panic drowned out the sound of Anthony's voice as she threw the car into Reverse, spun the wheel and shimmied out of the crush, scraping the SUV's fender in the process.

The big vehicle bucked when it came up against her sturdy Gremlin, and Tess almost had them clear when she heard the shots. Two loud cracks in the night. The wheel jerked in her hands. One—or was it two?—tires blew. She hung on and braked hard to change direction again, but this time the stop cost.

Men swarmed them, men who didn't look like any gang members she'd ever seen on the news.

"Keep the doors locked and stay inside." Anthony flung his door wide, jumped out and slammed it shut behind him.

"Anthony!"

He was gone. The solid *thunk* of the closing door jump-started her heart again, helped her think through panic.

Slamming the lock button down, Tess grabbed his cell phone off the seat to hear the woman on the other end trying to urge her onto the line. Tess shouted, "Send the police" into the receiver as she yanked open her glove compartment. Damn man. He was one to six out there. And they had guns.

Digging for her pepper spray, she grabbed the canister just as her driver's window exploded.

Tess had all she could do to scramble away from the narrow wooden club that suddenly appeared. Cold chunks of shattered glass bounced off her cheek and head before she brought her arm up to protect her face. She dropped the phone.

Rough laughter exploded outside, muffled thumps that might have been someone hitting the ground. Anthony? More shattered glass as the club cleared away debris. She thumbed off the pepper spray's safety while scooting farther toward the passenger's seat.

A black-clad arm shot through the broken window. A strong hand latched onto her forearm like a vice. Tess allowed herself to be pulled upright just enough to catch sight of the hooded face… She shot the pepper spray.

Some of the blast must have made it through the holes in the ski mask because the man's grip slackened. He reared back, whacking his head on the doorjamb with a solid crack. In that split instant, Tess repositioned herself so when he came back at her she could defend herself.

She planted her heel in his face and earned a muttered curse. Kicking again and again, she dodged his attempts to grab her, clutching the canister in case he caught her. She couldn't see the phone, couldn't spare a glance to find it.

Finally, his fingers bit into her ankle, and she clawed at the door, resisted by grabbing the handle and hanging on. She kicked hard with her other foot, trying to break his hold.

Strength won out, breaking her grip on the handle just as the passenger's window exploded above her head. She spat away tiny chunks of broken glass that clung to her lips, crying out when the attacker at her feet jerked her sharply toward him.

He fumbled one-handed with the lock. With her leg bent at an odd angle halfway through the window, all she could do was clutch the steering wheel to resist. She gritted her teeth against a blast of pain as he pulled open the door and broken glass caught her calf.

Tess knew he meant to pull her through next, and she managed to lock her arm in the cage of the steering wheel and get some weight behind it.

She leaned on the horn.

The blast of sound shrieked through the night reassuringly solid and loud, and she had the wild thought that no late model car had a horn that could come close to competing with those made in the seventies.

She leaned on that horn again, and again.

"Stop the bitch." A harsh command was growled out.

Tess clung to the steering wheel with steel in her arm, managing to break his grip. She bucked and kicked so her attacker couldn't grab her again.

Out of nowhere, a bat slammed into the windshield, hard enough to depress and web the tempered glass. Within seconds, the hatch window exploded, raining glass into the front seat.

She didn't know why these men were vandalizing her car, could only cling to the wheel, ram her fist into the horn, and keep kicking out at her attacker.

Then hands reached in from the passenger side for a fistful of hair. Her head snapped back painfully, and she cried out, giving way to the pressure before it ripped her hair out by the root.

"Get her." A rough voice broke over her head.

The attacker at her feet yanked the door completely open and the lower half of her spilled to the ground.

He was on her in an instant. She couldn't disentangle her hand from the steering wheel quickly enough, and felt her wrist snap as she was dragged off the seat.

The keening horn faded to silence. For a stunned instant, Tess could only absorb the shock of the pain, the blood throbbing so hard in her ears, she thought she'd be sick.

Another powerful pull, and she slithered off the seat, striking her head on the floorboard on her way down. White light exploded behind her lids, but cleared in time for her to see him rise above her.... With her undamaged hand, she sprayed another blast of pepper spray.

He roared a curse and staggered backward, giving her a chance to roll free. Cradling her injured wrist against her chest, her skin slick from sweat, Tess let adrenaline fuel her across the pavement. When she cleared her fender, she saw what was happening in the street, and her heartbeat stalled.

The ski-masked men huddled around Anthony.

Another man joined them, swinging his way through

the group with that wicked bat, but Anthony halted a blow with the tire iron, sending the bat spinning from his attacker's hands. Another lunged. Anthony staggered, rolling onto his back and bringing the man down with him.

It took Tess a second to recognize that while he might be fighting too many men, he wasn't struggling. He was a blur of skilled motion, striking out at one after another. He wielded that tire iron, blocking a blow then smashing it into the face of another, knocking him momentarily out of the fight.

She could only stare as he launched himself onto one of the attackers in a move she'd only seen in the movies. He came down on top of the man, landed a solid blow with his fist, then rolled away leaving the guy sprawled motionless on the ground.

But Tess stared a minute too long and forgot her own attacker. He'd recovered and launched himself on top of her, pinning her to the pavement. Her injured hand caught underneath her and a volley of pain was the last thing she knew.

ANTHONY COULDN'T GET TO Tess. Every time he fought off one thug, another had to be dealt with. But he'd heard her cry and couldn't look to see if she was all right. He couldn't lose his concentration, not with her safety in the balance.

These were no ordinary thugs—they were thugs with some skill, which meant they had money behind them. Not enough skill to take him down, but enough that if he screwed up, they'd overpower him by their sheer numbers.

He wouldn't screw up.

Nailing the back of some guy's head, he felt the tire iron vibrate as it struck a blow that took another thug out.

He wouldn't screw up.

The fifth one rejoined them, which meant Tess only had to contend with one. Not the one with the gun. That one he'd been keeping busy so he didn't have a chance to retrieve the weapon Anthony had kicked out of his hand. It had skittered beneath a parked car, and he needed to get it first to end this fight.

Blocking a blow with a bat, he found himself restrained as the thug with the silver eyebrow studs grabbed him around the throat. Silver Stud must have thought he had the upper hand because he didn't press his advantage.

Mistake.

Anthony drove the tire iron backward, catching him in the stomach. The force of the blow sent him reeling backward, and Anthony broke free. He dropped to the ground and rolled toward the car. If the gun hadn't flown too far underneath…

"Assholes," someone yelled from a window over a shop. "I'm calling the cops."

Thank you.

Tess's quick thinking with the car horn had called attention to them, and that yell bought Anthony the few precious seconds he needed to stretch his arm beneath the car, feeling the concrete beneath his splayed fingers, searching….

A kick to his back knocked the breath from his lungs. Before he could maneuver around to gain his feet, the bat caught the side of his face a stunning blow.

His head exploded and it was all he could do to shake off the sudden daze. He didn't resist when violent hands dragged him to his feet. He didn't do anything as one of the thugs held him by the throat and the others gathered around to kick his ass.

Then Anthony leveled the automatic pistol at one of the approaching thug's legs, fired, then brought the weapon back to rest against the cheek of the guy who held him.

He heard a sharp intake of breath, and nudged the gun in a silent demand. "Let go."

The arm around his throat eased off. Without moving the gun, Anthony spun and caught the thug around the neck. Shielding himself behind the guy, he said, "Call off your friends."

The sight of his buddy on the ground clutching his bleeding knee seemed to be all the incentive this one needed.

"Back off," he yelled.

The one standing closest took a step backward. The one beside Tess bolted behind a parked car, safely out of Anthony's line of fire. He held the gun steady and took in the scene in a glance. Two on the ground disabled. One injured. One gone.

And Tess sprawled beside the Gremlin, unmoving.

"Get against the car." Anthony struggled against a surge of red heat, a need to fire this gun and end this fight so he could get to Tess. "Hands where I can see them. Now start talking or I start pulling this trigger. Who sent you?"

He barely noticed the sirens as police cruisers surrounded the intersection or the visibars that flashed in the darkness.

11

"WE HAVE YOUR STATEMENT, and we'll be in touch," the detective told Anthony. "Don't worry. Once we get those guys booked, I'm sure they'll start talking."

"You'll tow the car to your impound lot until I can make arrangements to get it home?"

The man handed him a business card. "It's already there. Call and talk to Jerry when you're squared. Now go see your lady and be glad you made out as well as you did tonight."

Anthony was glad, but when he arrived inside the emergency room to find Tess still unconscious, he didn't feel as though they'd made out well at all.

His chest constricted around a breath as he took in the glossy dark hair tangled around her head, such a stark contrast to the linens on the gurney and her too-pale skin. To his relief, her beautiful face showed no signs of the attack, but she seemed small lying there...*vulnerable.*

"She'll be fine," an unfamiliar voice said.

Anthony glanced at the doctor. The nurse beside him seemed old enough to have a few years of experience behind her, but this guy didn't look much older than Anthony himself.

"Why's she still out?"

"Shock. That's to be expected with the concussion and arm trauma. I'll keep her here for the rest of the night so we can keep an eye on her."

Anthony's gaze zeroed in on Tess's arm. He hadn't noticed that—the white plaster cast blended in with the sheets.

"Broken?"

The doctor nodded. The nurse whispered something to him and both their gazes riveted onto Anthony's face.

"You need to be x-rayed," the doctor said. "I'll send your friend to a room, so we can take a look at you."

"I'm fine."

"You don't look fine. You need stitches on that cheek, and judging by the swelling, you sustained some head injury, too."

If Anthony was being honest, he didn't feel fine. His head felt ready to explode. The skin on his face felt swollen and tight, and he suspected he might have cracked a rib or two.

He didn't feel like being honest.

"I'm fine," he insisted. "I'll go up with Tess."

The nurse frowned. "If you don't let the doctor stitch that cheek, it'll scar."

He just leveled his gaze at her. She shook her head in disapproval and said, "At least let me clean it."

The doctor handed her antiseptic, and he submitted to her ministrations while waiting for the transportation aide to arrive.

Tess didn't awaken as they wheeled her upstairs to a regular floor, and Anthony paced outside the room as the nurse got her settled. He used the time to make the phone call he'd never expected to make.

Ray Macy picked up on the fourth ring, his voice gravelly with sleep. "Yeah."

"This is Anthony DiLeo, sir. I didn't live up to my end of our deal," he said simply, truthfully. "Tess and I were involved in an attack in San Francisco. She'll be fine, but she got banged around some. The doctor wants to keep her in the hospital for the rest of the night to keep his eye on her. I need you to contact her father and let him know where she is."

To Ray Macy's credit, he handled the news well. Maybe it had to do with a family member in crisis. Anthony knew well enough from his own that when something went wrong, family stuck to the business at hand—fixing the problem. There'd always be time later for guilt and blame, and he appreciated Ray Macy not making him feel any worse than he already did. If that were even possible.

By the time he'd relayed the hospital information and disconnected the call, the floor nurse was exiting Tess's room. Anthony decided that he must look like shit, because she glanced his way and gave directions to the coffeepot in the patient pantry room then told him she'd leave pillows and a blanket so he could get some sleep, too.

Anthony thanked her and headed to the pantry, where he grabbed himself a cup of joe and dialed the number of someone he could count on, someone who, with a P.I. background, could help him figure out what to do to protect Tess.

He wasn't waiting around for the police to get those thugs into lockup. He wanted to know who'd come after them and why.

It might be the dead of night in New Orleans, but a sleep-drugged voice answered on the third ring.

"Anthony."

"Hey, princess. Getting your beauty sleep?"

"You all right?" Alarm sharpened her drowsy tone.

He leaned against the counter, amazed by the relief that swept through him, by how much he'd needed to hear a familiar voice right now. The voice of someone he didn't have to impress or prove himself to, someone who wouldn't ask for explanations the way his family would. He needed to hear *her* voice, and he hadn't known how much until she was on the other end, just *there*, waiting.

"Yeah, I'll live, but I need your help."

"Of course."

Of course.

He could practically see her sitting up in bed to shake off sleep, scowling as she wished for some jet-fuel java to speed the process along. The thought made him feel better, in control.

Just hearing her voice helped him understand that the way he felt right now wasn't about being busted up in a fight. It was about the woman lying inside the hospital room down the hall. He cared, damn it, so much that he was in over his head. He recognized how this felt. He worried about keeping Tess safe, questioned whether he could. She'd already been hurt because he hadn't been able to protect her.

But he felt better talking, so he explained what had been happening with the rally, the letters Big Tex had received, the attack and what he'd learned from their attackers.

Harley listened, occasionally asking questions, annoyed that the police couldn't offer any more. She didn't ask for anything except the necessities about Tess, but she would know that this woman was important enough for him to call her, that he wouldn't trust anyone but Harley to help him protect her.

She'd get the significance of that.

"I'll start the preliminary work just as soon as I make some coffee," she said. "I'll catch a flight to San Francisco in the morning. Hopefully the police won't jerk me around, but it doesn't matter. I need to follow the trail from there before it gets cold and find out who springs these guys from lockup."

"This won't screw things up for next week, will it?"

"If I get tied up, I'll fly back for the day."

"You're sure?"

She gave an exasperated huff that came through loud and clear over two thousand miles of bouncing satellite signals. "Why are you asking me stupid questions at three in the morning when I haven't made coffee yet?"

He smiled. He needed reassurance right now, needed to know she'd help him figure this out.

Of course.

It was that simple.

"You don't let her out of your eyesight, Anthony, and I'll find out what's going on."

"Thanks, princess."

"Take care of you, too. Promise?"

He heard the concern in her voice and for a moment he just absorbed the feeling, drew strength from it. "Promise."

"I'll call." She disconnected, and he stood there, savoring the knowledge that he was no longer alone.

Harley was there as she always was, not only to help him sort out the threat against Tess, but to help him sort out his feelings, feelings that suddenly seemed bigger than he was. When he finally made his way to Tess's room, he closed the door and sank into the chair beside the bed, the weight of the night's events settling on him as if it had been strapped across his back.

The room's only light glowed softly above her head, spilling a muted glow across her face. Her lashes clustered on her cheeks, dark semicircles against her pale skin that drew his attention to the faint smudges beneath her eyes, evidence of too many sleepless nights.

He'd been responsible for that, too.

His gaze traveled to her arm propped gingerly on a pillow, the slim fingers extending beyond the smooth edges, the neat pink nails. That cast symbolized the violence of the night.

So many questions rattled around in his head. About the attack. About Tess. But he wasn't alone. To hell with the stupid police. Harley would help him, leaving him free to take care of the most important thing right now—keeping Tess safe.

Hooking his arms on his knees, Anthony leaned forward, finding the position relieved the pounding pressure in his face. Tess exhaled a restless sigh, and he watched as she turned her head to the side, as if she could sense his presence.

She'd held her own tonight, kept her head and raised the alarm, doing her bit to help when he'd been outmanned in that street, unable to keep all their assailants busy.

What bothered him the most was the thought of her being scared. It was a physical ache that hurt more than potentially cracked ribs, split skin or a bruised face.

He needed to hear her say she'd be okay, needed to see that familiar challenge flare in those big green eyes, a look

that said she would take whatever life threw at her and tri-
ple it. He needed to see her smile.

That need kept surprising him.

Their attraction had taken him off guard. He hadn't expected to get this sucked into a woman ever again. But as
he sat in this hospital room watching her sleep, rehashing
the events of the past week, everything about him hurting,
Anthony understood what he wanted from her, finally recognized what was happening between them. He'd gotten
the one thing he'd never thought he would.

A second chance.

TESS STILL SLEPT when Ray Macy and Big Tex Hardaway
arrived shortly before dawn.

Anthony rose to greet them, grateful he'd abandoned attempts to sleep and made for the patient coffeepot long ago.

In his Stetson and hand-tooled boots, Big Tex Hardaway could have walked off a television set, and there was
no missing Penny Parker's genius at capturing this man's
presence in her advertising campaign. Like his TV alter
ego, Big Tex was larger than life, brawny rather than tall,
with a strong grip and an easy smile.

Tess looked nothing like her father, except for the flash
of challenge in his green eyes. The man's gaze traveled
over Tess with a look that hit Anthony as the way every
father should look at his daughter.

Adoring, with a little possessive and a lot of smitten
thrown into the mix.

Anthony nodded to Ray Macy, expected to feel the
weight of the man's stare. After all, he'd promised to care
for Tess the last time they'd spoken, and here they were
inside a hospital.

To his surprise, he didn't see accusation in Ray Macy's face. "I hear we owe you a thanks."

"We talked to the police and the doctor on our flight in." Big Tex stepped back from the bed. "And I checked out everything I could find out about you."

Anthony appreciated the honesty but wasn't sure how to respond, so he went straight to the heart of matters. "Then you know the attack wasn't random."

"Heard all about it from the police. Also heard you questioned the attackers."

How ironic that after all the effort he'd put forth to get in front of this man, Big Tex's first impression of him would involve a street fight and a gun. "I didn't learn as much as I'd hoped. They were paid to rough up Tess's car and knock her out of the race. According to the ones I talked to, she wasn't supposed to get hurt."

"But you were. The police think that's significant."

Anthony thought so, too. "Someone's trying to make a point, but I couldn't tell you what it is. Forcing Tess out of the race doesn't make sense. It's not like there's any prize money at stake here, and since I've only known her a week, I don't have a clue where I fit in. Obviously, my first concern is her safety, so I called in some private investigator friends of mine. They're with Eastman Investigations out of New Orleans.

"You can check them out. It's a reputable firm that does a lot of work with government agencies." Pulling one of Harley's business cards from his wallet, he handed it to Big Tex. "I know about the letters. Do you think they could be connected?"

"Could be," Big Tex said noncommittally and let his words trail off into a silence that got heavier by the second.

Anthony braced himself. The man's intensity clued him in on what was coming next—an interrogation.

Sure enough, Big Tex looked him dead in the eye and said, "Son, I've got some questions, and I'd like straight answers."

"Shoot, sir."

"Until four days ago, I'd never heard your name. Now, all of a sudden, you're running the rally with my daughter, protecting her from bad guys and concerning yourself with who might be after her. Seems like an awful lot going on since you showed up. Should I be worried about you?"

Anthony knew his answer would lay the whole foundation for his relationship with this man. A week ago, he'd wanted that relationship to be all about business.

Now, a lot more rode on his answer.

"I understand your concern, sir. I'm new to the equation, and it looks like I didn't walk in at the best of times. Ray said as much before the rally. Like I told him then, all I have is my reputation to vouch for me, and my word that my intentions toward Tess are honorable."

Big Tex's expression didn't budge, and Anthony knew this man was no one's fool. He'd cut his way through the ranks to his current success with shrewd business tactics and people savvy. At the moment, he was passing judgment on Anthony.

But he hadn't thrown him out yet. It was a start.

"Penny told us you were chasing Tess around the convention to talk about some sort of business," Ray said. "Care to tell us more about that?"

The moment of truth.

Anthony had yet to bridge the distance between bed buddy and serious contender with Tess. If he explained his

AutoTexCare plan and the reason he'd sought Tess out in the first place, he'd only reinforce her belief he was more interested in her father than he was in her.

On the other hand, if he didn't answer this question and fast, he sensed these two were about to send him packing.

Anthony didn't think he had enough leverage with Tess yet to override a veto from the two most important men in her life. And when he glanced at her as she stirred on the bed, he knew there was only one answer he could give, anyway.

The truth.

"I'd rather not tell you about my business with Tess just yet. It isn't a secret or anything mysterious." He gave a dry laugh. "It's not a big deal at all, really, or it wasn't at first. But now there's a problem she and I need to work out."

"DiLeo, that's convoluted as hell," Ray Macy shot back. "Just answer the damn question."

Anthony shrugged. They'd have to take it or leave it on this. He had something to prove to Tess and that came first. "I wish I had more to vouch for me than my word. I don't."

Ray Macy scowled harder, but Big Tex eyed him levelly and asked, "What problem?"

"I want to keep seeing your daughter after this rally is over, but our business is in the way."

Ray Macy gave a snort of undisguised humor, as if out of anything in the world Anthony could have said he'd picked about the stupidest.

Given the circumstances, Anthony would have to agree.

"Do you think she wants to keep seeing you?" Big Tex asked.

"I do." *If* Tess was willing to give him a chance to prove she'd become a lot more important than his AutoTexCare plan.

Big Tex stared, gauging his worth, calculating the risks. Anthony could see the moment he'd made his decision, recognized the determination in those strikingly familiar eyes.

"You do have something more than your reputation to vouch for you. Your actions. You protected my little girl last night, and from the looks of you that took some doing. Keep your secret for now and work out your problem." He extended his hand. "Don't do me wrong, son. You'll regret it."

Big Tex had a father's look all over him, a look that promised he'd blow through Anthony like a category five hurricane if he did anything to hurt Tess.

It was a chance, and that meant another step in the right direction. They shook. "You won't regret it, sir. I'm just glad she'll be okay."

Big Tex flipped Anthony's hand over to reveal the cut knuckles and bruised fingers. "And how many attacked you again?"

"Six, Daddy," Tess said in a groggy morning voice. "They had guns."

Only one gun that Anthony knew of, but he didn't correct her. He stepped aside as Big Tex and Ray Macy went to her. Tess had called them mother hens, but they looked more like bodyguards flanking her bed. They also looked like two relieved men, both of whom loved her very much.

Quietly retreating from the room, Anthony gave them some privacy, drained by his own sense of relief, by how much he wanted to feel as though he belonged in that room.

But he didn't, not yet, no matter how much he cared about her. So he walked to the patient pantry, tossed the cold dregs of coffee into the sink then poured more. Downing it in a swallow, he threw the cup in the trash and headed to the nurses' station to consider his next step.

As far as Anthony was concerned, he and Tess were in this together, and they should solve it that way. Whether or not the reason for the attack began with letters to Big Tex, he'd almost gotten his head broken last night. That gave him some rights.

And no one would get close enough to hurt Tess again. They'd have to get through him first. *If* he could convince her to stick close…

"DiLeo." Ray Macy stepped out of the room and motioned him back. "Tess wants you."

He liked the sound of that and headed down the hall, feeling hopeful that something good might come from this brush with bad luck, after all.

He tried to get a read on Big Tex, but didn't know the man enough to guess his mood, except to recognize the air of tension was gone.

Moving to the side of the bed, Anthony inclined his head as Big Tex retreated, joining Ray Macy. Neither man left the room.

Tess watched him with a sleepy smile, and she reached up to take his hand and pull him down beside her.

Twining his fingers through hers, he held on, needing the anchor of touch. "You're one helluva driver, *chère.*"

Green fire flashed in those beautiful eyes as she examined his bruised fingers. Until that moment, Anthony hadn't fully appreciated how much he needed to see her smile to trust she'd be okay.

"Where did you learn to fight like that?"

"Did I mention my brother Damon owns a dojo and holds black belts in four disciplines?"

She gave a soft laugh. "No, you didn't. Is Damon older or younger?"

"Younger."

"So you've spent your whole life trying not to let him kick your butt?"

He smiled.

She smiled back. But her smile faded as she searched his face, and he could see how bad he must look reflected in her expression. "Why didn't you let them stitch that cut?"

"Now what makes you think I didn't *let* them?"

"Right. Did they treat you at all or did you sit here all night worrying about me?"

Funny how easily she saw through him, and since he couldn't think of any reply, he said nothing.

Tess wasn't having any part of it. "Daddy's here. Did you tell him about your service—"

"About my service center?" He forced a laugh. "Figured I'd have plenty of time to impress him with my credentials after we tracked down who was responsible for last night."

She eyed him curiously, but let the subject drop. "Daddy and Uncle Ray filled me in. My car's a mess, isn't it?"

He supposed a girl had to have priorities. Here she sat in a hospital bed with a cast on her arm after a night spent sleeping off shock, and her first thought was her car.

No, he corrected himself. Her *second* thought was her car. Her first had been about him.

Anthony found that promising, too.

"Nothing that can't be fixed, *chère*. I told the police to impound it, so she'll be safe and sound until you decide what you want to do."

"Have her towed home, I guess. I don't know of anyone around here I'd trust to do the work."

"We'll take care of it, sweet thing," Ray Macy said from the door. "Don't you worry your pretty head about her."

"Thanks, Uncle Ray." She gave an absent nod. "I'm so sorry you got caught up in all this, Anthony."

She thumbed his swollen knuckles, another absent gesture that fueled his resolve not to let her go.

"I'm not worried about *me*. But our trip's been cut short, so what about you coming back to New Orleans for a while?"

She just blinked in surprise. Anthony could practically feel the stares boring holes through the back of his head and hoped he wasn't pushing his luck *too* far.

"With everything that's just happened, the safest place for my daughter is at home," Big Tex said.

"I disagree, sir. If Tess heads back to her normal routine, she'll be predictable, and that's exactly what she doesn't want to be right now. At least not until my friends get a lock on what's going on." He turned to face the men, and found not one but *two* stares that could have drilled holes through his skull. "And to be frank, I can't convince her that she wants to keep seeing me with you two around."

Big Tex and Ray Macy scowled.

Tess laughed that silvery laugh and said, "Not to worry, Daddy. Anthony earned his chance to convince me, and I've been dying for a ride in his Firebird."

12

"I'M SURPRISED you didn't ask one of your brothers to pick us up from the airport," Tess said, resting her head on his shoulder as the taxi drove through the dark streets.

Daddy had insisted they all fly out of San Francisco on his private plane, which had dropped him and Uncle Ray off in Lubbock before continuing on to New Orleans.

Tess knew he worried about not bringing her home. He'd have much rather Anthony disembarked in Lubbock instead of taking her to New Orleans. But she'd wanted to go. Daddy's compromise had been a flight together to discuss investigation strategy and get to know Anthony.

"Don't be," he said. "If everyone knows I'm home, we'll spend the next few days bombarded with company. I promised your father I'd keep you safe and make sure you got some rest."

"So you're mother-henning me, too?"

He only rested his cheek on the top of her head, but Tess didn't doubt if she could see his face, he'd be smiling. Macho man loved this, no doubt. But even worse was that her protest came purely by rote. Having Daddy, Uncle Ray and Anthony around her all day had proven just how much she'd wanted them there.

Whoever was behind the attack had achieved his goal.

The violence had unnerved her, and Tess wondered if Anthony sensed she was still reeling. She knew her daddy did. That had been the only reason he hadn't given her a hard time about going to New Orleans with Anthony. He might not understand how she could feel safe with a man she'd only just met, but he knew she did. And he seemed willing to trust that.

That in itself felt like an accomplishment of sorts. For so long she'd dismissed his worries as invalid, considered his concerns a parental side effect of losing her mother. And while he definitely was overprotective, Tess had to admit she'd lost her perspective, too.

This was something she'd have to sort out—after they'd figured out who was behind the attack.

Snuggling closer, Tess let her eyes drift shut, trying to feel bad because she'd dragged Anthony into a situation that had turned into such a mess. She'd insisted the doctor check him out and he'd finally agreed. His ribs hadn't been cracked but bruised. Ice packs and antiseptic had taken care of the worst of the cuts and swelling, but he'd waited too long to have the gash stitched. He'd have a nice scar to remind him of the choice.

But as bad as she felt, Tess couldn't lie to herself. She was glad they were still together. The idea of an anonymous someone wanting to hurt Daddy and the people he loved, and even the people around her, was frightening, but she flat-out refused to live as an emotional hostage.

Between the San Francisco police department, Anthony's investigator friends and Daddy's chief of security at AutoCarTex, they would uncover the threat and put a stop to it. Until then, she'd enjoy her time with Anthony and let him play mother hen if that's what he wanted. He had another chance to impress her daddy, and he'd earned that chance.

She enjoyed the ride through the city, the sound of Anthony's voice as he directed the driver along a street in the Art District to his place. Though it was late, street lamps washed the facades of what appeared to be businesses that had been converted into town houses.

The taxi pulled up in front of an iron fence and ivy-covered gate. Tess waited while Anthony got out, unfolding himself as though every muscle in his body screamed with the effort. He extended a hand to her and helped her out behind him.

"You're sore, aren't you?" she asked.

"Sat too long on the plane."

While her father's plane often made speedy travel possible in a pinch, it wasn't exactly a spacious ride.

She circled the taxi to grab her own bags, knowing Anthony would do the honors if she let him. He shot her a look that convinced her he knew exactly what she was doing, paid the cabbie and grabbed his own bags. "Come on, *chère.*"

The taxi pulled away and he led her through the gate and up the steps to where a lone light shone on the portico.

Tess followed him upstairs, flipping lights on and off as he gave her the nickel tour.

She liked his place. The warehouse had been converted into a contemporary design with a ceiling shooting three stories straight up and a loft-style arrangement with a master suite on the second floor and a guest room and another that Anthony used as an office on the third.

His master suite took up the entire second floor and

much of that square footage went to an outdoor patio that turned his view into a jungle.

"Wow, you've got a green thumb," she remarked, peering through the glass doors to the wild arrangement of plants and trees that she could make out with the solar-powered lights.

"I've got a plant service."

She laughed. Dropping her garment bag beside his in front of the closet, she caught him before he moved away, ran her hand along his shoulders. "How about a massage? I've still got one good hand left. I can help loosen you up."

He turned to her, and the tenderness in his expression made her heart melt. Reaching for her broken arm, he lifted it to brush his mouth across her fingers. It was a featherlight kiss that managed to ripple through her as softly as a caress. This man had calmly soothed her panic when she'd been frantic to outrun that SUV, had fiercely protected her. She was struck by the desire to pamper him, to ease his aches and be as possessive of him as he'd been of her.

"Will you let me make you feel better?" She met his gaze above their clasped hands, and the longing in his bedroom eyes mirrored her own.

"If it involves my spa."

"My pleasure."

She unpacked their bags as he headed onto the patio to remove the protective cover and get the jets whirring to life.

After hanging clothes haphazardly in the closet and making piles on top of his dresser, Tess went on a research expedition for something to drink. She headed back downstairs, seeking out light switches to lead her way through the house that struck her as totally Anthony. Contemporary. The leather furniture seemed comfortable yet created a stylish look that suggested a designer had helped decorate the interior. Yet Anthony had imprinted himself all over the place, too.

Meticulously assembled models of classic cars on shelves above a desk. Framed photos in various disarray on practically every surface of the room. Someone had hand-crocheted a bright afghan that he'd tossed over the back of a recliner.

Sports equipment—baseball judging by the bat—had been tossed on the foyer floor, suggesting he'd walked in the door, dropped everything and hadn't given it another thought.

Tess decided this was a house he lived in, Making her way into the kitchen, she dug through his cabinets, taking stock of all the empty space, smiling when she thought about his familiarity with fast food. There was something about seeing these little things that added to the strange sense of reality she'd had ever since opening her eyes in the hospital. On the road Anthony had seemed like a fantasy man with his incredible mouth and oh-so-noble gestures.

But after last night… Tess wasn't sure exactly what it was, but last night had somehow changed everything. She'd known he had a family, brothers, a business, but seeing his home, pictures of people important to him, seeing him tired and hurt from the fight made him much more…*real*.

She opened and closed cabinets, looking for something to wrap her cast. She lucked out and found plastic garbage bags. Bypassing a bottle of burgundy in a wine rack on the counter, she went for the fridge, where she found lots of condiments and more empty shelf space. She grabbed two bottles of water.

Heading back upstairs, she found Anthony pulling towels from a linen cabinet.

"I like your house. It looks like you." She held up the bag and said, "Almost all set. I couldn't find any tape."

"Upstairs in the office." His gaze slid to the water bottles. "Didn't I have any wine?"

"You took painkillers."

"Not since we left San Francisco."

She hadn't taken any since, either, but Tess didn't have a clue how long it would take the medication to clear their systems. Slipping her arms around his waist she pressed her hips suggestively against him. "I won't take chances. I want to make love to you, not send you back to the hospital."

"Making love definitely sounds better."

"If you can move, of course."

"I can always move enough for that, *chère*." To prove his point, he ground a promising erection against her. She tipped her face up to his for a kiss, enjoying this unfamiliar tenderness, wanting to explore it.

She meant just to give him a gentle peck, but his mouth covered hers slowly, heavily almost, and she could taste his weariness. She held him even tighter. He sighed.

The sound broke against her mouth, and she drank it in, savoring his warm breath, the unfamiliar feel of his swollen lips. She pulled away then, gliding her hands around his waist to work his shirt from his jeans. With her one bum hand, and his bruised ribs, it took both of them to get the shirt over his head, and when they did, she tossed it onto the bed.

Leaning forward, she pressed her mouth softly against the bruised skin on his ribs, felt him tremble.

"Does that feel a little better?" she asked, unfastening his jeans and freeing the sexy body part that she was so enjoying becoming acquainted with.

"Do I look like I need to be taken care of?"

She wouldn't want to crush Mr. Macho Man's pride so she simply said, "I owe you."

"For what? We're only together because you gave me a chance to impress you, remember?"

"You impressed me above and beyond last night."

He exhaled sharply when he leaned over to help her lame attempts to get the pants down his legs one-handed. "I don't think I impressed you enough."

She peered up in time to catch him looking at her cast.

"Trust me when I say I can't think of another man I'd have wanted to be with last night, Anthony. I mean that."

"Your father and uncle wouldn't let anything happen to you."

"They'd have been two against six, and trust me, neither of them fight like you do. Can you imagine last night with Daryl? He'd have opened that mouth of his and wound up getting us both shot. Guaranteed."

That earned a chuckle. "Okay. You got me there."

He actually swayed on his feet and braced himself when she tugged off the last of his pants. She tossed those onto the bed, too.

"You said the office is upstairs."

He glanced absently at the door. "Yeah, I'll go grab—"

"*You* get in the tub. I can find the tape."

She headed out of the room without giving him a chance

to argue. The man was dead on his feet, and she needed to get in the spa with him before he fell asleep and drowned.

The stairway continued at the second-floor loft, and the top floor had another landing with two doors. Inside the office, a massive desk housed a late model computer setup and a variety of office equipment. Like the rest of his house, this room was stylishly decorated, but judging by the piles of paper scattered over every surface, Tess guessed that he spent a lot of time in here.

Sitting in his cushy leather chair, she scanned the desk, debating where she would hide if she were a roll of tape. Her gaze fell on a photograph displayed on a shelf beside the monitor, a spot where he might slide his gaze often while he worked.

Carefully retrieving the photo from the shelf, Tess glanced into the face of a beautiful redheaded woman who'd been captured in a candid moment, laughing, her blue eyes sparkling with humor. Tess could only see her from the neck up, but didn't need to see more to know this woman would be delicate and exquisitely feminine. It was all over her fine-boned features, the graceful way she tipped her head when she laughed.

He'd mentioned a sister, but she didn't look a thing like the man Tess had left climbing into the spa downstairs.

"Who are you?" she whispered into the quiet while replacing the frame on the shelf.

Silence was her only reply.

A roll of mailing tape hid in the desk drawer, so she grabbed it and a pair of scissors before returning to the patio where Anthony sat submerged in the spa. He cracked an eye open when she came in.

"Find what you needed?"

"Yep." Quickly removing her clothes, she deposited them beside Anthony's then tried to fashion a protective plastic covering for her cast.

"Come here, *chère,*" he said, and she went to sit on the rim of the spa. "Let me do this. I'm the mechanic, remember?"

"I could never forget how good you are with your hands."

He smiled at that, his ego swelling visibly. Fashioning a watertight wrapping to her elbow, he secured it with tape.

"Feel good?" he asked.

"Perfect." She slid into the water, pleased when he pulled her onto the seat beside him.

Dangling her cast on the outer rim, she let her legs twine with his, skin meeting skin as she stretched out against him in the hot bubbly water.

He sighed, leaned his head back and closed his eyes. "Oh, man. I needed this. You feel so good."

Tess only rested her head against his shoulder, careful not to press hard against his ribs. They faded into companionable silence, letting the hot water soak away the stiffness.

Solar lights lit the patio, casting the lush summer night in a bluish glow, and the peaceful sounds even helped chase away the memories of violence.

She must have dozed because suddenly he caught her cast and directed her arm back toward the ledge. She felt dreamy and relaxed and...*content* in a way she couldn't ever remember feeling before. With him she didn't feel restless or bored, and she wanted to understand why, *needed* to understand.

Idly stroking her fingers across his tight tummy, she asked, "That picture on your desk. Who is she?"

"A friend."

"A *friend* friend or a *date* friend?"

He didn't answer right away, just stared into the night, but the jaw he clenched tight hinted at what she'd already guessed—whoever the woman was, she was important.

"A friend friend who became a date friend who's a friend friend again."

Okay. Tess waited, hoping he'd offer something more about a woman who'd apparently been in his life awhile. But they faded into silence again.

She debated cooling her curiosity, accepting what he offered and not pushing for more. He didn't have to explain himself to her. They'd signed on for a fling, and that didn't entitle her to answers.

"Tell me about her, Anthony." Her curiosity wouldn't cool. She was getting more than she bargained for with this man, and wanted to understand what was happening between them.

"She believed in me so much that I believed, too."

It wasn't at all what Tess had expected, but that simple statement held so much power, confirmed the impact this woman had had on Anthony's life.

He was silent so long that Tess thought that's all she'd get, but then he said, "Watching her conquer the world showed me I could do anything I wanted to do, be anything I wanted to be. All I had to do was believe in myself."

Tess had recognized that confidence in him from the first, began to understand. "Were you together long?"

"On and off for ten years."

Whoa. The "on and off" part raised a few questions. She

couldn't imagine what would keep bringing two people back together for that long, but she had no frame of reference. She'd never dated anyone for more than a few months, had always found some reason to move on.

That raised another important question, but not one Anthony could answer. One she'd have to tackle herself. "When did ten years end?"

"A long time ago." He stared off into the night. "Nearly five years."

For some reason Tess felt much better. "Do you mind if I ask why?"

"She didn't settle. She still doesn't."

More simple words, but the emotion in his face convinced Tess that he meant this woman hadn't settled for what he'd had to offer, hadn't settled for *him*.

She was surprised by how many emotions that thought stirred up. Sorrow for what was clearly a painful memory. Disbelief that any woman would toss this man's love away. And envy that the redhead in the picture had the power to hurt him so much.

Tess stopped asking questions then. Each one she asked left her wanting to know why she'd never cared so much for a man. Her heart felt heavy with more than hurt for his pain. For unfulfilled promises. For lives that felt empty.

And she wasn't sure whether she meant his or her own.

But now…with Anthony, she understood what it felt like to want and liked how it felt to be wanted back. A feeling of such promise that she tipped her mouth to his throat, pressed a kiss to the pulse beating there.

Snuggling against him, she let the bubbling quiet and their nearness soothe away everything but the pleasure of being together. And when he finally asked, "You ready to get out?" she smiled, excited at the thought of climbing into his bed.

Getting out of the spa, she grabbed a towel, dragging the soft cotton over her skin, sensing Anthony's gaze on her. She put on a show, liking the way he made her feel, more than beautiful, as if she was the most important thing in his world.

He helped her remove the plastic from her cast, then it was her turn to watch when he stood in an eye-catching if drowsy display of dripping male. Tess brushed aside his hands. "Let me."

He half sat on the rim of the spa while she ruffled the towel along his shoulders, down his arms, gingerly patting his ribs, the broken skin on his hands. She explored him with an unfamiliar sense of possession, of power, to ease his pain, to bring him pleasure.

He groaned softly when she worked the towel over his groin, lingering passes along wet skin that earned an immediate reaction. So she sank to her knees to press whisper-soft kisses in the wake of her touch. He groaned again, threaded his fingers into her hair and hung on.

Tess laughed and nuzzled her face against his groin again, nipped her way along that tender spot at the juncture of his thigh, dragged her tongue along puckered skin.

"Is this payback for the broken arm?" he asked.

"Yes." And to prove it, she licked the underside of his penis, gratified when his growing erection jumped toward her mouth like a pleasure-seeking missile. "Now let's go to bed, so I can pay you back some more."

She didn't have to tell him twice, and when they slid beneath the sheets, they became a tangle of glowing skin and drowsy eagerness. With a burst of energy that came from nowhere, he rolled and braced himself on top of her, staring down with a satisfied smile.

"What?" she asked.

"I wanted to see how you look in my bed."

"Tired, I'll bet."

"No, *chère,* you look good…good enough to eat."

She laughed, wishing he could have obliged her but with those swollen lips…Tess slithered her legs around him instead, aligned herself….

"What are you doing?"

Her fingers around his erection answered that question. He swelled in her hand, his body recognizing what she had in mind. Dragging him against her moist heat, she took aim, and fired. He arched his hips to go the rest of the way.

Tess sighed.

Anthony sighed.

And they lay in the darkness, swaying gently against each other. Their motions dreamy and lazy and sweet. Their bodies fitted perfectly as the night closed in around them.

Tess stared into his face, resisting the urge to kiss his mouth, watching her pleasure mirrored in his expression.

Their breaths broke in soft bursts as they rose toward fulfillment, the feeling so amazing and complete that she knew all these tender emotions—the curiosity, the hurt, the ecstasy—could come with only this man. Only Anthony.

Swaying full-bodied against him, she dug her fingers into his butt when he rallied the energy to drive harder, riding all those places that made her ache, only to withdraw in sleek strokes, an ebb and flow that wound her toward fulfillment. Then she exploded with him, lazy, crazy bursts that went on and on.

Only Anthony.

13

TESS DIDN'T LEAVE Anthony's place for another two days. Anthony had insisted—and she'd agreed—that since they'd been cheated of their minivacation from the real world, they deserved to indulge their convalescence.

When food had become an issue, they'd ordered pizza delivery, and for two glorious days and three glorious nights, they'd done nothing more than make love, soak in the spa, sleep, munch on reheated pizza and work their way through a bottle of ibuprofen.

Tess enjoyed this break from reality and, aside from telephone calls to Daddy, the time passed in a blur of dreamy pleasure and incredible orgasms, where she spoiled Anthony and let Anthony spoil her. And in between she tried to make sense of how she felt about him.

Eventually reality intruded.

"Good morning, *chère*," Anthony whispered close to her ear, a burst of tingly warmth that seemed the perfect way to start a new day. "I ate the last slice of pizza before bed last night, so I'm heading out for breakfast. Any requests?"

"Protein."

He trailed kisses over her temples, down her cheek. "Sleep. I won't be long. I'll lock you in with the security system and wake you when I get back."

Those feather kisses made her want to drag him back down into bed, but to do that, she'd have had to move. No go. After spending so many days depleting as much strength as they'd regained, Tess found it all too tempting to roll over and go to sleep. She was pretty sure he'd almost killed her with his particular brand of mouth therapy sometime during the night.

Or had that been the night before last?

Death by orgasm. No doubt Penny would say, "Way to go!"

Tess must have slept again because the next thing she heard was a male voice. She didn't bother opening her eyes, only vaguely aware of the rich masculine sound and a hunger that seemed out of proportion with how awake she wasn't. She wondered dreamily what Anthony had managed for breakfast, heard a steady stream of talk that grew louder as footsteps thumped up the stairs.

He said he'd awaken her, but if he expected her to open her eyes without sprinkling her face with more of those tempting kisses, the man had another think coming.

Then came a knock.

Her eyes opened, and Tess stared at the door. Were Anthony's hands so full he couldn't get the door? She tried to rally the energy to get up, but as sleep cleared her brain, she realized the voice on the other side of the door only *sounded* like Anthony.

She shot from zero to sixty in a blink.

Bolting upright, she clutched the sheet to her chest, undecided between hunkering down or bolting for the bathroom. Another knock. More chatter. The image of being caught bare-assed as she raced across the room froze her to the spot.

Then the door opened.

"Is there really a woman in here?" a male voice asked, a voice familiar, yet strikingly unfamiliar.

Tess had a moment of panic as she watched the door open wider, but decided to whack anyone who got close enough with her cast. A head appeared, followed by broad shoulders, and a face that was Anthony, but wasn't. Younger and leaner, this DiLeo brother—and there could be no doubt he was one of Anthony's brothers—wore his hair *really* long and grinned a faster grin.

"Well, hello, green eyes," he said. "We didn't believe Anthony when he said he had a woman up here. But you're a woman all right, and a gorgeous one."

We?

Before Tess had a chance to reflect on who else might be here—please, God, not his mother!—or to wonder why no one believed Anthony had invited a woman home, another tawny head popped through the door.

This brother—and there could be no missing that here was yet another of Anthony's brothers—shouldered the door even wider to give her a glimpse of an older and brawnier version of these cookie-cutter DiLeo siblings.

This one wore his hair short and wasn't nearly so quick to grin. In fact, as he raked his gaze over her, he seemed to be summing her up before saying, "He was telling the truth."

"Do you believe it?"

The older DiLeo only shook his head, and they both turned back to stare at her as if they'd never seen a woman in their combined lifetimes.

She glanced at the bedside clock, tried not to think about the impression she must be making, so clearly naked in the middle of their brother's rumpled bed.

"Good morning, gentlemen." She wouldn't win this race if she didn't get behind the wheel. "The name's Tess. Anthony stepped out. He said he wouldn't be long."

They exchanged glances as if they'd never heard a woman talk before today, either.

"Tess from Texas." the younger brother said.

The older brother leveled his gaze her way again, and she was relieved when he didn't budge from the doorway to do something gentlemanly like shake her hand. "Dominic DiLeo. Anthony's oldest brother. This is Damon, the family pain in the ass. I tried to catch him before he got upstairs. My apologies."

"Like you could catch me, Nic." Damon laughed. "Actually, I'm the brother who's not happy that Anthony caught the prettiest gal between here and Houston."

"Lubbock," she corrected.

He inclined his head. "We heard Anthony got back to town. When he didn't call, we decided to find out why."

"When did he get back?" Nic asked.

"Thursday night."

"Did you come back with him, green eyes?"

She nodded.

"He told us he had company, but we didn't believe him." Nic gave her the first thing that resembled a smile.

"You saw him? He's on his way home?"

"Not anytime soon."

Damon's grin almost made her afraid to ask why. "Why?"

"He's downstairs. Handcuffed to Nic's cruiser."

"Handcuffed?"

Nic nodded. "I'm surprised you didn't hear him. He didn't go down without a fight. Never does."

Another fight?

She wasn't sure whether or not to take them seriously and wanted a peek outside for herself. However, these two didn't look as if they'd be voluntarily leaving this room in the immediate future. They were checking her out, and she got the sense they were also taking her measure.

Concern for Anthony finally won out, so hanging on to the sheet for dear life, she swung her legs around and stood, whipping yards of high-thread-count sateen around her. Then as regally as if she'd crossed the finish line a car length ahead of the pack, she made for the window.

Sure enough, there was a NOPD cruiser with visibars flashing. Anthony leaned against it, still holding a bag— presumably their breakfast. He bristled with attitude, and she bit back a smile when he saw her. Pushing away from the car, he motioned to a hand still firmly attached to the door handle.

Clutching the sheet in place with her cast, she wrestled the window open with the other. "Are you okay?"

"Tell them they're dead."

No need to ask who "them" was.

"Tell him that busted-up face of his has me real worried," Damon shot back.

Nic's stoic gaze zeroed in on her wrist. "Does that cast have anything to do with what happened to Anthony's face?"

She nodded.

Damon swore. "I told him to get his ass into the dojo more than twice a week. He might have done a better job protecting you, green eyes."

Tess had no idea if Anthony had even called his family while they were on the road. If he had, he obviously hadn't said anything about the attack. She didn't want to interfere with how he handled them, but she wasn't going to stand here and listen to his brother abuse him, either.

"If you're the brother with black belts in four disciplines, then you should know he held his own just fine. Six men with guns attacked us in San Francisco. Anthony had nothing more than a tire iron and me with my pepper spray."

"You're...*defending* him?"

She wasn't going to dignify *that* with a reply, especially when Nic's frown had deepened into a scowl. "So what happened to the six men with the guns?"

"Three out cold. One ran screaming. He questioned the others."

"This wasn't a random attack?" Nic asked.

"No, but if you want more information, you'll have to talk to him." She glanced back through the window. "And just out of curiosity, when do you plan to let him go?"

"As soon as you're ready to leave."

"Where am I going?"

"It's Sunday," Damon said as if that explained everything.

Nic glanced at his watch. "Mama will have dinner on the table in about thirty minutes. Better get a move on."

Tess wanted to make a good impression with Anthony's family—better than this first meeting anyway—but her clothing choices were limited since they hadn't gotten out of bed long enough to wash a load of clothes. Even a quick shower was out of the question. The hassle of wrapping her cast aside, Tess wouldn't leave Anthony handcuffed on the street any longer than necessary. Although she wouldn't have minded making these two wait one bit.

So she settled for heading into the bathroom to perform damage control, and reemerged an impressive ten minutes later, fully dressed with minty-fresh breath and neatly made-up face and hair that wouldn't frighten kids or dogs.

Nic had moved to stand beside the window, but Damon still stood beside the door, eyeing her with a wicked look.

"The loveliest lady in Lubbock, I'd say."

"Ready, Tess?" Nic glanced down at the street again, looking as though he wanted to get this show on the road.

Served him right as far as Tess was concerned. "In a sec. I want to grab a few things for Anthony. He didn't shower yet."

Nic and Damon exchanged glances again, but Tess didn't understand what *they* didn't understand. They'd attacked the man on the street before he'd even had breakfast.

Nic nodded to Damon, who dutifully went to the closet. Tess grabbed Anthony's duffel bag—still half-packed since they hadn't gotten around to unpacking yet, either—and dumped everything except his toiletries on the bed.

"No, not that one," she told Damon, who was pulling a polo-style shirt off a hanger. "Something that buttons."

"Why?"

"He bruised his ribs. It's hard for him to lift his arms."

"Oh, the poor baby." Damon slipped the shirt back into the closet and got another. "Is that what you've been doing here, green eyes—nursing my big bro back to health?"

Tess realized that Damon wasn't only the family pain in the ass, but very protective of his big brother. She liked what that said about him, and found her mood softening a little. A very little. At least until they uncuffed Anthony.

"If you must know, we've been nursing *each other* back to health. Doctor's orders."

That won a laugh from Nic, which Tess guessed was a rare occurrence. "Here's hoping he feels a lot better when he sees you, Tess. Otherwise he'll have to jog alongside my cruiser because I'm not unlocking those handcuffs."

To her relief, Anthony's mood did seem to improve the minute he laid eyes on her. Those big brown eyes melted over her in an apology he didn't need to make.

"You okay?" she asked.

"I *almost* made it with breakfast," he said wryly, narrowing his gaze at his brothers, who were still standing on the stairs.

"I hear your mom will have dinner on the table soon."

He tossed the bag onto the back dash. "Whatever she's cooking will beat this shrimp étouffé from Toujacques."

"Shrimp étouffé for breakfast?"

"You said you wanted protein, *chère*."

She smiled gratefully then motioned to Nic. "He seems in fine spirits. Let him go."

"What, you don't have the energy to jog home, big bro?" Damon smiled, but not Anthony, and she didn't miss how Nic gave his younger brother a head start to lock himself inside the front seat before he released Anthony.

They climbed into the back, and Tess scooted close enough to whisper, "First an ambulance. Now a police cruiser. Being with you is a thrill a minute."

"Told you we'd have a good time together." Anthony pounded on the Plexiglas divider separating the front seat. "How the hell did you two find out I was home?"

Damon slid open a panel. "The Gooch saw you at the casino. He called the house to find out if Mama had cancelled dinner since you were raiding the VIP bar."

"The Gooch?" Tess asked.

"A friend," Anthony said. "I'm not sure whose, though. He just showed up one day and never left. But leave it to him to still be gambling this late on a Sunday."

"What, you expected him to be in church?" Damon asked, and something about that made all three brothers laugh.

Tess remembered what Courtney Gerard had said about being adopted by the DiLeo family, and felt an unfamiliar zip of…*something* at the thought of meeting Anthony's family—extended or otherwise—a crazy mix of nerves and excitement.

Anthony's family home was a modest two story in a residential neighborhood skirting the French Quarter. The yard was meticulously cared for with a colorful array of blooms dripping over the fence. Cars crammed the driveway and overflowed onto the street, and while the place looked barely large enough to raise a family with six kids, it had a friendly feel that said, "Welcome."

"You grew up here?" she asked Anthony as Nic maneuvered the cruiser into a tight space on the street.

He nodded, and she liked this glimpse into his life, another piece of the puzzle that was Anthony of the noble gestures and the wicked mouth. She could see him and his brothers running wild around this place with their friends growing up, wondered at the woman who ruled this roost single-handedly and raised such a nice son.

She might even be warming up to Nic and Damon. Even though they'd handcuffed Anthony to the car and left him standing in the street, they were all clearly fond of each other with an easy camaraderie that was fun to watch.

"Let me go warn Mama that you've brought a girl home. I don't want her to have a heart attack." Damon hopped out of the cruiser and shot off down the stone walkway.

"Damned big mouth." Anthony snorted in disgust as he hauled his duffel bag over his shoulder and extended a hand to Tess.

"You should have called," Nic chided.

"I would have when I wanted to see your ugly mug."

They reached the front door just as Damon burst down a hallway, yelling, "Anthony got back into town on *Thursday*."

His hand tightened around hers possessively as he led her into a huge kitchen filled with people. Tess didn't even get to look around before a woman with a hint of Italian in her voice demanded, "*Caro mio,* you made it home, but didn't call?"

Anthony didn't get a chance to reply before Damon drew up against the woman with the tawny blond hair, standing in front of the stove. He kissed her cheek. "Anthony *and Tess* have been nursing each other back to health, Mama. Doctor's orders."

"Tess?" Mrs. DiLeo turned around to have a look for herself. "What doctor?"

She was a small woman, who hardly looked big enough, or old enough for that matter, to have reared these DiLeo boys. Her gaze zeroed in on her son's face and her expression dissolved into a frown. "Anthony, you been fighting? And who's your girl?"

With another of those reassuring smiles, Anthony looped his arm through Tess's and led her in state across the kitchen.

Mrs. DiLeo might have been physically petite, but there was nothing small about her presence. Meticulously groomed, from stylishly short hair to designer sandals, she was a beautiful woman with smooth olive skin and dark snapping eyes. This kitchen was obviously her throne room.

"Mama, this is Tess Hardaway. Tess, my mother, Angelina."

"It's a pleasure, Mrs. DiLeo." She extended her hand.

Anthony's mom shook with a no-nonsense grip, and didn't let go. She drew Tess toward her for a closer look. "You're a beauty. You've been taking good care of my Anthony?"

"I've been trying, ma'am. He's giving me a run for my money."

A smile twitched around Mrs. DiLeo's mouth as her hand slid from Tess's. She reached up to gingerly touch the healing wound on Anthony's face. "You think that looks dashing, don't you?"

"Is that why you wouldn't let the doctor stitch you up?" Tess asked.

Anthony flashed a smile that made her feel all flushed and fluttery and aware that not only his mom, but also everyone in the room hung on to their every word. "It worked, didn't it? You're here, *chère*."

"Of course I'm here." Tess rolled her eyes. "You begged me to come, didn't you?"

There was a beat of silence before snickers erupted around the kitchen, and even Tess couldn't suppress a smile when his mom nodded approvingly.

"Call me Mama, Tess," she said. "Everyone does. Now grab a seat and let's eat."

Two places at the table miraculously appeared, and suddenly she and Anthony plunged into the thick of things.

Tempting dishes appeared. Wine flowed. Conversation happened and laughter rang out. Tess was reminded of feeding time at the Critchley ranch, always a chaotic affair whenever she had the good fortune to show up in Mrs. Critchley's big kitchen at feeding time.

Tess met Marc, the brother in between Anthony and Nic, a man with a rolling laugh and a penchant for adventure as he blew in and out of town with his work as a bounty hunter.

She met Vince, the youngest, whom everyone called Vinny despite his repeated corrections. He'd just come off his shift at Charity Hospital, where he was doing his residency, and still looked sleep ruffled around the edges from a nap on the living-room sofa.

No sight of the one and only DiLeo daughter, but Tess did meet the Gooch, a startlingly attractive man who was close to Nic's age. He might radiate testosterone like the rest of this crew, but his wavy black hair and icy green eyes set him miles apart. And that glinting gold earring…he looked like a rogue.

She remembered what Anthony had said about not knowing when he'd first showed up or to whom he belonged. But the Gooch clearly belonged. She had no clue what his real name might be, but he sat at this huge table telling stories, as much a part of this family as any of the brothers.

There was a nail tech from Mama DiLeo's hair salon and two of Anthony's mechanics, who'd contributed freshly baked Italian bread and cannolis from the only bakery in town, consensus was, that could make a decent cannoli.

There was a lot of good-natured ribbing—especially when someone brought up the subject of work.

"You own a dojo, Damon," Marc said in a tone dripping disdain. "When the hell are you going to get a real job?"

"When you stay home long enough to take your turn on Mama detail," Damon shot back.

"What's Mama detail?" Tess asked.

"Mama doesn't drive, so we all take turns as chauffeur," Anthony explained. "Except for Marc, who's conveniently never here when his week rolls around."

"What did I tell you?" Damon shot a scowling Marc a smug look. "Like I make this stuff up."

Nic shook his head as if they all were crazy. "I can't figure this. Would be easier for Mama if she just took the driving test. Then she wouldn't have to put up with any of you."

"Makes perfect sense to me," Tess said. "What mother would want to miss out on having her boys drive her around? Especially when it seems to make you all feel so important."

Mama DiLeo raised her wineglass in salute.

Marc hooted with laughter. "I think I'm going to like you, Tess. You won't take any of Anthony's shit."

She sank back in her chair and whispered for Anthony's ears alone, "What shit?"

"No shit, *chère,*" he said in that whiskey voice. "What you see is what you get with me. My brother's an idiot."

She sipped her wine to contain a smile as Marc eyed them as if he suspected he was the topic of their discussion.

Then the family moved on to another topic for debate, giving her enough time to eat before they demanded the details of her meeting with Anthony.

Tess wasn't in public relations without good reason, and when the spotlight shone her way, she ran with it.

"Y'all know the Nostalgic Car Club hosted their annual convention in town last week, right?"

Several nods, and Nic narrowed his gaze. "Ran a bunch of fools through lockup because they couldn't keep their speedometers under a hundred while driving through my town."

"No one should have been doing a hundred except at Dixie Downs, Nic. That's the only time I drove a hundred. You have my word." She held up her hand in a gesture of honor.

Anthony laughed, but Damon sank back in his chair and eyed her curiously. "What were you doing on the track, green eyes?"

"Lapping the best of them. At least until I looked in my rearview mirror and saw this man's Firebird in my draft."

That raised a few eyebrows and Tess knew she was on a roll. She reveled in it, describing the scene with animated hand motions. "So I start blipping him, you know, just playing a little to see what he's made of, and, wham, the second I slide coming out of a turn, he shoots around me and I'm riding his bumper all the way to the finish line."

As Tess's words faded, all eyes turned to Anthony. He opened his mouth to comment then jerked forward in his chair when Marc slapped the back of his head.

"Didn't we teach you anything?" Marc said. "You don't beat a lady on the track. You're lucky she's even talking to you."

"Jeez. It wasn't my fault." Anthony rubbed the back of his head. "She provoked me."

"Ah, what did you do to provoke him, Tess?" the Gooch asked in a Cajun drawl that made her think of pirates in the bayou.

"It wasn't me, it was my car. He thinks it's ugly."

"I *never* called your car ugly."

"What do you drive?" Vince asked.

"A purple Gremlin," Anthony said, and there wasn't a man at that table who didn't wince.

It was enough to hurt a girl's feelings. "Let me tell you about my purple Gremlin, gentlemen. She gave this man and his muscle car a run for his money."

"*You* gave *Anthony* a run for his money on the track?" the mechanic named Sal asked incredulously.

"Not her car, trust me." Anthony sounded more than a little defensive. "But Tess isn't any normal driver, either. Tell them who taught you to race, *chère*."

"My uncle."

Anthony snorted. "Her uncle, the *Maverick*."

More silence, then all at once...

"*You're Ray Macy's niece?*"

"*Number seven? We call him the exterminator.*"

"*He kicked some royal ass the last time he came to town.*"

Tess grinned. "Didn't help me this time around. I lost."

"Idiot." Marc took another swipe at Anthony that he neatly dodged.

"Couldn't be that big an idiot," Mama DiLeo said matter-of-factly. "Tess is sitting at my table for Sunday dinner."

"Anthony more than made up for his poor manners on the track."

"What'd he do—jog a lap naked?" Damon asked.

A retort sprang to her lips, but Tess bit it back, not sure his mom would appreciate knowing how attractive she found her son in the buff. "He started by making a very generous contribution to my favorite charity."

Nic frowned. "My cheap brother? I don't believe it. This one squeezes pennies until they cry."

"I think our Anthony was trying to impress his young lady." Mama DiLeo glanced between them.

Tess just smiled and scooped up the last bite of her eggplant Parmesan, trying to act casual beneath Mama DiLeo's knowing gaze. Anthony laughed, and no sooner had she rested the fork back on her plate than he stood and took her plate.

He returned shortly with more of the exquisite eggplant and set the plate in front of her. "Was I right, or was I right?"

There was no missing the man's pride in his mother's cooking, and she said, "You win. This sauce has ruined me for any other."

"You'll just have to make sure you're around a lot on Sundays, *chère*."

The innuendo in that statement and the invitation in his eyes made her feel all fluttery again, but it wasn't until after Anthony reached for the breadbasket that Tess realized everyone else had fallen silent.

"Excuse me," Marc said. "Did my brother just get off his ass in the middle of dinner to serve this woman?"

"Good thing there's a doctor in the house," Vince said. "He's going to give someone a heart attack if he keeps this up."

"Behave, you two," Mama DiLeo admonished. "Anthony's impressing his young lady, and I won't have you all scaring her off." She winked at Tess then rose from the table, collected her dish and headed for the sink. "I raised a gentleman. Anthony, at least, knows how to take care of a lady."

Tess definitely wouldn't argue that. She felt comfortable sitting beside him with his family and friends, liked seeing him interact with the people he cared about, liked that the people he cared about accepted her with no questions asked. To Tess, that said a lot about how much they loved and respected him.

Talk inevitably got to the attack. Nic wanted details, so she and Anthony relayed the events of that night, and how the San Francisco police were investigating the attack locally despite Anthony's belief that the threat had followed Tess into town.

"I called Harley and asked her and Mac to investigate," Anthony said. "Haven't heard anything yet, but she said they'd drop everything to start following the trail before it got cold. I expect to hear from her soon."

"I'll give her a call and see if she needs my help cutting through any jurisdictional bullshit with the San Francisco police. That might save some time."

"Thanks, Nic," Anthony said.

"Am I hearing this right?" Damon let his fork clatter to his plate, the devil all over him. "You called Red from San Francisco, but we had to drag you out of bed after you'd been home for three days?"

Tess took her cue to get up from the table and remove their plates to the sink. Damon was a troublemaker, and she simply couldn't face a public discussion about how he and Nic had caught her in bed this morning. Not in front of an audience that included their mom, even if she seemed to be enjoying the show.

"I needed Harley on the trail," Anthony said. "If I'd called, half of New Orleans would have shown up at my place."

Tess heard a few snorts of laughter and one disbelieving, "Yeah, right."

"I already told you we needed rest. Doctor's orders, remember?" she asked, feigning innocence. "Anthony shouldn't be left handcuffed to a car on the street in his condition."

"Dominic Joseph and Damon Francis, you *handcuffed* your brother to the car?"

Suddenly they were in the hot seat, each attempting to blame the other for the idea. Unfortunately, Mama DiLeo didn't seem too interested in their explanations, and Tess felt a momentary pang of regret when she remembered Anthony's story about the knife. Then again, better Nic's and Damon's butts, than a conversation about her in Anthony's bed. Merciless, true, but it looked like every man for himself with the DiLeos.

Or every woman. And Tess wanted to get off to a good start.

"Nicely done." Anthony joined her at the counter as she was buying time by pouring coffee.

She pressed a mug into his hands. "As long as Mama doesn't start hurling silverware."

"She always misses. Intentionally. Got a helluvan arm, that woman does."

Tess remembered the baseball gear in his foyer and wondered if he'd inherited that arm, but before she got a chance to ask, Mama showed up.

"*Caro mio,* I took care of your brothers, but you didn't say how your work went? Did Tess's father see your proposal?"

Tess listened curiously, surprised when Anthony didn't answer but exploded away from the counter, swearing and sloshing coffee over the rim of his mug.

"Goddamn it, Mama." He set the mug down, making even more of a mess. Swinging around, he glared accusingly at his mom, who only smiled, raised a pair of shears and...*his ponytail.*

Tess stared as everyone dissolved into laughter.

Anthony rubbed the back of his nape, scowling. "Now you've got to give me a haircut."

"Come to the shop tomorrow." Mama waved him off and headed to the trash to deposit the tawny locks. "You know I hate cutting hair in the kitchen. I like my chair and mirror—"

"Come on, Tess," he said. "We'll have to skip dessert. If we hurry, I can catch Lou at the barbershop."

Mama scowled. Anthony scowled back.

A power struggle waged, and everyone in the kitchen had a ringside seat.

Anthony tossed his hands up in exasperation. "Here I finally bring a girl home, and now we have to leave—"

"Oh, all right." Mama tossed up her hands, too, and started issuing orders. "Vinny, get my salon bag. Tess, Gooch, Sal, let's get this food off the table before it winds up covered in hair."

Everyone leaped into action, and Anthony winked as he grabbed a chair and spun it into the center of the kitchen.

"You're it, Marc," he said. "Think you'll be around long enough to take your turn this time?"

"Damn things I do for this family," Marc grumbled in reply, running a hand through his hair.

Damon laughed as he sidled up against her at the sink, where she began scraping plates for the dishwasher.

"Marc's turn for what?" she asked.

"Mama's a hairdresser, green eyes." He lifted his long

ponytail. "She's been after *this* since I grew it, so the rest of them take turns growing their own puny ones to distract her. Even the Gooch."

"And now it's Marc's turn?"

Damon nodded. "It's become a family game."

But it was more than a game in Tess's eyes. Anthony's long hair wasn't a sign of rebelliousness, but an act that showed how much he cared for his brother. And as she loaded the dishwasher, she thought about brothers who took turns chauffeuring their mother around, who grew out ponytails for surprise haircuts and involved themselves in each others' lives.

While it might be every man for himself with the Di-Leos, this family clearly stuck together when it counted.

Tess liked what that said about them.

She liked it a lot.

Vince returned with Mama's salon bag and a package of multicolored permanent markers that he plunked down on the counter beside her. "While Anthony gets his hair cut, we'll sign your cast. The thing's so white it's blinding me."

Leave it to a doctor to notice. Tess was too busy noticing how Anthony's haircut shaped up. The close sides seemed to emphasize the sculpted lines of his face and make him even more striking. He looked different, but she liked the difference.

"I can't believe Anthony didn't do the honors." Damon agreed, snatching a blue marker. "He knows cast etiquette better than the rest of us."

Marc showed up and snatched the marker out of his hand. "Not better than you. Didn't you beat him when you broke your hand trying to karate chop cinder blocks or something?"

Damon frowned. "I don't think so. Mama, who broke the most bones?"

Just looking at this crew, Tess had no trouble imagining frequent visits to the emergency room.

"Frankie," Mama said. "She beat Damon with her broken ankle."

"I remember that." Marc gingerly directed Tess's arm to the counter for support then went to work on her cast like an artist. "She pulled the whole damn drainpipe off the side of the house trying to sneak out at night."

She. Frankie must be the one and only DiLeo sister.

"And she walked around with that broken ankle for a week so Mama wouldn't know," Vince said.

My brother doesn't deserve you. Marc wrote the word *doesn't* in bright orange for emphasis.

He beamed at his handiwork, and Tess wondered what she'd gotten herself into here. Not only would this cast be a permanent part of her wardrobe for a few weeks, but everyone seemed to assume that she was on her way to becoming a permanent fixture in Anthony's life.

But she only smiled as Damon wrote in green marker. *Green Eyes, you're the loveliest lady in Lubbock.*

Nic wrote a more conventional: *Hope you get this cast off soon!* Vince wrote underneath it: *It's getting uglier by the second!* with a big yellow smiley face.

Even the Gooch joined in with a *Welcome to the family.*

Vince grabbed the red marker before Sal could. "Let's save this one for Anthony so he can draw little red hearts."

Tess glanced at Anthony with his wet hair and styling cape covering all that yummy terrain between his neck and knees. He narrowed his gaze at his youngest brother then looked at her…and the pleasure softening his handsome face made her want to hand him the red marker herself.

14

"THIS BIG DAY YOU HAD TO get back for is a trip to school?"
Tess stared out the Firebird's window as Anthony wheeled
into a parking lot, clearly in the throes of first-day mad-
ness.

"Not a trip to any school. Today is my goddaughter's
first day at preschool."

"Oh, well, that is big news."

"Yep. Sure is."

He made a parking spot on the grass at the back of the
lot beneath a sign that read No Parking. Tess just rolled her
eyes and followed him inside, mulling over his casual dis-
regard for parking laws and his devotion to the people he
cared about.

She liked how much importance he placed on a little
girl's big day and that he wanted to share that day with her.

It was another piece in the puzzle that was Anthony.

He led her inside an old but well-maintained building,
and they battled their way down a crowded hall.

Tess had no idea who they were looking for, but she
knew when they found his goddaughter because a child's
voice rang out. "Uncle Anthony!"

Anthony sank to his knees just as a small redheaded
missile launched herself into his arms.

He hugged the child tight, pressing a kiss to the top of her head. "Hey, little princess. All set for your big day?"

"Mommy gave me braids." Stepping out of his arms, the little princess shook her head from side to side to display two long braids that looked as if Mommy had to wrestle a lot of hair to make them. Fine red curls were already creeping out, and all the shaking dislodged a few more.

"I like 'em. But then you're always gorgeous."

"I know," she said matter-of-factly, earning a smile from her doting uncle. Then her clear gray gaze riveted to the plastic box he held. "Is that for me?"

"I'd never show up on your big day without a present." He snapped open the box to reveal a small fresh-flower corsage.

She bounced on her tiptoes excitedly as he slid the corsage onto her tiny wrist. "It's roses. Look Mommy, it's my favorite."

Tess glanced up to notice the couple who appeared behind the child. They admired her new acquisition and reminded her to say thanks. Tess recognized the woman from the office photo.

She was even more beautiful in person. Somehow Tess had known she'd be delicate and exquisitely feminine. She was. With glossy red hair waving around her face, she had deep blue eyes that took Tess's measure in a glance. She smiled, a polite smile, a curious smile rather than a friendly one.

Her daughter flung herself into Anthony's arms with a heartfelt, "Oh, thank you, Uncle Anthony."

"My pleasure, little princess."

When she finally let him go, he stood and greeted her mother. "Hey, princess." He kissed her cheek. "You're here, so I guess that means you didn't have any trouble getting back."

Big princess and little princess.

"I caught the red-eye," the woman said. "No problem."

Anthony shook hands with the dark-haired man at her side then turned to her. "Tess, Harley and Mac Gerard. They're with Eastman Investigations. Harley's been in San Francisco investigating the attack."

Harley was his on-again, off-again, nonsettling ex?

Tess hadn't realized they were one and the same. That definitely said something. She wasn't sure what.

"Pleased to meet you both." She extended her hand in greeting to Harley first. "Appreciate the help."

Harley inclined her head. "If you've got a few minutes when we're done here, we'll bring you up to date."

"You found something," Anthony said, not a question.

"Hit the mother lode last night around nine."

That sounded promising, Tess thought. She also thought that compared to his wife, Mac Gerard seemed downright friendly. He welcomed her to New Orleans and thanked her for sharing in his daughter's excitement. She didn't miss the possessive arm he kept around his wife.

"It's a big day. Glad I could be a part."

Little Princess was clearly getting tired of the conversation and wanted some of the attention for herself. She stepped in front of her parents and extended her hand to Tess. "I'm Julia Antoinette Gerard. Julia for Daddy's grandma. Antoinette for my Uncle Anthony. But you can call me Toni."

"It's a pleasure to meet you, Toni. That's a very lovely name. Congratulations on starting school."

"Thank you," she said, politely. "Did you hurt your arm?"

"I broke my wrist. What do you think of my cast?" She held her arm out for inspection and hoped Toni couldn't read.

"Can I color on it, too?"

"I'd love for you to. All Uncle Anthony's brothers did, but not your Uncle Anthony. Maybe he will if you do."

Toni accepted Tess into her circle of acquaintances without another thought then pulled away to greet a long-haired woman in a gauzy dress who made her way through the crowd.

"Aunt Delilah!" she squealed. "Where's Uncle Joe?"

"Sleeping, babe. I'd have had to blast a cannon to get him out of bed before noon, but he wanted you to have this."

She whipped out a red bandanna from her purse and Toni dissolved into peals of joy. "Is it his?"

"Just like it."

Which appeared to be good enough for little Toni. Harley helped her daughter fasten the bandanna around her neck while Mac slid the camcorder off his shoulder and started taping.

Tess stood with Anthony, watching the proceedings, glad he'd brought her along today. She hadn't made sense of the whole Harley thing yet, but she liked meeting more people who so obviously cared about him. People he cared about in return.

It seemed like such a full way to live life, made her own too-busy days seem sterile and empty by comparison. Suddenly it didn't seem like such a big mystery that she'd been so bored with everything lately.

She wasn't bored now.

As Tess stood beside Anthony, she acknowledged

what she'd known instinctively from the first moment they'd met.

This man was special.

"Aunt Courtney," Toni said with another rapturous squeal. "You're here."

Courtney Gerard scooped her niece into her arms and gave a little spin. "Of course I'm here, silly. You didn't think I'd miss your first day of school, did you?"

She gazed over her niece's head in greeting then tipped her cheek for kisses from Harley and Mac. "Hey, baby bro. How are you and Mom holding up?"

"About as well as you'd expect," Harley said.

Mac gave his wife an affectionate squeeze. "She's been second-guessing our decision to start Toni in this program."

"Nothing to second-guess. You waited the extra year." Courtney kissed her niece's cheek. "Toni's four now. A big girl all ready for an adventure."

"Agreed," Mac said. "And three hours for three mornings a week is the perfect amount of adventure."

Tess stifled a grin. Since the big girl looked raring to go, she guessed Mom was the one who couldn't handle any more. She remembered what Courtney had said at the Christmas in July event and reasoned through the connection. If Mac was Courtney's brother, then she was connected to Anthony through Harley. One more indication of how entwined their lives still were, which raised more questions that needed answers.

Courtney finally set Toni down, kissed Anthony and turned to her. "I thought I warned you about getting wrapped up with this man's family, Tess?"

"You did, but the first day of preschool is big stuff around here. Couldn't miss it."

"You got that right, but I want to know if he's brought you home for dinner yet."

Tess nodded.

"Then it's over. You'll never get away now." Courtney shook her head in feigned sympathy.

Harley watched them closely, and Tess sensed that she had just as many questions as Tess. "You've met already?"

"Tess invited our entire Big Buddies chapter to an event at the car club convention last week," Courtney explained. "It was incredible, Harley. Parade of classic cars through town. The whole park done up like the North Pole. Huge picnic. Rides. Everyone had a blast."

Tess appreciated Courtney's enthusiasm, and that she had something positive to recommend her to this woman. She might not yet understand the relationship between Anthony and Harley, but she and her family were clearly an important part of his life.

And just as she had while standing inside Mama's kitchen yesterday, Tess found herself wanting to understand who these people were. She *needed* to know if she wanted a place for herself among them.

And Tess thought she just might.

"I'm on the board of the Nostalgic Car Club—"

"Do you have an old car?" Toni asked. "Like Uncle Anthony?"

"Not quite as old as your uncle's, but mine's a very pretty purple like your dress." At least that much hadn't changed after the beating it had taken in San Francisco.

Their discussion about classic cars was cut short when the bell rang and a teacher appeared in a doorway to invite the remaining parents into the classroom. Tess couldn't help feeling for Harley as she tightened her grip on her daughter's hand and faced the teacher with suddenly misty eyes.

She wasn't the only one who noticed, either, because Mac passed off the camcorder to Anthony. "Would you do the honors?"

Anthony didn't miss a beat. He aimed the camera as Mac wrapped his arm around his wife and led his family inside.

The Aunts Courtney and Delilah followed, but Tess hung back, wanting to give them some privacy in the crowded classroom. Yet no sooner had Harley and Mac queued up to greet the teacher than Toni broke away and headed back into the hall.

She reached for Tess's hand. "I like you. Uncle Anthony looks at you like he looks at Mommy, only not sad."

Tess took the little hand, not sure what to say, so she let herself be led inside to be part of the family. And when she found herself dragged to an elementary-size table to pose for Anthony with the aunts and Toni, she felt the craziest pride to be the woman who could make this little girl's uncle smile.

ANTHONY RESISTED THE URGE to interrogate Harley and Mac in the parking lot and suggested a nearby Starbucks instead. "It's so damn hot, the patio should be empty. We can talk there."

Not only did Harley look in need of caffeine, but a distraction couldn't hurt. She'd managed a brave face while kissing the little princess goodbye, but she hadn't gotten out of the classroom door before Mac had to steer her down the hall because she was too teary eyed to see straight.

Special days were big days for moms, too.

Turned out he was right on both counts. The patio was empty, and Harley ordered a high-test brew that Mac suggested she pour over ice. Anthony wished he'd taken the suggestion. He started sweating before he'd even pulled a chair for Tess.

"The San Francisco police didn't catch the assailant who got away from you on the street," Harley told them. "And there was no tracing their vehicle."

"Stolen?" he asked.

She nodded. "Naturally. But someone posted bail like clockwork on the others, so you were right about these guys having money behind them. The judge set some pretty steep numbers so whoever sprang them not only had big bucks, but also knew how to cover his tracks."

"Seriously." Mac gave a low whistle. "I spent the last two days unraveling the money trails. *Separate* money trails. This guy didn't miss a beat."

Harley looked pleased. "But Mac did it, and we got a name."

"Who?" Tess wanted to know.

"Daryl Keene."

That clearly wasn't what Tess had expected. She sank back in her chair, obviously stunned.

"Harley thought Tess might know him," Mac said. "He's a member of the Nostalgic Car Club."

"Oh, I know him, all right."

"He's been pursuing Tess, and not taking no for an answer," Anthony explained. "I can tell you he wasn't happy when I came on the scene."

Tess scowled. "I know Daryl was annoyed when I asked you to drive the rally, possibly even angry, but enough to arrange that attack? What would be the point? I wouldn't date him before, and he can't be foolish enough to think I'd date him after what he did to you and my car."

Anthony's gaze slid to her colorful cast. Daryl might not have intended for Tess to be harmed, but he'd damn sure meant to scare her. And putting her in harm's way was just as bad in Anthony's book. Yet, he couldn't see the point, either.

"Is this guy mentally unbalanced?"

Harley shrugged. "Nothing I came across to suggest it, but what if a date with you wasn't his *only* incentive?"

Anthony knew by the gleam in those baby blues that Harley had something. "You said you hit the mother lode. What?"

"While Mac was working on the money trails, I was tracking down how your assailants got to town. They all came in on the last morning of the rally, hours before you were expected to arrive. You declared your route with the car club that morning. I talked to a guy…what was his name—"

"Ralph," Tess supplied.

"That's it. Ralph told me Daryl Keene had to fix a flat, so he didn't get on the road until a good fifteen minutes after the rest of the contestants."

Mac set his cup back on the table. "He was hanging around after everyone else had left. It's possible he could have found out what route you were driving. This Ralph told Harley he was so busy breaking down the place that he wasn't paying any attention to what Keene was doing."

"If your assailants knew your route, it couldn't have been hard to spot you. Your car's unusual."

Anthony swallowed a laugh. "No doubt about that."

"Ha, ha." Tess narrowed her gaze. "What does Daryl want?"

Harley took a long sip from her iced coffee, eyed them above the rim, clearly enjoying a chance to build the drama.

"Pleased with yourself, aren't you, princess?" he asked.

Mac rolled his eyes. "You have no idea. She killed my cell battery last night going on about how this clue panned out."

But judging by the look on Harley's face, Anthony could just guess. "You're killing me here."

Harley smiled. "Once Mac got Daryl Keene's name, I had something to run with. I wanted to track all of your assailants back to Tulsa and some connection to this guy. Seemed pretty clear-cut. But it turned out that none of these guys was from anywhere around Tulsa, so I had to do some more digging."

"And," he prompted.

"And it turns out that none of them are even from the same towns, but there is a commonality here."

"Which is?" Tess asked.

"They're all from towns where Keene Motors has a dealership."

"Really? That's interesting."

Harley nodded. "I thought so, too. So I call Mac and we start digging into these guys' finances. Not a one of them has any connection to Keene Motors, but they're all on the books in a bunch of low-end jobs that in no way account for the money they've been tossing around the past year or so. Started running searches, and you wouldn't believe what we came up with."

"Nothing too conspicuous." Mac continued. "We got

one guy's name on a furniture-delivery invoice. Made a few phone calls and found out he walked into a showroom one day and paid for twenty grand worth of furniture in cash. Another one paid off the second mortgage on his mother's house."

"Individually, none of this would raise an eyebrow," Harley said. "But when you look at it together, you've got to ask—"

"Where are these guys getting this cash?"

"Bingo," Mac said.

"So I start making some phone calls to people with law enforcement connections in these areas, and guess what I find?"

"What?" Tess asked.

"That we've got another commonality. There's been a rash of auto thefts for the past year that the police can't seem to shut down."

Mac smiled. "So Harley gets me looking into Keene's financial transactions. Remember, this guy laundered enough money to post those bonds like a pro."

"And we find out that Daryl Keene has been sending a lot of money out of the States."

"Let me guess," Anthony said. "For about a year."

Harley nodded. "The way I figure it, he's averaging about twenty stolen cars a month through his father's dealerships and pocketing about four hundred grand in profit."

Tess shifted her gaze between them. "You're kidding? Stolen cars?"

Mac shook his head. "Gets even better."

Harley smiled triumphantly, plunking her cup back on the table and leaning forward excitedly. "I don't have solid evidence yet, but I'd bet money this Daryl Keene is just the tip of the iceberg. He's been running cars through all five of his father's dealerships and sending them *out of the country.*"

"Whoa," Anthony said.

"Whoa is right," Mac agreed. "We're talking international organized crime."

"All right. I get all this about the auto thefts," Tess said. "But where do Anthony and I come in? Why would Daryl want to destroy my car and hurt him?"

"I can't prove this," Harley said. "But if Daryl Keene is raking in this kind of money off five of his father's dealerships, just think about what he could do with his foot in the door at AutoCarTex."

Anthony agreed. "Even though Keene Motors has service departments, they deal mainly in new cars. It would be a helluva lot easier to run stolen cars through a business that deals in used vehicles. AutoCarTex would look like a gold mine."

"What do you think, Tess?" Harley asked. "Any of this ringing a bell? You know this guy."

"It could explain why Daryl wouldn't take no for an answer. I always suspected something more had to be going on." She gave a soft laugh. "Figures he only wanted me to get to Daddy."

"Now how do you know that, *chère?* The man might be a thief and an idiot, but he is male."

"Are you trying to make me feel better?"

"You're oversensitive about this," Anthony said. "You think everyone wants to get to your father through you."

"They do. You included."

"Excuse me. I didn't say word one about AutoTexCare, even though I had plenty of opportunity. Didn't you notice?"

"I noticed. I figured you wanted to wait until we re-solved all this, so you'd have Daddy's proper attention." She reached out to pat his hand. "I understand, Anthony. I know you worked hard pulling your proposal together. It doesn't deserve to get lost under everything that's happened."

She was serious. Sinking back in his chair, he opened his mouth then closed it again, before finally giving a snort of disgust. "Tess, that's not the reason at all. I was placing *your* safety above *my* work. I was showing you that you mean more than an introduction to your father."

Surprise flashed in those beautiful green eyes. "Oh."

"Jeez." He shook his head, not believing how she'd misinterpreted his actions. When he glanced around to find Harley and Mac watching them as if they were en-joying the show, he warned, "Don't even go there."

"Wouldn't dream of it." Harley raised her cup in salute, and Mac laughed.

Tess shook her head as if to clear it, a smile playing around her lips. "Right before the convention Daryl e-mailed me that he'd be coming to Lubbock to scout out a dealership for his daddy. I'll bet he's expanding his dad-dy's business since things haven't been going so well with me."

"Which might explain the attack," Anthony said, "if he wanted to undermine me with you. I wouldn't look so hot getting my ass kicked while your car got damaged and we lost the race."

"If that's what Daryl was after, then it was a stupid idea that didn't work," Tess said fiercely as she gave his hand a reassuring squeeze. "I'd bet the ranch he didn't expect you to take out six guys with guns."

There'd been only one gun and one of the guys had gotten away. But he didn't correct her, not when she seemed to enjoy defending him. Turned out he really liked the way she went all soft around the edges when she did.

He heard Harley sucking loudly on her straw, knew she was trying hard not to laugh. He didn't look at her, and asked instead, "Do you think Keene Motors is responsible for the letters Big Tex has been getting?"

Mac shrugged. "I spoke with Tess's father and had him fax copies along with the results of the handwriting analysis and the tox reports his security chief ran. I didn't see a connection, which brings us back to motive. I don't see one."

"Unless Daryl was just looking for a way to get Daddy involved," Tess said. "He's been around the car club as long as I have. He couldn't miss how Daddy gets his back up whenever I get too far out of reach. I mean, it's kind of hard to miss how protective he is."

"That's definitely a possibility." Anthony agreed. "Keene Motors brought the letters up when you asked me to drive the rally."

She nodded then looked at Harley and Mac. "So what happens now?"

"The million-dollar question," Mac said.

"We'll turn over our evidence to the San Francisco police so they can prosecute your assailants. They'll have enough to investigate Daryl Keene's involvement, too, so my guess is they'll all sing loud to get the police to cut some deals."

"Ethically, we're obligated to report our suspicions about Daryl Keene's involvement in an international auto-theft ring to the proper authorities, too," Mac explained.

"But we'll need to document our work for you, so we wanted to get the heads-up from you first."

"Any problem with that?" Anthony asked Tess.

She shook her head. "None. Do what you need to do, and thank you both for all your help. I'm so relieved to know that everything will be taken care of, and Anthony will be safe."

"I'll be safe—" He broke off when he saw her smile and realized she was teasing. "Big Tex will be pleased, too. Maybe now would be a good time to pitch my idea."

She laughed, her green eyes sparkling. Anthony glanced around the table feeling very pleased with the morning's revelations. Pleased, but not surprised, that Harley and Mac had come through for him in such a big way. And pleased by how Tess seemed to fit so perfectly into his life.

They cleared away their cups and headed to the cars together. Mac caught Anthony when he passed. "Not bad. Only two more hours to kill until we can pick up Toni from school."

"I heard that," Harley shot back.

Anthony smiled, feeling incredibly lucky today, despite bruised ribs and a smashed-up face that *still* hurt. He hoped that luck held. Now that they'd figured things out, Tess wouldn't have any reason to stay around....

Unless he could convince her she belonged here.

"SOMETHING CAME UP AT the garage so Anthony had to leave," Tess told Courtney later that day on the phone. "I offered to go along, but he insisted I stay locked inside his house with the security system on. I know you're working, but you must get off soon, or at least take a dinner break. I could hop a cab—"

"He locked you up?" Courtney asked in mock horror. "What was the man thinking? Just sit tight, Tess. I'm on my way to break you out."

"Then pick someplace good because dinner is on me."

"Hope you're hungry."

Tess was hungry, and Courtney made good on her promise. Not thirty minutes later they were being seated inside a lush French Quarter restaurant where the dinner special turned out to be shrimp étouffé.

Tess considered that a good omen.

They chatted over French coffees while awaiting their meal, and Tess explained what Mac and Harley had discovered about the car-theft ring.

"Your brother and sister-in-law are amazing," she said honestly. "I can't believe they solved this thing so quickly."

"They're quite good at what they do," Courtney agreed. "But what I find amazing is how much the proper funding and resources can accomplish. Imagine if the system could afford to put that sort of manpower on a case. It's overwhelming to think about."

There was a lot of subtext in that statement, which Tess guessed came from Courtney's experience working in the system. She volunteered as the president of the Big Buddies Society, but her day job was in social services. And Tess knew firsthand from her own work that most good causes were understaffed and underfunded, making organizations like the AutoCarTex Foundation essential for raising corporate donations.

"No argument there, but I still think a lot had to do with Mac's and Harley's skill. Not to mention how they dropped everything so the trail wouldn't get cold."

"Well, I'm glad they came through for you. But to be

honest, there never was any question. They'd be there for Anthony no matter what."

Had the opportunity not presented itself so perfectly, Tess might have squelched her curiosity, but since it had...

"Courtney, do you mind if I pick your brain a bit about your brother and Harley? I would never ask you to discuss anything you're not comfortable discussing, so just tell me to hush and I'll ask Anthony. It's just that he's been so vague I didn't want to push—"

"What do you want to know?"

Tess sipped her coffee, letting the words form in her mind before she let them out of her mouth. "Anthony told me that he and Harley dated on and off for a really long time. I'm trying to piece together what happened so I know what I'm getting myself into here. They seem really close, and everybody seems so surprised that I came back to town with him. I'm confused."

"If it's any consolation, it's not you. Confusion happens a lot around the DiLeo family."

"Yeah, I'm beginning to see that."

Courtney brushed her hair back and got straight to the point. "You're getting into something with Anthony?"

Like everyone else she'd met in Anthony's life, Courtney obviously cared a great deal, and Tess was again struck by the loyalty and love he inspired. "You know, when I met you at the convention, about the very last thought on my mind was getting involved with anyone. I had a lot of reasons—reasons that I thought were really valid—but after being with him...well, my reasons don't seem so important anymore."

Not when she had to ask if she really wanted to live her life alone? When she looked at Anthony, and all the people who loved him, it seemed clear that if she didn't let herself get involved, she'd never stop feeling restless and bored.

Tess shrugged and met Courtney's gaze. "I can't tell you what I'm getting into here. I know how I feel, but I don't know where Anthony stands. We haven't talked about anything."

"You don't know where he stands?" Courtney raised her brows, a look of such genuine amusement that Tess was suddenly sure she'd missed something obvious. "Oh, honey, you're right. We do need to talk. I'm just glad you had sense enough to call."

"Give it to me straight."

"Okay, first things first. Harley and Anthony did date. But they weren't meant to be together like *that* forever."

"They still seem to care a lot for each other."

"They do. I think they always will. He's an important part of her life, and she is of his. I can only tell you what my brother has told me, so please keep this to yourself or he'll know where you got it."

"Of course."

"Mac says it was a commitment thing. Harley and Anthony grew up together and started dating when they were young. They were busy with school and careers—doing what most people their ages do. Mac thinks they assumed their relationship would always be there. Anthony wasn't ready to commit yet, and Harley settled for what he had to offer and never pushed for more. Then my brother walked into the picture, and that was that."

"She didn't settle. She still doesn't." The memory of Anthony's explanation replayed in her memory.

"Your brother's okay with how close they are?"

"What's not to be okay with?" Courtney laughed. "You've seen Harley and my brother together. And remember they're together 24/7 between work and home. They're wild about each other, and that's only more rock solid since Toni got here. My brother knows how important Anthony is to Harley and vice versa. He respects that, and he respects Anthony."

Tess thought about the picture on Anthony's desk, the way he'd called Harley from San Francisco when he hadn't called his family. "I don't think it has always been that way for Anthony."

Courtney shook her head, looked a little sad. "I was new to the family at the time so I really can't say what was happening, but it looked pretty rough from where I was standing."

"Anthony told me it's been a long time—over five years. And in all that time he hasn't met anyone special?"

"He dates. I ran into him at a play once with a girl named…what was her name?" She smiled. "I don't remember. She was pretty, though. Long blond hair. Sweetest Prada shoes."

Tess laughed. "I'm beginning to understand why everyone was so surprised when he brought me home."

"Anthony *never* brings a date home. That's a long-standing arrangement from his Harley days. To hear his brothers tell it, he hasn't brought a woman to his new place, either."

"Oh, he didn't mention that his place was new."

Courtney shook her head. "*New* is relative. He bought that place off Mac and Harley's boss about two and a half years ago."

"What's that all about?"

Courtney shrugged. "Mama tells everyone to back off and stop making jokes. She said when Anthony finds the right girl he'll bring her home."

The *right* girl.

If Anthony hadn't brought a girl home in all this time, then what did that make her?

A crazy feeling mushroomed inside, one of those stomach-swooping feelings she hadn't felt…she hadn't ever felt. Not until Anthony DiLeo steered his shiny red muscle car across the track and stepped out with a blinding smile.

"Well," Tess said, and she barely recognized the giddy sound of her own voice. "That certainly explains why everyone has been making such a big deal about my staying at his place. I feel so much better. I was really starting to get nervous."

"About Anthony?"

"Look at him. He's drop-dead gorgeous, available, romantic, successful…. Why wouldn't he bring women home? I couldn't imagine he was gay, but I've been known to be wrong."

Courtney let out a laugh that drew attention from a nearby table. "Don't say that word around any of the DiLeo boys."

"Got it."

She smiled over the rim of her cup. "So are you getting an idea of where Anthony stands on the issue yet?"

"I think so."

And even better—she was getting a much better idea of where she stood on the issue, too.

15

ANTHONY HEARD THE CAR when it pulled up on the street in front of his place. Heading toward the door, he peered through the glass to see Tess emerging from a car he recognized—Courtney's. And she had the sense to keep driving after letting her passenger out. Tess gave a wave then headed through his front gate just as he stepped onto the portico.

Twilight cast her in shadows that bleached the color from her pretty sundress and made her seem beautiful in a surreal sort of way. The breath caught in his throat, a stunning combination of pleasure and relief.

"Couldn't you leave a note?" he asked.

She stopped, looked surprised. "I did. It's on the mantel."

He scowled, but didn't say anything. He didn't have to. That smug look on her beautiful face assured him that she knew he hadn't thought to look there.

"Were you worried about me, Anthony?"

He scowled harder.

She laughed that silvery laugh, stepped lightly up the stairs and kissed his cheek. "You were, weren't you?"

"Yes."

Okay, so he admitted it. He could have called her on her

cell, but it was sitting on the charger in his kitchen. He wouldn't have even left her at all if that important job hadn't just arrived in his garage. He'd needed to assess the damage so Sal could place orders for the parts. He'd be doing the work himself, but he didn't want Tess to know.

She breezed past him into the house. "You know, I used to get crazy when everyone worried about me. Seemed like that's all Daddy and Uncle Ray ever did. But I like when you do it. Isn't that interesting?"

What he found interesting was how she unzipped her sundress while walking into his living room. The back parted, giving him a clean shot of her creamy skin and a pink bra strap.

He flipped the lock on his door and followed, reminding himself that he was annoyed. "So what were you off doing with Courtney?"

Tess slid her dress down her arms and let it shimmy to the floor. His gaze raked up long, long legs, over her heart-shaped bottom with the pink thong strap disappearing between her cheeks, her trim waist, the matching bra strap that suddenly sprang open with an easy maneuver.

Stepping out of the circle of sundress at her feet, she went to the mantel, her strappy heeled sandals throwing her posture just enough so sleek muscles shifted with every step and her firm bottom swayed temptingly. She reached for a letter then turned to face him....

Another shrug and the pink bra slithered away and her breasts sprang free, a breathtaking display of rosy nipples and plump curves that proved he wasn't the only one being affected by this show. Not by a long shot.

"Here you go."

She handed him the letter, fingertips grazing his in a brush of warm skin. Anthony knew she expected him to open it and read the explanation for himself, but she distracted him yet again when she started rocking her hips to slip her thong panties down, down, down…

As he watched her bend over to unhook a strap from her heel, he forgot all about explanations. He would have forgotten his own name if it hadn't been embroidered on a work shirt hanging on the coatrack within eyesight.

There was no way he could concentrate in the face of this sexy assault, and he had the wild thought that if she planned to distract him like this every time he worried, he was in big trouble. This woman would run roughshod all over him, and wouldn't his brothers just love that?

That was, of course, supposing she hung around awhile, and *that* thought knocked some sense into him. He shook his head to get his brain cells working again, but when she draped herself across his leather couch, wearing nothing but her brightly colored cast and those strappy little sandals, his ability to reason went the way of his blood flow—south.

She hiked a foot over the chair arm, dangling her shoe sexily and giving him a glimpse of the goods between her thighs, all that sweet skin she'd kept cleanly shaved since Vegas…

"Go on, read my letter," she prompted.

The paper had been folded in half, a crease down the middle, his name on the front, but his fingers felt stiff as he unfolded it—all his blood had drained to his crotch.

Anthony,
Ran to dinner with Courtney to chat. Call me on
Courtney's cell if you need me. Be back soon.
Tess

Nothing earthshaking in here and he felt a little foolish.
But those few brain cells that weren't totally fixed on the
sight of her spread out on his couch—and she looked better than any fantasy calendar babe even without a car or a
timing wrench for props—locked onto a keyword. "*Chat*
about what?"

"About you."

That redirected the blood flow a bit. "What about me?"

"I wanted to know more about your relationship with
Harley."

"So you asked *Courtney?* What was the problem with
asking *me?*" He suddenly remembered his annoyance and
thought he understood the reason for her striptease.

"If you'll give me a chance to explain, I will, but you
have to come over here."

This was another trick. Tess had already dismantled his
brain with her sexy assault, and he guessed he'd be in for more
of the same if he gave in. But when she lifted her arms to him,
all that sleek skin beckoned, and he thought…what the hell?

He was living on borrowed time until he could convince
her there was a lot more in store for them than just a fling.
So far the only thing he had going for him was sex. He
wouldn't pass up a chance to get close. Especially when
she was *so* naked.

Sinking down on his knees beside the couch, he at-
tempted to hang on to his annoyance. "Let's hear it."

Slipping a hand around his neck, she idly fingered his

nape, a casual touch for touch's sake, as if she just liked touching him. "You were pretty vague when I asked about Harley before. I got the impression it wasn't easy for you to talk about her, and once I realized you'd called her and Mac for help when you hadn't even called your family, well…I wasn't sure if I should push you to tell me."

"But you wanted to know."

She nodded. "It's obvious you care a lot. I wanted to understand, so I could figure out if there's a place for me in your life."

A place in his life. He turned his face to press a kiss on her wrist, tasting the softness of her skin, not wanting her to see how much her admission meant.

They hadn't discussed anything about the future. He'd had no idea her thoughts were traveling down the same roads. Knowing who she was and how much she chafed against her father's well-intentioned smothering hadn't left him thinking he stood a chance….

"Courtney only told me that you and Harley grew up together and never got around to committing. That's all she said."

Anthony thought she sounded worried that she might have gotten Courtney into hot water, and he didn't say any differently. He was too busy figuring out what to tell her to reassure her he was over his past and more than ready to move on with his future.

The truth. That was all he had.

"Harley and I dated for so long that I honestly didn't remember a time we weren't together. We were young, so marriage was way off in the future, something we both figured would happen one day when we got around to it. But we had things to do first, school, work…you know, *living.*

I was so busy worrying about what I wanted, I wasn't paying enough attention to what I had. I just figured she'd always be there. Sure, we dated other people in between being together, but we had rules."

Tess's hand slid around his throat then down to his shirt's buttons. She loosened his collar, keeping her gaze fixed on her task, then slipped a button through a hole, then another.

He gave a laugh when she tried to shove his shirt over his shoulders one-handed, knew what she was trying to do—distract him some more.

She was succeeding. He sat up, helped her drag his shirt off.

"And…" she urged.

"And the situation with Mac came out of left field for all of us. She and Mac worked together. Had I been paying attention, I'd have realized she was in over her head. I didn't."

"That must have been hard."

He shrugged. "I knew she never meant to break the rules, no more than she'd planned to fall in love with Mac Gerard. But she did, and I loved her enough to want what was best for her. Even if it wasn't me."

"That's very honorable."

"It might sound that way, but it wasn't. Trust me. I was a total asshole."

She eyed him doubtfully.

"Not at first, maybe. I went through the motions because I knew she'd needed me, too. But afterward, I put distance between us. A lot. Even though I knew staying away hurt her. But she didn't call me on it. And I knew she wouldn't—because she felt like she'd broken the rules, too." He kissed Tess's hand, liking the feel of her warm skin, liking the way her hand felt in his. Solid. Real. "That's where the asshole part comes in. I was just vengeful enough to let her keep on thinking it."

"And she loved you enough to let you." Not a question.

He nodded. "She wanted me to make peace with the curve life had dealt us, even if it broke her heart in the process. My mother, on the other hand, didn't have nearly so much patience. She slapped me upside the head and told me to grow up. She said, I'd made my bed and now I got to sleep in it."

Tess ran her hand over his chest, a simple touch that reassured him in a way he hadn't realized he'd needed to be reassured. "At least it wasn't a knife."

He gave a laugh. "Yeah, but she didn't say anything I didn't deserve to hear. Nic, either. He gave me the mother of all lectures, but Damon…*shit*. He kicked my ass in the dojo and didn't talk to me for three months."

"Then what happened?"

"I learned to accept that life does exactly what it's supposed to, whether I agree or not. I love her, Tess. I always will. She's a part of who I am and has been for most of my life. But it's different between us now. We're in a new place, the place where we're meant to be. It might have taken me awhile, but I see that Harley couldn't have become who she is without Mac. I've made peace with that."

"Then how come you haven't brought a woman home?"

"Courtney had herself some fun at my expense tonight, hmm?"

"Don't blame Courtney. I picked her brain. I mean, let's be real, Anthony. The way your brothers keep making jokes about you bringing a girl home. If I hadn't already slept with you, I'd have thought you were gay."

He blinked.

A wicked smile curved her lips. "Well, you are pretty enough to be gay. *Usually.*"

She trailed her fingers along the healing cut on his cheek, and he caught her hand, launched himself on the couch so she couldn't get away.

"I'll give you *gay, chère.* And I'll give it to you underneath me."

Kneeing his way between her thighs, he settled on top of her so she could feel every inch of him—including the erection that wouldn't leave room for any doubts about his sexuality.

Looping her arms around his neck, she melted against him. Heat coiled inside, an urgency he'd never known, a feeling natural and right.

"For your information, I haven't brought anyone home because the women I dated were just dates. No one special. I figured I'd only get one shot at true love, and I already blew it."

"Courtney said your mother told everyone you'd bring home the right girl when you met her." She met his gaze and he could see the vulnerability behind the bravado in those beautiful green eyes. "So did you?"

"For some reason I can't begin to understand, I've been lucky enough to meet the *right* woman, the woman I'm supposed to be with."

"You think I'm the *right* woman?"

He brushed his lips across hers softly, savored the feel of her trembling in reply. "I know you are, *chère.* And I'm the *right* man for you. It's a damn good thing that I came up with my proposal or we'd have never met. But no job is worth more than what we have together. I learned that lesson the hard way. I won't take chances with you."

"Why haven't you said anything?"

He shrugged, tried to look more casual than he felt. "We haven't had enough time together. I only knew that I didn't want to let you go, and I was going to keep coming up with reasons why you shouldn't go home until I could convince you that we belong together."

She arched against him, riding his erection until he groaned aloud. "Anthony, I live in Lubbock, and have a job, too, I might add. Just because my daddy owns the company, doesn't mean I can take leave indefinitely."

His only reply was another downstroke. He might not be able to feel skin yet, but this was the next best thing.

She saw right through his game. "So what were you going to do to keep me around?"

"Hold your car hostage."

"What?" She tried to push him back so she could see his face, but he wouldn't budge, not when she felt so soft and *right* underneath him.

"You told your uncle to take care of your car repairs. I convinced him I was the only man he could trust to do the job."

"Is that where you went today?"

He nodded, feeling very pleased with himself when she nuzzled against him, obviously very pleased herself. "She was delivered safe and sound. I've already ordered parts."

"How long will repairs take?"

"Can't say. Repairing a classic is like art, *chère*. Can't rush art."

"You expect me to stay in town until you're through?"

He nodded. "I didn't think you'd want to leave your car when she's wounded."

"How bad?"

"She'll be as good as new the next time you see her."

"You won't even let me see her?"

He shook his head, nibbled the frown from her mouth with a bunch of small kisses. "She's in good hands."

Her expression visibly melted. Her arms tightened around him and she whispered, "Can we really make this happen?"

He stopped kissing and propped himself up on an elbow to stare down into her face. "We've got a few logistical problems, but I'm willing to do whatever it takes to be with you."

"I live in Texas and you live here."

"*Even* if it means I have to move to Lubbock and get a job as a mechanic in your father's service department. You'd date me if I were a mechanic, wouldn't you?"

Her fingers found his nape again, and she toyed with the hair there, drawing out the suspense, even though her wistful smile told him everything he needed to know. "You'd give up your family and friends to be with me?"

"I wouldn't exactly give them up. I just won't be around as often for Sunday dinner."

"What about your AutoTexCare plan?"

"What about it?"

"You'd give that up, too?"

"I won't take chances with you, Tess. Not for my job. Not for anything."

She slipped her legs around him, a move that spread her thighs wider, drove him a little deeper. "Daddy's going to be real disappointed, then. He thought your idea was brilliant."

"What?"

Arching her hips, she rode him a neat stroke, shivered when she caught a spot that must have felt really good.

"How would your father know about my AutoTexCare plan?"

"I told him all about it at the hospital."

Anthony exhaled heavily, wondering why he'd ever complained about being bored. Ironic how life had tossed him exactly what he'd asked for, and now he'd fallen in love with a woman who was a surprise a minute.

"So all this time when I thought I was proving I wanted you and not an introduction, I wasn't proving a damn thing?"

"You'd already proven yourself to me." There was a tenderness to her voice that told him just how serious she was. "I wasn't sure what I wanted from you, Anthony, but I knew I wasn't ready for us to be over yet."

"I got that part—you wanted to stay in San Francisco for a few extra days, remember?" Slipping a hand underneath her, he lifted her against him, another stroke that tortured him with thoughts of being inside her.

"We'd have had fun."

"We have had fun."

"Yeah. We have. I like your life. I want to be a part of it." She gave a dreamy sigh and pleasure melted over her face when she closed her eyes and let the rhythm of their rocking hips take over. "But I think you should officially present your proposal to Daddy before we try to figure out how to handle our logistical problems."

"Then I will. If he's interested, I can see a bunch of ways we might maneuver our work situations so we can be together, either here or in Lubbock."

"It'll all work out."

"Just like it's supposed to."

Anthony believed that. Tess had gotten under his skin, and when she tipped her beautiful face to his and said, "Kiss me," he could feel their future spread out before him, a promise, a challenge, the thrill of a lifetime.

Epilogue

TESS ALLOWED ANTHONY to lead her through the service center, his strong hands clamped over her eyes so she couldn't see a thing. But he led her along at a steady pace, holding her close so there was no chance she'd stumble and fall.

Having his hard body surround hers again felt so right. In the month and a half since they'd met, she'd grown familiar with the way his strong arms felt around her, the way he smelled, all freshly masculine, all Anthony. She hadn't realized when signing on to be a couple that she'd miss him so much when apart.

But she had, and that had been just one surprise as they'd spent the past month working, negotiating, arguing and making up again, while they merged their lives and careers.

She'd just arrived back in New Orleans after yet another trip to Lubbock, but this time she was here to stay.

It was the perfect solution. He owned a successful business that he wouldn't give up even though he had taken on the job of getting Daddy's service up and running with his AutoTexCare plan. She'd been wanting to spread her wings for a long time. New Orleans was far enough from Lubbock while not being too far. Daddy had his plane and his dealership here. Not to mention there were always road trips and cell phones....

After a week apart, Tess had wanted to head straight home to reacquaint herself with the man she'd lain in bed at night thinking about. Thank goodness for cell phones! When she hadn't been able to sleep in the wee hours, she'd dialed Anthony's number and they'd talked, or argued, or heated up the signal by sharing some very sexy dreams.

But right now the man wanted no part of anything except giving her a present. He'd promised to have her car completely restored as a welcome gift to her new home, and he'd apparently accomplished his goal.

When he finally brought her to a stop, she took advantage of the moment to lean back against him, to revel in the way all his hard places molded perfectly against her. He removed his hands from her face. "All right, you can open your eyes."

"First tell me—is she still purple?"

"You don't trust me, *chère?*" He sounded hurt.

"I do, but I know you think my car's ugly."

"I never said your car was ugly." He breathed the words against her ear, and she sighed aloud.

He chuckled, sending another warm blast through her, and said, "Okay."

Anthony had parked her car between the bays so it became the focal point of his big garage. On its hood was a bright red bow the size of a truck tire.

Her Gremlin was indeed still purple, its paint waxed to a highly glossed finish, all the new glass sparkling in the overhead lighting. There wasn't a trace left of the damage he'd had to pound out of her body after the tussle with the SUV. Tess would never have known the rear quarter panel wasn't brand-new.

And seeing her car and his meticulous attention to detail seemed to symbolize just how much he loved her.

"Oh, Anthony." She breathed the words on another sigh, feeling all warm and wonderful and so very pleased with life. "You do incredible work."

Shimmying close, she wrapped her arms around his neck and pulled him down so she could press appreciative kisses along his throat. She'd been waiting all week for a taste of him, wouldn't wait any longer. "I'll want to reward you, you know."

"I'm counting on it, *chère*."

"We'll have plenty of time together now."

He buried his face in her hair, inhaled deeply, leaving her no question that he'd been just as starved to see her. "I don't know about that. Corporate sent the specs for the new location. I'm looking at a lot of work to get the prototype service department up in time for construction to begin."

"As if you didn't live for challenges." And she knew that implementing his AutoTexCare plan in their new locations would be a piece of cake—especially since he was arranging for side-by-side offices in the new local showroom.

She had no doubt AutoTexCare would prove to be everything he thought it was and exactly what her daddy needed. After he got the prototypes up and running, he'd start looking at the next challenge of implementing his plan in the existing locations.

He brushed a kiss onto her hair. "So how did things work out with your staff?"

He'd known how worried she'd been. Moving the foundation out of AutoCarTex headquarters wasn't any problem since she operated independently anyway, but the others in her office…

"Found perfect positions in corporate for my office staff and it turns out that Hal wants to come here. He said New Orleans is much more along the lines of what he's used to. I didn't realize it, but he hated Lubbock and liked working for me. Coming here will solve his problem."

Anthony tightened his grip around her, pressed a kiss to the top of her head. "So everything worked out."

"Just like it was meant to."

Even the situation with Daryl was resolving itself. His thugs had done as Harley predicted and testified against him to cut their own deals. Turned out the auto-theft ring was operating out of all his father's dealerships, including the one here in New Orleans.

Eastman Investigations had been hired to assist local law enforcement in building the case, so even Harley and Mac were in on the action, which Tess thought a nice perk for their loyalty to Anthony.

Daddy had already scheduled his first trip to town at the end of the month under the pretense of checking out the new location. As construction hadn't started yet, Tess saw right through his ploy, but thought it would do him a world of good to get out of Lubbock for something other than business for a change. She was looking forward to seeing how he liked Mama DiLeo's good Italian cooking.

"So where is everyone around here?" she asked, rising up on tiptoes to look over his shoulder.

"It's Sunday, *chère.* Shop's closed."

"So there's no one here? No one at all?"

"Just you, me and your purple Gremlin."

That sounded promising. "Maybe I'll give you my reward right now."

"First you have to look inside your car."

She eyed him suspiciously. "What's more important than your reward? I'm *very* grateful, you know?"

He gave her butt a squeeze and launched her in the direction of her car. "This is."

Oh, my, my. Another surprise.

Tess couldn't imagine what he'd done inside. Naturally, she'd assumed he'd had the interior detailed since glass had been everywhere, but she could sense his excitement as he dogged her heels across the garage.

Peering inside at the pristine interior, she noticed that he'd even replaced the utility tray on the floor with an upscale model the same color as her seats. He didn't miss a trick, and again his thoroughness, knowing how much he wanted to please her, caught her in all her soft spots, and made her even more excited to please him back.

Then she caught sight of the tiny jeweler's box inside the tray. "Oh, Anthony. That's not what I think it is, is it?"

"Open it and find out."

He stepped aside so she could open the door, pleased that he'd even repaired the hinge that had made the heavy door creak. Grabbing the box, she sat down on the edge of the seat, feeling wobbly kneed in a way only this man had ever made her.

With his mouth. With his love. With his surprises. Anthony DiLeo was a thrill a minute.

He braced an arm on the roof above her and smiled down, watching her with excitement in his warm brown eyes.

She flipped open the box.

A diamond winked at her from an unusual platinum setting. Before she could make sense of what this meant, Anthony knelt in front of her, plucked away the box and removed the ring.

Reaching for her cast, he slipped the ring onto her third finger and said, "Marry me, Tess."

Their gazes met, and the tenderness she saw in his expression stole what was left of her breath. His beautiful face, the strong sculpted features, the glorious golden skin, the fading scar on his cheek, all reflected every bit of the love she felt.

"Marriage? I hadn't thought that far ahead."

"I have." He slipped his fingers through hers and gave a squeeze. "I bought my new place intending to put the past behind me. Now that I've met you, I have a future, so I want it to be our home. Not just the place you live."

The future with him suddenly swelled before her, so filled with promise that she felt tears prickle her eyes. She lifted his hand and pressed her mouth to his work-rough palm, a kiss that conveyed what no words ever could—how much she loved him.

"Yes."

He pulled her up and into his arms then, sealing the deal with a kiss that led from one thing to another and yet another.

Tess had no idea how long they stood there, wrapped in each other's arms, making out against the side of her car, but her shirt was in wild disarray and he had an erection as hard as her rear axle by the time they stopped.

"Wow," was all she could say.

He flashed that blinding grin and lifted her hand to admire his ring on her finger. "*Wow* is right."

She laughed, liking the sight, too. She'd even gotten a new cast just two weeks ago. And this one Anthony had filled with little hearts—not red, but purple.

"You're going to laugh," she said. "Or be offended. But this ring reminds me of my rims."

She positioned her hand to compare the ring to her sparkling alloy rims. "See what I'm talking about? There's something about the way these tiny diamonds shoot out from the solitaire. Am I crazy?"

He didn't reply, and she glanced around, unsure if she'd find him smiling or scowling. His bedroom eyes caressed her with a look of such promise that Tess couldn't wait for their future to begin. In bed. Soon.

"Very good, *chère*. I had this designed for you by one of Mac's friends. I brought her here to find something about your car for inspiration. She took one look at your rims, and there you have it. I wasn't sure it worked."

Laughing, Tess slipped away. She wasn't going to wait for the future and a bed. Not when she had *now* and a *hood*. She was going to perform a sexy striptease and act out one of his dreams. A well-deserved reward. "It's perfect."

And it was.

* * * * *

HER PERFECT HERO

Kara LENNOX

Texas native **Kara Lennox** has earned her living at various times as an art director, typesetter, textbook editor and reporter. She's worked in a boutique, a health club and an ad agency. She's been an antiques dealer and even a blackjack dealer. But no work has made her happier than writing romance novels. She has written more than fifty books. When not writing, Kara indulges in an ever-changing array of hobbies. Her latest passions are bird-watching and long-distance bicycling. She loves to hear from readers; you can visit her webpage at www.karalennox.com.

In memory of my uncle, Captain Henry "Pearly" Gates, who was a Dallas firefighter for many years.

Chapter One

Tony Veracruz climbed off Engine 59 pumped full of adrenaline for which there was no outlet. Around midafternoon his crew had been called to a house fire in South Dallas. But by the time they'd arrived another company had had the small blaze under control and there'd really been nothing for him to do.

Back at the station, he halted traffic on busy Jefferson Street so Lt. McCrae could back the engine into the apparatus room. He willed the alarm to buzz again, but annoyingly it remained silent.

For the past ten or so hours in the August heat he'd gone on one call after another, including the rescue of a kid stuck in a drainage ditch. All of which had, thank God, distracted him from thoughts of Daralee.

Now, with nothing to keep his brain occupied, he could think of nothing else. He wished he could banish her from his head. She was finished with him, and nothing he could do would bring her back.

For the past week, ever since their breakup, the only thing that could wipe her from his mind was the sound of that alarm.

As he followed the engine into its bay and prepared to close the door, movement across the street caught his eye.

"Hey, Ethan," he called to his fellow firefighter and lifelong best friend. "The lights are on at Brady's."

His announcement got the attention of everyone within earshot. The guys who'd been on the engine joined him in the open doorway to gaze at the illuminated beer signs in the front window of Brady's Tavern. The signs had been dark for the past two weeks, ever since Brady Keller, third-generation owner of the best bar in Dallas's Oak Cliff neighborhood, had died peacefully in his sleep.

"Maybe it's opening back up," Ethan said.

Tony shrugged. "We can only hope."

Oak Cliff had once been its own town, but Dallas had swallowed it up more than a hundred years earlier. It comprised a large area across the Trinity River from downtown and came with a diverse population and plenty of character. Those who lived and worked there tended to think of themselves as different—outside the mainstream—from other Dallasites. In turn, Dallas proper didn't think all that much of Oak Cliff.

Brady's was an Oak Cliff institution, and Tony had frequented the bar since he'd acquired his first fake ID at age seventeen. Located just across the street from the fire station, it was a favorite hangout for cops and firefighters.

And good ole Brady Keller had been as familiar a fixture as his tavern's sticky wood floors and antique shuffleboard table. He'd always been there, ready to listen, commiserate and even serve up an occasional beer on the house, provided your tale of woe was sad enough. Whenever Tony broke up with a girl—which happened with alarming frequency—he'd headed straight for Brady's, where he could distract himself with a game of pool, a sporting event on TV and a cold one. Until the bar had closed its doors.

Fire Station 59 had gone into mourning at the news of Brady's death, especially when the For Sale sign had gone up.

"Did you see who's inside?" Ethan asked.

"I think I can see someone moving around," said Priscilla Garner, another of Tony's good friends. She, Ethan and Tony had gone through firefighter training together. Now they all lived on the same block, worked the same shifts and watched each other's backs. As the three greenest rookies, they took a lot of grief from the veterans. "Maybe someone bought the place."

"I saw who went inside," said Otis Granger, who'd had a stool with his name on it at the bar. Otis hadn't gone on the last call. "Two girls, and they didn't look like bar owners to me."

"Girls?" Tony's interest immediately picked up.

"Well, women, if you want to be politically correct," Otis explained. "But one of them was a teenager, I think."

They were all hoping someone would buy the

place and open it up just as it had been. Brady's business had fallen off some in recent years as newer, trendier bars had opened in Oak Cliff, but none of his regular customers wanted to see the bar change.

"I think we should find out who they are," Ethan said. "Brady must have family—someone to inherit. He talked about a sister."

"Tony, go talk to them." Priscilla gave him a little shove.

"Why me?"

"Duh… They're female. I don't know if you've noticed, but you have a certain effect on women."

Otis and Ethan broke out laughing, but Tony didn't. Whatever effect he had, it never lasted. His longest romantic relationship had ended after only a couple of months.

"Just go find out who those women are," Priscilla urged. "They must be related to Brady somehow. Ask them what their plans are. Maybe you can impress on them how important it is to sell Brady's to someone who'll reopen it and keep things the same."

"Ethan, why don't *you* talk to them?" Tony argued. "You're the great persuader around here."

"Yeah, he managed to convince Kat to marry him," Otis said drily. "Like she couldn't have done a lot better."

Ethan puffed out his chest, as he did at any mention of his beautiful new bride. They'd been married less than a month. "Okay, I'll talk to the ladies."

Just then, the door to Brady's opened and one of the women emerged.

Even from a distance, Tony could see she was gorgeous—tall and sleek, with golden hair that blew in the breeze. She wore snug faded jeans that molded themselves to a body made for love and a clingy cropped shirt that showed off her trim waist and breasts that bounced slightly as she strode down the sidewalk.

She stopped in front of the For Sale sign attached to the front window, then reached behind the iron burglar bars and yanked on the paper until it came loose. She pulled it free and rolled it up, tucked it under her arm, then went back inside.

"Hold it," Tony said. "Changed my mind. I'll talk to her."

"Uh-oh," Priscilla said. "Watch out, Tony's on the prowl."

He gave Pris a disdainful look. "Daralee and I just broke up. You don't honestly think I'm ready to get involved with someone else, do you?"

Tony's fellow firefighters laughed so hard at this that Otis nearly fell onto the concrete floor and Ethan had to support himself against the truck.

"What? I can't believe you're laughing about my messed-up love life."

"Messed up," Ethan agreed, "until the next girl comes along. You've been mooning about Daralee for, what, a week?"

"We had a good thing going," Tony said more to himself than Ethan. "I really thought..." He stopped.

No time for regrets. That woman with the gold hair was undoubtedly the new owner of Brady's, and someone needed to talk to her before she changed anything. "Cover for me if Captain Campeon notices I'm gone." Without any further hesitation, Tony loped out of the station, darting between cars on busy Jefferson Street, toward the gorgeous goddess of a woman who—unknowingly—waited inside Brady's to meet him.

Brady's Tavern occupied a two-story building that must have been close to a hundred years old, and the brick looked as if it hadn't been cleaned since coal stoves went out of vogue. A flock of pigeons had taken up residence under the eaves and the evidence of their frequent presence covered the cracked sidewalk.

The bar's door wasn't locked, so Tony pushed it open. A wall of hot, stuffy air, heavy with the scent of stale beer, slapped him in the face. "Hello? Anyone home?"

A teenage girl bounded up to him like an eager puppy. "Hi. Who're you?"

"Tony. I work at the fire station across the street. Are you the new owner of Brady's?"

She nodded. "Well, my mom is. This place is so cool. Do you play shuffleboard?"

"Not only do I play, I was the Brady's Tavern shuffleboard champion two years running. Where's your mom?" Surely the woman he'd seen removing the For Sale sign wasn't this girl's mother.

"My mom is Brady's sister. Was. Whatever."

"Then Brady was your uncle. It must have been tough losing him so unexpectedly. He was a great guy."

"Not according to Mom. She said he was a drunkard black sheep who couldn't be trusted with a dime." The girl rocked back on her heels, apparently not realizing she'd insulted someone Tony had considered a friend. And her mother's information was outdated. Brady had quit drinking twenty years ago.

"Could I speak to your mom?" He looked around the bar, which seemed strangely empty without the usual smattering of cops, firefighters and "siren sisters"—the female groupies who were turned on by any man who wore a badge or wielded a hose. But he didn't see the blond woman.

"My mom is at work. But if it's anything to do with Brady's, you'll want to talk to Julie."

"Julie?"

"My sister."

Ah. That made a whole lot more sense.

"She's counting the glasses or something. Trying to decide what to keep and what to get rid of."

Then he'd better talk to her right away before she did something stupid—like throw away the Daryl Jones memorial ashtray.

Tony heard some clinking going on behind the long carved-wood bar and figured that had to be where Julie had disappeared to. He made his way to the bar, his feet *schlup-schlupp*ing with every step on the sticky floor.

Ah, it was good to be back here. Brady's was lit

up like a Christmas tree, with its vintage signs. They covered almost every available bit of wall surface and illuminated the interior, which was crammed full of tables and chairs, pool tables, dartboards—guy heaven. Every corner had a TV, and when the place had been open all of them were always tuned in to a smorgasbord of sporting events.

A lonely silk ficus tree lurked forlornly in a corner, covered with dust. Supposedly one of Brady's girlfriends had put it there one time, trying in vain to class the place up.

"Excuse me, Julie?"

She popped up from behind the bar, a pair of yellow rubber gloves on her hands. Looking startled, she stared at Tony for several seconds of charged silence. She had the most amazing amber eyes. He'd never seen eyes that color before. She reminded him of a golden fawn or an unspoiled woodland nymph.

"Yes?" she finally said. Her low, sexy voice sent shivers down his spine and a rush of blood through his veins.

Tony shook himself out of his daze. How could he be attracted to this woman when his pain over losing Daralee was still so fresh? It was just hormones playing a nasty trick on him. "Hi, I'm Tony Veracruz. I work at the fire station across the street, and we were just wondering...are you going to keep Brady's? We saw that you removed the For Sale sign."

She cocked her head to one side. "Do you want to buy it?"

"Believe me, we've talked about it. But the price tag is a bit high for us working stiffs. We just really miss the place—and Brady. He was a great guy. It was terrible losing him so suddenly. You're his niece?"

"That's right. Julie Polk." She extended her hand across the bar's polished surface, realized she still had gloves on, removed the right one hurriedly and tried again.

Tony took her hand, and rather than shake it as he would a man's, he squeezed it. It was a lovely little hand, with perfectly manicured nails polished a pearly pink. Tony's stomach gave a peculiar swoop.

Julie's mask of detached politeness slipped and a flicker of awareness passed over her face. So she felt it, too?

The teenage girl, who'd come to lean against the bar resting her chin on her folded arms, cleared her throat.

Julie extracted her hand from Tony's. "This is my sister, Belinda. I heard her talking to someone, so I assume you've already met."

"I did have the pleasure, though she didn't volunteer her name. It's a beautiful name, too." He'd almost named his daughter Belinda, so he wasn't deliberately laying it on thick.

Belinda blushed furiously. Though her hair and eyes were darker, she looked much like her sister—which meant she was probably already breaking hearts in all directions.

"So your mother is the new owner of Brady's?" Tony asked Julie.

"Yes. She and Brady owned it together, but she's been more of a silent partner. They weren't very close."

"That's too bad. It's sad when families drift apart." He was thinking about his own family. Due to his parents' multiple marriages, Tony had lots of stepsiblings and half siblings, some of whom he'd lost touch with. "So your mother has decided not to sell?"

"Frankly Mom really doesn't care. She's asked me to deal with it for her." Julie put the second rubber glove back on and resumed her task, which appeared to be counting beer mugs and entering the tally on a clipboard. She gave him a nice view of her denim-clad bottom in the process, which Tony fully enjoyed—until he realized Belinda was smirking at him. He diverted his gaze to the picture of the naked lady above the bar.

"But you are going to reopen?" Tony persisted.

"It would be a shame for the business to leave the family after we've owned it for three generations."

That sounded promising. "Yeah, there's a lot of history here. Who are you gonna get to run the place? Brady had a guy working for him, Alonzo. He'd be a great manager."

"You don't think I could run Brady's?" she asked, challenging. She put the clipboard down and devoted her full attention to their conversation.

"Well, you're…" Tony stopped himself before he

misstepped. Some women had accused him before of being a male chauvinist pig. But it wasn't because he didn't think women deserved equal rights or that they weren't as smart and capable as men. The opposite was more like it. He thought women should be treated better than men. And he didn't think any woman as beautiful and refined as Julie Polk should have to sling beer and deal with groping, drunk customers.

"I'm what?"

"Too pretty to work at a joint like this."

Her gaze fell, her long lashes casting shadows on her smooth cheeks. "Thanks, but I don't have the resources to hire someone else to run the place. And since I'm currently between assignments, as they say, I'm the logical one to take on the job."

"More power to you, then." Tony grinned. Brady's was coming back! The guys at the station would be over the moon. "And don't worry," he added, "you've got lots of friends in the neighborhood who'll help you out. So when are you planning to reopen?"

"Oh, I'd say it'll take a few weeks to refurbish the place, work out the menus…."

"Menus?" Brady had served microwave nachos, popcorn and beer nuts. You didn't need a menu for the basics. "You're going to change Brady's?"

"Brady's is not going to be Brady's." And a big smile spread across her face, dispelling the polite, almost icy mask she'd been wearing and transforming her into an angel. Tony was so entranced with how she looked he almost missed what she said next. "It's going to be Belinda's."

"Belinda's...Bar?" he asked warily.

"Belinda's is going to be the coolest tearoom in all of Dallas."

Julie gathered that sexy Tony Veracruz was not happy with her announcement. He stared, his jaw hanging open, for several seconds as he processed her news.

Lord, he was gorgeous. Those well-defined cheekbones, that smooth olive skin and brown eyes a girl could drown in. Funny, she'd always thought her ex-fiancé, with his aristocratic clean-cut blond handsomeness, was the best-looking guy around. But Tony's earthier looks struck a chord deep inside her.

When he'd said she was pretty, the compliment had given her heart palpitations. But how silly was that? He probably told a half-dozen women a day they were pretty.

"Did you say...?" Tony's voice trailed off.

"Yes, isn't it great? I'm turning Brady's into a tearoom."

"On Jefferson Street?"

"The perfect place, don't you think? Oak Cliff is in the middle of a renaissance. I see revitalization all around us. The historic district is right across the street. Those mansions in Kessler Park are only a mile away. Then there's the Bishop Arts district— lots of sophisticated restaurants and bars going in there." She was using all the same arguments she had used to convince her parents to okay this venture, though truthfully they hadn't cared much what she did with Brady's so long as it brought in some cash.

The moment she'd seen the place, despite its coat of grime, the thought had flashed into her mind: Julie Polk, owner and manager of the classiest tearoom in town. Wouldn't Trey be surprised? When she'd given him back his ring, he'd told her she would never make anything of herself without his help. But she was going to show him and his whole family how wrong they were.

Besides, she also wanted to transform Brady's into Belinda's for herself. After her disastrous broken engagement, she needed something she could call her own; something no one could take away from her.

She resumed counting beer mugs. They were nice, heavy glass ones, and she could use them as iced-tea glasses. Almost everything else would have to go, though. She'd been doing a quick-and-dirty inventory since she and Belinda had arrived this morning, and the results were depressing.

"But Brady's is a neighborhood institution," Tony argued. "You can't close it for good."

"I don't really have a choice," she said practically. "I know absolutely nothing about running a bar. I do, however, know a great deal about managing a tearoom." She'd spent a year as manager of Lochinvar's, the oh-so-tony tearoom inside Bailey-

Davidson's, the upscale department store owned by her ex-fiancé's family.

Belinda's was going to be much cooler than Lochinvar's, which had been around for fifty years and attracted mostly older matrons. Belinda's was going to bring in the younger women, the rich hipsters who frequented Hattie's and Caribe in Bishop Arts—the ones who knew Oak Cliff was the cool place to be, the ones who thought Deep Ellum was just a bit too grungy and Highland Park too stuffy.

"But Brady's is a gold mine," Tony argued, following her along his side of the bar as she moved to count the next shelf of glasses. "It's packed most nights with hard-drinking men and women who buy lots of beer."

"What a charming picture. Anyway, I've looked at the books. The place might have been crowded, but the customers weren't spending enough money. Brady's profits were way down. There's almost no money in the accounts either."

That didn't surprise Tony. "Brady spent it as fast as he could make it. He was a soft touch. He gave money away to any hard-luck story that came his way. He even hosted free Thanksgiving dinners for the homeless."

"He did?" Julie was surprised. According to her mother, Brady had never done anything that didn't directly benefit Brady. "That sounds so nice."

"You didn't know him?"

"Not really. Anyway, the point is, the books don't lie." She'd been taking classes at community college with an eye toward a degree in business management. She knew a bit about accounting. "Brady's was barely breaking even."

"Okay, so maybe the place isn't a gold mine. Yet. But with the right management skills…" He looked pointedly at Julie.

"I've done the research. The demographics are changing. A more upscale establishment on this street will be cutting-edge. Belinda's should be extremely profitable, even with the investments I'll have to make to refurbish the place." Julie was counting on some quick profits. Clever Belinda, with her perfect SAT scores, was going to attend an Ivy League university. And since the Davidsons had withdrawn their pledge to finance Belinda's education, it was up to Julie to figure out how to pay the staggering tuition by next fall, only a year away.

Even though Belinda was certain to get some sort of scholarship, there would still be huge expenses. And her parents couldn't contribute anything. They could barely take care of their own bills.

The real-estate agent had told Julie it could take months or even years to sell Brady's for a fair price. And all the mortgages and liens Brady had on the building would eat up the proceeds from any purchase.

Opening the tearoom was a much better idea. She could sell everything—and there were some collectibles tucked in and around Brady's, like the cigar-store Indian and the vintage pinball machines and neon signs. With the proceeds and her own little nest egg, she could transform this place into a posh yet cozy oasis that would provide her and her family with income for years to come.

Eventually, she would have to pay off Brady's creditors. Fortunately, however, they'd been willing to work out terms when she'd explained she wanted to get the place back in business.

Julie had done the math. She really could manage this.

"You can't do this," Tony said. "Please, Julie, I'm begging you. You'll be destroying a piece of Oak Cliff history."

Julie stopped counting beer mugs. She kept losing track, and who could blame her when this gorgeous man was distracting her? She wondered exactly what he'd be willing to do to get her to change her mind, then immediately banished the thought. She'd broken her engagement less than a month ago. She was still reeling over her fiancé's betrayal and the astounding realization that he and his whole family had expected her to brush his indiscretion under the rug. She had no business letting sexy Tony Veracruz heat up her blood.

"Mr. Veracruz, look around you."

He did. "Yeah?"

"This place is a dump. It's a dive, a blight on a neighborhood that's trying to come back. I'm going to improve it, beautify it, make it a showplace Oak Cliff can be proud of."

"Well, I'll admit Brady's could use a good scrubbing."

"What it could use is a nuclear explosion. That's what it would take to get the dirt off these floors. Everything reeks of stale beer and cigarette smoke."

"You could clean the place up," Tony tried again. "We'd help you."

"I'm sorry, Tony." And truly she was. Brady's had probably been the sort of place where some people felt they belonged. Like Cheers, only grittier. Finding a place to fit in, to belong, was important, and she should know. She'd been trying to figure out where she fit her whole life.

Not in Pleasant Grove, the blue-collar suburb where she'd grown up in a housing project. She'd always known there was something better for her out in the world and she'd thought she'd found her place working at Bailey-Davidson's. She'd devoted nine years of her life to it—watching, studying, improving herself, moving up the department-store career ladder, slowly accumulating college credits so that she would eventually qualify for higher management positions.

She loved that store. She loved being around the beautiful clothes, the delicate bone china, the designer bed linens—oh, how she loved the linens department.

Most of all, she'd loved being around all those well-educated, refined, soft-spoken people. And when Trey Davidson had noticed her, accepted her, when his friends had welcomed her into their circle—even though she couldn't claim an Ivy League affiliation or a single drop of blue blood—she'd thought she'd found her place. Up-and-coming Bailey-Davidson's executive and wife to the store's heir apparent.

A dream come true.

Except the dream had turned into the proverbial nightmare, and Julie had once again found herself afloat in a strange sea in which she didn't belong, wondering what she would do with her life.

Belinda's could be *her* place. Her creation, her universe. She could surround herself with beautiful things, fine foods and people who appreciated the same things she did.

Tony Veracruz, she guessed, would not be one of those people. Which was a pity. Let Marcel at the Bailey-Davidson's salon cut Tony's hair, then put him in an Armani suit, and he'd fit right in at any office in any glass high-rise in the city. But Julie suspected that sort of life didn't appeal to him. She could tell he liked himself the way he was and liked where he was in life.

Which was fine. That was part of his appeal, actually—the fact that he was obviously so comfortable in his skin.

His gorgeous skin.

"How 'bout I take you out to dinner tomorrow?" Tony asked. "We could get some burgers. You could tell me more about this tearoom idea of yours."

Oh, she was tempted. For one thing, she hadn't been out to eat at a real restaurant in weeks because she'd been hoarding her pennies.

But she had an idea that if she let Tony take her out, even for an innocent hamburger, before long he would be telling her more about what a great place Brady's was and how wrong she was to change it to a tearoom, and she would start to doubt herself.

She didn't need that. She'd doubted her judgment enough after finding out the man she loved had been lying to her for months—maybe longer. She needed to surround herself with people who would encourage her and support her and help her make Belinda's a resounding success.

Julie wouldn't have cared so much about this venture if it was just about herself, but she would do whatever it took for Belinda. Her sweet, brilliant baby sister was going to have the chance to make something fantastic of herself, and nothing was going to prevent it. Not the miserable, self-serving Davidsons, not her parents' apathy and certainly not a fireman who was sentimental about a run-down eyesore of a neighborhood bar. Even if he was sexy as hell.

"I'm sorry, Tony. I appreciate the invitation, but I have so much to do," she said coolly. Which was true enough.

"Another time, then. I better get back to work." He flashed her a dazzling grin, turned with a jaunty wave and exited out the squeaky front door.

She hoped he wasn't serious about asking her out again. She might not have the strength to turn down his next invitation.

Chapter Two

"I never met Uncle Brady, did I?" Belinda asked as she and Julie climbed the stairs to the apartment above the bar where Brady had lived.

"No, I don't think you ever met him." She only had a vague memory herself of a big bear of a man who showed up at Thanksgiving with a fruitcake, drank too much wine and was asked to leave. "He sent Mom a little check every once in a while—her part of the 'profits' from the bar. But he and Mom hardly ever talked. Mom sent him a Christmas card every year, but he never reciprocated."

"Tony said he was a great guy."

"Brady probably gave Tony free beer." But Tony had painted an image of Brady that Julie couldn't get out of her mind. A soft touch. Generous and kind. Sure didn't sound like the mooch her mother had described.

"How much do you think we'll get for all that stuff downstairs?" Belinda asked.

"I'll have to do some research, but I bet those vintage signs will fetch a good price."

"What about those green glass lampshades? Trey has some of those, doesn't he?"

Julie gave an unladylike snort. "Trey's are reproductions. Ours are the real thing. In fact, maybe I'll keep those. They'll look pretty in the tearoom, don't you think?"

Belinda shrugged. "Will you keep the jukebox?"

"No, that I'm going to sell. It's an old Wurlitzer, and the vinyl records alone are worth a fortune."

Rather than sounding excited about the prospect, Belinda gave a sad little huff.

"What?"

"Oh, it's just a bit tragic thinking about tearing the place up."

"Belinda, you must be joking. It's disgusting."

"Yeah, but that guy Tony was right. If you scrubbed it up, it wouldn't be so bad."

"Don't even think about it. I'm not running a bar." Even if she had the experience or knowledge, she preferred the idea of improving the neighborhood. Brady's had been an eyesore, no doubt drawing unsavory characters. Belinda's was going to be beautiful. Maybe the firefighters were unhappy about her planned changes, but she bet most of the residents around here would be delighted.

"I know, I know," Belinda said. "I'm just saying it's a little sad, that's all."

Julie tried several keys from the big key ring the lawyer had given her mother, finally locating the right one. She'd been avoiding the place where her uncle had died, but she knew she had to check it out. She was planning to live here while she oversaw the renovations—and maybe afterward, too. It would save her a long commute to work, plus she would have her privacy back. Living in her parents' tiny house, where they were all on top of each other and getting on each other's nerves, wasn't going to work for much longer.

This apartment would do until she could afford something better. Someday, she'd like to have her own house. It didn't have to be anything as grand as Trey's Highland Park house, where she would be living now if she hadn't canceled the wedding. But she wanted a front porch. And flower boxes in the windows. And a real backyard, maybe with a deck where she could sit outside on a Sunday morning and read the paper, a golden retriever by her side.

Still, a one-bedroom apartment rent-free wasn't bad. She held her breath and pushed open the door.

Brady's living space was surprisingly neat, clean and spartan, given the excessive grime and clutter of the bar. Julie had always heard Brady described as a man who couldn't be trusted. *Lazy, slovenly, a freeloader*—those were words her mother commonly used to describe Brady. Yet that image didn't match his digs.

Julie poked around to see if there might be any valuables, but aside from a couple of old paintings and some vintage Fiesta dishes, nothing jumped out as a real treasure.

The bedroom was empty except for a dresser. Someone had removed the bed in which Brady had expired, which was a huge relief. No way would Julie have been able to sleep there.

She returned to the living room and sank onto a worn sofa. It was pretty soft—she could sleep on this. And Belinda would be happy to get her own room back at their parents' house. The sisters had been sharing a room and a bed, just like old times, for the past couple of weeks.

"So what do you think?" Belinda asked. "Can you live here?"

"Sure. I've lived in worse places." Her first apartment—when she'd gotten her first real job as a stock girl at Bailey-Davidson's—had been one ratty room in the attic of an old East Dallas house. She'd done her cooking on a hot plate.

Brady's living quarters were a palace compared to that but something of a comedown from her last place—a classy Park Cities town house she'd rented from the Davidsons. Still, she had a little money to live on, the proceeds from returning all the wedding presents—the ones her friends and family had refused to take back. And Trey's parents had given her a handsome "severance check" in return for her silence about his little secret, which she'd been happy to accept—not that she ever would have gone blabbing about the illegitimate child he'd conceived with his mistress even as he'd been planning a lavish wedding to Julie. Gossip like that would only make *her* look dumb. Her stash was enough to keep her going until the tearoom opened.

"The view is certainly nice," Belinda said dreamily.

Julie glanced out the window to see what her sister was talking about. All she could see was the fire station, a hundred-year-old brick monstrosity in need of a good sandblasting.

Then she looked closer and realized the blinds to the second-floor window were open; inside a man was pulling off his T-shirt. "Belinda!"

"What? I can look, can't I?"

Julie joined her sister at the window. The man picked up a barbell and started doing some curls. It was none other than her firefighting Adonis. "He's doing that on purpose."

"Oh, like he knew we'd be up here, staring out the window? Get a grip, Jules. You're paranoid."

Maybe she was. But her reaction to Tony Veracruz had unnerved her.

She'd once felt that way about Trey. He'd flirted with her shamelessly, focused all his attention on her, swept her off her feet. She'd fallen in love, hard, with a man she thought she knew. Handsome, smart, ambitious, funny, generous...

Unfaithful.

Feeling all gooey inside over a man, getting caught up in flirtation and charm—none of those offered any guarantee of that man's deep-down character. Julie would do well to remember that and to focus on building a secure future for herself without relying on anyone else.

Tony looked out the window, saw them staring and flashed that cocky smile.

Julie abruptly closed the blinds.

"Hey!" Belinda objected.

"He's too old for you."

"But not for you. Earlier, he was checking out your butt."

"Really?" Despite herself, Julie felt a little thrill. "He probably checks out every girl's butt."

"He didn't look at mine. Besides, he's going to be your neighbor. You have to be friendly."

"No, I don't." Tony Veracruz was trouble with a capital *T*, and she certainly didn't need any more of that.

"So are you going to tell us what happened?" Priscilla asked. As busy as their shift had been earlier, activity had died down completely. Pris was killing time in Station 59's exercise room, running on the treadmill.

Priscilla was a maniac when it came to fitness and she'd guilted almost every firefighter on their shift into working out more. It was humiliating when a wisp of a woman like Pris could lift more weight than you.

Tony had found it difficult to admit to his co-workers the horrible news about what was happening to Brady's Tavern. They'd given him a task: convince the bar's new owner to reopen Brady's just as it was. And though he knew he had nothing to do with Julie's decision to turn Brady's into a tea-room, he still felt as if he'd let down his comrades.

Mission failed.

Not only that, but beautiful Julie Polk had said no when he'd asked her out. Oh, she was interested. She'd acted a little fluttery when he'd told her she was pretty, and he'd felt some definite vibes flash through the air between them. But she'd been prickly, too. Her mind was so filled with plans for her tearoom that romance was way down on her priority list.

He knew darn well he shouldn't be thinking about romance either. He was still smarting from Daralee's sudden rejection. He'd thought their relationship was going somewhere. They'd been so crazy about each other. Now he knew he'd been nothing but a boy toy to her, someone to irk her exhusband. When that hadn't worked, he'd become history.

But just looking at Julie sent his hormones into a frenzy. Could he help it if he liked having a girlfriend? Still, the next time he fell head over heels for someone, he wanted the same feelings in return. He didn't want to be a low priority or an after-thought.

"Earth to Tony," Priscilla said impatiently. "Did you hear me?"

Sooner or later everyone would find out about Julie's plans. He might as well break the news. "I heard you. It's just too horrible what she's doing to Brady's."

Priscilla gasped. "Is she tearing down the building? Granted, it needs work, but isn't it a historical landmark or something?"

"She's doing worse than that. It's sacrilege."

Now he had Ethan's and Otis's attention, too. And Jim Peterson's. "Would you just tell us instead of being a drama queen?" said Peterson, pedaling at a leisurely pace on the stationary bike.

"She's turning Brady's into a tearoom."

Otis dropped his barbell with a clang. Ethan's jaw sagged.

Priscilla, however, didn't appear horrified. "A tearoom. Right here in our neighborhood."

Ethan groaned. "Only you, Priscilla, would find this news welcome."

"I would miss Brady's, but a tearoom could be good. I could do lunch there."

Otis threw his sweaty towel at her. "And where exactly are us men supposed to hang out?"

Priscilla turned off the treadmill and slowed to a stop. "At least maybe we could get some healthy food there. A salad or…" Loud groans cut her off. She shrugged. "I can't help you if you won't help yourselves."

"Pris, maybe *you* should talk to her," Tony said. "Woman to woman. Tell her how important Brady's is to this neighborhood. It's important for us and the cops to have a neutral place to meet and talk things over."

Pris gave Tony an appraising look. "If you can't convince her, I don't have a chance. Is she married?"

"I don't think so." He hadn't seen a ring, anyway.

"You're just gonna have to try harder," Ethan said.

"Seduce her," Otis added. "Once she's sleeping with you, she'll have to listen to you. Chicks are like that."

Priscilla threw the sweaty towel back at Otis. "Typical male logic. *Men* think with their gonads. Women think with their brains."

"Just give it the old college try," Ethan said. "Get to know her, let her get to know you and then convince her to reopen Brady's. We're sick of seeing you mope about Daralee. About time you found a new girlfriend."

Tony couldn't deny he wanted to give Julie another try—smart move or not. Since meeting her a few minutes earlier, he'd had a hard time remembering exactly why he'd thought he was in love with Daralee. But cold-blooded seduction wasn't his game. He liked women. He didn't like the idea of using them, even for a good cause. And then there was his own much-stomped-on heart to think of.

"I'd love to have a new girlfriend," Tony said more candidly than he'd meant to. He focused on Ethan. "I want what you and Kat have. But I'm not sure Julie's the one to provide it. She's a tough cookie."

Ethan shook his head as he wiped down the weight bench he'd been using. "If you go in with that attitude, *expecting* to strike out…"

"Look," said Otis, "here's what you do. You harden your heart. Every time you look at Julie, you think Daralee. You remember how bad she treated you. You remind yourself that women are evil incarnate."

"Hey," Priscilla objected.

"Present company excluded," Otis said quickly. He'd been one of the ones to object the loudest when the fire station got invaded by a woman, but he and Priscilla had formed an unlikely friendship, surprising everyone. "If you feel yourself softening even a little bit toward this Julie person, you come talk to me and I'll set you straight."

Tony supposed Otis would be the one to do that. He had three ex-wives. "If you're such an expert, why don't you seduce her?"

"Me?" He gave a loud, hearty laugh and patted his gut. "That girl isn't looking for a fat, old black man. She's looking for a young stud like you. Besides, my Ruby would kill me if I went near that sweet young thing."

The P.A. system crackled to life. "Dinner is now being served in the kitchen," Lt. Murph McCrae's gruff voice announced. "Come get it now or go hungry."

The firefighters didn't have to be asked twice. They tromped down the stairs in a hungry stampede. But before they could sit down, the alarm sounded. And before they'd even climbed into their turnout gear, a second alarm went out.

"Sounds big," Tony said, pushing thoughts of Julie out of his mind for the moment. Another dose of adrenaline surged through his body. He was on the ladder truck today with Ethan, the captain and Jim Peterson. He hadn't been to many big fires, and just the thought of descending on a big conflagration got him as excited as a young kid at an amusement park.

This one was big, too. It was at a run-down autobody shop, which meant gasoline, oil—potential explosions.

"IC to Ladder 59," came the incident commander's voice over the radio. "Need y'all on the B side of the building on ventilation. Start getting those walls down, if you can."

Captain Campeon, on the ladder truck, abruptly ordered a change of direction, and the truck turned down a side street, raced through an alley and parked in a vacant lot just behind the burning building. Tony chugged the remainder of a bottle of water. On a hot day like today, it paid to stay hydrated.

"Grab your tools, rookies," Campeon ordered. Tony did as he was told, collecting an ax and a pike pole. Then he took up a position at veteran Jim Peterson's elbow. That was his only assignment—stick to Peterson like bubblegum. The hot August sun would roast him alive inside his turnout gear if he stood out in it for long.

"Basque," Campeon barked, "get a ladder up to that roof. Peterson, Veracruz, get the window."

The window was barred, but it was easy enough to break the glass using their pikes. As soon as they did, smoke poured out and that was when they heard a dog howling inside.

Tony hated the thought of a helpless animal dying in a fire. Normally, firefighters would rescue pets if it was possible to do so without dramatically endangering themselves.

"Hell, let's see if we can get to him," Peterson said. The back door was solid-core steel, but the walls were thin corrugated tin. Tony whacked at the wall with his ax and then Peterson yanked at it until they had an opening.

"Ladder 59 to IC, there's a dog inside. Request permission to enter and try to get him out. Not much fire back here."

"Affirmative, Ladder 59."

"I'll go first," Peterson said to Tony, pulling on his air mask as he set one leg through the jagged opening.

With his own breathing mask in place, Tony climbed in right after Peterson.

They'd no sooner gotten inside than a blur of brown fur rushed at them. It flew through the air and latched on to Jim Peterson's arm, growling furiously. The dog, a pit bull mix, wasn't huge, but it was determined.

Peterson fell back on his butt, cursing wildly. "Get this damn thing off me!"

Tony gave the dog a kick. And when that didn't dislodge it, he prodded it firmly with the flat side of his ax. He didn't want to kill the creature, but he didn't want it to maim his superior, either.

The dog remained firmly attached.

"Ladder 59 to IC," Tony said into his radio, trying

not to sound panicked. "We need some water back here, fast!"

But the call for help was unnecessary; two men were already approaching with a hose. They saw the situation for what it was and blasted the dog with a hard stream of water.

The spray nearly drowned Peterson, but the dog let go. It leaped through the makeshift door and was gone. Tony had never seen a dog run that fast.

"You okay, Jim?" Tony asked, helping Peterson to his feet.

"No. Damn dog has sharp teeth and the jaws of death."

Just as they were emerging through the opening in the wall, an air horn sounded, the signal to evacuate the building. It was too dangerous to remain. Tony was surprised: the building hadn't looked all that bad inside.

An ambulance had already pulled around to the vacant lot in back as Peterson and Tony emerged. Peterson yanked off his mask, his face tightened in pain. Tony couldn't see any blood—until Peterson took off his coat.

His arm was a mess.

Once the paramedics took over, Tony located Ethan and Captain Campeon. They were as baffled as he was about why they'd been told to clear the building. The fire seemed to be under control.

A few moments later, however, they found out why.

Two incendiary devices had been found at opposite ends of the structure and one on the roof. By

now, everyone knew what to look for; this was un-
mistakably the work of their serial arsonist. Planting a vicious attack dog on the scene was his latest
trick to inflict bodily damage on firefighters. Not as
showy as the deadly warehouse fire, in which the
roof had been rigged to collapse, but still clever and
mean. And there was no guarantee he hadn't planted
other booby traps inside. At the previous fire he'd
set a pipe bomb that fortunately hadn't detonated.

A fire marshal's Suburban showed up as Tony
and Ethan cleaned and loaded their tools, talking in
hushed voices about the arsonist. Captain Roark
Epperson, lead investigator on the case, stepped out,
his face grim.

Tony knew Epperson from the training academy;
he'd been an instructor there. He also knew
Epperson from hanging out at Brady's Tavern.
They'd crossed swords over the shuffleboard table
a few times.

The ambulance took Peterson to the hospital for
stitches and a shot of antibiotics, so Tony took the
rare opportunity to sit beside the captain.

"Epperson's gotta be taking this hard," Campeon
said as he pulled their truck out of the alley. They
drove slowly past the front of the building. Roark
was standing in the street, talking to one of the remaining firefighters. "Hey, is that Priscilla he's
talking to?"

"Yeah," Tony and Ethan said together. Priscilla
had been riding on the engine.

"How does he know her?"

"He was our arson instructor at the academy," Tony answered. "And we've run into him a few times at Brady's."

Campeon snorted. "Brady's. Damn shame. That niece has no idea the disservice she's doing to the community by destroying that bar." He turned to Tony. "Didn't I hear you were doing something about that, Romeo?"

"He's flakin' out on us," Ethan said. "He struck out once, so he's not even gonna try again."

"I didn't say that," Tony argued. In truth, he was still making up his mind.

"You gotta try," Campeon said, showing a rare degree of humanity. Normally he remained stoic and stone-faced no matter was going on around him. "You gotta get through to her. A tearoom? Holy cripes."

All right, Tony would do it—for Brady's. After all, his captain had just given him an order, right? He would seduce Julie Polk. He would pretend he wanted to help her get her tearoom open, but while he was doing it he would share stories about Brady's that would appeal to her sentimentality. He would use every strategy he could think of to get her to change her mind.

Most importantly, he would *not* fall in love with her. He would not set himself up for more heartbreak.

Chapter Three

Julie was afraid this time she'd bitten off more than she could chew. In her zeal to maximize profits from the liquidation of her uncle's estate, she'd decided an auction was the way to go. She'd done her research and estimated the value of most of the collectibles, putting a reserve price on anything really worthwhile so it wouldn't walk out the door for nothing. Then she'd hired an auctioneer, picked a date and paid for an expensive display ad in the newspaper as well as in a local antiques-and-collectibles weekly.

The auction was two days away—and the bar was still a wreck. She'd had every intention of getting in here and cleaning things so that the items would fetch the highest prices. She'd also planned to get a ladder and take down the tin ceiling—each panel was worth at least ten bucks. But she'd ended up staying home to care for her dad for a couple of days instead when the woman who regularly looked in on him developed a cold. Since Julie had been living back at home for several weeks, she'd felt it was the least she could do. Otherwise her mom would have had to miss work.

Now her dad's caregiver was back, but Julie was so far behind she knew she'd never catch up. She had a dozen different cleaning products, a bucket full of old rags and not nearly enough time or elbow grease to do the job. Belinda, working double shifts at her summer waitress job this week, wasn't available.

Well, nothing for Julie to do but jump into the project and get as much done as she could. She'd found an old ladder in a back closet. She could take down at least one of the ceiling panels and shine it up so bidders could get a good look at the intricate pressed pattern.

She climbed the rungs and balanced herself precariously at the top. With a screwdriver and a hammer she tried to pry one of the tiles loose, but they'd been up there for almost a hundred years and they weren't coming down easily.

Finally she managed to get the hammer's claw wedged under one corner. She pried with all her strength but got nowhere.

The front door opened and a shaft of morning sun cut through the bar's dusty interior. Belatedly, Julie realized she should have locked the door behind her. This part of Oak Cliff wasn't a hotbed of violent crime, but a girl couldn't be too careful.

A man stepped inside, silhouetted in the doorway, and for a few moments Julie couldn't see his features. Then she recognized the broad shoulders, that muscular chest, the dominating presence. She took in a deep breath. It was Tony.

Even as she'd teemed with ideas for Belinda's tearoom, making lists and budgets and plans, Tony Veracruz had never been far from her thoughts. And at night when she couldn't sleep—and these days, she never could sleep—he invaded her fantasies.

She'd told herself it was harmless to imagine what he looked like naked, that she would have few if any dealings with him in the future, so long as she kept her blinds drawn. Given her flat refusal to even talk about reopening Brady's or consider accepting his offer of dinner, she hadn't expected him to return, invading her solitude and setting her heart vibrating like a tuning fork.

She started to say something—and then everything happened at once. With an ear-splitting noise, the tin panel above her pulled partly free, revealing a wooden beam seething with termites.

Dozens of them fell into her hair.

She screamed and dropped her hammer, then lost her balance. Clawing at the air as she fell backward, she braced herself to hit the hard wooden floor. She wondered in the split second she was airborne how many bones she would break.

But she didn't hit the floor. Instead, she fell into a strong pair of arms as perfectly and neatly as if she'd fallen into a hammock.

How had he gotten there so quickly? It took her a few moments to realize she was okay; she wasn't going to die after all. "What are you doing here?" she asked inanely.

"Is that any way to greet a man who just saved your life?"

"Put me down, please." She still had a head full of termites. She had to get them off her.

"You could have broken your neck. Why didn't you ask someone to help you with this?"

"Oh, you mean a big, strong man—because I couldn't possibly wield a couple of tools?"

"Well, obviously you…"

"I'm perfectly capable! Or I was, until an entire nest of termites flew into my hair."

"Termites?"

"There are a couple on your arm now."

He quickly put her down and brushed at his arm, while she shook the rest of the insects out of her hair. Ugh. Her skin was still crawling from the sight of those awful bugs.

"Got any Raid?" Tony asked.

"It's going to take more than bug spray, I'm afraid." She mentally added a termite inspection, fumigation and possibly expensive repairs to her working list of things to take care of. For now, though…where had she seen bug spray? The storeroom? She walked back to look.

Tony was right at her heels. "You're taking down the ceiling?"

"I'd planned to auction off the ceiling, along with all this other stuff. But I didn't know there was nothing but bare rafters behind the tin. I guess I'll have to leave it. Ah, here it is. For crawling and flying insects. I think termites are both."

Tony took the can from her. "I'll take care of this." He climbed up the ladder and sent a toxic fog into the space above the ceiling panels. "You know, the tin ceiling is part of the ambience," he argued as dead bugs fell to the floor. "Anyway, this is a historical landmark. You can't go tearing it up."

Julie stood well away from the bug shower. "I checked with the landmark commission. So long as I don't make material changes to the exterior, I'm okay. And a tin ceiling isn't exactly the ambience I'm looking for."

Painted tin ceilings were funky and kind of charming, but Julie was going for classy all the way. She'd wanted to do textured plaster.

She mentally adjusted her picture of Belinda's to reflect a tin ceiling—painted a pale yellow so as not to call attention to itself. It would be okay.

Then she realized something was on her foot—something alive. Immediately thinking *termite,* she started to kick until she realized it was a half-grown Dalmatian puppy gnawing on her shoelace.

"Excuse me," she said, yanking her foot away, "have we met?"

Tony came down from the ladder. "This is Bluto. His mom is Daisy, the fire station mascot. I usually give him a walk on my days off."

"They let you keep puppies at the fire station?"

"Only in a dog run in the back. And only temporarily. The pups had to go. Bluto is the last one."

"So you brought him here?"

"I saw the lights on and thought I'd stop in and see how it's going." He looked around. "You still have a lot of work to do, I see."

"Rub it in, why don't you?" Her attention was torn between gorgeous Tony and his cute puppy, which wagged its tail so hard its entire body wiggled.

She couldn't help it. She bent down to pet the pup, and it jumped all over, licking her face in a frenzy of love. Her parents hadn't allowed any pets, seeing them simply as more mouths to feed. And once she was on her own, she'd never considered getting a dog or cat.

"Hi, Bluto." It was much easier to be warm and friendly to the puppy than to Tony. Safer, too. She wasn't normally *un*friendly, but she knew she had to be on her guard with Tony for two reasons: he wanted something from her she couldn't give, and she wanted something from him she didn't dare ask for. If he had any idea how attracted she was to him, he could use it against her.

"So you live around here?" she asked.

"Just down Willomet. Less than a block."

They were neighbors.

A noise above her yanked her attention away from the pup. She looked up just in time to see the ceiling panel she'd been working on detach itself completely and head straight for her.

Tony grabbed Julie and the dog and yanked them both out of the way. The heavy piece of tin, with its knife-sharp edges, crashed to the floor right where she'd been standing, leaving a gouge in the wooden planking.

Now she reacted. She'd almost died—twice in two minutes. Her knees went wobbly, and if Tony hadn't put his arms around her, she'd have sunk to the floor.

"That's twice I've saved your life," he said, his voice husky.

For an insane moment, Julie thought he might kiss her. She'd fantasized about it often enough over the past couple of days. But then the moment passed, sanity reasserted itself and Tony released her, leaving her tingling.

Could a brush with death cause these peculiar feelings? She sure hoped she had an excuse for wanting to lose herself in a man's touch when she was supposed to be concentrating on her tearoom.

With no small effort, Tony pulled himself out of the sensual fog that Julie had put him in. He'd felt so drawn to her, as if he wanted to kiss her. Thankfully he'd realized how inappropriate that would be and had let the woman go, taking a step back to put her out of temptation's reach. This seduction had to be executed with care.

Ethan had said to make friends with Julie, get to know her. That wasn't Tony's normal approach. He usually liked to sweep a woman off her feet, flirt mercilessly, prove to her how strongly he was attracted to her. He'd always figured the friendship could come later, when the sexual pull wasn't so overwhelming that it occupied all of his brain cells.

But so far that friendship part had eluded him. Yeah, he was friends with Priscilla and Ethan's wife, Kat—and Natalie, the mother of his little girl. As far as his love life went, though, something always went wrong before he could become friends with a lover.

So maybe he would try being friends first. There was more than one way to seduce a woman, and he wouldn't quit until he'd tried them all.

"Th-thank you," Julie said, recovering some of the color in her face. "I do appreciate the life-saving maneuvers."

"That's what firefighters are for." She looked amazing, standing there with her heaving breasts and her rosy cheeks, her golden hair mussed from shaking. She was trying to pretend that being so close to him hadn't had much effect, but Tony knew better.

Then she pulled herself together, all business again. "As you pointed out, I have a ton of work to do. So if you'll excuse me…"

"That's why I'm here. I thought I could help."

She narrowed her eyes suspiciously. "Why would you offer to help when you hate the idea of my tearoom?"

He shrugged. "Never could resist a damsel in distress." He looked around. "And you are in distress."

He could tell she wanted to argue. But her need for an extra pair of hands and some elbow grease won out. "If you really want to help, the wooden Indian would make a good start. He's covered with so much nicotine I can't even tell what color he's supposed to be." Then she added, "But you won't soften me up. I won't change my mind about the tea-room. So if that's your agenda…"

"Agenda? You've got to be kidding," Tony said, his conscience pinching him a bit as he picked up a cleaning rag. At least if he helped her clean, he had an excuse to stick around and get to know her better. And she could get to know him. Once she thought it through, she'd realize what a great guy he was— saving her life, helping her scrub this place down— and she might be more willing to listen to his reasons for wanting to revive Brady's Tavern.

Or he might just make love to her. Right now, that seemed a far more intriguing goal than changing her mind about keeping Brady's intact.

"I'm not sure how Sir Edward will feel about tak-ing a bath," Tony said as he tackled decades of filth.

"Sir Edward?"

"The cigar man. He used to belong to an English-man who owned a cigar shop down on Jefferson. When that gentleman fell on hard times he closed the shop—and he didn't have enough money to pay off his bar tab. So Brady—that would have been the second Brady, your grandfather—took the Indian as payment."

Tony watched Julie from the corner of his eye. She paused in her efforts to clean years of scum off one of the high round tables that dotted Brady's. "Really? How interesting."

She didn't sound sarcastic, at least. So she enjoyed local history. That had to be a good thing for the campaign to save Brady's.

"Are there more stories like that?"

"Dozens." Tony gave up on the Indian and walked back to the bar. "Where's the ashtray that was sitting here?"

"The big ugly one that possibly used to be brass?"

"Yeah."

"I didn't figure anyone would want it, so I threw it away."

Tony clutched at his chest and pretended to gasp for air. "Threw it away?"

"Was it special?" She actually sounded concerned.

"It was the Daryl Jones memorial ashtray. Jones was a legendary fire chief, back in the days of prohibition. When he died, they took the old fire bell down and made an ashtray out of it. He and Brady—that would be your great-grandfather—were good friends."

Julie winced. "And they made his bell into an *ashtray?* Isn't that kind of disrespectful?"

"Since Jones was a chain-smoker, no. I can't believe you threw it away. I'd have bought it from you. Any of the firefighters would have."

Without a word, Julie disappeared into the back room. He heard her digging around and a minute or so later she emerged triumphantly with the ashtray in hand. "If you'll help me clean, you can have the ashtray for free."

"Deal."

As they worked, Tony told her more stories. The

billiard table had come from Dallas's first bowling alley just before it was torn down. The dartboard had been a gift from a baseball player in the 1950s.

Tony showed Julie a bullet hole in the wall that was reputed to have been put there by the famous bank robber Clyde Barrow, of Bonnie and Clyde fame, when Brady's had been a speakeasy.

Julie paused often to take notes.

"That popcorn machine behind the bar came from the Texas Theater down the street."

"No kidding? Hey, they've renovated that theater, haven't they?"

"Yeah, and it looks great." Now he was getting somewhere. "Oak Cliff is renovating everything. People are really starting to appreciate the history of this area. Preserving rather than tearing down." *Hint, hint, Julie.*

"That's marvelous! I bet the theater owners would love to buy back this machine and display it there."

Tony sighed. "What are you writing all these stories down for?"

"The auctioneer says that anything with historical significance will get a better price. So tell me more."

Tony realized his efforts to convince Julie not to tear up Brady's might actually be counterproductive. His stories made her even more inclined to parcel out all these wonderful old things.

Watching her as she scrubbed the filth off an old hurricane lamp—probably something left over from the days before the bar had electricity—he had a hard time remembering what his mission was. He just wanted to kiss her.

Still, he made one more try. "I understand your wanting to get money for all this stuff," he said carefully. "But doesn't sentimental value count for anything? Separately, you have some semivaluable collectibles. Together, you have a legend—your family's legend at that. This is the place your great-grandfather opened a century ago. Doesn't that mean anything to you?"

She looked stung by his harsh question, at first, and then she looked mad—and he knew he'd gone too far. She threw down her rag and marched over to him, getting right in his face.

"I'm sorry that you guys have lost your hangout. Truly I am. But I have to do what's right for me and my family. My living family, not a bunch of dead guys. And even if you try to deny it, it'll be good for the neighborhood, too."

He started to say something, but she cut him off.

"I am not going to change my mind. What do I have to do to convince you?"

Bluto chose that moment to jump against Tony's leg and yip.

"Maybe you should take him for that walk," Julie suggested, her voice softening.

"Yeah, I'll take him back to his mom. He's looking for a good home, by the way."

"That's all I need—a dog to make my life complete. Why don't you keep him?"

Tony laughed. "I already adopted one." He hooked Bluto's leash to his collar and the dog proceeded to drag him toward the door. "Goodbye, Julie. But I'll be back."

As he stepped out into the August heat, he acknowledged that this battle was going to be a lot harder than he'd first thought. But Julie wasn't immune to him. She'd enjoyed the stories he told. Maybe, after she had time to think about it, she would change her mind. And if not...

He could at least get the word out about the auction. Every off-duty cop and firefighter in Oak Cliff would want to attend and grab a piece of Brady's.

As Tony crossed the street, intending to return Bluto to his dog run behind Station 59, he realized he'd forgotten to take the Daryl Jones memorial ashtray.

JULIE HAD BEEN HOPING for a good crowd at the auction, but the mass of people crowding up to the bar to register and receive their bidding numbers exceeded all her expectations.

She'd done everything she could think of to publicize the auction, including the well-placed ads. She'd asked her auctioneer if she should have the sale at an auction house, but he'd discouraged her from that. The bar itself was plenty big enough. The location was easy to find and she would save the costs of renting a hall and transporting the goods. Plus, she would get some locals who would bid on items for sentimental reasons.

The crowd was made up mostly of men in jeans and T-shirts. They didn't look like collectors or antiques dealers. But, then again, how would she know what such people looked like?

The one man she'd been most anxious to see wasn't in the crowd, however. Tony had left abruptly two days earlier, without his darned old ashtray. She felt bad about the way they'd parted, with her all mad. She shouldn't have let him get to her. If she were one hundred percent confident in her plans, his arguments should have just harmlessly rolled off her back. But the truth was, she was scared to death of what she was attempting.

Maybe she'd managed a tearoom, but she'd never started her own business from the ground up. She was a mass of insecurities.

The quality of her sleep had deteriorated still more, because she couldn't get the feel of Tony's embrace out of her mind—nor the way he'd looked into her eyes just before releasing her.

But she had to. Getting involved with a sexy firefighter—or any man, for that matter—wasn't in her plans.

An older man in a suit approached her and she pointed to the clipboard sitting on the bar. "Fill out your name, address and phone there and I'll assign you a number."

"I'm not here to buy, Ms. Polk."

She looked up sharply, alarmed by his stern tone. "Then what can I help you with?"

He held up a badge for her to see. "I'm the fire

marshal. There's a strict limit of one hundred people for these premises, in terms of fire safety, and you've already exceeded that limit."

"A hundred?" Surely that was wrong. The number seemed very low to her. Her building wasn't huge, but it wasn't a broom closet, either. "Are you sure?"

"It's posted by the door. This old building is a historic landmark, which means we take extra care. Have you had the sprinkler system inspected?"

"I'll be doing a complete renovation, and fire safety will be my number one priority," she assured him. "But for the auction, I can't just go kicking people out who've already registered."

"I'm afraid you'll have to, ma'am. Unless you want me to do it. But then I'd have to charge you a hefty fine."

Julie was steaming. The firefighters were behind this, she was sure of it. They'd probably been searching for some way to foil her auction—and they'd found it. Maybe the maximum occupancy was a hundred, but she doubted it had ever been enforced until now.

She supposed she had no choice but to comply with the fire marshal's order. The auction was starting in fifteen minutes.

So she went to the auctioneer's microphone, turned it on and announced that all those who hadn't registered, plus those with numbers higher than ninety-seven, would have to leave because of the fire code. Including herself, Belinda and the auctioneer,

that made one hundred. Her announcement produced lots of grumbling, but everyone complied.
Once the extras had left, there was plenty of room
in the bar. She smelled a rat, especially when the fire
marshal shot her a victorious smile.

He parked himself at the door, keeping careful
count of all those who came in and those who left.

As the auction progressed, Julie was increasingly
disappointed in the results. She'd been to a few similar
events before, and usually there was heated bidding,
at least over some of the items. But with her auction,
once someone bid, the rest of the crowd stayed maddeningly silent. She'd put modest reserve prices on
the more valuable things, and most of these did not
achieve the minimum bid and so remained unsold.

The auctioneer was sweating, talking up indi-
vidual items, sharing the stories Julie had written
down for him. Finally, though, he shrugged his
shoulders and shot her a bewildered glance, validat-
ing her own feelings that this was an aberration.

Was it fixed? She took a closer look at the pre-
dominantly male, casually dressed crowd, and an
awful realization occurred.

They were firefighters. Cops and firefighters.
Every single blasted one of them. And they were
cooperating, to ensure she did not succeed.

Her face grew hot. How could they be so hateful?
Such bad sports? Couldn't they accept that Brady's
was gone now and leave her alone? How could anyone get so riled up over a stupid old bar, even if it
was a historic landmark?

She caught the eye of one man who'd bid on the wooden Indian and gotten it for a hundred dollars when she knew it was worth a lot more. But she'd purposely set her minimum bids low because she wanted this stuff gone. He gave her a potent, malevolent look, confirming her suspicions.

There wasn't a thing she could do. It was probably illegal for a group of people to get together and refuse to bid against each other, but who was she going to call? The cops? They'd arrived early and gotten in line, ensuring they would fill in all the low-numbered slots, and the fire marshal had done the rest of the work to keep out legitimate collectors and antiques dealers.

The auction was over in less than two hours, and she watched dejectedly as items from Brady's went out the door—the neon lights, the rickety tables and chairs, the dartboards and pool tables, the TVs, even the liquor. A bottle of aged scotch was the one thing that had elicited spirited bidding.

Clem, the auctioneer, approached Julie with a sheepish look. "I'm really sorry, Ms. Polk. I don't know what happened. I gave it my best shot, but these folks just weren't in a bidding mood."

She patted his arm. "It's okay, Clem. I know you did your best. Just bad luck." And some conniving firefighters.

Chapter Four

The fire marshal had gone, and a woman entered the bar, heading straight for Julie. She was about Julie's age and very beautiful, with light brown hair subtly highlighted with gold and a complexion that indicated she took care of her skin.

Her clothes were good quality, too. Lord knew, Julie could spot such things. The woman also looked vaguely familiar. She'd probably shopped in the department store or eaten in the tearoom.

"Are you Julie?" the woman asked.

"Yes, that's me." Julie held out her hand, and the woman shook it in a businesslike fashion.

"Priscilla Garner. I understand a number of your items didn't meet their reserve prices."

Julie mentally snapped her fingers. *Priscilla Garner, of course!* Julie should have recognized her. Her parents were friends of the Davidsons. "Yes, that's right."

"I'll take them off your hands."

"You'll pay the reserve?"

"Well, no. But I'll give you something for them."

Julie figured she couldn't afford to be on her high horse. Maybe she'd set those reserve prices too high. She and Priscilla did some horse trading, and in the end they reached an agreement. Julie would be getting a little more than half what she'd hoped for, but it was better than nothing.

The one thing she hadn't sold was the carved wooden bar, and she was secretly glad about that. No one was willing to pay the steep price she'd put on it, and she wasn't about to take less. Once she'd polished it, it was pretty impressive. She could incorporate it into the design of the tearoom. She'd already decided she would play up the historic-landmark angle. With the money she'd raised—quite a bit less than she'd planned on—she didn't have many options but to make lemonade from the lemons she was stuck with.

The place was almost deserted. Clem had taken off, Belinda had gone to her waitress job and only a few of the bidders remained, working out how to transport and pack some of the larger items they'd bought.

And that was when Tony showed up.

Earlier, she'd been feeling conciliatory toward him, but now that she'd figured out the firefighters' conspiracy, she hardened her heart. He was the enemy.

She pretended not to see him as she cleaned up some glassware that had mysteriously "accidentally" gotten broken. But he apparently wasn't looking for her. He stopped to talk to Priscilla, who'd been heading for the door, intent on finding help in moving the items she'd purchased.

Julie couldn't help but overhear their conversation.

"Hey, Pris. I thought you couldn't get in."

"I couldn't, but I came in after the auction was over. I made a deal for some of the unsold items. I got your shuffleboard table." She headed on out the door.

So Priscilla was in league with the firefighters. If Julie had known that, she'd have told the woman to go soak her head. But, no, that probably wouldn't have been wise. Priscilla and her crowd were exactly the type of people Julie wanted to attract to the tearoom. She'd better be careful.

Tony walked up to Julie, his footsteps bouncing, as if nothing was wrong. "Looks like you had an accident."

"No accident. Someone did it on purpose."

"What happened?" He seemed concerned, but it was probably an act.

She looked up at him, leaning on the broom handle. "A conspiracy to ruin my auction, that's what."

"Really?"

She had to hand it to him, his look of concern would have fooled anyone who didn't know better. "Don't play dumb. The firefighters got here early to fill up all the slots, then they cooperated to keep the prices down."

Tony's face fell. "Are you sure? Maybe they came early because everyone wanted a piece of Brady's for themselves. Lots of memories were made here."

"What about the cooperative bidding?"

"Firefighters are loyal to each other. Maybe they just didn't want to bid against each other."

"Or maybe they wanted to wreck my auction."

"Maybe. But I don't think so. Priscilla helped you out, didn't she?"

Julie nodded. "Yeah, she did, sort of. But she's not a firefighter."

"As a matter of fact, she is."

"You're kidding." So much for counting on Priscilla and her friends to patronize the tearoom. If she was one of *them*, she probably would prefer bellying up to the bar at Brady's instead of eating quiche and fruit salad at Belinda's.

"I went through training with her," Tony said, "and she's a lot tougher than she looks. She's also my neighbor and landlady."

The undeniable fondness in his voice made Julie bristle. Nothing was more guaranteed to rile her up than a faithless man. "I see. Does she know you asked me out to dinner?"

Tony grinned. "Jealous?"

"No, I'm not jealous! How could you think—"

"Hey, take it easy. Pris and I are just friends."

"Oh." Now she felt silly. She *had* sounded jealous. No, she'd actually *been* jealous. "What are you doing here, anyway?" Julie asked, unable to keep the sharpness out of her voice. "Come to enjoy the aftermath of the train wreck?"

"I wanted to find out how the auction went."

"Now you know. But don't think a bad auction is going to stop me. My plans for Belinda's are going ahead full steam." She might have to scale down her renovation plans. The chandeliers and the mosaic-tile floor would have to wait. But she'd make this happen somehow.

"I'm sorry. About the auction, I mean."

"Save it. You know you just came in here to gloat." Julie went back to her sweeping. It was tempting to poke him with the broom handle, but she'd probably end up being charged with assault. No, the classy owner of a classy tearoom would just ignore her detractors and wait for them to go away.

"You've had a long morning. Why don't you let me take you out to lunch?" Tony asked.

"No, thank you. Why don't you go home and enjoy your new shuffleboard table? I bet Priscilla would play with you."

"I told you, Priscilla's just a friend. But I do think it's cute that you're jealous."

"For the last time, I'm not…" She stopped and made herself calm down. The smile on Tony's face did little to lower her blood pressure, however. He certainly had his nerve showing her that sexy grin when she was in such a foul mood.

She'd already had one career ruined because of a man and she was determined to learn from her mistakes.

"I want you to leave now," she said. "You're not welcome." She picked up a stray piece of broken glass, intending to toss it in the trash, and somehow she managed to cut herself. "Ouch. I'm blaming this on you, too."

"Let me see." He grabbed her hand and inspected the cut. "Damn, that's no little scratch." He led her to the sink behind the bar and ran cold water over her hand. She was acutely aware of the feeling of his hand holding hers, the faint smell of soap and shaving cream and the commanding way he took charge of the situation.

He looked at the cut again. "You should get stitches. I'll drive you to—"

"No, thanks. It'll be fine."

But the cut between her thumb and forefinger hurt like the dickens and it was bleeding at an alarming rate.

"It'll never stop bleeding," Tony said.

"I don't have insurance," she admitted. She'd declined the expensive COBRA health-insurance policy Bailey-Davidson's was legally required to offer when she left employment there. And while she'd checked into some other policies, she hadn't actually gotten around to signing on the dotted line.

Stupid. Irresponsible. She just had too much to do, and some things had fallen between the cracks.

"At least let me walk you across the street. The fire station has first aid."

"The fire station? You guys would probably pre-fer it if I bled to death." Which was what just might happen if she didn't do something. She'd soaked through three paper towels already.

Tony took offense. "Hey, maybe the firefighters are a little ticked off about losing Brady's, but that doesn't mean they wouldn't do their jobs. They take this stuff seriously."

Julie realized she was being unreasonable. "All right. But if I end up with gangrene, that's your fault, too."

The bar was empty now. Julie gave Tony her keys. He locked the door for her while she put pressure on her cut and then he solicitously walked her across the busy street, his arm around her waist.

She couldn't pretend she was unaffected by the care he gave her. Only minutes earlier she'd wanted to assault him with her broom handle. But now her feelings were quite different.

Hormones, she reminded herself. She couldn't afford to let herself get distracted by hormones. He was a cute guy, so what? Trey was a cute guy, too, and look where her attraction to him had gotten her.

Unemployed and living above a bar.

The reception Julie got at the fire station was cool at first—until they realized she was injured. Then the firefighters couldn't move fast enough to help her. They cleaned the cut with some brown antiseptic, which stung so severely it brought tears to her eyes, then skillfully applied a butterfly bandage. When they were done, she was no longer bleeding.

"I wouldn't use that hand for a couple of days,"

a firefighter named Carl warned her, "or you'll open it up again. You really should have stitches."

"I'll be careful. And thank you."

"Hmph," he said. "If you were really grateful, you'd open Brady's back up."

"Okay, I'm out of here."

"Where you going?" Tony asked.

"Back to work. I have a tearoom to renovate."

"Have you eaten?"

Breakfast was such a distant memory that she had no idea what she'd eaten. And it was past lunchtime. Between lack of sleep, exhaustion, blood loss and her empty stomach, she was swaying on her feet.

"I'm taking you home and feeding you," he said without waiting for an answer.

She wanted to object but found she didn't have the strength. Fine. She'd let him take her home. If he had food in his fridge, she was all for it. "Just know this—I'll be watching, so no trying to poison me."

"I'm not trying to kill you, Julie," he said as if she'd been serious. "I have *much* more interesting plans for you."

She should have been put off by his innuendo. Instead, a shiver of anticipated pleasure rippled through her body, and she realized she should have turned down that lunch invitation. Now it was too late.

"I can drive you if you're feeling too shaky to walk," Tony said, and his concern nearly did Julie in.

"I'm fine, really. You said it was only a block."
But she had reason to regret being so stoic as they
made their way down Jefferson in the broiling
August heat. She had to focus, to put one foot in
front of the other and not trip on the cracked
sidewalk.

Fortunately Willomet Avenue was lined with live
oak trees, planted by some forward-thinking urban
pioneer several decades earlier. The slow-growing
trees were now a respectable size, providing shade
from the sun. Julie breathed a sigh of relief, feeling
enough improved that she could appreciate the
historic district's quaint, brightly painted homes.
Though the area still had some houses in sad shape,
most of them had been lovingly restored.

When Tony took Julie's elbow and gently guided
her up the front walk of a house painted in three
shades of blue toward the end of the block, she saw
that his was one of the larger, nicer homes on the
street. She'd once thought she'd like to live in an
elaborate Victorian home, but the cleaner, sleeker
lines of this early-twentieth-century house made it appealing.

"Pretty house," she couldn't resist commenting.

"Thanks. I can't take much credit. Priscilla has
gone a little nuts fixing up the place. She owns the
house and lives upstairs, but she rents the downstairs
unit to me."

"The flowers are beautiful."

"Now those I can take credit for. The yard is
all mine."

It looked great. The lush green grass was neatly trimmed, while holly bushes and geraniums dressed up the front yard and lined the porch railings.

Julie could see herself living in this neighborhood. She'd always thought she was a Park Cities girl at heart, but this neighborhood would be so convenient. As soon as Belinda's Tearoom started making money, she could think about upgrading her living arrangements.

"So you garden on your days off?"

"Women garden. I do yard work."

The inside of Tony's house was nothing special, from a decorating standpoint. It was furnished almost sparsely, with simple, unpretentious wood furniture and a rug here and there over the oak-plank floors. But Julie had to admit she liked the feel of the place. With the high ceilings, spacious rooms and dark wood, it was a cool oasis on this sizzling day. It proclaimed a certain comfort. She could feel at home here and put her feet up.

Not at all like Trey's home. She remembered when she'd first seen it, she'd been afraid to touch anything.

Tony pulled off his Texas Rangers cap and stuck it in his back pocket. "Let's go see what we can scare up in the kitchen." He led her past a living room with some puffy furniture—not the latest style but comfortable-looking.

In the kitchen, Tony opened the fridge and started pulling out packages and jars. "How about a sandwich? I have turkey, bologna, salami, some leftover meatballs…."

"It all sounds good." Her stomach rumbled. "Anything." He could have offered her cat food and it would have sounded appealing.

He pulled out a chair for her at the kitchen table. "You sit and relax. You might want to hold your hand up above your heart so it won't throb. Does it hurt?" His concern seemed genuine. Maybe she'd been too hard on him.

"It's not bad."

He fixed them both hot meatball sandwiches and poured tall glasses of Coke. Julie tore into her lunch as if she hadn't eaten in weeks. Just as Tony was about to sit down, though, someone knocked at the kitchen door and he went to open it. Priscilla stood there, dressed in shorts and a Dallas Fire Rescue tank top. She held out a small basket. "Tony, there's a big yellow-jacket nest on my balcony. I know it's girlie of me not to deal with it myself, but I'm allergic to wasp stings. Can you get rid of it?"

"I just sat down to lunch."

"They're coming into my apartment," Priscilla said. "I brought you some of my mom's fudge-raspberry-mousse croquettes as a bribe." She held the basket so Tony could smell the chocolate.

"The sandwich will be here when you get back," Julie said, taking pity on Priscilla. After the termites, she couldn't help but be sympathetic with anyone having problems involving bugs—particularly yellow jackets. Their stings were extremely painful, not to mention life-threatening for someone with an allergy.

Priscilla looked past Tony. "Oh, I'm sorry. I didn't know you had company."

"It's okay," Julie said. "Tony just saved me from bleeding to death, so he's in savior mode."

"All right, I'll take care of the wasps," Tony said. He fished out some bug spray from under the sink. "Priscilla, you stay here. I don't want you getting stung."

"Gladly." She slipped into the kitchen, put her basket on the table and sat in the chair Tony had just left. "Is this a meatball sandwich? Tony makes the best meatballs." And she took a bite. "Mmm. Oh, Julie, what happened to your hand?"

"I cut it on broken glass. That's why I'm here, actually. Tony seems to think it's his sworn duty to play doctor and feed me simply because he was standing there when it happened."

Priscilla laughed. "That's a firefighter for you." And she took another bite of Tony's sandwich.

"Did Lorraine Garner actually bake those with her own hands?" Julie studied the beautiful and dainty pastries, impressed. Priscilla's mother was well known for her baked goods. If you got a basket of cookies or a cake from the Garners for the holidays, you were considered blessed. Lorraine Garner indicated who was in and out of favor—not just with her but with the elite of the city—by who was chosen and who was neglected on that holiday-basket list. Invitations to share food at her home were even more highly desired.

Mrs. Davidson, Trey's mother, had been snubbed last Christmas.

"You know my mother?" Priscilla asked.

"I know *of* her. I haven't actually had the pleasure of meeting her. But I did taste one of her chocolate truffles once, at the home of a friend. Unbelievable."

"I'll tell her you said so. Unfortunately, I didn't inherit any of my mother's culinary skills."

"I'm not much like my parents either," Julie said. She had no idea where she and Belinda had gotten their drive and ambition. Not from their father, who had lost a leg to diabetes and had done nothing to rehabilitate himself, preferring to sit in his wheelchair all day and watch TV. Not from their mother, who worked hard but was content with a dead-end job at a dry cleaner's so long as she could come home to her nightly beer, her crocheting and her tabloid newspapers.

They weren't bad people, just worn down by hard lives. Now that Julie was older, she understood how hard they'd worked to keep their heads above water. She wanted to make sure they were taken care of as they grew older.

The tearoom could help her do that.

"You know, you look awfully familiar," Priscilla said. "Did you go to Highland Park?"

Not hardly. Normally, Julie was a bit cagey about her humble roots. But since she didn't sense an ounce of pretense in Priscilla, she felt compelled to open up. "No, I went to Aaron Burr High." Everyone knew it was a rough high school, both in terms of academics and safety.

Priscilla didn't react, though she had to wonder how a girl from the Grove would have come to move in the same circles as a friend of her mother's.

"You probably saw me at Bailey-Davidson's," Julie said. "I used to work there."

"Oh, yeah! I remember—" Then she stopped short, and Julie could almost see the wheels turning in her head as she struggled to remember some snippet of gossip, trying to put the pieces together. Trey's family, determined that their precious son wouldn't be tainted by scandal, had told everyone that Julie had called off the wedding for unknown reasons. But Trey himself had hinted that Julie had experienced some sort of mental breakdown. "I remember seeing you at Lochinvar's."

"Yes, that's right," Julie said, relieved.

Priscilla took another bite of Tony's sandwich. By now it was half gone. But Julie couldn't really blame her. Her own sandwich was delicious, and she was feeling a hundred percent better. Her head was no longer swimming, her hand didn't hurt quite so much and she was relaxed for the first time in days.

And she liked Priscilla, even if she was a fire-fighter and in the enemy camp. She seemed so effortlessly classy but friendly, too. That kind of class got into your pores when you were a child, Julie theorized. No matter how hard she tried, no matter how many fashion and decorating magazines she studied, she would never achieve the aura that Priscilla just naturally radiated.

Maybe she could sway Priscilla to her side.

Surely someone with her background could appreciate what Julie wanted to do with the tearoom.

"This house is very nice," Julie said, feeling a change of subject was in order. "I really like the clean, streamlined feel." She couldn't help again comparing it to Trey's house, where elaborate detail was almost a religion. There, every surface was covered with expensive knickknacks. Once, Julie had accidentally broken a small dog figurine. Trey had swept up the shards and assured Julie not to worry about it, but Mrs. Davidson, who'd been there at the time, hadn't been able to resist informing Julie that the figurine was a collectible worth several thousand dollars. Julie had almost fainted.

She didn't think there were any two-thousand-dollar china dogs in this house. She felt comfortable here. In fact, though a few minutes ago she'd protested that she didn't have time to come here for lunch, she now found herself wanting to linger. She was tired of the smell of stale beer and cigarette smoke, which she'd been inhaling for the past week as she'd prepared for the auction. Even after much cleaning, the smells remained in small pockets of Brady's—like when she opened a long-unused drawer, for example.

Tony's place, in contrast, now smelled like meatball sandwiches. But when they'd first walked in, she'd been aware of citrus furniture polish. She loved that fragrance. She even wore a citrus perfume.

"Thanks," Priscilla said. "There's still a lot to be done."

"Do you think Tony's okay?" Julie asked. "He's been gone a while."

"I think he's staying outside on purpose. He wants us to bond, woman to woman, so I can convince you how important Brady's Tavern is to the community and talk you into keeping it just as it was."

Julie sighed. "I appreciate your honesty. And I sympathize with the loss of a place where everyone felt comfortable. But *I* wouldn't have felt comfortable there."

Priscilla finished off Tony's sandwich. "I guess I should make another one of these. How did he do it?"

"He just put some meatballs and cheese on a roll and stuck it in the microwave."

"Okay, I can do that." Priscilla went to work. "I sometimes felt a little uncomfortable at Brady's," she admitted. "And secretly—" she dropped her voice to a whisper "—I'm thrilled you're opening a tearoom."

"You are?"

"Someplace quiet and pleasant where I can get a salad and a glass of wine and not have to listen to loud country music and breathe cigarette smoke in the process. I liked Brady's and I confess I did hang out there. It was fun, and playing darts and shuffleboard helped me to fit in with the guys. But sometimes things change, and change isn't always bad."

"Exactly. I'm so glad you understand."

"But I did want to talk to you about something else." She hesitated, then plunged ahead. "Tony."

"Oh, Tony." Julie waved a dismissive hand, though her heart beat a little faster at the mention of his name. "I can handle Tony. I'm immune to his charm. I just got rid of one man, so I sure don't need another. I might never need another."

"Small world. I got rid of one not too long ago, too."

Oh, it was so, so tempting to tell Priscilla what a skunk Trey Davidson was. But she'd promised the Davidsons not to spread it around.

"I found out he wasn't being totally honest with me." Which was the excuse she had settled on. It wasn't a lie, but it wasn't the whole truth either.

"I'm sorry. Guys can be real jerks. But Tony isn't one of them. The fact is, he likes you. He *really* likes you."

Again Julie's heart quivered. No, no, no, she wasn't going to listen to this. "Tony seems like a nice guy," she said noncommittally.

"He's an exceptionally nice guy. One of the rare ones. You're angry with all the firefighters right now for what they did at your auction, and I don't blame you. But fixing the bidding wasn't Tony's idea. He didn't even know about it, I'm sure. He might want the old Brady's back, but he would never hurt someone else to get his way. That's just not Tony's style."

Julie said nothing. She didn't know what to believe.

"Just promise me you'll be gentle with him. Don't hurt him."

"What? Excuse me? He's totally against me trying to live my life, my dream, and I'm supposed to worry about hurting him?"

"I know this won't make sense to you right now, but at some point it will. Just promise me you'll remember this conversation. Because no matter what it might look like on the outside right now, I predict Tony Veracruz is going to fall in love with you."

Chapter Five

Julie nearly spit out her drink, but somehow she managed to swallow without choking. "Love? Are you kidding me?" She wasn't sure men were even capable of love. Lust, yes. She would never completely understand Trey's reasons for wanting to marry her, but lust had been a part of it. She also suspected he'd appreciated her utter devotion to him. She'd been so in awe of him, maybe he'd thought she would be a doormat and let him have his way in everything. But she knew now his motives had had little to do with love.

"I'm not kidding." Priscilla didn't add anything else.

Feeling awkward now, Julie drained the rest of her cola. "I really do have to go. I appreciate the lunch and the conversation. More than you know." Ever since her breakup with Trey, she'd felt isolated, with only Belinda for commiseration. Most of her friends had been Trey's friends, and they'd naturally sided with him.

Today, for the first time in a long time, she'd felt welcomed. Odd that it would be firefighters who made her feel that way.

She stood and took her dishes to the sink, considering how she might slip out without having to see Tony again. But even as she decided that would be too rude, Tony returned, smiling victoriously. "Those were some ticked-off wasps. But they're gone now."

"You sure?"

"Sure, I'm—hey, what happened to my sandwich?"

"It was getting cold, so I put it in the microwave," Priscilla said quickly. "Thanks, Tony. See ya!" And she escaped.

Tony shook his head and laughed. "She's a piece of work. And whatever she told you about me, it's not true. That bucket of water we dumped on her from the second floor didn't hurt her at all, no matter what she says."

Julie grinned. If Tony had any idea what Priscilla had *really* said about him, he'd probably flip. "Priscilla had many interesting things to say about you—none of them having to do with a bucket of water."

"Then forget what I just said. I would never dump a bucket of water on an unsuspecting colleague."

"Uh-huh. Tony, I really have to go."

"Don't you want to go out and see my puppy? His name's Dino, and he's even cuter than Bluto."

"Another time maybe." Julie was surprised at how much she wanted to stay and loll away the afternoon with Tony and his Dalmatian pup. What was wrong with her? She had work to do, a tearoom to renovate, numbers to crunch, advertising and promotion to dream up. She absolutely did not have time to loll.

"I'll walk you back to Brady's, then."

"Belinda's."

"Whatever."

"Belinda's. Say it. Belinda's Tearoom."

"I just can't. I would be a traitor to my kind."

"Fine. I'll walk alone."

He screwed up his face. "Belinda's Tearoom. There, I said it." Then he did walk her back to the bar. And when she reached the front door, he tried to steal a kiss.

She ducked her head, refusing to let his lips make contact, no matter how badly she wanted that kiss herself. Weak, weak, weak.

"Tony, this wasn't a date."

"It felt like one." He took a step closer, backing her against the door before she could get the stubborn lock to turn. "I've been thinking about kissing you ever since I watched you take a bite of that sandwich. The way you closed your mouth around it, then sighed with appreciation..."

"Tony, really!" This guy was just too much. Equating eating a sandwich with a kiss? Ridiculous!

"Just one kiss and then I'll leave you alone."

"Forever?"

"Now you wound me. You'd be sad if you never saw me again."

She wanted to tell Tony that nothing would give

her more pleasure than to rid her life of him and all firefighters. But it was such a lie she couldn't say it. She *would* be sad if she never saw him again. He'd gotten under her skin.

Now he had a hand on either side of her, trapping her between his arms. "Look me in the eye and tell me you don't want to kiss me."

She looked him straight in the eye. But again the words wouldn't come. Because all she could think about was his mouth and how she'd imagined it would feel against hers. And how it would feel now...

"You can't say it, can you?"

"I don't want to—" That was all she managed to get out before his lips caught hers midsentence and her world tipped on its axis. Before she knew what was happening, her arms had slid around his neck and she was straining to press her body against his, so warm and hard and masculine. And the way he smelled—like soap and laundry detergent, with a hint of musk and maybe a trace of smoke. His mouth was insistent but gentle, too, teasing responses from her rather than demanding them.

He was getting exactly what he wanted. She felt as if her bones were melting.

Only a honk from a passing motorist brought her back to her senses. She forced herself to pull away, to put some steel in her backbone and stop this nonsense.

Tony obviously sensed her change of mood and gave her a parting nibble at the corner of her mouth.

"Will you please stop kissing me?"

"I gave you a chance to say you didn't want it."

She ducked under his arm and out of his light embrace. "I tried. You didn't give me enough time."

"All day wouldn't have been enough time."

She finally got the lock to turn and opened the door. She stepped inside and turned, effectively blocking the doorway. "You're pretty sure of yourself."

He shrugged, and a fleeting ghost of doubt flitted across his handsome features. "You might be surprised."

"Goodbye, Tony." She forced herself to shut the door. She could not let him distract her or sway her and she would not feel sympathy toward him and his firefighter friends for losing their hangout. She had to keep focused on her goal. Security for her parents. An education for her sister. A place for her to belong. A place that would prove to Trey just how much she didn't need his money or his influence.

Perhaps most important, she had to stay in control of her own destiny and never again pin her hopes on someone who had the power to send all her plans crashing down around her ears.

Car accident. Vehicle on fire. People trapped inside. Those were words to strike fear in any firefighter's heart—or, more accurately, not fear but an adrenaline rush that quickened the step and put more speed and purpose into his actions.

Engine 59 was less than a minute away. Tony, on paramedic duty, was right behind the engine in the "box"—the ambulance. A plume of black smoke from the fire led them straight to the accident at the busy intersection of Twelfth Street and Hampton, where traffic was now tied up in knots. Both engine and ambulance drove up on the sidewalk to get through.

When they reached the scene, things looked bad. Two cars, one on fire, civilians screaming and running around trying to get the doors open on the burning car and then retreating quickly from the intense heat. Tony wanted nothing more than to charge into the blaze and get to the people in the burning car. Training went right out the window as he started to do just that, but Lt. McCrae yelled at him to get back.

In seconds, McCrae and Priscilla had a small booster line in hand and were using a fog to attack the flames that came out from under the hood. They beat back the blaze just enough that Ethan could get in and get the driver's door open, and that was Tony's signal to go into action, finally. The car had just one occupant, a teenage boy behind the wheel.

"He's alive," Ethan announced, his relief evident.

Tony, who'd learned to keep a pocketknife on hand, cut the seat belt. He did his best to support the boy's neck and head while Kevin and Ethan got him onto a backboard. Once he was out of the car, Tony put a C-collar on him and they got him onto a stretcher.

Meanwhile, Otis got the hood open with a crowbar. Flames whooshed out, then just as suddenly disappeared as the hose line found the source of the blaze and extinguished it.

Tony's patient was bleeding from a cut on his head, where he'd hit the steering wheel. The old car didn't have air bags, but his seat belt had probably prevented a more serious injury. He was breathing but unconscious, whether from inhaling smoke and fumes or from a concussion it was hard to tell.

Back in the box Kevin drove while Tony tended to their patient. "BP one hundred over forty-two, respiration fourteen," he reported to Bio-Tel, the service that had a doctor on hand to provide medical advice. "Both pupils respond to light." He put pressure on the cut, which was bleeding profusely, then started an IV as the ambulance jerked and swayed and bumped its way to the closest trauma unit at Methodist Medical Center.

Once the basics were covered, Tony found the kid's wallet in a back pocket and reported the name and age. The poor kid hadn't had his license more than a couple of months.

Minutes later, the boy was delivered into the capable hands of the ER doctors. Tony took a deep breath and waited for the metabolic crash that inevitably came after a life-or-death sprint to the hospital. All that adrenaline, then nothing. He filled out the required paperwork, reported to the dispatcher that they were clear, then prayed for another call.

But nothing else came in, so he and Kevin returned to the station, where Tony's gaze was inevitably drawn to Brady's—or what used to be Brady's. The weathered sign was gone now.

For the past two weeks Tony and the rest of the firefighters had been watching various workers tromp in and out of the old tavern—floor sanders, electricians, plumbers and thankfully even an exterminator. Today, the outside of the building was getting a sandblasting, years of grime disappearing to reveal the true creamy color of the bricks.

The only thing worse than watching Brady's disappear before their eyes was catching glimpses of Julie, striding to and from her little blue Mini Cooper, always with purpose and determination in her step. Sometimes she carried various supplies with her—tools, wallpaper books, tile samples. Sometimes just a briefcase bulging with papers.

Tony had to admit she was making it happen. She had a plan and she was carrying it out with the precision of a military general. He wanted to get inside and see what she was doing, but so far, every time he'd wandered by on his days off, the door to the former bar had either been locked or barred with yellow caution tape and a sign indicating it was a hard-hat zone. In two weeks, he hadn't once managed to catch Julie and talk to her.

But she was always in his thoughts. A few days ago someone had casually asked him if he'd heard from Daralee, and he'd had to struggle a few seconds to even remember who Daralee was. All he could think about was Julie. And as before, the only thing that took his mind off his romantic troubles was work and more work. The slow shifts were torture.

The only good news was he was spending so much time at the weight bench, where he had a good view from the window overlooking the building across the street, that he was building some new muscles.

Finally, early the following morning, just as he was getting off his shift, he saw Julie's car drive up and park at a meter in front of her building.

Though he was grimy from putting out a kitchen fire and he hadn't had a chance to shower yet, he didn't delay. He sprinted across the street and caught her just as she was getting out of her car.

Startled, she looked from side to side for an escape route before finally resigning herself to a conversation. "Hello, Tony."

"Morning. You've been avoiding me."

"I don't have time to argue with you about my tearoom. I have things to do, places to go, people to meet." She headed resolutely for the front door, keys in hand. But she stopped before she reached it, perhaps remembering what had happened the last time he accompanied her toward that door.

"Tony, I'm really in a rush."

"What's up? Anything I can help with?"

"Help? Ha. You only have one thing in mind, and it's not helping me. You'd like to stop me from opening Belinda's. And I'm not going to let you."

"You're partly right. I do have only one thing on my mind. But it has nothing to do with your tearoom."

Her face flushed pink and she looked away. "If that's true, than there's even more reason to avoid you. I don't have time for your nonsense."

"You didn't think that kiss was nonsense. Admit it, Julie, you've hardly been able to think of anything else." If the kiss had affected her the way it affected him, that was how it worked.

She still wouldn't meet his gaze, which gave him some hope that he was right. She wasn't made of ice.

While her guard was down he took the keys from her hand and strolled toward the building, and she had no choice but to follow.

Tony opened the door and held it for her to enter. She did so quickly, but not before he felt the heat of her body and caught a whiff of her citrus scent. If he didn't have his way with this woman soon, he was going to expire from the wanting.

He followed her into the darkness and waited for his eyes to adjust, but then Julie turned on the lights and he got his first really good look at Belinda's Tearoom.

It was a strange sensation looking around at the changes, because the place still felt like Brady's—but not quite. All of the tables and chairs, neon signs and games were gone. The floor had been sanded bare.

The most dramatic change, though, was that the far back room of the bar had been walled off. Anyone who didn't know the history of the place would swear that wall had always been there, it blended so seamlessly with the rest of the space.

"What happened to the back room?" he asked.

"That's where the kitchen is."

It was depressing to realize the old Brady's was gone for good. But Tony wasn't giving up yet. If he could just spend some time with Julie, he was sure he could get her to understand why the tearoom was a bad idea. "You've made good progress," he said finally.

That obviously wasn't the observation she'd been hoping for from him, because she frowned. "You can't do better than that?"

"It's a big, empty space. I'm sure somehow you'll make it look like a tearoom. But it won't be Brady's, and I can feel the Ghosts of Brady's Past hanging out in the corners, cringing."

He expected her to shoot back a retort. But instead she hugged herself and shivered. "I wish you hadn't said that. You know, I'm living in my uncle's apartment and sometimes I think I can feel him there. Disapproving. I know it's my imagination, but after everything you've told me about Brady—about how generous he was and how everyone called him a friend—I'm feeling bad about destroying the place he helped to create."

Then, as if just realizing what she'd admitted, she suddenly turned all business. "Would you look at the mess those floor guys left! They were supposed to clean up everything before they took off yesterday." She started picking up discarded scraps of wood and bent nails.

Tony hadn't in a million years expected her to

make such an honest admission. He found himself wanting to sympathize, sharing her need to fulfill her dream. But he hardened his heart. The guys wouldn't speak to him for a week if they knew.

"It's not too late, you know. You could still make this a bar, and it wouldn't have to be grungy like before. Have you been to that new place in Bishop Arts?" He grabbed a broom and started sweeping up sawdust because it didn't feel right just standing there, doing nothing, while she worked. "It's really fancy. They serve those multicolored fruity martinis for eight bucks a pop. You don't think there's a heckuva profit margin there?"

"Turn Brady's into a martini bar?" Julie made a face. "I don't think Uncle Brady would like that any better. Besides, I told you, I don't know anything about running a bar." She paused and stared at him suspiciously. "You guys would freak if I turned this place into some high-priced beautiful-people bar. Is this some new game you're playing, using reverse psychology or something?"

Tony shrugged as he found a dustpan. "It doesn't have to be that fancy. I miss Brady's. Everybody does. But I like you and I want to see you succeed with this venture and make a profit. A bar is going to do better than a tearoom."

For about a half second her amber eyes glowed a little warmer, and he thought she believed him. But then she dropped her protective shutters into place, just as if she'd dropped the blinds on her window as a barrier between them.

"I do want to make enough money so that I can send Belinda to college and help out my parents."

"And that's a good thing. I fully support that."

She grabbed a trash bag that was already half-full and started pitching lumber scraps into it. Tony dumped a load of sawdust in, too.

"You smell like smoke," she said.

"I just got back from a kitchen fire. I was on my way home to shower when I saw you." He tied up the ends of the trash bag, which was now full. He'd been thinking about kissing her again, but she'd reminded him of his unkempt state. "Where's your trash?"

"It's back here." She led him behind the bar to a storage room, where a huge plastic garbage bin was already overflowing with refuse. "Oh, shoot, just drop that bag anywhere. I need to take my trash out to the alley. So what happened with the kitchen fire?"

"It was at Norma's Café—you know, that diner over on Davis?"

"Everyone knows Norma's, even people who don't live in Oak Cliff. Best chicken-fried steak in town—so I hear."

"But your lips never touch fried food, I take it."

"I wouldn't say that," she admitted. "I love Norma's. Was the fire bad?"

"Nah, just a little grease. They'll be back open by tomorrow."

"Oh, that's good."

"Norma's is your competition. I thought you'd want to see them closed."

She seemed disturbed by his suggestion. "Is that the impression I've given you? Tony, number one, Norma's and Belinda's appeal to completely different clientele. But number two, I would never wish a fire or anything else bad on anyone. Ever."

"You're right. I'm sorry, that wasn't fair." Tony helped Julie wrestle with the trash bin. "I can handle this if you'll get that last bag. Anyway, the fire was out in about thirty seconds. But I got a little steam burn. See?" He showed her a bright red crescent on his wrist. "Rookie mistake. I put my gloves on too quick and left a gap."

She felt an urge to kiss the red mark on his arm as she shook her head. "I don't know how you do it. Placing yourself in danger, saving people's lives. Don't you find it hard? What about those fires that aren't so easy? Or when people are seriously hurt, even killed. Your job makes my plan to open a tearoom seem…I don't know…silly and insignificant."

She tied the top of the bag in a knot and walked it toward the back door, which led to the alley.

Tony laid a hand on her arm, halting her. "Tearooms aren't silly. The world needs tearooms. Just like it needs neighborhood bars."

She rolled her eyes. "I was starting to like you a little bit."

He grinned and wrestled the trash bin out the back door, then held the door open for her.

"You don't have to be such a gentleman, you know."

"Can't help it. Anyway, you're still injured." He

pointed to her bandaged hand. "You shouldn't be doing all this heavy work." He'd noticed that she had her hand wrapped up in new bandages, rather inexpertly, but she seemed to be using it okay.

"It's almost healed now. Doesn't hurt at all." She opened the Dumpster lid and he heaved the bag inside. They both turned back as the lid slammed shut—and froze in their steps.

Someone had spray painted a message on the back wall in three-foot-high letters: *Bring Brady's back or else.*

Chapter Six

Julie's hands flew to her mouth as she took in the graffiti.

Tony felt sick.

"Well, that's just lovely," Julie said finally. "Did you get what you came for? Was my reaction suitably dramatic? Would it make a better story if I fell to the ground in tears?"

"Julie, I don't know anything about this." He reached out to touch her shoulder, knowing how hurt and frustrated she must feel at being attacked, but she stepped away from him.

"Don't touch me."

"I didn't do this."

"But you know who did."

"No. I have no idea." But he sure would love to find out. Applying a bit of romance to sway Julie's thinking wasn't exactly aboveboard, but it wasn't criminal. This was way over the line. If he found out who did it, the guy was going to be in a world of pain.

Julie trembled with outrage. Tony wanted to help her, comfort her. But his comfort was about as welcome as an electric shock.

"I can fix this," he said. "Kids spray paint this wall all the time. Brady just painted over the graffiti."

"*You're* not fixing anything. *I'll* fix it. And you can put the word out. If I find out who did this, I'll make his life miserable."

That went double for Tony, but he doubted Julie was in any mood to believe him. Words were cheap. He was going to have to *do* something to prove he wasn't her adversary.

"I'll get to the bottom of this," he said.

Less than a minute later he was across the street, back at Station 59, where the guys from the A shift were attending to their morning rituals—cooking breakfast, drinking coffee, checking out the day's news. He knew a couple of them but only casually, so he started by shaking hands and introducing himself.

"What, you just can't get enough of this place on your own shift?" one of the men ribbed him.

"I was just across the street at Brady's, talking to the new owner," he said. "Someone spray painted graffiti on her back wall."

A couple of the guys applauded and another whistled. "Good job. Was it you?"

"No, it wasn't me." His strenuous objection earned him a few curious stares. "I know everyone's ticked off about what's happening to Brady's. But don't y'all think committing malicious mischief against Julie is going a little far?"

"Julie, is it?" asked a lanky lieutenant. "Whose side are you on, Rookie?"

Tony sighed. *Rookie.* It had been a while since he'd had to deal with that moniker. Ethan, Priscilla and Tony had filled the vacancies at Station 59 caused by the deaths of three firefighters killed in the warehouse fire set by the serial arsonist, and resentments had run strong their first few weeks. But the three rookies had proved themselves. They'd all been in fires, they'd done their duty and gradually their colleagues had come to give them grudging respect.

Suddenly Tony was green again.

"I'm not on anyone's side," he said. "I'm trying harder than anyone to convince her to reopen Brady's just as it was. But she has definite ideas about what she wants to do with the bar, and no harassment is going to change her mind."

"So are you accusing someone here of painting this chick's wall?" one of the guys demanded.

"I'm not accusing anyone. I have no idea who did it. But if you know who did it, I hope you'll tell that person he's not helping matters."

"How do you know it was a 'he'?" the lieutenant asked. "Maybe it was a siren sister."

And maybe it was the Easter bunny. But Tony doubted it was anybody but a fellow firefighter. Maybe a cop, but probably not.

"I'm just saying it's not helping, that's all." He decided to cut his losses and get the hell out of there before the mood got any more hostile. He needed a shower and some sleep. Then he was going to buy some paint and get rid of the ugly words on Julie's wall, whether she wanted his help or not.

WHEN JULIE STEPPED OUT into the alley that afternoon to toss yet another bag of garbage into the Dumpster, she was surprised to encounter a man on a ladder painting her back wall. Her immediate reaction was to jump to the conclusion she'd caught her graffiti artist red-handed—until she realized the man was Tony, and he was painting over the last of the hurtful words with a nice neutral beige that almost matched the natural color of the bricks.

He turned when he heard the door and grinned. "Hi, there."

"Tony, I told you not to bother."

"I make a habit of doing what I'm told not to do. It gets me in a lot of trouble."

"The really irksome thing about you is you seem to *like* trouble."

"Most firefighters do, I guess."

She watched silently as Tony obliterated the last of the awful red letters. Her relief at seeing the graffiti disappear felt like a cool gust of wind.

"Tony, why are you doing this?"

"Because I feel responsible," he answered without hesitation. "I don't know who painted your wall, but it must have been a firefighter. Whoever he is, though, he doesn't represent all of us. I think you should know that not all firefighters would stoop so low as to break the law. We're not all bad."

"I never thought all firefighters were bad." But maybe she had. Maybe she had generalized, assuming things about Tony based on his occupation, the way people had once assumed she was unworthy or even stupid because she didn't wear the right shoes and didn't speak with the right inflections.

She felt a little guilty when she realized that. "It looks very nice. Thank you." Truthfully she'd had no idea when she was going to get around to painting over the graffiti. She hadn't wanted to waste any of her precious renovation budget on something so stupid, so she'd planned to do the painting herself. Now she didn't have to worry.

He smiled again. "You're welcome."

She felt herself softening toward Tony. Though she knew that was a dangerous development, she couldn't seem to help herself. "Come on inside and get something to drink. You can sit at the bar and pretend you're at Brady's."

"It won't seem like Brady's unless you're serving warm beer. And you'd have to be wearing a miniskirt and halter top, like Brady's waitresses did."

"Not in this lifetime. You'll have to settle for cold lemonade and faded jeans."

His gaze traveled in a leisurely path down her body to look at those jeans, and her face warmed. If another guy did that, she would feel affronted. But Tony's look was so...appreciative. It made her feel beautiful and sexy rather than insulted by his boldness.

She was about to step back into the building when something caught her eye, a small red spot on her beige brick wall. She stepped closer to get a better look, while Tony cleared his throat.

"Um, you weren't supposed to notice that."

It was a little red heart, only a couple of inches across, painted on one brick. Beside it Tony had signed his initials.

"See, my original plan was to paint over the graffiti and move on before you saw me. So it would be a big surprise. But then I decided to leave a clue."

"So I could thank you."

"I was secretly hoping you'd be so grateful you'd want to go out with me."

Hell. How was she supposed to respond to that? With his big brown eyes and his earnest manner, she wanted to take him home and feed him like a stray puppy.

And then give him a warm place to sleep. If they ever got around to sleeping.

He did make it pretty hard to stay mad. "Lemonade," she said, strengthening her resolve. He wasn't a puppy, he was a man. A firefighter who hated her tearoom and wanted his dingy old bar back.

Tony opened the door for her, and she had to brush close to him to get inside. He had a knack for making her do that. She couldn't help noticing that he no longer smelled like smoke.

From the small fridge behind the bar she produced a couple of cans of lemonade. But there was no place to sit. Every stick of the old furniture had been sold, and the new tables and chairs she'd ordered wouldn't arrive until the renovations were completed.

Tony solved the problem by vaulting onto the bar. He sat facing out, his legs dangling. "Come on up, the view is fine."

Since she needed a break and didn't want to sit on the floor, she followed his example, sitting just close enough that she could feel the heat radiating off him.

She'd never seen the tearoom from this angle before. It looked enormous. Not quite as big as Lochinvar's, but the size was still intimidating.

"So tell me about your tearoom. What kind of food are you going to serve?"

"I'm still working out all the details, but I'm planning on an eclectic menu. Specialty salads, soups, quiche, then a few heartier seafood and chicken dishes."

"No burgers?"

"No, but there'll be a few sandwiches."

"Ribs?" he asked hopefully.

"Definitely not."

"So no guy food."

"The menu will be designed to appeal primarily to women, but there is no law that says a guy can't eat a salad or a club sandwich."

"What about liquor?"

"Wine only."

He sighed. "You know, you might actually attract a few businessmen if you put some token items on the menu that appeal to men. Steak, chili, burgers, maybe some designer beer—"

"I don't want tables full of noisy men who've been drinking. Then the women won't want to eat here. I want refinement. Quiet conversation. I want my customers to appreciate the decor and the background music. I'm thinking of hiring a harpist to come in once or twice a week during lunch, to really give the place some atmosphere."

Tony groaned.

"You're not scaring me. It's not meant to appeal to you."

"Just how many tea-drinking, itty-bitty-sandwich-eating, harp-music-listening women of leisure do you think live in Oak Cliff?"

"Not necessarily women of leisure. Working women will come here on their lunch break. I intend for the service to be quick."

"Oak Cliff working women won't be able to afford your prices, not on a regular basis."

"You don't even know what my prices are."

"I can guess."

"You're not scaring me," she said again. "I know what I'm doing." Not for the first time since she'd committed herself to this idea, however, she had some doubts. What if Tony was right? What if her concept was just too high-end for this working-class neighborhood?

No, she wasn't going to worry about that. What did Tony know? He didn't have any restaurant experience.

"I'm not trying to scare you," he said. "Honestly. I'm trying to help you attract more customers so you can stay open."

"Stay open?"

"Something like ninety percent of restaurant start-ups close within the first year."

"Now you're scaring me." She'd encountered the statistic before.

He slipped an arm around her and scooted closer. "I'll stop. Tell me more. Will you be open for breakfast?"

"Just lunch, at first. Once I get the hang of that, I'm planning to offer a limited breakfast—pastries, coffee and tea."

"Bagels with cream cheese?" he asked hopefully. "No one around here serves a decent bagel. Crispy on the outside, chewy on the inside…" He nibbled her ear. "I'd be here every morning if you served a good bagel."

"I'm beginning to think what you really want is hot Julie on a platter." The blood rushed to her face. Had she really just said that?

"Mmm, that sounds even better than bagels. I'll be here an hour early for that."

She couldn't believe this guy. He didn't even deny he wanted in her pants! But she also couldn't believe herself. She was sitting here letting him nibble her ear and her neck, making no move to escape. She opened her mouth to tell him to stop, but what he was doing just felt too good.

She reached up a hand to push him away, but then she remembered the little red heart he'd left on her wall and her own heart just melted. Along with a few other strategically placed body parts.

"Tony," she implored, but he ignored her, planting

little kisses along her jaw. Eventually, he reached the corner of her mouth. If he actually kissed her on the lips, she would be a goner. Her body was already clamoring for more Tony. Her breasts strained against her bra, her nipples hard and achy. And the heat building at the core of her being was like a furnace in the basement of an old building, long disused but raging back to life with the touch of a lit match.

Trey had never made her feel quite like this, like a bowl of melting gelatin. Common sense, good judgment and willpower had left the building.

But, honestly, what could happen? They were sitting on a hard wooden bar. Would it hurt to make out? They were already making out. She had her tongue in his mouth—that was making out.

When a loud banging noise finally penetrated her lust-fogged mind, she realized someone was knocking on the door.

"Ignore it," Tony said. His hand was up her shirt, caressing her breast, and she wanted more than anything to do what he said. But she couldn't.

"It's the man here to install my new stove." She was shocked by the breathy croak of her own voice. "I have to let him in."

Reluctantly Tony relinquished his hold. He withdrew slowly but without arguing further.

Julie hopped off the bar, found the shoe she'd dropped and ran for the door, where a man with a handcart waited impatiently. "Thought you were in a hurry to get your kitchen done," he said as she let him in.

"Sorry. I didn't hear you knocking at first." Which was true. Her brain had been so filled with Tony there hadn't been room for anything else. "I'll open the back door for you."

She had no business dallying with Tony. The installer already knew exactly what to do, so she left him to his business. It wasn't as if she didn't have a million other things to attend to. But first she had one little matter to take care of.

Or maybe not so little.

Tony stood with his back against the bar, arms folded, looking just this side of smug. "Lucky we were interrupted."

"Lucky? You're glad?"

"When I make love to you," he said in a low voice, "I don't want it to be on a hard wooden bar. We're going to have a soft bed, rose petals, champagne…."

"Oh, please." Though she couldn't deny the picture he painted had its appeal.

"I want to take you out for a steak dinner," he said, not the slightest deterred by her negative attitude. "Wine, violins, the whole nine yards."

Her mouth watered. She hadn't had any dinner more elaborate than tuna casserole or mac-and-cheese since she and Trey had broken up. "Then you were going to seduce me."

"Make love to you." The way he said it, all soft and sexy, made her skin itch for his touch. How did he do that? One minute she was sure she wanted to sweep him out of the bar, and the next she was drooling to be in his arms again. "I want you to wear your sexiest dress and your highest pair of heels so I can show you off."

Julie walked behind the bar, careful to keep more than an arm's reach away from Tony, and gathered up some cleaning rags that needed washing, stuffing them into a plastic bag. "I'm not a prize poodle."

"Julie, why are you being like this? What's wrong?"

Julie made herself stop and think. She *was* being harsh. And unfair. If a man ran hot and cold as she was doing, it would make her furious.

"I'm sorry, Tony. I know I'm being inconsistent. But having a guy in my life right now—it just won't work." She didn't add that her plans particularly didn't include hooking up with a firefighter. It wasn't that she had anything against Tony or his occupation. In fact, she found it very brave and noble. But it just didn't fit in with the vision she had for her future.

"Why not?"

"Belinda's is taking up a hundred percent of my time and energy right now. Anyway, we don't even know each other." He'd flirted with her, but he hadn't told her anything important about himself.

"So if I don't take you out to dinner tomorrow night, what will you do instead?"

"Sew curtains." The price of custom window treatments was so outrageous that Julie had decided she would have to make her own. She'd sewn her clothes as a teen; it was the only way she'd been able to afford to wear the styles and fabrics that appealed to her. Even when she'd been able to buy high-quality clothing, she'd still occasionally made her own creations, which had earned her many compliments.

No one had ever suspected. But her sewing habit was an embarrassing little secret she'd kept from Trey.

"You can do that?" Tony asked. "That's really talented. And are you going to be sewing curtains every night for the foreseeable future?"

She carried her bag of laundry into the storage room, where an ancient but serviceable washer and dryer occupied one wall. "If I'm not sewing curtains, I'll be painting or sanding or texturing. I'm building a mosaic countertop around the sink in the ladies' room and a stained-glass pane for the window over the door. I have a million projects." She stuffed the dirty rags into the washer, emphasizing how very busy she was.

"So I could bring over a bucket of chicken and help you. I can't sew, but I can sand and paint—I can even do laundry—and you wouldn't have to pay me with anything but your charming company."

She almost said yes. He was so darn cute and he could charm the skin right off a snake. But she made herself shake her head. "Even if I had the time, I'm not ready to date. I just broke up with a guy. It was a couple of weeks before our wedding and I found out…" Her throat still closed up when she thought about it. It had been such a shock. Her whole world had shifted and a new reality had taken over in mere seconds.

She wouldn't be marrying Trey Davidson. She wouldn't be changing her name or moving into Trey's Highland Park home. She was single again. Alone. She hadn't really belonged in that world of privilege. She'd only been a guest, one who could be ejected at the whim of her host.

And eject her Trey had. He was the one who'd cheated and lied, yet somehow he'd managed to blame her and justify his anger toward her.

"He was unfaithful, huh? Bastard."

"Not just unfaithful. He had a child. But the very worst thing was he refused to take responsibility. When he found out she was pregnant, he cranked up the family's legal machine and tried every way possible to get rid of the woman, right down to having her deported."

"Jeez. It's a good thing you didn't marry the guy. But what does that have to do with us?"

"I'm on the rebound."

He shrugged. "So am I. I just broke up with someone, too. We weren't engaged, but it was serious. Well, sort of."

"So we're both on the rebound. Recipe for disaster."

"I can't think of a better way to get over a bad affair than to find love with someone else."

Love? She remembered the strange prediction Priscilla Garner had made, then pushed it out of her mind.

"You see, Tony, I made a mistake. Not just with whom I picked as a partner but why I wanted to be with someone in the first place. I placed my entire future in someone else's hands rather than relying on myself. I need to find out what I can do with my life—on my own."

"So bottom line…you're telling me you just want to be friends?" He pulled a face at that old hackneyed expression, and she couldn't blame him.

But was that what she wanted? Friends? How could she have Tony around as a friend when she was so attracted to him? Could she keep her hands off him? Did she really want to tell Tony to go away and not come back, that she was a loner and wanted to stay that way? Could she take a couple of days to think about it?

But she already knew the answer to that question. If she gave Tony an inch, he'd take a mile. He'd be in her life, in her bed; she would fall in love, and everything would be topsy-turvy until he decided some other woman had something she didn't.

"Just friends."

"Okay, then." He looked sad for a moment, and she almost blurted out that she'd changed her mind. But then he grinned. "You're a really good kisser, anyone ever tell you that?" And without giving her a chance for a comeback, he gave her a two-finger salute and sauntered out the door into the hot afternoon.

Chapter Seven

Tony tried to shake off Julie's rejection as he made the short walk home. Not even the prospect of seeing Jasmine for the first time in two weeks could completely cheer him up, though it helped. She would be here in about an hour, he reckoned. Just enough time to take another shower, then run to the store and buy some of those double-fudge brownies she liked.

Jas was a chocoholic in the making. Tony tried to be a good dad and not let her indulge herself too much, but this was a special occasion. His daughter had been visiting her grandparents in Galveston for the past two weeks—the longest she and Tony had ever been separated.

When he got home with the brownies, he opened a can of fudge icing and frosted them, then put some colored sprinkles on top, because she liked those, too.

As he put on the finishing touches, Priscilla knocked on the back door and let herself in. "Well, aren't you domestic."

"Do you have, like, some sort of specialized food radar? 'Cause I swear, every time I have something good and I'm just about to eat it, you show up."

"Actually, I wanted to ask you if you would quiz me for my test. It's on drugs and drug interactions, poisons, antidotes and overdose protocol. I need help, and Ethan's not home."

Priscilla and Ethan were working toward their paramedic certification, a requirement for all Dallas firefighters. Tony didn't envy them, having to go through a solid year of training while they were still adjusting to the job of fighting fires. Fortunately he'd been a paramedic before he applied to the fire department.

"I wish I could help you study, Pris, but Jasmine will be here any minute. I haven't seen her in two weeks and I want to spend some time with her."

Pris smiled at the mention of Jasmine. Everyone loved her. She was such a sweet, loving, uncomplicated kid. A lot of people said she was like Tony in terms of her personality, which always made him feel proud. But if that was the case, the poor girl was probably in for some heartbreak when she got older.

"So what have you been up to?" Pris asked as she opened the refrigerator. She never came into his kitchen without opening his fridge and swiping something, since her fridge was notoriously empty. Considering she brought him goodies from her mother's kitchen, though, he couldn't complain too bitterly.

"I was painting over some graffiti on the back wall of Brady's. You wouldn't happen to know who's responsible, would you?"

"Don't look at me." She closed the fridge and opened the freezer, finally settling on a cherry Popsicle.

"I just thought maybe you'd heard something. This campaign to stop Julie from opening the tearoom has gotten way out of hand."

"What about you? Have you given up on the cold-blooded-seduction thing?" Pris asked.

Tony sighed. "It's not my style. I tried to stop myself from falling in love with Julie, but I can't just *not* feel anything for her. I mean, she's so…she's just so… Damn, Pris, what am I doing wrong?"

"She's not interested?" Pris asked. "I find that hard to believe. I saw the way she looked at you."

"Yeah, the way a lot of women *look* at me. Apparently I'm okay to look at. Or make out with. In some cases, I'm okay to have sex with. But that's it."

"Oh, Tony. I'm sure that's not true. What happened?"

"Julie gave me the 'just friends' speech. You know the one."

"'The timing's wrong. It's me not you'?"

"That's the one." Tony, having temporarily forgotten the brownies were for Jasmine, took a bite out of one. "She's all into this 'on the rebound' stuff. Her last boyfriend was some jerk who cheated on her, and now she thinks all guys are like him. She won't go out with me. So what did I do wrong?"

"Well, you do come on a little strong."

Tony stopped just as he was about to take another bite. Too strong?

"I mean, don't take this wrong, but I think you might scare a woman to bits because you're so… intense. And persistent."

He thought intensity and persistence were good things.

"Are you in love with Julie?" Priscilla asked suddenly.

"I'm trying not to go there. But I could be. In a big way. I mean, what if she's The One?"

"You think every girl you meet is The One. It's called infatuation. Not that infatuation can't develop into love, but you don't know Julie well enough to have such strong feelings about her. A few weeks ago you were in love with Daralee."

"Now *that* was infatuation."

"But you thought she was The One, didn't you? And I think you scared her off. You did the same thing with Karla."

Karla. He hadn't thought about her in forever. She'd been a secretary at the firefighter school. And, yes, he'd thought she was The One, too.

"And before that—"

"Okay, I get—"

"You see the pattern, right?" Priscilla asked.

"That women break up with me after a few weeks? Yeah, I've got that down."

"Because real, lasting relationships don't build overnight. And most women know that. Maybe they think you're a player. Maybe they don't believe you're sincere. Because frankly, Tony, you're a catch. Any girl would be lucky to have you and keep you. The only thing I can figure out is that you're scaring them away because you're just too damn good to be true."

Tony put the half-eaten brownie aside. His stomach hurt. "You think?"

"I don't know. I've been trying to figure it out. I've also wondered why there's no chemistry between you and me."

"Because we're friends. I'd never want to mess that up."

"So you think you can't be friends and lovers at the same time?"

"I was being friendly to Julie," he argued. "I painted over her graffiti."

"Because you wanted to soften her up. So she'd go to bed with you. And let's face it, you have an even darker ulterior motive. You want to mess up her plans for the tearoom."

"I do want to change her mind, for her own good as well as ours," Tony said. "If she would get to know me better, if she could trust me, maybe she would believe it when I tell her the tearoom thing is a bad idea."

"So you have ulterior motives. Why don't you try being friends, no strings attached?"

"I can't stop wanting her. It's not like a faucet I can turn on and off."

"I know. But here's the deal—if you had an ironclad guarantee that you and Julie will never, ever get together, would you still want to spend time with her?"

"Yes." That was easy.

"Then do it. Be her friend. Get it fixed in your mind that there's absolutely no possibility of hooking up with her. Let her really get to know you like I know you. Then maybe when she's over being hurt by the jerk and she's ready to date again, she'll think of you. But don't make that your focus."

"I can't keep my hands off her."

"You not only have to keep your hands off her, you have to stop flirting. No sexual innuendos. Nothing you wouldn't do in front of Jasmine."

Tony wanted to ask Priscilla what was left to talk about. But the front door opened, signaling Jasmine's arrival, and he needed to focus on his daughter.

He went to greet her as she ran inside, arms outstretched. He picked her up in a bear hug and swung her around. This relationship, at least, was in his life for good. And for a couple more years, at least—until Jasmine reached puberty and became a moody teenager—their relationship was entirely good and uncomplicated.

"I missed you a lot, Jazzy."

"I missed you, too, Dad."

He set her down. "Just look at you! You're all tan."

"I spent almost every day at the beach. Where's Samantha?"

"At her dad's for a few days before school starts."

"Oh." Jasmine was clearly disappointed. Ever since Kat and her daughter Samantha had moved in next door, Jas and Samantha had been inseparable. Although Jas was a couple of years older, she adored Samantha and treated her like the little sister she'd never had.

He understood nonblood family ties. The only real family Tony had known as a kid was Ethan and his mom, who'd sort of unofficially adopted him. At least Tony had had a place to crash when things at his own house got ugly.

Tony picked up his daughter's suitcase and followed her down the hall to her room. She would be anxious to put everything away and get settled in. She was a fastidious child, always wanting things neat, clean and organized.

"Want to go for a bike ride?" he asked.

"Ugh, it's too hot."

"We could swim at the rec center." He set her small suitcase on the bed and opened it for her.

"Dad, could you not hover quite so much? I just spent two weeks with Gramma and Grandpa wanting to be with me every second. I need some space."

Tony groaned inwardly. Now he was smothering his own daughter. Was he the only person in the world who didn't need "space"?

"Okay, Sweetie. I'll be out in the yard. After you unwind a little, you can tell me all about your trip."

But out in the yard doing what? It occurred to him that he really had no nonwork interests beyond his backyard. Ethan had his home-improvement projects to keep him busy and now he was talking about buying a boat. Priscilla was always involved in something—recreational shopping, visiting with her friends, charity work, getting a pedicure. And they were both in the thick of paramedic training, which kept them busy.

Tony liked to run and ride his bike, but in the heat of summer he was done with those activities by eight in the morning. When he'd been with Daralee, he'd filled his off days with her. And after their breakup, he'd spent his leisure time mooning over her, plotting to get her back. Then he'd discovered Julie, and his focus had switched to her.

Maybe if he had more varied interests, women like Julie would find him worth something beyond a roll in the hay.

He wandered into the living room, his gaze falling on a bookshelf lined with leather-bound volumes. Priscilla, trying to class his place up a little, had filled Tony's bookcase with more of an eye toward decor than reading pleasure.

Moby Dick. That was an action story, right? They'd even made a movie out of it. He pulled the book off the shelf, found himself a comfortable chair and started to read.

Tony hadn't read a novel since he'd been forced to in high school—and even then he'd relied on Cliff's Notes to pass the test. He found the tiny print and dense prose slow going, but he persevered. If he was going to be friends with Julie, they would have to have something to talk about. Maybe they could talk about books.

That sounded *so* boring. But much as he hated to admit it, he knew Priscilla had a point. He was doing something wrong where women were concerned. He couldn't just keep doing what he'd always done and expect different results.

So, all right, he would be Julie's friend—and he would do it right this time. He would not touch her or flirt with her. He was still hoping to change her mind about the tearoom, but he was beginning to think that was a lost cause. She wouldn't listen to reason and neither would she fall for any emotional pleas. So he would treat her as he did Priscilla, whom he liked and respected. He wouldn't smother her.

In fact, he decided, he'd go even further. If she wanted anything more than friendship from him, ever, she was going to have to make the first move. He was done forever being the seducer, the hunter, the aggressor. He was, from this day forward, Mr. Aloof, Mr. Hard-to-Get. No more handing his heart on a platter to every good-looking woman who batted her eyelashes at him.

If Julie changed her mind, she was going to have to seduce *him*.

THREE DAYS LATER JULIE was ashamed to be standing at the bedroom window at precisely seven o'clock, just when Tony got off his shift. He usually came out the front door of the station and walked to the corner of Willomet, where he turned and headed for his home down the block.

She made sure she was hidden behind the blinds, but it turned out not to matter. This morning he didn't spare her building a glance. He was with Priscilla and Ethan, and the three of them seemed wrapped up in conversation, laughing about something. It was almost as if Tony deliberately avoided looking her way, though that was probably granting herself way too much importance. After the old "just friends" speech, she doubted he was going to think about her much at all.

He'd probably moved on to his next conquest.

Guys like Tony had women standing in line to date him, to sleep with him. He'd probably had his pick of candidates. Why would he waste even a moment's thought on Julie when she'd been so clear with her rejection?

She'd regretted her actions a million ways to Sunday. Though in her mind she knew she'd done the right thing, her heart was arguing with it. Tony was a good guy, as Priscilla had said. How often did one of them come along? Yes, he wanted her, but she wanted him, too, so they were even. Besides, that wasn't the only reason he'd painted over the hurtful graffiti on her back wall or helped her clean up the bar. He liked helping people. Why else would he be a firefighter?

She'd loved Trey—or she thought she had. But what had attracted her to him was his self-assuredness, his clever mind and—if she were being completely, brutally honest—his wealth. Or at least the security his money represented. She'd told herself

Trey was generous. He'd always been taking her out to nice places and surprising her with expensive gifts. She'd told herself he was a hard worker and a good friend.

But looking back, she could see the flaw in her reasoning. It was easy for guys like Trey to be generous. Buying her little baubles was no hardship when his bank account was practically unlimited. But when had he ever been generous with his time?

Would Trey have painted a wall for her? With his own hands? Not likely.

As Tony and his housemates disappeared around the corner, she sighed. She envied them their friendship. After her split with Trey, she'd lost most of her friends, too, even the women. Why would they ally themselves with a penniless, jobless person when they could continue hobnobbing with Trey, riding around in his Porsche, drinking upscale beer and lemon martinis while soaking in his enormous hot tub?

At least she had Belinda. Her little sister was growing up. She had thrown herself wholeheartedly into the tearoom venture with Julie, putting in a lot of hours of drudge work when she wasn't at her waitressing job. Sometimes, she called at odd hours when she had a brainstorm about the decor or the menu or advertising. Yeah, she was still into rock bands and clothes and boys, but Julie sensed a new maturity in Belinda.

She would go far. And Julie and the tearoom

were the keys to helping Belinda reach her potential. Unlike Julie, who had always banged up against the limits of her poor upbringing and her lack of education and training in social graces, Belinda faced no limits. And Julie intended to make sure things stayed that way, no matter what the cost to herself.

Julie forced herself to walk away from the window and start her day. She headed for her tiny shower with its three minutes of hot water, and along with yesterday's grit she washed away her pensive mood. She didn't have time to ponder life's puzzles today. She had walls to paint. She stuck a few pins in her hair to keep it out of her face and out of the paint. Then she headed downstairs, gearing up for the task at hand.

Once she reached the tearoom, she paused a few moments to savor the transformation taking place. The construction had been completed—she'd really only moved one wall so she would have room for a kitchen. And she'd hired a neighborhood guy to paint the tin ceiling, because he'd offered and the price was right. But the walls were all hers.

She spread out her plastic drop cloth, positioned the ladder and opened the first can of the beautiful soft gold paint she'd selected. She thought it would give the place a sort of Tuscan feel.

She'd only covered a few square feet when someone knocked on her front door. She didn't think she had any deliveries scheduled for the day and at first she considered ignoring it, but then she couldn't deny her own curiosity. She climbed down from the ladder, wiped her hands on a rag and padded to the front door, making sure she didn't have any paint on her feet.

Her heart slammed into her chest. Tony. What was he doing here? Even more surprising, he had a little girl with him.

She opened the door. "Hey, how's it going?" he said with a friendly smile, just as if they hadn't parted company on such an awkward note three days earlier.

"It's going fine. And, no, I haven't changed my mind about opening a tearoom." Just in case he'd come over to argue his case again. "I'm painting."

"We know, we saw through the window," the little girl said. "Can we come in and look?"

"Sure. Y'all can tell me if you like the color, although it's too late if you don't. I've bought six nonreturnable gallons of the stuff." She opened the door wider to let them in, but she snagged Tony's arm as he entered. "Are you going to introduce me to your friend?"

The girl giggled.

"This is my daughter, Jasmine."

"Oh." Julie struggled to put the world right side up again. Okay, so Tony had a child. He'd been married before. No big deal. She wasn't antidivorce or anything. It's just that she hadn't thought of him that way. Until this moment he had been, in her mind, the typical bachelor, free and unattached.

But he was a father.

"I guess I never mentioned Jasmine before," he said.

"No, you didn't." Julie found a smile for the adorable young girl. "Hi, Jasmine. I'm Julie."

She was tall and slender—and beautiful, with thick black hair piled carelessly on her head. She looked like Tony around the eyes, but the upturned nose and wide mouth had perhaps come from her mother. She was dressed in baggy blue shorts, a Marine World T-shirt and glittery flip-flops.

"It's nice to meet you, Julie," Jasmine said, polite as can be, extending her hand, which Julie shook. "Do you really own this place?"

"Did you think I made it up?" Tony said.

"Actually, my mother owns it," Julie replied, "but she's an absentee owner. She hasn't been here in years."

Tony looked around. "You planning to paint this whole place by yourself?"

"Do you have any idea what painters charge?" she countered. "It's a big job, but I'm up to it. And Belinda's going to help later."

"We could help, too," Jasmine said. "I know how to paint. I painted my room at home. Purple. It is so cool."

"I appreciate the offer, but you don't have your painting clothes on," Julie pointed out. "If you've painted before, you know how messy it is." She already had dots of gold decorating the old T-shirt she wore.

"We could go home and change," Tony said.

"That's really nice of you, but… Do you really want to help? I mean, every step I take toward getting the place renovated is another step closer to my opening Belinda's Tearoom—which goes directly against your best interests."

Tony grinned. "Not necessarily. Brady's Tavern could have gold walls."

"Pretty much anything would be an improvement over, well, I'm not sure what to call the current color. Cloudy dirt?"

"More like pukey beige."

Jasmine giggled.

"We'll go change clothes and be right back," Tony said. "Hey, it's that or we'll have to go home and pull weeds."

"Oh, no, not that!" Jasmine said. "I hate weeding. Save me, Julie, please?"

Julie really was in no position to turn down free labor, even if she doubted Tony's motives were completely pure. "Okay. If you really want. I have lots of brushes."

Jasmine clapped her hands together and dragged her father out the door. It was so funny what some children got excited about.

Tony, a dad. That would take some getting used to. The girl had to be nine or ten, at least, which put Tony in his early thirties, probably. She'd thought he was closer to her own age of twenty-five.

By the time the two returned in their old clothes a few minutes later, Julie had prepared an area for Jasmine to work on—a half wall that served to break up the dining room a bit, so it seemed cozier. She gave the girl a wide brush and a coffee can of paint, as well as a bit of instruction.

"I can do this, really," Jasmine said. "I'll be neat, too."

"Knowing her, she won't spill a drop," Tony said so only Julie could hear. "She is the tidiest person in the world."

Julie put Tony to work with a roller, while she started the more detailed brushwork near the wood trim. Both father and daughter worked a while without complaint, seemingly happy. And, true to her word, Jasmine was very neat and very thorough. She didn't cover a lot of territory, but what she did, she did well.

When Julie's path crossed Tony's and her ladder was almost on top of him, she couldn't resist commenting about Jasmine. "I can't believe you didn't tell me you had a daughter."

"It didn't come up," he said. "Anyway, I thought you and I might be…well, you know. And us single dads learn not to blurt out the truth about our kids right out of the gate. Some women don't want to compete with children."

"It wouldn't have bothered me," Julie said. "I like kids."

"Well, anyway, Jasmine's not something I would hide for long. I'm very proud of her. She's the…the shining light in my universe. Sometimes I'm amazed that two ordinary people could have produced such an amazing child."

Seeing the way Tony lit up when he talked about her, Julie softened. Just because Trey wanted to duck his responsibilities as a father didn't mean every man felt the same way. "Does she live with you?"

"I share custody with Natalie, her mom. Our arrangement is pretty loose, especially in the summer. I want to spend time with her now, before she turns into one of those sullen teenagers and I'm not cool enough for her."

"How old is she now?"

He grinned. "Nine going on thirty. I can't keep up with her."

Julie couldn't deny the appeal of this new Tony. Before, he'd been charming in a Casanova sort of way. But now she felt she was seeing more of his true nature. And she had to admit she liked what she saw. And then there was the way his old T-shirt stretched across his shoulders made her want to touch him.

She resisted the urge. Her body hungered for some physical contact with him, even something perfectly innocent. But he'd been giving off definite we're-just-friends-now vibes. She was the one who had told him it wouldn't work, and he'd taken her at her word. It would be wrong for her to suddenly change her mind. Probably foolish, too. She had made her bed, as her mother was fond of saying. Now she could lie in it. Or *not* lie in it with Tony, at any rate.

But, damn, she missed the flirtatious winks, the compliments, the lingering looks.

She shook her head in frustration with herself.

This was what she wanted, wasn't it? She didn't have time for a relationship. She had a tearoom to open and she needed more time to grieve the canceled marriage to Trey.

Why, then, did she feel so sad and empty? So bereaved?

Julie moved to a different spot, closer to Jasmine. "When does school start?" she asked.

"Ugh, next week. Too soon."

"You're going into fourth grade?" Julie guessed.

"Uh-huh."

"I remember fourth grade. That's when stuff gets really interesting. Do you have a favorite subject?"

Jasmine brightened. "Science. And math and creative writing. I have a really good teacher for those classes, Mrs. Jeffries. I think I might want to be a doctor someday. And maybe go to Africa and cure some terrible disease."

"That's very noble," Julie said, impressed that a nine-year-old would think that far ahead. "Makes my wanting to serve people quiche and crepes seem kind of unimportant."

"People have to eat," Jasmine said pragmatically.

Julie laughed. "Yes, they do."

"Anyway, I might become a supermodel instead of a doctor."

Julie smiled. That sounded more like a little girl.

They broke for lunch, and Tony insisted on buying a pizza. Julie insisted just as hard that it should be her treat; they were doing her a huge favor, after all. So they compromised and split the cost.

After lunch, Jasmine seemed a little less enthusiastic about painting.

"I think you guys have done enough," Julie said. "Why don't you go have some fun? Belinda's coming over after her shift at work and she'll help me, so I won't be alone."

"Daddy, you did say something about swimming this afternoon."

"You're right, I did." He checked his watch. "I guess we should go."

"Thanks for letting me paint," Jasmine said to Julie. She was an exceedingly polite child. Someone was raising her right. "When I come here to eat, I'm gonna tell everyone I painted that whole wall all by myself."

"And a beautiful wall it is," Julie said.

"See you around," Tony said. No wink. No sexy grin. Just a wave.

Julie watched them as they crossed the street and disappeared down Willomet Avenue, her heart heavy. Part of her wanted to be included in their intimate circle. But she had to be practical.

Chapter Eight

Belinda arrived just as they left, wearing a baggy pair of overall shorts and a tube top that revealed a little butterfly tattoo on her shoulder. Julie had just about fainted when she'd first spotted it a few weeks ago.

Belinda threw her purse behind the bar. "Was that Tony?"

Julie sighed. "Uh-huh. And his daughter. He's got a daughter."

Belinda's jaw dropped. "Wow. He doesn't seem, you know, dadlike."

"You wouldn't say that if you saw the two of them together."

"Really. What were they doing here? I thought you guys had decided it wasn't going to work out."

"We did. He's just being a good neighbor." And Julie related that morning's events while she set up a painting area for Belinda.

"Now, excuse me, but a guy doesn't spend half a day painting your restaurant—a restaurant he claims he doesn't want you to open—unless he wants something from you. Like sex."

"I dunno, Bel. It didn't seem that way."

"You sound sad."

"I am a little. I shouldn't even be thinking about a new guy right now. But I can't help it. He was cute and sexy before and he really got under my skin. I saw a new side of him today."

"'Cause he has a kid?" Belinda wrinkled her nose. "Doesn't appeal to me at all."

"I didn't think it would me, either." She shrugged again. "Can't explain it. But, I can't help but wonder if I've made a terrible mistake."

A FEW DAYS LATER TONY dropped by again, this time without Jasmine. "Hey, the paint looks great."

"Thanks." It had taken Julie the rest of that first day and all of a second to get it done, but she was pleased with the results. The texturing she'd done had given the walls a sort of antique look. Today she planned to tackle the bar. It was a beautiful thing, solid oak and intricately carved with lions' heads and leaves, but it was scarred and in desperate need of refinishing.

"I'm heading for The Home Depot to get some stuff for the yard," Tony said. "Since you probably go there every day, I thought I'd ask if you needed anything."

Well, how thoughtful. "I really can't think of anything just now. I'm in debt to that store up to my eyeballs anyway. Oh, but there is one little thing you could help with. The bar has a few built-in drawers, and one of them is completely stuck. Maybe you could put a little muscle behind it and yank it out?"

"Sure. Show me."

Was she inventing excuses to keep him around? Yeah, maybe. The drawer really was stuck, but with a hammer she'd probably have been able to get it open on her own. He looked so good in his khaki shorts and soft-blue pocket tee that she had to stick her hands in her pockets to keep them from straying.

She led him behind the bar and pointed to the stubborn drawer.

Tony rubbed his hands together. "Let's see if all the pumping iron pays off." He bent down, grabbed the drawer handle and gave it a mighty yank.

Nothing.

"Guess I have to put some weight behind it." He spread his feet, then gave an even harder pull. The drawer came loose so suddenly it caused Tony to topple backward—right into Julie's legs. Julie grabbed at the edge of the bar and managed to slow her fall, but they both ended up in a heap on the floor. She heard Tony's elbow hit the hardwood planks.

"Are you okay?" Tony immediately asked.

"I'm fine, but how's your elbow?"

As he sat up, he rubbed his arm. "I guess I smacked it pretty good." They both looked at the drawer. It was in pieces. "Julie, I'm sorry. I broke your drawer."

"Never mind about the drawer. I broke your elbow."

"It's fine," he insisted. "I'll have a bruise, that's all."

"Let me get you some ice." She tried to extricate herself and stand up, but he grabbed her hand and tugged her back down to the floor.

"Julie, it's fine."

Oh, he shouldn't have touched her. She felt the warmth and strength of his hand all the way to the pit of her stomach. And he hadn't let her go.

They were only inches apart. Their gazes locked, and she thought for sure he was going to kiss her again. But then he seemed to shake himself out of the sensual spell. He released her hand and looked away. "Maybe ice is a good idea."

Yeah, they should cover their bodies with it. Because nothing else was going to put out the fire.

She touched his face. She couldn't help herself. Wise or not, she wanted him to kiss her. It was hell seeing him and not being able to touch.

"You're making things difficult," he said.

"I don't mean to." And when he still didn't kiss her, she leaned in and kissed him.

Whatever had been making him hesitate vanished. He returned her kiss like a sailor who'd been at sea far too long. As for her, she couldn't hold back or temper her response with restraint. She'd opened Pandora's box.

"I suck at this 'just friends' stuff," she said between fevered kisses.

"Me, too."

In some dim recess of his brain Tony knew this

probably wasn't a smart move. Julie didn't know her mind; she was very likely to reject him again and to regret any kind of intimate contact. But if this was his last chance to convince her they had some amazing chemistry going for them, he wanted to do it right.

He deliberately slowed down the kisses, exploring her mouth in a leisurely way, nibbling her full lower lip. She tasted of something spicy, something exotic he couldn't put a name to.

Although she'd started this, he took full command of it, angling their mouths just right until they fit together, then drinking in the kiss as a man dying of thirst would drink from a well. He slid his fingers into her hair, then one by one found the pins holding it up and slipped them out until the soft strands of golden silk cascaded over his arms.

"You have any deliveries scheduled for today?" he murmured in her ear.

She shivered delicately. "No."

"Any workmen on their way over?"

"Uh-uh."

"Is the door locked?"

"Uh-huh."

He pushed her down onto her back and kissed her some more. "Are you going to tell me to stop?"

She didn't answer for quite some time, choosing instead to kiss his neck. His blood surged hot through his veins.

"No," she finally whispered.

"No what?"

"No, I'm not going to stop you."

"Okay, then." Their fate was sealed. By some miracle, Tony was about to make love to a willing— eager—Julie Polk. He wasn't about to question his good fortune.

He had her paint-spattered T-shirt off in no time. Underneath it she wore an ivory-colored silky wisp of a bra that left little to his imagination, but off it came, as well. Her breasts were creamy and so flawless he was almost afraid to touch them. When he did, Julie closed her eyes and gave a trembling sigh.

"Too many clothes," Julie said.

"I can fix that." Shorts, shirt, shoes, socks, underwear, everything was gone in seconds flat. When Julie looked amused by his rapid-fire striptease, he added, "Firefighters have to learn to dress and undress quickly." He smiled, then cupped her chin in his hand and kissed her again, more aggressively this time. She would never mistake his desire for her as passing for lukewarm.

He considered moving somewhere more comfortable than a hard floor, but then decided that he didn't care if she didn't. Besides, relocating might cause one of them to come to their senses, and he didn't want to risk that. He'd have made love to Julie on the back of a camel, if that was what was the only available option.

He unzipped her shorts and pulled them down her legs. He could undress a woman pretty quickly, too. He paused only briefly to admire how she looked in silky bikini panties that barely covered anything, then they too joined the pile of discarded clothing.

Suddenly, she stiffened and pulled back. "Oh, no."

"What?" Tony thought he would die if she changed her mind now.

"I don't have any birth control." She sounded both relieved and miserable.

"Got it covered—uh, no pun intended." Thank God. For ten years he'd never gone anywhere without protection, whether he thought he would need it or not—not after he'd unintentionally gotten Natalie pregnant.

He honestly hadn't come here with seduction in mind. He'd been holding fast to Priscilla's advice to treat Julie as a friend. But he sure was glad he'd been prepared for anything.

He pulled her on top of him to save her the bite of the wood floor, then reveled in every inch of her bare skin as it touched his. He wanted to feel her everywhere at once. He ran one hand across a smooth flank, then gently cupped one breast, testing its weight, letting the hard nipple scrape across his palm.

His arousal stirred with eagerness.

Julie couldn't believe this was happening. She'd had a lot of mixed feelings about Tony and had wondered if she could change her mind, but she had never imagined they would suddenly come together on the floor behind her bar. She might as well have been tied to railroad tracks, for all the ability she had to halt the inevitable outcome.

As if she really wanted to.

Tony maneuvered so deftly she never even realized it until she felt the press of his arousal against her. He'd already taken care of protecting her—when had he done that? She couldn't remember. But he didn't enter her right away. Instead, he smoothed her hair away from her face and looked deeply into her eyes.

"You know I'm crazy about you, right?"

"Um…" At this point, did it matter?

"I am. I don't just go around making love because I have the chance to. It means something to me. It's important that you know that."

"Uh-huh." Sorry, she was no longer verbal. Her brain was preoccupied with other, more important things. Like processing the ten million sensations coming from below her waist. But she stored his words away for later examination.

"I won't hurt you, will I?"

She was going to hurt *him* if he didn't enter her in the next ten seconds. But all she could do was shake her head. What, did he think that she might be a virgin?

She poised herself over him, her invitation impossible to misunderstand.

Tony grinned. "All right, then." But he didn't rush. He pulled her down on top of him slowly, inch by inch, allowing her to appreciate each new sensation as it came.

He filled her completely, stretched her until she was sure she couldn't accommodate any more, then pushed again.

Oh, she'd had no idea, no idea at all it could feel like this. To her utter surprise, she reached a climax before he'd even started to move. She writhed ecstatically on top of him, trying to keep her cries to a minimum because she was actually shocked by the strength of her response to him.

"Let it loose, Julie," he said. "There's no one here but us." But then his grin faded as his rational side lost control of the situation and his body took over. He thrust into her over and over, rocking them back and forth and side to side and every which way. Her foot caught a broom and sent it toppling with a crash just as Tony reached his own crescendo.

After a few moments of gasping for breath, he laughed. She laughed, too, a lovely release of tension. Weren't they a pair? She sagged against him, her fingers tangled in his hair as their breathing slowed.

"That was one for the record books," he said. "I've heard sex compared to falling off the edge of the world before, but for a minute there I thought I really did."

"I guess we could have gone upstairs first," she said, feeling the first tendrils of embarrassment at the way she'd just acted—like a cat in heat. "But it wouldn't have been much better. I put all my money into the tearoom and I couldn't afford the luxury of a bed."

"A bed is a necessity, babe, not a luxury."

"I'm starting to see why."

He stroked her back, sending aftershock chills through her body.

"So really," she asked drowsily, "how come you just happened to have a condom in your pocket?"

"Be Prepared—that's my motto."

"You were never a Boy Scout."

"How do you know that?"

"Because you were too busy feeling up Girl Scouts to work on merit badges. And besides, they don't give out merit badges for seduction."

He laughed. "You think you've got my number, but you might be surprised. Were you a Girl Scout?"

"Campfire Girl." For all of a couple of weeks, until her mother found out she would have to pay for a uniform. "I need a shower."

"Want some company?"

"No! I… I mean, this is weird. I need time to think about it."

Tony sighed. "I wish women wouldn't think so much."

"Someone has to or we'd still be living in caves. Maybe men are credited with most of the great inventions and advances in society, but only because women told them what to go out and invent."

Tony laughed again, but he did let her go. She rolled to the side and sat up. "I'll be right back, okay?" She pulled on her T-shirt, underwear and shorts—she couldn't wander about naked in the tearoom, not when someone could look in if they had a mind to—and retired to the ladies' room to freshen up. She heard the door down the hall close and knew Tony was doing the same in the other washroom.

She felt more relaxed than she had in a long time.

She washed her hands with vanilla-scented soap, which filled the whole bathroom with a wonderful fragrance. When she was done, she emerged to find Tony leaning against the bar, fully dressed. Her wonderful mood immediately evaporated when she saw the look on Tony's face.

"Julie, there's something I have to tell you."

"What?" she asked warily.

"The, um, condom broke."

"What?" She closed her eyes, then opened them again, panic rising in her chest. This could not be happening. They'd been careful. They'd been responsible. "How did that happen?"

"I'm not really qualified to explain latex failure."

"How can you joke about this? It isn't funny. It's horrible! An unplanned pregnancy is just what I need right now."

"I'm sorry. It's not on my agenda either."

"Well…well, what do we do?"

"I don't know that there's anything to do right now."

Her head started to spin, but there was nowhere to sit down. She put a hand on the freshly painted wall to steady herself. "So we just have to wait to see if I'm pregnant?"

"I'm sorry," he said again, which didn't help. Logically, she knew it wasn't Tony's fault, but she was angry, and he was the closest target.

She sank to the floor and put her head in her hands.

Tony was beside her in an instant. "Hey, look at me."

She couldn't. She was horrified. She'd never

done anything else this crazy and irresponsible in her whole life.

He lifted her chin up and forced her to look at him. "It'll be okay."

"Easy for you to say. You're not the one who's probably pregnant as we speak." She lowered her head into her hands. He wasn't the one whose life would be irrevocably changed if she had a child out of wedlock. She visualized herself working in the tearoom, seating her customers and refilling iced-tea glasses, her stomach looking like a beach ball and no husband in sight.

Wouldn't that impress her high-society clientele?

Meanwhile, he would be off in macho land, on to his next conquest, maybe *engaged*. No, that wasn't fair to color every man with the same brush. Just because Trey had tried to weasel out of his paternal responsibilities didn't mean Tony would do the same thing.

Really, she had no idea what Tony would do if faced with an unexpected child. She didn't know him that well. He *seemed* like a good guy, a good dad to Jasmine. But Julie surely couldn't rely on her own judgment when it came to men. Trey had seemed like a good guy, too.

"You do want kids someday, right?" he asked.

Julie sensed her answer was important to him, so she made it as honest as she could. "Sure, of course. But not now! Anyway, that's not why I'm upset. I'm upset because I did something stupid. I should know better. What a horrible example I'm setting for my sister!" She pressed a hand to her abdomen and willed her panic to go away. Panic wouldn't help anything.

"Do you share everything with Belinda?"

"No, but if I'm pregnant, I won't have to share."

"The chance of that is small."

"Not that small." She sighed. "If I bring a child into the world, I want it to have the benefit of two parents. Two married, committed parents."

Then she remembered that Tony's daughter didn't have that and she backpedaled a bit. "I'm not criticizing the fact you're a single dad, believe me. I'm sure you must have tried to make things work, and it seems like you're doing a great job with Jasmine. Still, to even risk having a child when I'm not in any position to be a good parent—that is just the height of irresponsibility. I broke up with Trey because he did that."

"You know," Tony said carefully, "if you just love your kids, it makes up for an awful lot. Working eighty-hour weeks to provide them with stuff doesn't hold a candle to loving them. Ethan grew up with only one parent. His mom didn't have much money, but she raised him right. They're still really close."

So Tony thought she would do fine as a single mother? *Thanks for the vote of confidence.* But it wasn't exactly the response she would have preferred.

Maybe he was right about one thing, however. One committed parent was probably better than two who didn't care as much. Her parents had gotten married "because they had to." They'd taken responsibility for Julie, but they hadn't been the most devoted mother and father.

Quality, not quantity, was the important thing.

Tony was gazing out into space, lost in thought. He'd mentioned Ethan's mother but not his own. Had he felt loved as a child?

"Tony, I think this was a mistake."

Her words made him flinch, and she immediately wished she had couched her feelings in softer terms.

"We can't take it back," he said.

"No. But we should have a little more sense."

"Aw, you aren't going to give me the 'just friends' speech again, are you? I don't think I could stand that."

Finally, she found a smile. "I guess that doesn't work very well for us, does it? But you can't expect… I'm not ready to… I have to give a hundred percent to the tearoom right now."

"You couldn't even spare one percent for me?"

"Would you really want that?"

"No. I'd like to be the most important thing in your life. I'd like for you to worship the ground I walk on. But given the likelihood of that at this point in your life, I'll take what I can get. At least until you get your life put back together."

She pinched the bridge of her nose. "It's a mess, isn't it?"

"Everyone's life gets messy at some point. But, Julie, I have to ask you something. Do you see any future in it? In us? I'm not saying we should get all serious right away, I'm not saying that at all. But I don't want to be your recreational sex buddy, your boy toy, your gigolo. So if you're saying to yourself, 'Tony's fun, but I could never take him seriously,' or 'Tony's okay till someone better comes along,' tell me now."

She looked at him a long time before answering. "Some woman did a real number on you."

"Not any particular woman," he said. "It's more like a syndrome. Women don't take me seriously."

"For the record, Tony, I'm not thinking any of those things. Right now it's hard to think about the future, at least not anything beyond paying next month's bills. But I don't see you as a diversion. I like you a lot. I want the chance to get to know you better. I certainly wouldn't rule out the possibility that we could be, well, you know…long-term. Someday. Who knows?"

Tony grinned. "That's all I need to hear."

Maybe not all. "I know I'm a little flaky right now. But you can count on one thing from me—I'll be honest. I despise game-playing of any kind. But I want the same from you. If we can just tell each other the truth, maybe this can work out."

He nodded agreement. "Yeah. Absolutely." But it seemed to her that his gaze got just a bit evasive.

Chapter Nine

Tony left because Julie virtually kicked him out, claiming she had work to do and she couldn't do it if he was around distracting her. But she'd given him hope. She'd agreed that they could be together, at least sometimes. Though he would never be content with just crumbs of her affection, he realized that for now that was all she had to offer and he was willing to live with it. For a while.

There was just one teensy fly in the ointment. It was that little speech she'd given about honesty and game-playing.

How would she feel if she knew that the reason he'd approached her in the first place, the reason he'd flirted and pretended to want to help her, was so he could manipulate himself into a position of influence in her life and convince her to reopen Brady's Tavern?

What if she found out? He was in for some merciless razzing from his fellow firefighters when they discovered he and Julie had hit it off. Most of them would only wish him luck, but not all of them. Some were still angry and spiteful that Julie had destroyed Brady's Tavern. Any one of them could let it slip, accidentally or on purpose, that Tony's interest in Julie hadn't originated from the purest of motives.

He should tell her himself, that's what he should do. Maybe she would think it was funny—that he'd set out to seduce her so he could convince her to preserve his bar and had ended up falling for her instead.

Yeah, right. Or maybe she wouldn't think it was so funny.

He would tell her anyway, he decided. So long as that secret remained between them, he wouldn't be able to rest. But he wouldn't tell her yet. Their relationship was too new, too fragile. He would give it a couple of weeks.

He planted some fall flowers in the bed in front of his house, then took Dino for a long walk. Now that the worst of the summer heat had passed, walks were a pleasure again. He let the pup's unbridled affection soothe him. Dogs weren't hard to figure out. Feed them, walk them, pet them, and they'd love you for life. Just like him.

A woman was a bit more complicated, and Julie seemed to be the most complicated of all.

Jasmine arrived that evening, weighed down by a half-dozen shopping bags in different colors. Oh, boy, a little shopaholic in the making.

"Daddy!" She dropped the bags and ran to hug him with all the delicacy of a freight train, and he stumbled backward as they threw their arms around each other.

"Hi, Jazzy. Looks like you bought out the stores."

"Mom took me school shopping today."

"Did you use my card?" Natalie had a VISA she used only for Jasmine-related expenses, and Tony paid the bill.

"Yeah, but we found some good bargains. Did you plant new flowers out front? They look good."

"Yeah, I did. Thanks. Nice change of subject, too." Tony was actually pleased she'd noticed. He'd become a complete yard nut since moving in here. Before, he'd always lived in apartments and hadn't given green things a single thought. But since Priscilla had provided him with any sort of outdoor tool he wanted, so long as he took care of the yard, he'd discovered a new calling.

"Have you seen Julie again?" she asked, the question laced with innuendo. Now how had she figured that out?

"I might have."

"She's sooooo much nicer than Daralee," Jasmine said.

He put his arm around her as they walked toward the kitchen. "You didn't like Daralee? I thought she was pretty nice to you. She bought you a ring, didn't she?"

"'Cause she was trying to impress *you*. She didn't like me at all. If you'd married her, she'd have sent me off to boarding school. I couldn't stand her."

That gave Tony pause. "What about my other girlfriends? Did you hate them, too?"

"Some of them."

He'd never considered how his social life affected his daughter. She'd always been very accepting of whomever he happened to be dating, never jealous or resentful. At least not that she showed him.

"From now on, I want you to tell me if you don't like some girl I'm dating, okay? I need to know these things."

"I like Julie. She's nice—and pretty. Then again, all your girlfriends are pretty."

"You say it like I have a harem or something."

"Also, Julie didn't treat me like a baby."

"I like her, too, kiddo. So what's the homework situation?"

"Done."

"Then you can show me your new clothes. How about that?"

"Okay. Mom said not to show you the price tags. But Daddy, I'm in fourth grade now. How I look is *really* important."

"How you act is more important, Jas." But he didn't feel like giving her a lecture now. "Come on, show me your new duds. I won't look at the price tags."

Tony sat on his daughter's bed, and Jasmine went into the closet to change into her various new outfits, emerging like a model on the runway, gliding across the room with her nose in the air and pirouetting for his inspection.

"Very nice," he said of her latest offering. "The skirt's pretty short."

"Daaaaaddy."

"Get used to it. You'll be hearing it a lot over the next few years. Okay, what else?"

"That's all," she said hastily.

"What's in that bag?" He pointed to a shiny pink bag that Jasmine had kicked off to the side.

"Uh, nothing, Dad. Just underwear and socks and stuff."

He looked more closely at the bag. "From Paris Intimates?"

"I got a bra, okay?" she blurted out.

Tony sat up straight. Had he heard right? "You're only nine years old!" Girls in his family did tend to mature early, but still.

"Almost ten, and I need it! It's really embarrassing!" She burst into tears and stormed out of the room. Moments later he heard the bathroom door slam.

Tony put Jasmine's pillow over his head and groaned. This could not be happening. He would have to spend the rest of his life *not* looking in the vicinity of his daughter's chest, because he didn't want to know whether it was true or not.

A FEW DAYS LATER AT the fire station, Tony had just cooked some french fries and dumped them onto paper towels when Otis strolled into the kitchen. "Smells good. At least you rookies are good for something."

"I don't see how you can smell anything but Ben-Gay, the way you slather that stuff on your old, creaking joints."

Otis narrowed his eyes, then laughed. "Touché. I hate it when rookies can't give as good as they get." He snagged a hot fry, tossing it back and forth between his hands to cool it. "So how are things going with juicy Julie?" He accompanied the question with a leer.

"Okay," Tony said, offering up as little detail as possible. In truth, things were better than okay. Over the past few days he'd been pitching in at the tearoom, helping Julie with various projects, and she'd let him. Though he'd have preferred to take her out to dinner—or even just walk to the park and feed the ducks—at least they were talking, getting to know each other better. Julie had seemed more relaxed and twice more they'd made love—on her lumpy sofa. Not as good as a bed but better than the floor. She had not mentioned the possible pregnancy again, but he knew it was on her mind.

It was on his mind, too.

"You get her into bed yet?" Otis asked.

Tony's whole face tightened. "That topic is not up for discussion."

"So you haven't," Otis said smugly. He put some water on to boil for tea, giving himself an excuse to hang around.

Tony practically bit through his tongue. Otis was deliberately maligning Tony's manhood to get a rise out of him, but he would not give up any details.

"I don't know how you expect to convince that gal to give up her tearoom if you can't even get her into bed."

Tony wasn't normally prone to violence. He'd always been known as the one with the cool head, the prototypical "I'm a lover, not a fighter" kind of guy. But he really wanted to punch Otis. His right hand clenched into a fist.

That was as far as it went, however. If he got involved in a fistfight with a senior firefighter—with anyone, really—while on duty, he'd be in the unemployment line faster than a bullet train. During the first year, rookies could be let go for almost any reason.

If he wanted to defend Julie's honor, he had to do it with words.

"You're still trying to bring Brady's back, right?" He sighed. "It seems pretty hopeless."

"So you're giving up. Man, I knew we shouldn't have sent a boy to do a man's job."

Tony's blood was slowly coming to a simmer, but he sensed a full boil was on the way. "You're welcome to try."

"Not me. I'm not her type. But maybe Carl Dutton. You know him?"

Tony was afraid he did. He was the guy who'd patched up Julie's hand when she'd cut it on the glass and he'd spent far too much time caressing her hand and arm, in Tony's opinion.

"Dutton's been talking about what a hottie Julie is ever since he fixed up her hand. Think maybe I'll tell him the field's wide-open, you've struck out."

Tony turned on Otis, pointing his spatula at him. "You tell Dutton to keep away from Julie. She doesn't need some stud sniffing around her door. She has enough on her plate."

Otis just laughed. "Veracruz, can't you tell when I'm jerking your chain? You got such a bad case for that girl it might as well be tattooed to your forehead. I warned you not to fall in love."

"Otis!"

Both men turned to see Priscilla standing in the doorway.

"Leave Tony alone. Anyway, he's not in love. He hasn't known Julie long enough to be in love. I've been trying to hammer that fact home to him, and you're going to ruin everything."

Otis smiled sheepishly. "Just havin' a bit of fun."

"And get your paws off those french fries or they'll all be gone before the dinner bell rings."

"Yes, Ma'am. Sometimes you sound just like my ex-wife."

"Which one?" Priscilla quipped as Otis set a pitcher of tea on the table.

Otis sauntered out, and Priscilla went to work slicing tomatoes for hamburgers. "You shouldn't let him get to you like that. You know he's just trying to get a rise out of you."

"I know. I don't mind him razzing me so much, but when he talks dirt about Julie, it gets to me."

Priscilla sighed. "There's something you should know. Some of the guys are getting together and pooling their money. They're talking about forming a partnership so they can buy Julie out."

"Really?" The thought was intriguing. If Julie

didn't have that damn tearoom to renovate and open and run, maybe she would have more time for him. He immediately recognized the selfishness contained in that thought, but there it was.

"You're in favor of the idea?" Priscilla asked, surprised.

"I think Julie's tearoom is destined for failure. As much as I'd like to see Brady's reopened, I also don't want her hurt. If she sold out now, she might come out better in the end." But he was pretty sure she wouldn't see it that way.

"There's more to the story. If she doesn't sell, they're talking about buying out her lien holders, then foreclosing if she misses any payments."

Tony winced. "Can they do that?"

"I don't know anything about property law, but Jim Peterson's wife is a real-estate broker, and she said it all depends on how the loans are structured. But it's a possibility."

"Julie could lose everything." That wasn't what he wanted, but he didn't think there was any way in the world she would listen to his advice regarding her property.

Later in the day, Tony talked to Jim Peterson. It was all true—the partnership papers were actually being drawn up. They called themselves the Brady's Consortium. "You don't like the idea?" Peterson asked.

Hell. He'd never felt so torn in his life. If he stuck up for Julie, he'd be seen as a traitor—and he already had enough problems being accepted on equal terms here at the station. But he couldn't honestly say he was in favor of putting pressure tactics on Julie. She was so determined to move forward with her plans. So determined that she wouldn't listen to reason.

"I like Julie," he confessed. "I can't help it. I don't want to see her hurt."

"Look at it this way," Peterson said. "If we let her alone, she'll fail on her own. Then she'll *want* to sell. But I guarantee she won't get as good an offer."

ABOUT A WEEK LATER THE partnership was a reality. Peterson, Otis, Bing Tate and a couple of guys from other stations and other shifts had put it together. They had an offer for Julie—and they wanted Tony to present it to her.

"Since I'm not part of the partnership, I'm not sure I'm the ideal candidate to talk to her," Tony said.

"She's let you in closer than anyone else," Otis pointed out. "She won't let any of the rest of us through the front door. C'mon, do it for Brady's."

"I'll try." But he didn't think he would get very far.

The next day he walked over to the tearoom with papers in hand. Who knew? Maybe Julie would welcome the offer. It seemed fair to him.

She greeted him with a big smile, and his heart lurched as it always did at the sight of her. But she had shadows under her eyes and she looked as if she might have lost weight. She was working too hard.

He let her show him her latest project—a mosaic

countertop made with broken china in the ladies' room. It was a real work of art. "You did that yourself?"

"Uh-huh."

"That's amazing." He had to admit he was impressed with the way things were coming along. All of the woodwork and the floor gleamed with new stain. She had tables and chairs now. Some of the walls had artwork on them. The curtains she'd been sewing, night after night, were finished and ready to hang.

"Listen, Julie, do you have a minute to talk about something serious? I have a business proposition."

"Huh?"

"Just… Let's sit down." They sat at one of the tables, and Tony explained the offer as clearly and succinctly as he could. Her face showed nothing. She was listening, but her expression was carefully blank.

"It's a good offer," he said. "The guys aren't trying to rip you off. You're in the best position right now—before you open. If you should decide to sell later, and let's say the tearoom isn't performing as you hope, the offer will go down." And then he explained about the contingency plan to buy out her lien holders. She needed to know all of it. "I also want you to know that I'm not part of this partnership. I have nothing to gain from this."

She folded her arms and glared at him. "Except to get your bar back."

"That's totally secondary at this point. I don't want to see you get hurt. I think accepting this offer would be the best route for you to take. You'd come out with some significant cash and you could start again somewhere else."

"Start again?" She looked at him as if he was crazy. "After all the work I've put into this? Let me ask you something, Tony. How do you feel about being a firefighter?"

He was thrown off by her question and had no idea where she was going, but he couldn't think of anything to do but answer honestly. "I love it. I love everything about it. I'm just a rookie, but I know this is what I want to do till I'm old and gray."

"And does it occur to you that I might have dreams, too?"

"Well, sure. Everybody's entitled to dream."

"Until recently, I had a career I loved. I was an up-and-coming manager at Bailey-Davidson's and I ran the tearoom there. I loved it. I loved everything about it—the food, the customers, the beautiful chandeliers, the soft music." She got a dreamy expression as she talked about her work.

He knew the basic facts of her previous employment. Her former fiancé and his family hadn't exactly fired her, but she'd been made to feel very uncomfortable and so she'd quit.

"I really didn't know what I was going to do after I left," she continued. "I'd worked at Bailey-Davidson's since I was sixteen. But then Uncle Brady died, and I got this wonderful new opportunity to open my own tearoom.

"Belinda's Tearoom is *my* dream. Owning a

grungy bar is not. Having a pile of cash is not. Sure, I have a brilliant sister to put through college and parents who are depending on this so they can retire with dignity. But I want this for myself, too."

She picked up the papers he'd laid out and shoved them back at him. "You can tell your pals where to stick this offer. I'm not selling."

Well, that hadn't gone well. But had he really expected anything different? Strangely he found himself smiling. He was *glad* she'd refused the offer. And for the first time, he was starting to believe she could make the tearoom a success. Anyone who was that passionate about a dream had an advantage over those just seeking a profit.

"Good," he said. "I hope Belinda's turns out to be the best damn tearoom on the planet."

She stared at him, puzzled, as if she didn't know quite what to make of his sudden about-face.

"I need to get back home," he said. "Jas and I have plans. You want to join us later?"

"I can't," she said. He was getting used to her refusals, though he still had to force himself not to try to cajole her into putting aside her work to have fun. She got cranky when he did.

As he was heading out the door, she called his name.

"Yeah?"

"I'm not pregnant," she blurted out. "So you don't have to worry about that anymore."

He let the news sink in, expecting to feel a rush of relief. But, strangely, he felt a bit let down.

"Hmm. As I recall, you were the one worrying, not me." No, he didn't want another unplanned child. But the thought of having a child with Julie—it wasn't really that scary. He wasn't sixteen anymore.

"You should tell her the truth," Priscilla pronounced during their next shift. They'd gotten stuck with bathroom duty again. It was particularly unrewarding working with Priscilla because she was the world's worst bathroom scrubber. It wasn't that she didn't try. She seemed to put a lot of energy into it. But her efforts were ineffectual. Tony always ended up remopping any floor she'd tried to clean.

Now he had the double pleasure of redoing her work and getting a lecture, too. He probably should have kept his mouth shut, but he'd wanted a woman's perspective on how Julie might react to knowing he'd never married Jasmine's mother.

"Lots of people have babies in their teens," Priscilla continued. "It's not like you did it on purpose. And you're a wonderful father to Jasmine."

"Thanks, but I suspect Julie won't see it that way. I didn't marry Natalie."

"But you would have. You were willing to, right?"

"Of course. It seemed like the only thing to do. But her parents discouraged that. And it was a good thing. We'd never have made it as a married couple. Heck, we'd broken up before we even found out she was pregnant." And he knew it was a lot of strain on a relationship, having a baby. He couldn't understand how any marriage survived it.

Priscilla was quiet for a few moments, leaning against her mop, staring out into space. Her sudden change of mood made him wonder what he'd said wrong. But then she shook herself out of it and returned to her mopping with renewed vigor, spreading dirty water around in circles and ruining everything he'd just cleaned. "But you've stayed on good terms and you've always put Jasmine first. I think Julie would admire that."

"Not given her history."

"What's her history, exactly? All I know is she broke up with a guy not long ago."

"Her fiancée got his housekeeper pregnant and then had the poor girl deported before she could give birth. Julie only found out two weeks before—"

Priscilla gasped.

"What?"

"Trey Davidson. I'd heard some rumors, but I didn't think they were true. He said his fiancée went psycho on him and that's why the wedding was called off. Is he the one?"

Tony tried to figure a way out of this. He wasn't supposed to spread the story around—Julie had made him promise not to.

"Don't worry," Pris said before he could confirm or deny. "I won't say anything to anyone. That's awful!"

"Not only did she lose her fiancé, but she lost her job and her town house."

"It's amazing she bounced back the way she has.

And it's amazing she would get anywhere near another guy so soon. That says something about your powers of persuasion."

Tony finished cleaning the last toilet. He took the mop out of her hands so she wouldn't mess up anything else. "Just for that, I'm going to finish your mopping for you." Or they'd never get out of that bathroom.

"Thanks. I'll go check on dinner."

She was even worse at cooking than she was at mopping. But he let her go. He'd been hoping Priscilla would encourage him not to tell, but no, she had to go and push him to be honest.

Things were going so well between Tony and Julie. Yesterday, Julie had actually decided to take a few hours off from her feverish preparations for tomorrow's grand opening. She'd called Tony, and they'd gone to Kidd Springs Park and had a picnic lunch, then played Frisbee with Dino. Later, they'd gone back to his place and made love—on an actual bed. They'd foraged in his kitchen for dinner, feasting on a strange array of leftover pizza, meat loaf and fresh pears. They'd talked about all kinds of things— even *Moby Dick* and *Ivanhoe,* his current reading project.

She'd stayed the whole night, and Tony had imagined how it could be like that every day. He could definitely get used to it.

If he told Julie all his dirty little secrets, it could end in a heartbeat.

He couldn't do it. Not yet.

Chapter Ten

At five in the morning, Julie opened her eyes and sat bolt upright, her heart pounding. She'd had a nightmare that a pipe had burst and flooded the tearoom.

She'd never been prone to prophetic dreams, but just in case, she raced downstairs in her pajamas to check. All was dark and quiet and everything looked fine.

Her chef, André, would already be at the farmers' market downtown, selecting meat, fish and produce. Lisa, her pastry chef, would be hard at work on a selection of desserts. And somehow it was all going to come together for her first day as a restaurateur.

It had to.

Many people had said it was impossible, but she was so close to running out of money that she needed to get Belinda's open and pulling in cash as quickly as possible. She had sold everything she owned just to get this far—including the baubles

Trey had given her. She had balloon payments to make to her lien holders in a few weeks, and André had demanded a month's salary in advance.

But despite all the setbacks and naysayers, today it was going to happen. She'd installed a professional kitchen in record time, had gotten city permits and even transferred Brady's liquor license so she could sell wine. She'd hired her staff and hung the sign. She'd put up her beautiful curtains, arrayed her brass coffee urns on the bar, arranged the dishes, linens and flatware.

She'd sent out invitations to the highest-income zip codes in Dallas, offering a free dessert to anyone who came in for lunch.

She suspected her first day would be hectic and have its ups and downs. But she knew this business well. She knew what ladies who lunched would like. She'd seen to every detail.

Julie showered and dressed with care in one of her favorite outfits—a designer skirt and silk blouse she'd bought at Bailey-Davidson's a few months ago. Even with her employee discount, the price had been outrageous. But it fit so well and made her feel confident, so it was the perfect choice for today.

As soon as she returned downstairs, her pastry chef arrived with a carload of beautiful cakes, pies and cookies. André, along with his two assistants, was busy preparing the soups and quiches and taking care of all the prep work.

Julie stood in her kitchen and watched her employees moving around the room as if they'd worked there for years. André barked out orders from time to time, and his crew scurried to do his bidding, but he was entitled to be a bit high-strung on this first day.

She double-checked the day's specials—mushroom-and-artichoke quiche, tomato-basil soup and carrot cake—and wrote them up on her chalkboard menu.

It really was happening!

She had made sure that Trey and his parents had received invitations. Would they connect Belinda's Tearoom with Julie Polk? Or would her invitation go right into the wastebasket without a second thought? She fantasized about the Davidsons showing up for the grand opening, unexpectedly encountering Julie or Belinda.

Wouldn't they be surprised?

Julie would be perfectly gracious, of course, acting as if nothing was wrong. Or even as if they were strangers—as if she'd already forgotten them.

She had another fantasy, too, that Tony would come for lunch today. Dressed in a suit, his unruly hair trimmed for the occasion, he would take her hands and exclaim, "You've worked a miracle. I never should have tried to talk you out of opening a tearoom."

Although he'd refrained from saying anything discouraging this past week, she hadn't forgotten his earlier predictions. She wanted to prove him wrong. She wanted to prove everybody wrong.

Tony had made some good points about the challenges Belinda's faced. But she couldn't help the yearning inside her—not just to have a business that made a profit but to have security and respect. To accomplish something, to make her mark.

As opening time drew near, the butterflies went crazy in her stomach. She checked with the kitchen every five minutes to be sure everything was on schedule, until finally André chased her away with a spatula and told her to stay out.

Everything was going too smoothly. It made her suspicious. Nothing was ever this easy for her—nothing.

Then the phone rang. It was one of her newly hired waitresses. "My car won't start," she wailed. "Now I have to wait for the auto club. As soon as they get here, I'll have them drop me at a bus stop, but I'm still going to be at least an hour late. Today of all days!"

Julie understood such things. "It's okay, Sara," she said calmly. "Just get here when you can." She'd scheduled five wait staff, including Belinda, so one person being late wasn't a catastrophe.

Then Tommy, one of her waiters, called in sick.

She'd known things were going too smoothly.

As she was pondering whether to drag one of the chef's assistants out of the kitchen and train him to wait tables, someone pounded on her front door.

An early customer? Surely not. She peeked out the window and saw a Hispanic woman with a baby standing there. The woman looked vaguely familiar, but Julie couldn't place her. She opened the door. "Yes?"

"I'm Eloisa." At Julie's blank look, she continued. "Eloisa Tinajero. I worked at dollar store." And she pointed down the street.

Julie finally recognized the woman as the sweet but insecure clerk from Dollar Olé on the next block, which had gone out of business the week before. She always *tried* to help, but she was hampered by the fact that her English wasn't too good.

"I need job," the woman blurted out rather desperately. "I cook, wait tables, wash dishes—anything. Dollar Olé close. I can't pay my rent."

The poor woman was almost in tears. How and why had she sought out Julie, and on this day of all days? "Come on in," she said. She would at least give the woman a hot cup of coffee.

"You give me job?" she asked hopefully.

Julie thought about it. She was short a waitress. But she needed servers who were experienced and polished—and who could speak flawless English. Still, Eloisa was neat and well groomed. She could at least refill water glasses and clear tables.

"All right. We'll try you out as a…an assistant waitress."

"Oh, thank you. You teach me menu, I can remember."

"What about the baby?"

"Josephina? She can stay with me. She good baby, never cry."

"No, no, she can't stay here. You'll have to find—"

But Eloisa didn't let her finish. She threw her

arms around Julie's neck. "Thank you so much. I work hard, you see."

Julie just closed her eyes. This was surreal. But the craziness was only beginning.

Eloisa made up a pallet for the baby in Julie's office. She nursed the baby and then put her down for a nap, and Josephina went right to sleep. Julie crossed her fingers that the infant's angelic behavior would continue.

Then she didn't have any more time to worry, because the rest of her wait staff was arriving. She gave them their assignments, then asked Annette, whose Spanish was good, to take Eloisa under her wing.

At ten to eleven everything was in place. The bakery case was filled with mouthwatering cakes and pies, cookies, brownies and dessert bars. The brewing coffee provided a subtle background scent. The piped-in music was a concerto.

There was no trace anywhere of that old stale-beer-and-cigarettes stench that had once permeated the place. Everything was clean, stylish, downright beautiful.

Belinda came to stand beside Julie and took her hand. "You really did it. It's an amazing place. I still can't believe you named it after me."

"It's for your future, after all. Let's rip the paper off the windows!"

They did, and in the matter of a few seconds, daylight was pouring in through the sparkling glass. Now it looked like a real restaurant. All they needed was customers.

"Let's go see if anyone's pulled into the parking lot yet," Belinda said. In her eagerness, she made Julie think of Christmas morning.

As they walked through the storeroom, one of the kitchen staff, Marc, came in to grab something from a shelf. He and Belinda collided, then stopped and stared at each other for a heart-stopping few seconds.

"Oh, hi, Marc."

"Belinda. You coming to hear us play tonight?"

"If you can get me in," Belinda said dreamily.

Oh, for heaven's sake. "Belinda," Julie warned once Marc had gone, "you're not going to clubs, are you? You're not legal drinking age yet."

"I don't drink," she said. "I go for the music." She lowered her voice. "And Marc is so gorgeous. I'm glad you hired him."

If Julie had realized Belinda had the hots for Marc, she would have vetoed André's decision to take him on. But she didn't have time to worry about that now. She grabbed her sister's arm. "Come on. We'll talk later."

Belinda seemed to shake herself from a daze. They peeked out the back door. The first car had arrived, a red Mercedes that Julie recognized.

"Uh-oh," she murmured.

"Trouble?"

Julie's stomach tensed. "Megan Von Snell, a former boss from Bailey-Davidson's."

Belinda frowned. "You don't think Trey sent spies to sabotage our grand opening, do you?"

What a horrible thought! "We'll see." They watched covertly as Megan, who'd arrived alone, followed the flower-lined stone path to the front door. Her face was hard to read.

Julie and Belinda quickly retreated through the kitchen and headed back into the dining room in time to watch Megan, in her red power suit, walk confidently past the windows. She paused outside the entrance to peruse the chalkboard menu, nodding with appreciation, and then entered the tearoom.

Her smile was strained as Julie greeted her.

"Julie. I couldn't believe it when I heard what you were doing and I just had to check it out. It was certainly a…brave move, opening in such a neighborhood."

Julie's spine stiffened at the affront to her new home turf. Although she'd only lived here a short time, she'd grown to like the neighborhood. There were so many different kinds of people—young, old, black, white, Hispanic, rich, poor, gay, straight. Here, there were people driving cars, riding bicycles and walking.

It was nothing like the Park Cities condo where she'd lived before losing her job, where the homes, the cars and the people had a certain…sameness.

But the last thing she needed to do was get into an argument with a customer. "The neighborhood is on its way up," she said cheerfully as she seated Megan by the window. "I'd recommend the salmon. It's very fresh."

Megan's smile warmed slightly. "Thanks, that sounds terrific. And a glass of Chablis."

Julie placed the order and then noticed something out the window. Several firefighters from across the street were gathering around a grill they'd set up in their driveway, which now had bright flames shooting up into the sky. One of the men carried a huge plate of what looked like ribs. She could only imagine what the air was going to smell like in a few minutes, and it wouldn't put her customers in the mood for salad or quiche.

To top it off, the guys had brought out a boom box, and with the flick of a switch Julie was treated to some particularly bad rap music. It wasn't loud enough to qualify as a nuisance—not that the police would do anything about it if she complained. It was just annoying, something her customers would *never* hear in North Dallas.

She had to do something. She alerted Belinda, asking her to hold down the fort, then left the tearoom and marched across the street. One of the doors to the apparatus room was open, so she entered there rather than ringing the bell at the front door. She found a couple of firefighters carrying a second barbecue grill toward the driveway. One of them was the one who had patched up her hand.

"Carl, right? I need to see your captain, please," she said succinctly. The two men looked at each other.

"He's pretty busy," Carl said uneasily.

"Take me to him now or I'm going higher. I'll go to the chief or the mayor if I have to. This is harassment and it's affecting my livelihood. I'd like to handle this matter quietly." Her threat was implied. If she couldn't resolve this immediately, things would get messy.

Something about her determination killed their cocky grins, and they took her to the captain's office. He was a silver-haired man with a big belly and he seemed to be busy with a great deal of paper on his desk.

"What is it?" he barked. Then he looked up. "Oh, excuse me. Can I help you?"

"You can tell those men out front to please turn down their music and to refrain from blowing their smoke across the street."

"Well, now, I can't order the wind to blow in any particular direction."

"But you can tell the guys to turn down the gangsta rap music."

The captain rolled his eyes. "Dutton," he said to Carl, who was lingering in the doorway to witness the fireworks, "tell whoever's out front to cut it out. Gangsta rap. Jeez."

"Thank you," Julie said, satisfied that at least one problem was solved. She returned to her tearoom, took a deep breath and rejoiced in the fact that at least a few of the tables were occupied.

"What is going on?" Belinda whispered as she passed by carrying a pitcher of raspberry iced tea.

"We're being harassed, that's what. But everything's under control now. Sort of."

Things remained under control for five more

minutes—until two men in overalls and straw hats entered the tearoom, wanting to be seated.

Julie recognized one of the men from the auction. More firefighters. Though their mode of dress was not exactly elegant, she had no choice but to seat the men. She hadn't posted a dress code anywhere, and to turn them away would be inviting a scene.

"Right this way, gentleman," she said with her most gracious smile, thanking her lucky stars that most of the tables in the front section of the restaurant were filled by now. She seated them in the back, where they wouldn't be immediately visible to anyone who was just arriving.

"Oo-ee!" one of them said as he passed by tables of well-heeled diners. "Ain't this sump'n fancy."

"Kinda reminds me of that whorehouse we visited in Nevada," the other one said, earning several outraged stares.

Julie was dying a thousand deaths, but she'd be damned if she'd let them see she was ruffled. She seated them and handed them each a menu. "Can I get your drink orders, gentlemen? How about some peach or raspberry iced tea or perhaps a glass of chardonnay?"

"Got any beer?"

"No, I'm sorry, we don't serve beer."

"Shame. Bring us some Cokes."

"Yes, sir. Your server will be right with you to tell you about today's specials."

For the next few minutes the men talked in loud voices, scratched themselves and belched. But their waitress treated them just like any other customers and they had to order if they wanted to stay. When their food arrived, they got considerably quieter.

"I think they like the food," Belinda observed.

Another battle won.

"Do you know if Mom's coming?" Belinda asked. Julie had made a point of inviting her parents. She knew her father wouldn't want to come. Aside from the fact he would hate this kind of place, he rarely left the house these days. But she'd thought maybe her mother might want to see what she'd done.

"She's not coming," Julie said. "She had to work."

"Oh, you'd think she could have taken time off just this once. How often do her daughters open a tearoom?"

"I don't think she really understands what we're doing here," Julie said, but her mother's lack of interest still stung.

"She doesn't try to understand," Belinda said. "Hey, look who's here."

Tony. For some reason, every bit of self-confidence Julie had been nursing deserted her. She'd invited him, of course, but she hadn't been sure he would come. His fellow firefighters would see it as a betrayal. In fact, they'd given him a real hard time about his friendship—relationship—with her.

And yet here he was. It was heartwarming to see him walk through the door, but scary, too. If her grand opening bombed, she didn't want him, of all people, to witness it.

Priscilla was with him. Julie greeted the two of them with a stiff smile. "Your brethren have been doing their best to spoil my grand opening."

"Oh, yeah. We saw." Tony nodded behind him, indicating the barbecue party across the street. "Just ignore them."

"It's pretty hard. Every time the door opens, I get a whiff of burning pork."

"Well, even if those guys are being jerks," said Priscilla, "we're here to support you."

Julie put a hand to her forehead. "I'm sorry, I shouldn't be so grumpy." She grabbed some menus and led them toward the back so they could see for themselves what she had to contend with.

"Bud." Priscilla greeted one of the men with a nod. "Didn't you tell me you wouldn't set foot in a tearoom? Charlie. Nice outfit."

"Traitors," the one called Bud said under his breath.

Julie seated the newcomers a couple of tables away from the straw-hat duo so they couldn't easily trade barbs.

"I can't believe they're being so mean," Priscilla said. "Those guys are normally pretty nice."

"They're behaving now," Julie said. "Once they got their food and realized it was good." She took drink orders and then said, "Thank you for coming. I know you're risking the wrath of your coworkers."

"We're trying to be good neighbors," Tony said.

"He just wants the free dessert," Priscilla added. "But I'm *dying* to try the food. I heard André Le Croix is working for you."

"He is," Julie confirmed. At an exorbitant salary, too. But if people liked the food as much as she hoped, it would be worth every penny. "Enjoy your meal. And please let me know if there's anything I can do better."

For the next little while she was too busy to think as she paused to chat with customers at each table. She hadn't drawn the crowd she'd hoped for, but it was early days yet.

Eloisa seemed to be doing well. She wasn't taking lunch orders, as she wouldn't be able to understand or answer questions about the food. But she was delivering and clearing plates, refilling water and tea and doing so with grace and poise.

An older matron signaled Julie, who hurried to her table. "Yes, Mrs. Blankenship. What can I do for you?"

"You know me?" she asked, surprised. "I wasn't aware we'd had the pleasure. Although you do look familiar."

"I used to work at Lochinvar's," Julie admitted.

"Oh, of course. Well, I was just a little curious about this place when I got the invitation. I didn't realize it would be such a long drive."

"I appreciate your taking the time to give us a try," Julie said diplomatically. "Are you enjoying the food?"

"I found the chicken a little dry but otherwise very passable."

Julie remembered that Mrs. Blankenship always complained about the food at Lochinvar's. *Passable* was a high compliment.

"I'll pass your comments along to my chef." His reputation as well as hers was riding on the success of Belinda's. Of course, he'd paid more for the raw ingredients than she'd budgeted—more than she'd been accustomed to paying when she'd managed Lochinvar's. But he was a genius. She'd tasted the chicken herself and had found it to be perfection.

A younger woman rushed up to the table. "Mother, you'd better come. The police are towing your car!"

Chapter Eleven

"What?" Julie said at the same time as Mrs. Blankenship.

"They said the meter was expired."

"Oh, for heaven's sake, half those meters on Jefferson don't work and they're *never* enforced."

"Well, the cops are out today in numbers," the young woman said. "A ticket I could understand, but towing?"

Julie stalked outside, and sure enough a tow truck down the block was dragging a gold Cadillac out of its parking space. Farther down, she could see another tow truck. Ah, and the smell of burning pork, stronger than ever.

Julie could throw a fit, but what good would that do? The police had the right to enforce parking laws, though she suspected their sudden attention to the area surrounding Belinda's was not coincidental.

For the rest of the afternoon, Julie waited for another shoe to drop. But she heard nothing more from the firefighters. The men in their straw hats paid for their meals and even left a hefty tip—and they looked a little ashamed as they made their exit. By three o'clock, when the last customer left, the dessert case was nearly cleared out and everyone was exhausted.

But it was over. She'd survived her grand opening.

She'd been wrong about the last customer leaving, though. One remained.

Tony had been lurking in the back, nursing a cup of coffee and lingering over his apple-pecan pie long after Priscilla had left.

Now he approached the cash register, where Julie was closing out the day's receipts. "If you have a couple more desserts, I'll buy them to take home. The pie I had was incredible."

"Thank you. I'm surprised to see you're still here."

"I stuck around in case any more of my coworkers decided to have fun at your expense. Plus, I enjoyed watching everything you've worked so hard for coming together."

"At least your buddies didn't give me any more trouble. But thanks for watching out for me." He looked so handsome in his creased khakis and starched shirt. She couldn't recall ever seeing him quite so dressed up. He'd gotten a haircut, too, just as in her fantasy.

Her heart did its mad flutter as she boxed up a couple of desserts. She added some chocolate cookies for Jasmine.

"Were your parents impressed with what you've done?"

"I invited them, but they couldn't make it."

"They didn't come to the grand opening?" Tony asked, surprised. "I mean, your mother owns the place."

"My mom had to work, and my dad doesn't go anywhere without her. He can't drive himself." Julie tried to filter the hurt out of her voice. Her parents had never understood Julie's ambition or Belinda's aspirations to attend "some hoity-toity school in the east," as they put it.

"I invited my dad to my graduation from the fire academy," Tony said. "But he didn't show."

She squeezed his hand in commiseration. "I guess our parents do the best they can."

A baby's cry coming from the kitchen reminded Julie she had another big problem to contend with.

Eloisa and Josephina.

Tony's head swiveled, his attention drawn by the sound. "Is that a baby?"

"Yes. Tony, you speak Spanish, right?"

"Yeah, sure. Why?"

"That woman who just came out of the kitchen with the baby is Eloisa. Could you explain to her that I'm very happy with her work and I'd like her to continue with me? But she's going to have to fill out papers. And she absolutely must find child care. I don't want to be hard-hearted, but I can't have a crying baby here."

"Sure, I can talk to her."

After Eloisa had finished tending to the baby, he motioned for her to join him at a table. She protested at first—she wanted to keep working. She intended to work until there was no more work left to do and she wasn't too proud to get her hands dirty. Her determination to do her job well made Julie think of herself when she was first out in the working world. She had always worked twice as hard as anyone else, asking questions, finding out what it would take to get a raise or promotion and then following instructions to the letter.

Tony, ever persuasive, took a heavy bus tray from Eloisa and set it down. The two settled at a table and carried on a conversation in rapid-fire Spanish, of which Julie could not understand a word.

She wished she'd paid better attention in her high school Spanish classes. She would dearly love to know what they were saying to each other.

Julie continued to count receipts, watching the two from the corner of her eye. Every so often Eloisa would point to Julie. And then she started crying, and Tony patted her on the shoulder.

Julie couldn't help feeling a twinge of jealousy. Eloisa was very pretty. And Tony, being a firefighter, had that rescue gene in him. Would he take her home and feed her?

After a few minutes more, Eloisa came over to Julie and hugged her. "Thank you, Miss Julie. I be here tomorrow early for papers." She looked uncertainly at Tony.

"She needs bus fare to get home," Tony said. "I can cover it…"

"No, no, her share of the tips is more than enough

to get her home." Julie pulled some ones from the petty-cash box and handed them to Eloisa, making a quick note for bookkeeping purposes.

Finally she managed to get Eloisa out the door. There was only a little bit of work left.

"You did really well today," Tony said. "Grace under pressure. And I liked the food. I actually ate quiche. It's not much different than pot pie."

"It's a miracle."

He laughed. But then he sobered. "What you did for Eloisa was generous."

"She's a good worker and a fast learner. I'd be stupid to turn her away."

"She doesn't have any references—her previous employer skipped town. She doesn't even have a permanent address and she speaks very little English."

"I was desperate for another waitress. I'm not a saint."

"Not every woman would be so open-minded. She's in a very bad place. Her husband left her, disappeared, took all their money. And then she lost her job when Dollar Olé closed."

Steam nearly came out of Julie's ears. She was tired of hearing about men who didn't take responsibility for their children. "All the more reason for me to help her out."

It amazed her how little she'd even thought of Trey the past few weeks. His betrayal, which only two months ago had devastated her and caused her to cry for days, hardly gave her a twinge now. "I have a good feeling about Eloisa. She just needs a leg up."

She started for the kitchen, but Tony caught her arm and pulled her against him. She resisted at first, but then she yielded, letting him kiss her.

"We should go out and celebrate," he said.

"Oh, Tony, I can't. I have so much… Ah, I wish you wouldn't do that."

He kissed her under her ear. "I've been really good, not bugging you."

"I know. But I've got work to do. It went well today, all things considered, but there are adjustments to make. André is a talented chef, but he's a bear to work for. Marc, his assistant, walked out in a huff a few minutes ago." She forced a smile. "But everything's okay."

"I guess it was a good thing you weren't too busy in the dining room."

"That's one way to look at it." After that flurry of early activity, customers had only trickled in.

"Are you worried?"

"A little. But it's just my first day. I have some ads running next week. And they're doing an article about me on the Oak Cliff Web site. I just have to survive until word of mouth starts to spread."

"It will. The food is really good here. Although I still say you need hamburgers and beer…."

She pulled away, thinking. Had she been too inflexible about her vision for Belinda's? "You know, maybe you're right. How hard would it be to add a hamburger to the menu? And maybe a few microbrewery designer beers."

Tony couldn't believe she would even entertain

the idea. She'd been dead set against it a few weeks earlier. Maybe things were going worse than he thought. "You know, if you need a loan or something, just to tide you over until…"

"Oh, no, no, no. I think that's a very bad way to start off a relationship."

"Why? I trust you. You're good for it."

"Unless the restaurant goes south. No, I already owe a lot of other people money. I don't want to add you to the list." She waved away his concern. "It's okay. Business will pick up next week, and I'll find someone to replace Marc."

"Still, the offer stands. I don't have a boatload of cash, but I have some."

"Thank you, Tony. But no." She looked at her watch. "Isn't Jasmine due home from school right about now?"

"Yeah, I guess I better go. Natalie told me Jasmine's been wearing makeup at school and washing it off before she comes home. We have to have a little chat."

Julie laughed. "Oh, man. Isn't she young for that? I didn't want to wear makeup until I was at least twelve."

"She is so advanced for her age I honestly don't know what to do."

"Man. I don't envy you when she reaches her teens."

It was on the tip of Tony's tongue to mention that, if he had his way, Julie would be Jasmine's stepmom by the time she became a teenager. But he stifled the comment. Priscilla was still coaching him, every chance she got, that he had to give the relationship time and let it grow at its own pace. He always wanted to rush things.

Priscilla still insisted he couldn't be in love with Julie, that it was too soon. Tony wasn't so sure. That ache in his chest every time he saw her and the fact that he shared her doubts and anxiety about the success of the tearoom—what was that if not love?

"Jasmine will be a handful. She just bought her first bra. I can't believe it."

"Wow. Does she really need it?"

"Her mother says she does."

"Do you get along well with your ex?" Julie asked casually.

"Oh, sure. Natalie's great." He toyed with the idea of confessing that Natalie wasn't really his "ex," at least not in the way Julie meant. But he decided now was the wrong time. Maybe tonight.

Julie sent Tony on his way with a smile and a promise, but when she turned back toward her tiny office, her heart was heavy. She'd put on a brave face, but she was worried. Certainly her opening hadn't produced the crowd she'd been hoping for.

She sat down at her desk and started totaling receipts, but her mind was so clouded with doubt she had a hard time making the appropriate entries in her bookkeeping program. She was exhausted. Happy that she'd survived her first day but daunted by the thought that she would have to get up and do it all again tomorrow.

What if she was wrong? What if this neighborhood simply wasn't ready for an upscale tearoom? She'd seen a few of the locals stop, look at the chalkboard with interest, then shake their heads and walk on. Had the prices scared them away? They were a little lower than what Lochinvar's charged for similar fare. But this wasn't Park Cities.

What did she know about running a business, anyway? A year at a tearoom with an established clientele and employees who'd been in the kitchen forever hadn't prepared her for the headaches she was facing at this moment.

She'd known from the beginning that failure was a possibility. But she'd brushed that reality under the rug as much as she could, confident that she could *will* Belinda's into being a success. Having Marc walk out because of André's temperamental outbursts had thrown her for a loop.

By the time she'd finished adding up the receipts, she was more depressed than ever. If she made this amount every day, she might be able to make her first payroll. But there wouldn't be much left for overhead. Worse, she had a balloon payment coming up. She'd been counting on sufficient cash flow to persuade a bank to let her roll it over into a longer-term loan. Now she put her head down on her desk and wept from exhaustion.

TWO DAYS LATER TONY was on duty, digging in to a dinner of grilled sausage, au gratin potatoes, coleslaw and pound cake. "A little heartier than what your girlfriend serves at lunch, I'll bet," said Bing Tate, who could be really annoying when he wanted to be.

Tony refused to be drawn into an argument. "It's good," Tony said. And it was. It was easy to see how some firefighters gained weight. Maybe Priscilla and Julie were on to something with their insistence on eating healthier fare.

The shift was dull. At close to midnight, Tony knew he should try to get some sleep. But he found himself in the fitness area, lifting weights and watching out the window. The last light had gone off in Julie's apartment an hour ago, after he'd spoken to her briefly on the phone to wish her good-night.

Otis joined him, hopping on the treadmill. Oh, joy.

"Got to run off some of those potatoes," he said. "You ever notice how we don't eat anything green around here?"

"You're starting to sound like Priscilla."

"Well, she's right about some things. Ruby says I ought to lose some weight. She doesn't think I'm sexy enough."

Tony didn't care to think about Otis and *sexy* in the same sentence.

"She dragged me to Belinda's yesterday."

"Really?" That was a shock.

"It wasn't half-bad. I could have eaten twice as much food as they put on the plate, but it tasted good."

"The portions are ladylike. On purpose," Tony said.

"Your girlfriend doesn't want men eating there?"

"Not so much. She likes to keep the atmosphere girlie. But a few well-behaved men, that's okay."

Otis laughed. "How's she gonna make any money alienating half the population?"

Tony shook his head. "Good question."

"I noticed she didn't have many customers."

"No."

"You think she'll stay open?"

"I don't know," Tony said. The thought of Julie having to close Belinda's...well, it made his chest ache to imagine her failing. But maybe the new ads and word of mouth would bring in more customers.

"I hope she makes it," Otis said, surprising Tony. "I still miss Brady's. But it's pretty amazing what your Julie's done with the place. I guess she's entitled to have her tearoom."

"I thought you guys wanted to buy her out?"

"We talked to some of the lien holders, but no one can agree on terms, so we're pretty well dead in the water."

There was one avenue the partnership hadn't considered. They could contact Julie's mother. She was the actual owner of the building and the business, after all. As little as the woman seemed to care about Julie's business, she might just accept a wad of cash. But apparently the Brady's Consortium hadn't realized that, and Tony wasn't going to tell them.

Tony's attention was drawn back to the window. A light downstairs. Was Julie up and prowling? He knew she had trouble sleeping sometimes. If she was awake, he would call her again. He liked hearing her voice.

But now he wasn't sure whether he'd seen a light at all. Maybe it was just a reflection from a passing motorist's headlights.

The treadmill wound to a halt, and Otis joined Tony at the window. "What are you starin' at?"

"I thought I saw a light. Shouldn't be any lights on downstairs this time of night. There. I did see something…."

"That's no light," Otis said. "That's a fire!"

Chapter Twelve

Tony had no memory of how he got downstairs, how he got into his turnout gear. Next thing he knew, he was facing Captain Campeon. "Julie's in there. She lives in the apartment above the restaurant. I'm going over on foot." He didn't wait for Campeon's okay. He took off at a dead run, dodging a car that ignored his signal to stop, speed-dialing Julie's number on his cell as he ran.

Her answering machine had picked up by the time he reached the parking lot in back. Maybe she wasn't home. But where would she be?

He banged on the separate door that led to her apartment. "Julie, pick up the phone!" he yelled into his cell. Then he shouted, "Julie, answer the door!" He got no response to either demand.

What if she had already been overcome by smoke? He had no way of knowing how advanced the fire was, but if they could see flames through the window, it might have been burning for hours.

Both doors in back were steel. No hope of getting

through them without serious tools. Every window was barred—the place was like Fort Knox. She had no fire escape, though Tony had at least bought her a rope ladder. But a ladder would do her no good if she was unconscious.

He'd made a stupid mistake arriving without any tools. Fueled by anger and frustration with himself, he ran back to the front of the building. The engine had pulled across the street, its red-and-white lights flashing eerily in the darkness. Ethan and McCrae were busy cutting through the front door with a K-12 rotary saw.

Tony peered through the windows. He couldn't see flames, but that might be because the tearoom was full of smoke.

He again reported to Campeon, who was now the official Incident Commander. "I can't raise her. Request permission to take a ladder to an upstairs window."

"Affirmative," Campeon said with his usual military precision. "Take Granger."

Tony snagged Otis and filled him in on their assignment as he pulled a wall ladder off Engine 59. He heard the door give way. Glass shattered. Smoke poured out. They got the ladder in place in record time. With his breathing apparatus on, his ax ready, Tony climbed faster than he'd climbed any ladder in his life. Otis trailed behind, his breathing labored. "Wait for me, eager beaver. Man, I got to get in better shape."

Wait, hell. With one sharp crack with his ax Tony

tore through the window screen and glass. In moments, he was through. "Julie!"

He was relieved to see the smoke was only a thin haze on the second floor. The bedroom was empty except for a chest of drawers. Still no bed. He opened the door into the living room, where the smoke was a bit thicker—and thicker still toward the door leading downstairs.

God, what if she'd been downstairs, tending to some detail? Maybe she hadn't been able to sleep and she'd gone downstairs to check on something?

Then he saw her. She was lying on the couch, fully clothed. "Julie!" he bellowed and he reached her in two strides.

She jolted awake. "Huh?"

Tony's knees nearly buckled with relief. "There's a fire downstairs. You have to get out."

She whipped her head around, still a bit disoriented. "A fire? In the *tearoom?*" She was vertical in a flash and heading toward the door. He tried to snag her arm as she passed, but his gloves made him clumsy and he missed her.

"Not that way!" he yelled. "The window."

But it was too late. She opened the door, and hot smoke billowed in from downstairs.

He yanked her away from the opening, which would help ventilate downstairs but wasn't too healthy for them up here. "The window!"

She looked at him as if he were crazy. "My tearoom is on fire. I'm not going to jump out the window like a scared rabbit."

"It's being taken care of."

"But how…?" She paused to cough.

"Are you coming or do I have to drag you?" Tony heard Otis reporting their situation to IC. She made a move toward the door again, but Tony held fast to her arm.

"My tearoom," she tried again.

So did Tony. He didn't want to have to drag her out the window, but he would if he had to. "Your safety is more important than a tearoom."

Her direct look challenged him, and then she slumped in defeat. Thank God.

"There's no one else here, is there?"

"No, of course not." Coughing now, she allowed herself to be led to the bedroom window, casting only a glazed glance at the broken glass on the floor.

Tony went out first, then helped Julie. "Careful, there's some sharp glass."

She made no response, but she was agile enough on the ladder to climb down on her own. Tony was there to prevent her from falling, but she didn't need his help. Otis followed.

Tony led Julie along the sidewalk, well out of danger. He pulled off his breathing gear. "Stay here. Don't move. And stay out of the way until we're sure this thing's out."

She peered through the darkness toward her building. "I don't even see any smoke down here. Tony, what happened?"

"We'll know more in a bit." He left her alone—he had no choice. He had a job to do, and his job wasn't to comfort her. But Peterson and Kevin Sinclair, on paramedic duty, were heading for her, so she wouldn't be alone for long.

When he reported back to Captain Campeon, he was relieved to learn the fire was under control. The flames had been limited to the storage room and office area. But the firefighters' work wasn't done. They had to continue spraying down hot spots and tearing into walls and ceilings to make sure every single cinder was cold and dead.

Civilians always complained about the damage firefighters did, even during a small fire—the water, ashy footprints everywhere and especially the holes—whether they were made for ventilation or to check for fire inside walls and ceilings, where it usually traveled. Tony could only imagine what Julie would have to say. But better some superficial damage than to walk away too soon, before the fire was truly out.

The captain had no further tasks for him other than to direct traffic and keep people away, which normally wasn't a problem for a small fire at this time of night. Still, there were always a few "blue lighters" who monitored the fire department's radio and came to watch.

After directing a car to maneuver around the engine, he glanced back to where he'd left Julie. She was gone.

"Damn. Otis, I'll be back in a second."

Otis gave him a knowing nod. "Okay. But if you're looking for your girl, she's over there."

"What?" He looked where Otis pointed. And there was Julie, practically spitting nails in the captain's face.

Not good. He knew people got emotional when they saw their homes or their businesses in flames. They said and did things they didn't mean. But it wasn't safe to lose your cool in front of Campeon. The guy had the compassion of a block of ice.

Tony knew Julie wasn't thinking straight. Damn, he should have made sure she was safely with the paramedics before leaving her.

He approached Julie and the captain cautiously, just as Julie was yelling, "I demand that you get those men out of my restaurant immediately. Just *look* what they're doing! Who's going to pay for this mess? The fire is out, why are they still stomping around in there, breaking things?"

"Ma'am," the captain said, "until that fire is out, you don't own that restaurant—I do."

Tony touched her shoulder. "Julie…"

She whirled around, not appearing happy to see him in the least. "What?"

Campeon grimaced. "Veracruz, control your girlfriend."

Tony tried to take her arm, intending to nudge her back to a safer vantage point. Though it looked as if the fire was out, it was wise not to draw premature conclusions.

Julie shook him off. "Control me? Look, just because you're sleeping with me doesn't mean you can *control* me."

Tony wasn't sure whether Campeon was about to explode or burst out laughing.

Bing Tate overheard the exchange and paused in his task of putting the saw back on the engine. He flashed an evil grin.

"I thought all along we sent in the wrong man," he said to Tony but loud enough that anyone on the whole block could hear. "If you'd given the job to me, this place'd still be Brady's."

Tony had never wanted to sock a man in the nose as bad as he did at that moment. Tate, not one of his favorite people to begin with, had timed his barb to inflict the maximum damage—when Julie was already in an emotional state, watching her tearoom turned into a shambles.

Julie narrowed her gaze. "What are you talking about? Tony, what's he talking about?"

"Hey," Campeon barked. "This isn't *The Young and the Restless.* You," he said to Julie, "get away from my fire and let me do my job. I want you across the street. I'll tell you when it's safe for you to reenter the building and I better not see you again until then or I'll have you arrested. And *you*—" he turned on Tony "—get back to your job!"

"Yes, sir."

Something in Campeon's voice made Julie back down. She shuffled away, but she couldn't resist one final barb. "Guess you guys got what you wanted after all. Congratulations."

Oh, man, did he have some explaining to do.

As he returned to his job of directing traffic, Tony

saw more bad news. Roark Epperson's car had pulled up behind the engine. It was standard procedure to call in an investigator on any fire that involved property damage. But the fact they'd called in Epperson—the big gun—meant someone really did suspect arson.

At least Tony knew the investigator would be thorough.

First making sure the captain was busy with other things, Tony met Epperson as he exited his SUV. They shook hands.

"What's going on here?" Epperson asked casually, still shaking off residual drowsiness. He'd probably been warm in his bed less than an hour ago.

"I can't tell you much. What I heard is that the fire was confined to two small rooms in the back of the restaurant. I was never inside, except on the second floor to get the owner out of the building."

"That woman who destroyed Brady's?" Epperson asked, cocking one eyebrow. "She was upstairs?"

Tony knew resentment still ran high among some firefighters. He also knew this wasn't the time or place to try to defend Julie. "That's the one. She's over there if you want to talk to her." Tony nodded across the street, where Julie had finally succumbed and allowed the paramedics to give her a chair and some oxygen. "But trust me, she doesn't know anything. I had to break a window to get to her." He nodded toward where Otis was taking down the ladder. "She was in a dead sleep and had no idea what was going on."

Epperson seemed a bit more alert as he pulled a notebook out of his back pocket and started taking notes. "You let her get dressed?"

"What? Oh, no, she was like that."

"Shoes, too?"

"She must have fallen asleep watching TV or something."

"Is her business doing well?" Epperson asked, again too casually.

Tony pinched the bridge of his nose. "She just opened a couple of days ago. So if you're thinking insurance fraud or something, you're barking up the wrong tree. Julie had nothing to do with setting the fire."

The investigator studied Tony. "Oh, wait a minute. You're the one who tried to get her to change her mind about Brady's by..."

"Damn! The department grapevine is about to strangle me."

Epperson grinned. "If you're sleeping with her, I can't believe a word you say, even if you are a brother." And he sauntered toward the soggy tearoom, leaving Tony cursing silently and wondering if he'd just gotten Julie in a whole lot of trouble.

Julie did need money. He knew she had a loan payment coming due before long. Still, it was utterly ridiculous to think she would destroy something she loved so much. But Epperson didn't know Julie. And the property owner was often the first suspect in an arson case.

Damn.

Now that the shock had worn off, Julie felt sick to her stomach. Her beloved tearoom, up in flames. They wouldn't even let her see the damage. Although the building was intact and there was no more smoke or fire, she could only imagine the damage inside. They wouldn't let her near the place. It was *her* tearoom, her building, but the firefighters were treating her like some pesky mosquito.

She could only watch from across the street while two paramedics hovered over her. They seemed sincere in wanting to comfort her, but at this pointshe didn't trust anyone's motives. They were probably suppressing the urge to dance a jig because Belinda's was burning. They probably thought it was what she deserved for destroying their precious bar.

Then there was Tony. The more she tried not to think about what that other fireman had said, the more it plagued her.

We sent in the wrong man.... If you'd given the job to me, this place'd still be Brady's.

What exactly had he meant by that? If she struggled, she could probably come up with an innocent explanation. But the play of emotions across Tony's face had said it all. First he'd looked stricken and then undeniably guilty.

So Tony had been "sent" to deal with her somehow. To reason with her? To intimidate her? He'd definitely tried the first, not the second. But somehow she suspected there was a lot more to it than that.

The determined approach of a strange man in

civilian clothes ended her speculations for the moment. She'd spotted his arrival a few minutes earlier. Though he hadn't been wearing any protective gear, he'd been allowed to roam freely and talk to anyone. Now, apparently, he'd decided to talk to her.

She didn't feel good about this.

She stood up as he drew closer, so he wouldn't tower over her. He still topped her by half a head. And talk about intimidation! Though he wasn't half-bad looking, the steely look in his eyes scared the hell out of her.

"Roark Epperson," he said, extending his hand. "I'm an arson investigator." The way he said it, it sounded like *ahs-sun investigatah*. Definitely not from around here.

She shook his hand distractedly, riveted by a sudden realization. "You think my fire was caused by arson?" The thought hadn't even occurred to her. Though she had no idea what had caused the fire, she'd assumed it was something like faulty wiring or a short—even spontaneous combustion, what with all the cooking oils and paper towels. Arson had never entered her mind.

"I won't know until I take a closer look. But don't worry, it's standard procedure to call in an arson investigator when the cause of a fire can't be easily determined. Many turn out to be accidental."

"But not all."

"That's what keeps me employed. Let's go inside the station, where I can get a cup of coffee and we can sit down." It wasn't an invitation, it was an order.

And though only a few minutes ago Julie had been feeling feisty and argumentative, all the starch had gone out of her now.

Arson. Who would hate her enough to want to burn down her restaurant? She wasn't winning a popularity contest with any number of people at the moment. But she couldn't imagine any of them taking their anger so far. A little graffiti was one thing. Burning down a building was something else entirely. Besides, who would have had access?

Roark Epperson brought her a cup of coffee in a chipped mug. "I added some milk. Hope you don't mind."

"That's fine." She took a sip. But when it landed in her stomach, it immediately started to burn, so she set the mug aside. "You didn't grow up in Texas," she said.

He smiled. "No. Boston."

"Ah, that's why you sound like a long-lost Kennedy."

He shrugged boyishly. But then he was all business. He asked her a few preliminary questions, establishing her identity and her status as the daughter of the building's owner, plus the fact she operated a business downstairs and lived above it. He asked who had locked up the restaurant, who'd been the last to leave. The answer to both questions was Julie herself.

"Belinda's has only been open...how long?"

She sighed. "Three days." Not even long enough for her to find out if she was any good as a restaurateur. "Oh, God, my employees. My sister! She quit a really good job at a steak house to wait tables at Belinda's. And poor Eloisa."

Epperson ignored her outburst. "When officers Veracruz and Granger entered your apartment to alert you, you were asleep—is that right?"

"Yes."

"On the sofa?"

"Yes. I don't actually have a real bed."

"So you went to sleep fully clothed?"

She looked down at herself. "I guess so. I honestly don't remember. But I've been working some ridiculous hours." She'd pretty well fallen asleep standing up in the shower the day before. Only the blast of cold when the hot water ran out had revived her.

"And last night, when did you fall asleep?"

"It would have been this morning. I know I was up past midnight. But the exact time...I just don't know."

"Were you with anyone last night?"

"No. I was alone."

He made a note, and she wondered why he cared about her clothes or her personal habits.

"Do you have any enemies, Ms. Polk?" he asked. The tone of his question was alarming.

"*Enemies* is a strong word. There are a few people who aren't happy with me right now, starting with all the Oak Cliff firefighters and cops who used to frequent Brady's. But despite the...animosity, I'd hardly consider any of them suspects. Besides, no one broke in. Did they?"

"How would you know? You didn't go out by the back door."

"I have an alarm. I'd have known if anyone broke through a door or window."

"You have a fire alarm, too, right?"

"Yes. And sprinklers." She felt sick at the thought of all those sprinklers soaking her beautiful tearoom.

"But you didn't hear the fire alarm."

She thought back to when Tony had awakened her. Was the alarm going off? Not the smoke alarm in her apartment. That thing was loud enough to wake the dead. But the one in the tearoom? Surely she would have heard that after she woke up. "I don't remember hearing anything. But I sleep hard and I was disoriented to wake up to the smoke—and two men dressed like aliens telling me to get up and jump out the window."

More notes. Epperson's face gave away nothing.

"Any disgruntled employees?"

"No one has worked long enough for me, to become disgruntled. Oh, well, I take that back. One of the kitchen staff quit the first day. But he was mad at my head chef, not me." Still, she provided Marc's name. Belinda would not be pleased.

"Anyone who applied for a job that you *didn't* hire?"

"Sure, there were lots of applicants. But no one stands out as a likely person to bear a grudge."

"What about ex-husbands, ex-boyfriends?"

"No ex-husbands…" She hesitated. Not in a million years could she imagine Trey or any of his friends or family stooping to something as sordid as arson. But Trey had been angry with her when she'd called off the wedding. Unreasonably angry.

"There is a boyfriend, I take it."

She told Epperson, as briefly as possible, of her broken engagement, and when he pressed her, she gave him Trey's name. "But there's no way. I mean, really. I haven't heard even a peep out of him or anyone connected to him since I moved out of the town house I was renting from his parents."

More scribbles in the notebook.

"You aren't going to talk to him, are you?" She couldn't bear the thought of them gloating over her failure. She didn't think they would deliberately harm her, but they weren't above reveling in her misfortune.

"If it's arson, I'll be talking with everyone until I find who did it. And that's a promise."

Julie thought it sounded more like a threat.

Chapter Thirteen

The sky was starting to lighten when Julie exited the fire station. Across the street, the firefighters were folding their hoses and preparing to retreat. Finally she could get in and see the damage.

But the odious Captain Campeon soon disabused her of that notion. "For now, we're treating this building as if it were a crime scene."

"The whole building? My apartment, too?"

"I'm afraid so. Someone can escort you upstairs to collect a few personal belongings if you'd like."

"Yes, I'd like."

A FIREFIGHTER WHOSE name tag identified him as K. Sinclair escorted her inside. Epperson grumbled about letting more people tromp through the scene of the fire, but in the end he let Julie pass. He warned her not to touch anything.

Julie took one step inside, skidded to a halt and tried not to faint. "Oh, my God!" It looked as though a herd of dirty, wet buffalo had stampeded through.

Tables and chairs were overturned, fine table linens trampled and everything was soaking wet. Yet she could see no evidence of anything burned except toward the very back, near the door that led to her office and the storeroom, where one wall and the ceiling bore ugly black scorch marks. "Oh. My. God."

"It's not as bad as it could be," Sinclair said. "We managed to keep the fire confined to the store—"

"Not as bad? The only way it could be worse would be if the building had actually burned to the ground. Everything is ruined." She looked around again, noting the sodden curtains and the smoke-stained upholstery on her chairs.

There was no point in arguing with anyone about this. The only person who would really get it was her insurance adjuster. Thank God she hadn't cut corners where that was concerned. Given the fact her building was a historic landmark, she'd had to pay higher rates. But her policy allowed for full replacement value of everything, including contents.

Upstairs in her apartment, there didn't appear to be any damage. But everything smelled like smoke, including the clothing she quickly packed up to take—who knew where? She'd have to return to her parents' house. They wouldn't be too thrilled. In fact, she had a pretty good idea what they'd say when they learned of the fire. They'd advise her to collect on the insurance and put the building up for sale. Given that her mother was the actual owner of the building, Julie realized she might be forced to do just that.

The firefighters would win.

She collected a few toiletries, her purse, cell phone and car keys. Unfortunately Roark Epperson was waiting for her downstairs, his hand outstretched. "Your car is part of the investigation just now, so I'll need your keys. I also need a phone number where you can be reached."

It just got worse and worse, but Julie gave him her cell number and handed over her keys. "How am I supposed to get home without a car?"

Tony, lurking nearby, stepped forward. "I thought you'd come stay with me. I'll be off duty in a few minutes."

She wasn't ready to face Tony. She was emotional, exhausted and she knew he'd been dishonest with her. She wasn't prepared to deal with that reality just now. Not until she found out exactly what that Tate guy had meant by "We sent in the wrong man."

She curbed her urge to fly off the handle. Getting emotional wouldn't help matters. "I don't think that's a good idea."

He led her outside, where they could talk privately. "No obligation, okay? You don't even have to talk to me if you don't want to."

"Look, Tony, I'm too tired and too upset to think rationally. I need to call my employees and let them know what's happened. Then I need to sleep."

"If this is about what Bing Tate said…"

"It is."

"I can explain. It's not what it looks like."

"Tell me, Tony, what does it look like?"

"If you'll let me explain—"

"Stop. Just stop. I can't take any more in right now. I mean, arson. Who could hate me that much?"

"Epperson's a good investigator. He'll figure out what caused the fire and who did it, if it's arson."

She squeezed her eyes shut, willing herself not to cry. She didn't have the luxury of falling apart now.

Tony put an arm around her. "Don't cry, babe. I know how much you loved Belinda's, but—"

"Don't put it in the past tense," she interrupted, pulling herself together. "I still love Belinda's and I'm reopening as soon as humanly possible. And if someone deliberately torched my building, I'll see him in jail."

In front of Belinda's, a pickup truck with a camper top had pulled up to the curb that the fire engine had just vacated. A woman in dark pants and a Dallas Fire Rescue golf shirt hopped out, greeting several of the men milling around with a lazy wave.

"Who's that?" Julie asked Tony.

"Captain Betsy Wingate. Dog handler."

"Dog handler?"

The woman opened the back of her truck, and a gorgeous black Labrador retriever bounded out, eager to play.

"Accelerant-sniffing dog. Come on, we need to clear the area. You can come over to the fire station and call someone to pick you up, if you absolutely refuse to come home with me. Or if you can wait a few minutes till I get off, I'll take you to your parents' house."

She didn't want Tony to see the run-down neighborhood where she'd grown up or the tiny place her parents and Belinda called home. She knew she shouldn't be embarrassed by her humble beginnings, but she was.

"Can I sleep on your couch?" she asked in a small voice, conceding defeat. She was just too wiped out to figure her way out of anything.

"If that's what you want, sure." Back at the station, he found his keys and handed them to her. "Sleep wherever you feel most comfortable. I'll try not to wake you when I get home."

Tony had hoped Julie would relent and sleep in his bed. But when he arrived at his house a few minutes later, he found her on the living room sofa wearing a polka-dot tank top and matching boxer shorts. Her hair was wet and tangled from a recent shower. It looked as if she hadn't even combed it. And she was already in a deep sleep.

His chest ached just looking at her. She seemed so peaceful. If there was any way he could have spared her from the pain tonight had brought... But, no, he was partly to blame. He should have been honest with her from the beginning.

If only that idiot Tate hadn't gone and blabbed. He hadn't gone into details, but obviously he'd said enough that Julie could fit together the missing pieces. Tony should have listened to Priscilla and told Julie the truth. Come to think of it, he never should have agreed in the first place to any half-baked scheme to derail the tearoom plans.

Tony had showered at the station, so he shed his clothes and climbed directly into bed. But he couldn't sleep. Though Julie had shared this bed only a couple of times, it felt empty when he knew she was right in the next room. After thirty frustrating minutes of tossing and turning, he got up, dressed and went to the kitchen to find something to eat. Julie was still sound asleep.

He called down to the station and asked if anyone knew anything more about the cause of the fire. The A shift was probably keeping an eye on things. But all anyone would tell him was that the accelerant-sniffing dog had gone home and Epperson was still on the scene collecting samples and taking pictures.

Figured. Roark Epperson never did anything halfway.

Tony knew it looked suspicious finding Julie fully clothed, her shoes already on, conveniently asleep on the sofa—ready to make a run for it if the fire got too close before she was "rescued." But what possible motive would she have? That tearoom was her dream. She had put everything into it. Every penny she had, every ounce of energy and imagination. She wouldn't let a slow start discourage her for long.

A throat clearing alerted Tony to the fact that he was no longer alone. Julie stood in the kitchen doorway, looking deliciously rumpled, those polka-dot boxers showing miles of slender leg.

He recovered enough from the sensual jolt to speak actual words. "Hey, you're awake." Brilliant observation.

"Can I have some of that coffee?"

"I'll get it for you," Tony said. "Sit down. Want some breakfast?"

"I don't think I can eat."

He poured her a cup and gave it to her black, the way he knew she liked it. He loved knowing little things about her—what toppings she ordered on her pizza, the kind of movies she liked to see, her favorite color. He'd always wanted to have a girlfriend to share private jokes with. And memories.

They'd only recently started to feel comfortable around each other, and he'd been looking forward to new discoveries, sharing new experiences, building those memories. But the whole thing would end prematurely if he couldn't convince Julie that his attempts to get to know her, to flirt with her, to seduce her, had been one hundred percent sincere—even if he'd had an ulterior motive.

Julie took an appreciative sip of her coffee, but it didn't help. She had never felt so wretched. Her entire life was falling apart, and how fair was that when it had already fallen apart once this year? Her restaurant was a shambles. Her boyfriend had lied to her. And to top if off, she was suspected of being an arsonist.

"Is there anything I can do to help?" Tony asked.

"Shoot me. Put me out of my misery."

"Now don't talk like that. You've faced some tough challenges before and you're not a quitter. You'll rebuild and you'll make Belinda's even better than before."

She sighed. Last night she'd been mad and spoken some brave words, but this morning it was hard to even think about rebuilding. "I wish I could believe that. André quit when I called him. He said he had another offer and he was taking it."

"So you'll hire another chef."

"When I think about how hard it was the first time…"

"You'll have more help this time. You don't have to do everything by yourself, you know." He watched her intently. "You sure you don't want something to eat?"

Maybe she needed something in her stomach after all. "Could I have some toast?"

"I can do that." He jumped to his feet and got busy.

She looked at her watch. "I better get dressed. Belinda's picking me up any minute." She turned, but Tony caught her hand and stopped her.

"Julie, don't leave. Stay here. Let me take care of you. Let me help you. I know you're having some doubts about me, but we can work them out."

"I don't know, Tony…."

"I'll tell you the whole story. But it's not what Tate made it sound like."

"So you weren't sent on a mission to seduce me and then convince me to reopen Brady's?"

Long pause as he put some white bread in the toaster. "Well, yeah, I was."

Her heart plummeted. If that was the case, it was every bit as bad as she feared. "Then there's nothing else to say."

The doorbell rang, and Julie jumped up to answer it, thinking it was Belinda. But when she opened the door, she found Jasmine instead.

The little girl smiled broadly. "Oh, hi, Julie." And she breezed in, a stuffed backpack slung over one shoulder. Apparently finding a woman in pajamas at her father's house wasn't an unusual circumstance. Something to consider.

"Jas, what are you doing here?" asked Tony, coming out of the kitchen.

"You said if I came over early today, you'd take me and Samantha to Six Flags."

"I didn't mean at the crack of dawn."

"Mom wanted to drop me off on her way to work. Hey, Julie, will you come to my room? I want to show you something."

"Jas," Tony said, "this isn't a good time to bug Julie. She had a fire last night."

Jasmine gasped. "That's horrible. The tearoom?"

"Yeah," Julie said.

"Was it bad? I didn't even get to eat there yet."

"She's gonna reopen. Don't worry," Tony said, sounding a lot more optimistic than Julie felt.

"Please, just come to my room for a minute." Jasmine took Julie's hand and dragged her, but she didn't really mind. Jasmine was so sweet; such an odd mixture, a little kid who desperately wanted to be older.

Tony shrugged helplessly as if to say he was no match for a female, even a pint-size one.

"What are you going to show me?" Julie asked as the little girl tugged her down the hall toward her room.

"Shh," Jasmine said. "It's a secret." She led Julie into her room and closed the door. The room was a pink-and-purple haven for a little girl, with stuffed animals and dolls peeking from every corner—as well as a poster of the latest teenaged heartthrob.

Jasmine opened the drawer to her bedside table and pulled out a red velvet pouch, which she opened reverently. She extracted a heart, about an inch wide, made of intricately worked Mexican silver. She looked at it for a moment, as if composing her thoughts, then handed it to Julie.

"It's an antique. My great-grandma brought it from Mexico."

Even Julie, who knew little about Mexican silver, could tell the piece was an example of exquisite craftsmanship. "It's lovely."

"My grandma, Helena, gave it to me before she died, for safekeeping."

"Your father's mother?"

Jasmine nodded, and Julie was surprised. She hadn't realized Tony's mother was deceased. Tony didn't talk much about his parents. Julie had gleaned enough information to know his home situation had been less than ideal and sometimes painful, so she hadn't pressed him for details.

"She died last year," Jasmine offered. "She had a bad liver."

"She must have loved and trusted you a lot to give you such a beautiful thing," Julie said, still studying the heart.

"But it's not mine to keep. It's supposed to get passed down to the wife of the oldest son in each family. Nana Helena told me to give it to whoever my dad gets married to."

"That's a lovely tradition," Julie said, wondering where all this was going and afraid to speculate.

"I want to give it to you."

Julie looked up, startled, to see Jasmine staring at her with unabashed adoration.

"My dad's had a lot of girlfriends," she said bluntly. "And every time I meet a new one, the first thing I think is, 'Could I give her Nana's heart?' And I always said, 'No way.' Until you. I think you're the one who's meant to have it."

Julie was so touched her eyes filled with tears. She and Jasmine hadn't spent much time together yet, and Julie felt unworthy of the child's affection and faith. She opened her arms, and Jasmine came in for a killer hug, the kind you remember always.

"I'm so honored," Julie said, meaning it. "But I think this is a little premature. We don't know what the future will bring." Boy, was that an understatement.

Jasmine pulled away so she could look at Julie

with her big, earnest brown eyes, so much like her father's. "There will be a wedding," she said with unwavering certainty. "But I want you to take the heart now."

Julie knew it wasn't right to take the heirloom when her future with Tony was in limbo. Still, she sensed Jasmine's determination. "I'll take it for now," she said. "But only for safekeeping and with the understanding that I might have to give it back."

Jasmine smiled. "You won't."

"Jazzy!" Tony called down the hall. "Let Julie go. Her sister is here to pick her up."

And here Julie was, still in her pajamas.

"Don't show it to my dad, whatever you do," Jasmine said. "It's a secret—only the ladies in the family know about it. Okay?"

"Sure, okay." Who was she to mess with a family tradition so complex? "But I was wondering… didn't your grandmother give the heart to your mother when she and your dad got married?" And had Natalie been forced to give it back?

"Oh, my mom and dad were never married," Jasmine tossed off casually as she unzipped her backpack. Then she leaned over and whispered into a stunned Julie's ear, "I was a looooove child. I'm not supposed to know what that means, but I do."

Then, as if the emotional conversation of moments before had never taken place, she started pulling neatly packed clothing from her backpack and hanging it in her closet.

Julie just sat there, her body frozen. Tony hadn't

married Natalie? Tony had gotten a woman pregnant and hadn't married her?

Had he not loved her? Had she been some one-night stand? Had he already been involved with someone else when he found out about the baby?

Memories of Trey intruded—his casual belief that he was entitled to take a lover if he wanted because he was a Davidson, and Davidson men took what they wanted. His sense that he was above having to take responsibility for a bastard child. His total self-involvement, a trait Julie had been completely blind to until it had hit her in the face.

Was she similarly blind about Tony? He seemed to her like the type to be loyal and true, to take responsibility for his mistakes, though she was loath to call Jasmine a mistake. But was she wrong? She'd already caught him in one deception, and though she couldn't specifically remember Tony telling her that he and Natalie had been married, he hadn't gone out of his way to explain the truth either.

Sure, he was a good father now. But how long had it taken him to get to that point? Had he resisted getting tied down? After their condom mishap, when she'd been so freaked out, he'd extolled the virtues of Ethan's mother. He hadn't seemed eager to assume any responsibility.

Tony found her a few minutes later, sitting on Jasmine's bed in a daze as Jasmine continued to hang up her clothes and talk about the planned outing to an amusement park. "Julie, your sister's here."

She shook herself back to the present and stood. She had to get out of there.

"Promise me you'll call me if you need anything," Tony said. "Even if you're mad at me."

All she could think about was escape. She had to think this through before she started blurting out accusations or jumping to conclusions. She ran out of the room, threw on some clothes and fled with Belinda, her heart pounding the entire time.

Chapter Fourteen

"Thanks for coming to get me," Julie said, studying her little sister. Belinda looked a little worse for wear. But *she* wasn't the one who'd been up all night watching the tearoom burn. "Are you okay?"

"Of course not. I'm bummed. Maybe you shouldn't have put my name on the tearoom. Maybe I'm a jinx."

"You're not a jinx. Don't worry, we'll get everything repaired and open back up. I have great insurance." If she wasn't in jail.

Belinda didn't seem that comforted. "You want to drive by and look at it?"

Maybe she should. Maybe it would look better in the daylight.

Belinda turned left onto Jefferson Street. The tearoom looked fine from the outside, except for the plywood over the door and a broken bedroom window. On closer inspection, Julie saw that her new awning was crumpled on one end.

"It's not horrible," Belinda said, parking at the curb.

"Wait till you see the inside."

The yellow tape was gone. In fact, the building appeared to be deserted. Had the investigation released the premises?

Right on cue, her cell phone rang. It was a voice and a name she didn't recognize from the fire marshal's office. "Your building's been released," he said. "We left the keys at the fire station across the street."

"Did you find anything?"

"I can't give you that information, Ma'am."

Damn. That didn't sound good. She repeated the information to Belinda.

"So you're staying here? You don't want to go back to Mom and Dad's?"

"I might as well face it now."

Belinda looked at her sister squarely. "You mean you got me out of bed after five hours' sleep for nothing? If you wanted to go to the tearoom, you could have walked."

"Well, I didn't know they'd let me back in so early. Anyway, why were you up so late?"

"Just, you know, hanging out."

"With Marc?"

"Jules, don't give me the third degree, okay?"

"How old is he? Twenty-three?"

"Twenty-one. When you were my age, you were moving into your own apartment."

True enough. Though Belinda was still in high school, she would be eighteen next month. "I guess you're smart enough to stay out of trouble."

Belinda made the universal groan of a frustrated teenager. "Of course I am!"

With Belinda by her side, Julie was ready to face the damage again. Things looked even worse in the light of day.

Belinda simply stood in the dining room, her mouth hanging open. "Oh, Jules, I'm so sorry."

"Yeah. Me, too." The actual fire damage had been confined to the storeroom and office area, which were a total loss—nothing but the blackened remains of furniture and other items, twisted into unrecognizable lumps. Her computer was a goner, but thankfully she had backed up all of her financial information and she knew it was safe.

Flames hadn't actually reached the dining area, but the firefighters had. They'd pulled down parts of the tin ceiling, and water from the hoses and sprinklers had soaked everything.

The only rooms that remained relatively unscathed were the kitchen and washrooms.

Julie called her insurance company, and an adjuster arrived a short time later. The slight thin-lipped man volunteered little information, walked around making notes on a clipboard and taking pictures. He gave Julie the unwelcome information that she would not receive any compensation until she'd been cleared of any suspicion of arson.

She'd expected as much.

Belinda put her arm around Julie's shoulders. "We can still get started cleaning. That doesn't cost anything. All we need is a bunch of garbage sacks."

"You're right," Julie said, rolling up her figurative sleeves. "We'll do what we can, work with what we have." That had always been her way. A tiny sliver of her old determination surfaced and pushed her into gear.

She raided the cash register, which miraculously was undamaged, and drove to the grocery store to buy trash bags and other cleaning supplies while Belinda started piling up debris.

When Julie returned, she came in through the back door—the only door that still worked—and thought she'd walked into the wrong place.

There was a party going on.

Belinda ran up to her. "Julie, look who came to help!"

It was Tony, plus three helpers—Jasmine, Ethan and Priscilla.

"Jasmine," Julie said, "what about Six Flags?"

"Samantha's got a cold, so she couldn't go with me. But it doesn't matter, 'cause I'd rather help you clean up the mess anyway."

Julie was so touched. These people didn't have anything to gain, but a neighbor had hit some hard times and they simply wanted do what they could. "It's so nice of you to help," she said to them, "but you don't have to…"

"We're helping and that's final," Priscilla said.

Tears came to Julie's eyes. So this was what it was like to have friends, real friends.

With so many helping hands and the use of Tony's wheelbarrow, it didn't take long to haul out the debris. Julie started to make a list of everything she would have to replace, plus some preliminary calculations on what it would cost to repair the walls, floor and ceiling in the damaged areas. She'd learned a lot about building costs during the remodeling.

Linens and curtains were gathered up for a trip to the Laundromat; they might be saved. Tables and chairs were righted, floors swept and mopped, every dish in the place sent through the dishwasher.

By the end of the day, Julie felt a thousand percent better. It didn't look so bad. Once the professional fire-damage people got done, it would look even better. Maybe she wouldn't have to stay closed more than a couple of weeks.

"Who's hungry?" Ethan asked. "I'm thinking the weather's nice enough that we should fire up your grill, Tony."

Tony looked at his watch. "Oh, jeez, I almost forgot. Nat's coming for dinner, and I invited Paolo, too."

"Paolo?" Julie asked.

"Natalie's husband."

"You have your ex and her husband over for dinner?" She couldn't imagine sitting across a table from Trey without her fork ending up in his throat.

"Nat and I get along great. And Paolo—he's terrific. I couldn't ask for a better stepfather for Jasmine."

Julie found Tony's attitude refreshing.

"You girls are coming, right?" Priscilla asked Julie and Belinda.

"Thanks, but I can't," Belinda said. "I have a date. In fact, I really should be gone now."

They all looked at Julie expectantly. "I can't come, either. I've got so much to do. But I really appreciate the invitation."

She could tell her answer didn't sit well with Tony. But he didn't argue. He just looked at her sadly.

They all left except Belinda. "Do you really have anything important to do?" she asked. "Or is something wrong with you and Tony?"

"Things are kind of a mess. He lied to me."

Belinda gasped. "He cheated?"

"Oh, no, nothing like that. But he…well, he wasn't really interested in me. The only reason he slept with me is so he could get me to change my mind about opening the tearoom. He had sex with me so he could get his stupid bar back."

Belinda snorted. "You mean he's faking? I don't think so. Anyway, he must have figured out pretty quick you weren't going to cave, even for him. Yet he didn't run screaming into the night."

Julie recognized the truth in that statement at once. If Tony was only interested in Brady's, why was he still hanging around?

"I guess I need to talk to him," Julie said. "We have to straighten a few things out. But I really do have something important to do."

There was something she'd been neglecting, and now seemed the perfect time to tackle it. She needed to take a hard look at her budget. It had seemed perfectly reasonable when she'd started out, but the actual numbers—both expenses and revenues—had changed so dramatically from her original plan she had no idea where she stood. All she knew was that the balance in the restaurant account wasn't where she'd hoped it would be. Now would be a very good time to make changes, if necessary.

"Maybe I can help," Belinda said when Julie explained her dilemma. She'd apparently forgotten about her date, if she'd had one to begin with.

Together, they analyzed the numbers for almost two hours and then came to a grim conclusion: the tearoom couldn't make a profit, given Julie's current business model.

"André's salary takes too big a bite out of the budget," Julie said. "Not to mention what he's spent on food. The man is insane."

"Can't you keep him on an allowance or something?"

"Oh, it's a moot point. He quit this morning. Took another job."

"Oh. You didn't tell me that."

"With so much else going on, I guess I forgot."

"So hire someone more flexible," Belinda suggested. "And less expensive."

Julie realized she might have to simplify the menu—and cut down on the kitchen help, too.

"As long as you're making changes," Belinda said, "maybe…well, maybe you should think about changing the name."

"Changing the name? Why?"

"Because it's your tearoom. Not mine."

"But you're my inspiration. This place is your legacy. It's going to send you to Princeton. Or Stanford. Or wherever it is you're applying for scholarships this week."

"Yeah. Um, there's something I've been meaning to tell you."

Julie gasped. "Did you get offered a scholarship?"

"Not exactly." Belinda opened her backpack and pulled out a wrinkled piece of paper, handing it reluctantly to Julie. Julie read it top to bottom three times and still didn't get it.

"General Educational Development... What the hell is this?"

"It's a GED certificate."

"I don't understand. You took the GED test?"

"I was bored out of my mind in high school—you knew that. I took the test a few weeks ago. Now I don't have to finish—"

"You're *dropping out?*" Julie shrieked.

Belinda flopped onto a smoke-stained chair. "Don't freak, okay? This is why I've been putting off telling you. I knew you'd be mad. Besides, it's not dropping out if you have a GED. It's like, you know, graduating early."

"But you can't get into a good college with a GED—"

"Well, I could. But I'm not going to college."

Julie felt woozy. She found her way to a chair and sank into it. "Maybe you'd better explain from the beginning."

"I'll go to college someday. But not now. Marc's band got this incredible opportunity. They're going on tour with the Chokers. I'm sure you've heard of them." Belinda nodded encouragingly.

"Actually, no."

Belinda sighed. "They've been on MTV and everything. Well, MTV in Germany. I'm going on tour with him. He might even let me sing a couple of songs. I'm leaving in a week."

Julie had thought there couldn't be any bigger shock to her system than a fire in her tearoom. But this surprise was right up there with an alien invasion. Her sister was a groupie.

"But, Belinda, you're so smart…."

"I'll still go to college. There's time for all that later. Oh, please don't be mad. You've always told me to live life on my terms."

"Yeah, 'cause I thought you wanted to go to college!"

"But I want to live a full life, too."

Julie wanted to argue, but she sensed it was futile. Belinda had that look in her eye that said she was going to do something, and no one would talk her out of it. "Just promise me you'll be careful."

"Sheesh, I'm not stupid."

"What do Mom and Dad say?"

"I had to get their permission to take the GED and they're cool with that, but I haven't told them about going on tour. I think they won't mind, though."

Unfortunately Julie suspected Belinda was right. They'd be happy to get Belinda out from under their roof. One less mouth to feed, though Belinda had been feeding herself pretty well for years.

"I have to go," Belinda said. "We're rehearsing tonight and I promised to bring them pizza." She gave Julie a lightning-fast hug. "Thanks for being understanding. But you should change the name of the tearoom. Maybe another name would give you better luck."

Julie had nothing to say to that. What was happening to the well-ordered life she had visualized when she'd first gotten the idea to open her own tearoom? She would be the captain of her own ship, she'd thought. Master of her universe.

Ha. What a joke. She'd been out of control since the day she'd walked into the dingy bar.

Once again, Julie was alone—just her and her tearoom. How many hours had she spent here in solitude, contemplating the realization of her dream?

Now, in hindsight, she had to ask herself, was running a tearoom all she'd hoped it would be? She had to admit she'd harbored hopes that Trey or someone from his family would come in, and she could rub their noses in it that she was doing just fine without their help, thank you very much.

But none of the Davidsons had cared a whit about her tearoom. And she recognized now how childish and vengeful her motives had been. Given the strange twists her life had taken, she was starting to see what was really important. Friends, family…

And Tony. Where did he fit in?

Though her feelings for Tony ran deep, she'd been careful not to label them. Tony had obviously been disappointed by women in the past, women who'd trifled with his emotions.

She hadn't wanted to be one of those women. She wanted to be straight with him, totally honest, so there would be no misunderstandings.

But then she'd learned of his cold-blooded plan to seduce her into reopening Brady's. On top of that, she'd discovered that Tony hadn't married Jasmine's mother.

But she hadn't bothered to learn the circumstances surrounding either of these matters, had she? She'd simply had a knee-jerk reaction. Tony obviously had a good relationship with Natalie and was a devoted father, and in that respect he was nothing like Trey. And as for the other...she at least ought to listen to what he had to say.

PRISCILLA ANSWERED Tony's door when Julie rang the bell, and she smiled a warm welcome.

"I come bearing gifts." Julie handed Priscilla two white bakery boxes. "Cheesecake and mud pie, saved from the smoke because they were in the fridge. If someone doesn't eat them, they'll just go bad."

"Are you kidding? Around here they won't last fifteen minutes, although I have to say, at the moment the clan is pretty stuffed. Come on in."

As Julie stepped inside, she heard the faint strains of beautifully played guitar music and slightly off-kilter bongo drums. "What's that?"

"That's Paolo. He plays part-time in a mariachi band. I'm not sure where the bongos came from—Ethan or Tony, probably. The girls are taking turns playing them. Come on, we're out on the deck."

The scene that greeted Julie when she stepped through the kitchen door was like something from another era—one of those Elvis beach movies, maybe. A handsome Hispanic man sat on the deck railing, gently strumming his guitar and singing a Mexican ballad. Jasmine, sitting cross-legged on a pillow, tapped softly on the bongo drums.

Everyone else was spread out around the deck, in lawn chairs or pillows, lazy from food and lulled by the music. Dino and an identical spotted pup were sprawled in unmoving heaps, their toys forgotten. Now that the sun was down, sitting outdoors was bearable, even pleasant, with a soft breeze bringing just a hint of cooler weather to come.

It occurred to Julie that this was probably one of those snapshot moments that might never be recreated.

Tony's eyes lit up when he saw her and he smiled. He lay in a hammock that was stretched across one corner of the spacious deck, and he motioned for her to join him.

She shook her head. No, not yet. She still had questions, and cozying up with Tony would only muddle her brain. She sat on a lawn chair near the hammock. Tony was close enough that they could talk softly without others hearing but not so close that they touched.

"He's very good," Julie said.

"Paolo? Yeah. He's even taught Jasmine to play a little bit."

"Sounds like he really is a good stepfather."

"Oh, yeah, the best. Jas is crazy about him."

"How does that make you feel?" Julie asked. Maybe it was a bit forward of her, but she needed to know Tony's views on his role as a parent.

"Truthfully? I feel lucky. Stepparents can be horrible—and believe me, I know. I had four altogether. Out of those four, only one treated me better than a stray dog. So if Jasmine has a stepfather who loves her and spoils her and treats her as his own, I'm happy for her. It just means she has more good influences."

"Do you ever feel jealous?"

He shrugged. "Not really. What I have with Jas is special. No one can take that away."

Julie felt a lump forming in her throat. Yes, she was emotional today, given all that was happening in her life. But the obvious love radiating from Tony was so moving. "You're a really good dad."

"I try, but it isn't easy. The fact her parents live in different houses has never seemed to bother her. But you always wonder if you're somehow unintentionally screwing up your kid's life."

"You and Natalie never married, did you?"

He sat up, looking surprised, probably wondering how she knew. "No, we didn't."

"Jasmine told me this morning. It freaked me out a little."

Tony groaned.

"It doesn't matter to me now," she said quickly, amazed it was true. "What matters is that you're a fantastic father to Jasmine. But I was just surprised. And I wondered why you hadn't mentioned it."

"It just didn't come up." Then he looked down and over Julie's shoulder, anywhere but directly at her. "No, that's not really true. I avoided mentioning it because I didn't think it cast me in a flattering light. The truth is, I wanted to marry Natalie. I assumed, at first, that was the only solution. But her parents were dead set against it. They said if she married me, she was on her own."

Julie was appalled. "She chose her parents over you?"

"Julie, we were sixteen. She was terrified."

"Sixteen!" She tried to imagine Belinda, not much older than that, pregnant and scared. Or even herself at that age. Sixteen was way too young to be married.

"It was good we didn't get married," Tony continued. "Her parents were right. The stress of having a baby is hard enough for adults, much less teenagers. We'd have never made it and we might have ended up hating each other. Instead we have a good relationship, which is good for Jasmine."

"She's a lucky girl."

"No, I'm the lucky one." In that moment, Tony's love for his daughter was so real, so obvious, it was almost a physical presence. And at that same moment, Julie realized she loved Tony. She knew that whatever schemes he'd been involved with, he'd never set out to hurt her. She would be a fool to let him go.

Tony was a person she could rely on. He wasn't going anywhere. He was solid as the building that housed her business and her home—enduring hardships and changes of circumstances but still standing strong.

She'd come so close to losing him by closing her mind, judging and letting the writing on her walls blind her from the truth. In fact, she might still lose him. But how to tell him, after all her waffling and all her flakiness, how she really felt?

Chapter Fifteen

As the evening wound down and little girls' eyes began to droop, tension began to build in Julie's stomach again. Soon she would be alone with Tony. They would have to talk. She would have to tell him her true feelings.

As Paolo packed away his guitar and Kat gathered up the pillows to take them inside, a voice called out, "Hello, is anyone home?"

Priscilla, who'd been lounging on a lawn chair, nursing a glass of wine, sat up so suddenly she spilled wine on her shorts.

The newcomer stood at the fence separating the driveway from the backyard. In the semidarkness Julie saw only the silhouette of a man's head above the fence.

Tony peered suspiciously at the intruder, then abruptly his face relaxed into a smile. "Roark. You just missed the party. Come on back, the gate's open."

As Tony went to greet his new guest halfway,

Julie sidled over to Priscilla. "What do you suppose he's here for?" she asked, fear making her voice shrill.

"Don't panic," Priscilla said. "I don't think he's here to haul you off to jail. He doesn't normally do the arresting. He may just be here to play shuffleboard or something."

But Julie didn't think so. Even as he shook hands with Tony and went through some sort of male-bonding trade of punches, his gaze sought out Julie.

Or maybe Priscilla. But if he was trying to catch Priscilla's eye, it was hopeless. The normally poised woman was frantically trying to get the red wine spot off her shorts with a damp paper towel.

Priscilla cursed in the dainty way only she could. "I've got to go soak these shorts before the stain sets in," she said, making a hasty escape before Epperson even reached the deck.

Julie just stood there, feeling like a sitting duck. She wanted to run and hide from whatever news he was about to give her—and surely that's why he was here, because he was coming right toward her.

"Ms. Polk."

"You're looking for me?"

"I tried you on your cell phone, but I kept getting voice mail."

Because the battery was dead and the charger burned up. "But still you found me," she said cautiously.

"The Dallas Fire Rescue grapevine is alive and

well. Someone on the A shift at Station 59 saw you headed this way."

Sometimes Julie wondered if the firefighters had anything better to do than watch her comings and goings.

"I wanted to see you face-to-face anyway," the investigator said, turning serious, and Julie felt a little shaky in the knees. She steadied herself against Tony, who'd moved to stand protectively by her side. Ethan, too, had stopped to greet Epperson and listen to whatever he had to say.

The air was charged with tension.

Then suddenly the man smiled. "Would you all stop looking at me like I'm an executioner? I've got good news. The official report will be filed tomorrow morning, but since I've put you through hell, I thought it was only fair to let you know now. I've made my official determination of the cause of the fire, and it's not arson. Apparently a nail went through an old wire during your remodeling and caused a short. It was probably smoldering there inside your wall for weeks."

Julie nearly passed out with relief. "So does this mean…?" She could hardly grasp it.

"You're off the hook. You should be able to collect on your insurance and rebuild in no time."

She wanted to throw herself at Roark Epperson and hug him, but she settled for a handshake. "Thank you. You have no idea how happy you've just made me."

"Hey, Roark," Ethan said, "We've got the old

shuffleboard table set up and ready to go. Seems you owe me a rematch."

"No kidding? Got some warm beer to go with it?"

Ethan grinned. "Would you settle for a cold one?"

As the two men stepped inside, Tony pulled Julie into a bear hug. "This is great! Everything's going your way now, I can feel it. Hey, you want to stay and play shuffleboard?"

"I really need to get home and get some sleep. Long day tomorrow. You're not working tomorrow, right?"

Tony shook his head.

"Come over in the morning. I'll fix you some breakfast—I've got lots of eggs to use up. And we can talk."

Tony immediately sobered. "Oh. You know, for a minute there, I forgot how bad I screwed up."

"Maybe not so bad. We'll get everything straightened out tomorrow, okay?"

"Anyplace, anytime you say, babe."

THE NEXT MORNING, bright and early, Julie was on the phone with the contractor who'd done her original remodeling. "You've got to fit me in, Sid," she insisted. "Every day I stay closed is another day closer to bankruptcy."

"You want I should get no sleep?" he asked, but she knew he would take the job. He loved to complain, but she sensed he would come through.

"Sid, someone's knocking at the door. I'll call you back." Let him think about it. She went to the tearoom's battered door, which Ethan had rigged to at least open, close and lock. Although she and Tony hadn't set a particular time to meet, she thought that was who she'd find.

She wanted to pour out all her doubts and worries, her mixed feelings about her future, and she knew without guessing at all that he would fold her into his arms and reassure her that everything would be okay. Belinda was a smart kid, he would say. She's entitled to follow her heart and maybe make some mistakes. She'll come out okay. The important thing was that she lived her life on her own terms, just as Julie wanted to do.

He would have ideas about how to fix her finances, too. He would remind her that he could float her a loan if she needed one. He would volunteer free labor—his and that of all his friends, whether they agreed or not.

So she was disappointed when it wasn't Tony standing on the sidewalk but Eloisa and Josephina.

Surprised though she was, she managed a smile for the other woman. "Eloisa! Come on in. I was about to put some coffee on."

"I do coffee," Eloisa said eagerly.

"You don't have to—" Julie tried to object, but Eloisa seemed not to hear. She made a beeline for the kitchen, and Julie followed her with a shrug.

"I know the kitchen good," Eloisa said. And, sure enough, she did brew a pot of coffee without any instruction from Julie. "I work in kitchen in Acapulco."

"Eloisa, if you're wondering about your job, you'll still have it when I reopen the restaurant. But that won't be for weeks yet. Three weeks, maybe more. You understand?"

"Yes, you give me job."

"In a few weeks."

Eloisa nodded. "But I work in kitchen, yes?"

"You want to be a sous chef?" Julie asked incredulously.

"Sous chef. That's chef's helper?"

"Right. An assistant chef." And in a kitchen serving the kind of gourmet food Belinda's did, it was a highly skilled position.

"No. I want to be top chef. André, he is mean and greedy. I do his job. A lot better and cheaper."

Julie resisted the urge to giggle. Eloisa, her head chef?

"I can cook," Eloisa said stubbornly.

"I'm sure you can." She could probably make great Tex-Mex food. But Belinda's was not a Mexican restaurant.

Eloisa shrugged. "I show you." And she proceeded, over Julie's fading objections, to cook up a delectable and innovative omelet with prosciutto, green onions and cream cheese. Not only was the food delicious, but Eloisa had produced it in less than five minutes, wielding her utensils with the ease of a practiced chef.

Julie, who held Josephina while Eloisa worked, was almost afraid to ask. "What else can you cook?"

"Anything. Lamb, chicken, uh…" She struggled for the word. "SpaghettiOs?"

"Pasta."

"Yes, pasta. Enchiladas so good you cry."

"Are you trained? Did you go to school?"

"School? To cook?" She dismissed that as fool-ishness. "I learn from Mama. And I watch Emeril on the TV."

Suddenly an idea struck Julie—a terrible, won-derful idea. It was crazy. It went against almost ev-erything she'd fought for all these weeks and months. But it made a kooky kind of sense.

She'd already decided she needed a different kind of chef and a simpler menu. Why not a casual tearoom by day? Fewer tables. Fewer staff. A shorter, simplified menu but still classy and appeal-ing to women.

A bar by night. A nice bar, a friendly neighbor-hood place. Clean. Inviting. Burgers and cold beer. Darts and shuffleboard. No smoking.

Brady's Tavern and Tearoom.

Now that she knew and understood this neighbor-hood better, she could see that it would fit right in. More upscale than the old Brady's, certainly, but not off-putting. Friendlier and less expensive than Belinda's. People could bring their kids. Men could order a burger.

"Ms. Julie?" Eloisa said. "What you think?"

"I think you're hired."

Eloisa dropped her spatula and threw her arms around Julie with a squeal.

The more Julie thought about it, the more she re-alized the answer had been in front of her all along if only she hadn't been so pigheaded. There'd been no need to choose between a bar and a tearoom. She could do both and double her profits.

She couldn't wait to tell Tony.

Tony. She loved him—oh, how she loved him. She'd gone to sleep last night sure of it and woken up this morning even more positive. But she'd taken his affections for granted. She'd been so ridiculously focused on her life, her problems, she hadn't given much thought to how all this was affecting Tony.

That was all going to change.

She promised Eloisa she would be in touch soon. They would have to work out a menu, which would be a whole new challenge, given the language barrier. Then, once she was alone again, she made plans—not plans for the new Brady's but plans for her and Tony. From this moment forward, Tony would be a part of all her plans.

If he would have her.

Unwilling to live with the suspense a moment longer, she picked up her cell and dialed Tony's number. She didn't care if she woke him up.

But no one answered.

Disappointed, she looked out the window—and there he was, striding with determination across the street toward her. She walked outside to wave a welcome, and he quickened his pace. He didn't stop until he was nose to nose with her.

"You just have to know one thing," he said. "I love you."

She took a step back in pure self-defense. If she didn't, she was going to be all over him. The smell of him made her think about sex—and she didn't think that should be her first priority.

"Oh, Tony." She tried not to cry. She had things to say. "You were right all along. Belinda's Tearoom was wrong for this neighborhood. A few blocks north in Kessler Park or even in Bishop Arts, maybe I could have made it. But not on Jefferson Street. Even if it hadn't been for the fire, I would have been broke in another few weeks." It was easier to start with the less personal stuff, she decided.

"You're giving up?" He looked like a kid who'd just been told Santa Claus is a myth.

"No. That's the good part. I've decided to reopen Brady's, but with a slight twist—Brady's Tavern and Tearoom. Eloisa's going to cook for me. I'm going to serve hamburgers."

Tony's eyes widened. "And ribs?"

"If you think it's a good idea." She shuddered a little at the thought. But her idea hadn't worked. She needed to listen to other people for a change. "The tearoom was sort of snobby, wasn't it?"

"That's not the word I would have used." But he said it cautiously.

"My mother said I was putting on airs. I was trying to prove something to Trey and his family, to be someone I wasn't."

Tony adjusted the collar of her shirt. "You were doing something that made you happy, honey.

You're entitled to live your dream any way you see fit."

"But it wouldn't have made me happy. It was one big headache. And when Trey and his family completely ignored me, I realized at least half the reason I had for opening a tearoom was bogus. Shallow."

"So what would make you happy?"

"I just want to belong somewhere. To be part of something that's bigger than me. I want some control over my life. But if I ever had any control over anything, it was just an illusion. My restaurant burned down, my sister is running off with a rock musician and on top of everything else…"

The words stuck in her throat.

He smoothed a strand of hair off her forehead. Oh, the feel of his touch. It would be so easy to fall into it, to let hormones rule.

"On top of everything else, I love you," Tony said again. "Or did you not hear me the first time?"

Julie was staring at him, her lips slightly parted, her chest rising and falling in rapid succession. He had no idea what she was thinking. Was she shocked? Horrified? He'd told her the unvarnished truth this time. He'd wanted no more deception between them.

"You can pretend I didn't. It sorta slipped out. Priscilla says I fall in love too easy. And maybe I do. But this time I know it's for real. And for keeps."

She continued to watch him with unnerving intensity.

He felt compelled to fill the silence. In direct opposition to his self-preservation instincts, he continued to blather. "I'm not even sure I know what love is. But I know I think about you all the time. And I worry about you, about whether you're happy, whether you're safe. And sometimes I just want to hold you."

That, he realized, was something new. He'd felt lust for plenty of women. But this tenderness? The tightness in his throat when he thought about losing Julie? He'd never known those feelings before. Was that love?

"I love you, too, Tony."

"You...you do?"

"Uh-huh."

"Don't you want to know about what Bing said?"

"It doesn't matter anymore."

"I want to tell you what happened anyway." He had to get it off his chest. "I didn't want anything to do with any plan to sweet-talk you into reopening Brady's. Until I saw you. Just the way you walked out the door of Brady's, your head held high, so full of purpose, your hair all shiny and gold..." He paused, looking off into space, a slight smile on his lips. "I wasn't willing to let anyone else have the job."

"So you had an ulterior motive."

"Yeah. Even if I hadn't, Julie, I'd have been at your door every day anyway. But over the next few weeks I saw how excited you were about the tearoom, how much you loved decorating every little corner and working out the menu and choosing your dishes and sewing those curtains, night after night. And you know what I realized?"

"That I was stubborn as a squirrel trying to get at the bird feeder?"

"No. I realized you had a right to follow your dream. Because it was making you happy. And being happy is a lot more important than making a ton of money—or catering to a bunch of cranky firefighters.

"If my only goal had been to change your mind about the tearoom, I'd have given up. But I was crazy about you from the very first day. It wasn't like I was faking anything, ever."

Julie felt the first pinpricks of guilt. He'd been crazy about her, and she'd treated him as an after-thought. Though she'd seen the potential, she hadn't felt she could invest everything in a relationship. Not when the last one had gone so badly.

"I guess the joke was on me," he said. "I didn't want my heart to get stomped on again and I swore I wouldn't fall in love with you. But I did."

Tony backed Julie up against the tearoom door, much as he had just before their first kiss. "So that's it. The last of the deep, dark secrets."

Julie sighed. "Is this the part where we get to kiss and make up?"

"If you insist."

He closed his mouth over hers, and his kiss was every bit as exciting as the very first one had been.

Unfortunately they had an audience. Applause, whistles and catcalls broke out from across the street, where most of the B shift was standing around in Station 59's driveway.

"Would you guys get lives?" Tony called out. Then he opened the door, nudged Julie inside and closed it again. "I really want to get naked with you."

"I can't. The contractor's on his way over here right now. But, Tony, I swear I'll never make this business a priority over you again. People are what matter. While I was busy obsessing over account balances, Belinda was off falling in love, and she never even told me. It's all going to change."

He caressed her face. "Don't worry about me. All I've ever wanted is the same thing you want. To belong. I don't think either of us were born into an ideal family. But look how lucky we are now. We get to make our own family. You, me, Jasmine."

Jasmine. Julie lightly touched the silver heart, still in her pocket. How had the girl known?

Julie wanted to say more. But her heart was stuck in her throat, preventing any words from emerging. She couldn't believe Tony was so understanding about everything, so willing to accept her, quirks and mood swings and all.

"So what do you say? I'm not a millionaire and I don't own any fancy department stores, but I'll love you more than any ten millionaires could. Let's get married."

"What?"

He grinned. "Priscilla would kill me right now, but I don't care. Let's get married."

There, he'd said it again. She wasn't hearing things. "Priscilla told me this would happen, you know. She warned me not to hurt you."

"You're not going to, are you?"

She shook her head. "I don't think so."

"I'm looking for a yes or a no here," he said.

"Yes." It was the easiest answer in the world.

JULIE'S INSURANCE company came through with a check almost instantly, and it was far more than she'd thought she would get. The cleanup and renovations to Brady's Tavern and Tearoom were moving along with amazing speed. Her beautiful wood bar, which she'd feared was damaged beyond repair, underwent a miraculous transformation. Laundering and pressing restored her curtains. And the professional cleaners got rid of the last of the smoke smell.

She set a date for reopening.

About half of her previous staff wanted to come back—which worked out perfectly. She hired Alonzo, formerly her uncle Brady's right-hand man, to manage the bar, which would now include a limited menu of burgers and barbecue, along with some mini quiches and stuffed mushrooms for the female diners.

It all fell together so easily, so beautifully, she wondered why she'd ever resisted this idea.

Belinda sent her postcards from the road. It still terrified Julie to think of her baby sister out in the big, bad world, but she sounded remarkably content and unnervingly adult.

It was a few days before the reopening—she refused to call it a grand opening this time, for fear of jinxing herself—and Julie was touching up the paint.

It still looked like her tearoom—but friendlier now. She'd gotten rid of the fussy table linens in favor of white butcher paper. The stuffy paintings she'd originally bought for the walls had been smoke- and water-damaged beyond repair, so she'd replaced them with artwork from Oak Cliff artisans, all of it offered for sale; yet another revenue stream, and as the paintings sold, the decor would change continually.

Tony was mysteriously absent. He'd spent almost every minute he wasn't on duty with her, helping her get ready to reopen. So his absence was noted—but not worried about. He liked to surprise her, and she liked to let him. Before, he'd held back a little, worried about overwhelming her with affection and scaring her off, as he had other girlfriends.

Now he just let it fly, and she lapped it up. She'd never felt so honored, so cherished, so loved without reservation. Her whole life was coming together like a jigsaw puzzle of the most beautiful, perfect sunrise.

Now she heard a noise at the door, and her whole being grew brighter as Tony entered, a big, dirt-eating grin on his face. But then he got a better look at what she was doing and frowned disapprovingly. He loped across the tearoom toward her.

"What are you doing on that ladder and not even holding on to anything? Jeez, the first time I met you you were falling off a ladder, and don't think I've forgotten. I told you I'd do the hard stuff." He steadied the ladder and held a hand out to help her down.

"Tony, I'm only on the second step." But she loved that he was protective. He'd made her promise to slap him down if he got carried away, but so far it didn't bother her a bit.

To humor him, she stepped off the ladder and laid aside her paintbrush. "Where've you been?"

His grin returned. "Wait until you see. You're going to take back every mean thing you ever thought about cops and firefighters." He ran back to the door and opened it. "Okay, guys," he yelled. "Bring it in."

Julie stared, slack-jawed, as Brady's antique shuffleboard table came in through the door. Close on its heels was the dartboard. Then several neon signs. And finally in came Sir Edward, the wooden cigar-store Indian.

Tony, directing the placement of each item carted in by at least a dozen off-duty firefighters and cops, kept glancing at Julie to see if she would object. But she was too amazed to do anything but stare. She'd been regretting her headstrong decision to sell all the quirky things that had made the old Brady's what it was, but she hadn't imagined there'd be any way to get them back.

Tony had managed it.

He joined her, sliding an arm around her waist. "You're not saying much."

"I'm in shock. How did you buy all this stuff back?"

"I didn't. They're giving it to you as a sort of housewarming gift for the new Brady's."

"And they were feeling a little guilty for ripping me off," she concluded.

"Yeah. That, too."

When the naked-lady picture came through the door, she finally shook her head. "I can't put *that* back up. This is a family establishment."

"How about in the men's restroom?" Tony cajoled. "She *is* a part of Brady's history."

She threw up her hands. "Fine. I'll drape her with scarves."

Tony laughed. "Brady would think that was hilarious."

It was funny, Julie agreed. This was going to be one funky tearoom.

But it was going to work. Somehow this strange amalgam of good taste and tacky honky-tonk nostalgia was going to work. It was a reflection of Oak Cliff itself—the old and the new, rich and poor, tasteful and tacky living cheek by jowl, each element becoming greater for being part of the whole.

Just as she was a more whole, more complete person for having moved here, for having fallen in love with a true hero.

She gave Tony an extra squeeze. "How would

you feel about having our wedding here? All my dreams in one place."

He grinned down at her. "Perfect."

* * * * *

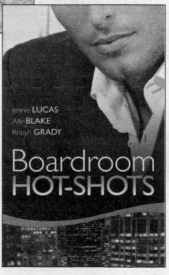